A FALL
OF
WATER

ELIZABETH HUNTER

A Fall of Water
Copyright © 2012
Elizabeth Hunter

ISBN-13: 978-1477578742
ISBN-10: 1477578749

This is a work of fiction. Names, characters, places, and incidents are the products of the author's imagination, or are used fictitiously. Any resemblance to actual persons, living or dead, business establishments, events, or locales is entirely coincidental.

Cover Design: Flash in the Can Productions
Edited by: Amy Eye
Formatted by: Amy Eye

For more information about Elizabeth Hunter, please visit:
ElizabethHunterWrites.com

FOR MY SON

May you love life
and be more than happy;
may you be good.

May your stories bring you joy
and your heart find peace.
I am blessed beyond measure
to be called your mother.

"Close your eyes, hold your breath…
And always trust your cape."

The fall of dropping water wears away the stone.

—LUCRETIUS

PROLOGUE

Cochamó Valley, Chile
2011

January

"What's that?"

Giovanni winked over his shoulder as he backed into the living room. "Another bookcase."

Beatrice rolled her eyes as Gustavo stumbled into the room. "Ha ha. Funny, it sure looks like a piano."

"And not one that was easy to get here," Gustavo said.

"Gio, why did you bring a piano to the house?"

"Because we're going to be here for at least a year, and I like the piano."

She shrugged and turned back to the fire and her book.

"And I thought maybe you would like to learn, too."

She glanced over at the two vampires. "I'm not very musical."

"I know," Gustavo said. "I've heard you hum."

"Hey!" She tossed a pillow at him, but he only laughed as he and Giovanni maneuvered the piano into a corner of the living room near the bookcases. It was a small upright, shiny black, and blended nicely with the dark wood and wrought iron, which decorated their mountain home. Much smaller than Giovanni's grand piano at their house in Los Angeles, she knew he would enjoy playing it just as much.

Beatrice heard footsteps crossing the meadow and rose to meet the visitor at the door. It was Isabel, carrying the bench for the piano.

"They forgot this!" she called as she climbed the steps. "I'm amazed it all made it into the valley in one piece."

Gustavo walked over and took the bench from her. "We didn't forget it, woman. We may have inhuman strength, but we still only have two hands apiece."

Isabel sat next to Beatrice and put her arm around the younger woman. "How are you? I haven't seen you since Christmas."

"Fine." She nodded. "Good. I've been doing a lot of reading."

"Ben's doing well. He and Father are thick as thieves."

Beatrice smiled. "Well, that's not a surprise. They're about the same age, mentally."

Isabel's laugh pealed out and Beatrice saw Gustavo look up, watching his wife with a small smile as he helped Giovanni.

"You're right, you know; you missed the wrestling match. I've never... I don't think there are words to describe that scene."

"I was sorry to miss it, but I didn't want to spoil Ben's fun by, you know, draining him or something."

Isabel nodded. "Good point. Nice of you to be so thoughtful."

"I try."

Isabel raised a knowing eyebrow. "Really?"

Beatrice took a deep breath and swallowed the lump that had risen in her throat. "I'm... trying."

Isabel leaned over and squeezed her shoulders in a quick hug before she rose from the couch. "I'll see you later. If you want a break from this one"—she pointed at Giovanni—"just use the radio."

"Thanks."

Giovanni scowled at Isabel. "Why would she want a break from me?"

Beatrice snickered as Isabel gave him a dry look, then pulled Gustavo out the door, muttering under her breath about "stubborn, donkey men."

Giovanni sat next to her on the couch, tossing more flames toward the dwindling fire, even though it was summer. He frowned and looked into the bright flames, which lit the dim cabin. "So, you really don't have any interest in learning the piano?"

Beatrice leaned into his shoulder and shrugged. "Like I said, I'm not musical."

February

"I'm sick of you!" Beatrice threw a copy of *Moby Dick* at Giovanni.

He caught it and slammed it on the coffee table, wincing at the crack of wood underneath the book. "It's a good thing that was a mass market edition, woman! And I'm not particularly thrilled with you right now, either."

She stalked toward him, shoving a finger in his chest. He could see her fangs descended in anger and feel her heart racing. "You know, at least you're not stuck up in this cabin, miles away from any other person. I can't even visit most of them because I'd probably end up drinking them for dinner! Add to that, I'm awake in here all day with nothing to do but read. You, at least, get to sleep for longer than a few hours!"

Giovanni stepped closer, ignoring Carwyn, who stared at them from the couch with wide eyes. "At least I don't blame you for things that are entirely out of my control, Beatrice. It's not my fault that you're awake most of the day."

"You don't even *try* to stay awake."

His mouth gaped. "You're being completely irrational right now. I refuse to continue this discussion—"

"Don't you use the professor voice on me!"

Giovanni saw Carwyn sneaking toward the door. "I'm just—" the priest stammered, "I'll be..." He slipped out and they paused, waiting for the sound of their friend escaping through the forest.

Giovanni waited for only a moment before he grabbed Beatrice, lifting her up as she wrapped her legs around his waist. "Nicely done, Tesoro," he murmured as his lips devoured the skin along her neck.

Her hands were already ripping his shirt. "I thought he was never going to leave."

"Mmm." He growled as she nipped at his collarbone. "Why is it so sexy when you yell at me?" They stumbled toward the bedroom and Giovanni nudged the door closed with his hip.

"Probably"—she panted as Giovanni tore her shirt down the front—"the same reason I find the professor voice strangely hot."

"Let's not question it, shall we?"

March

She sat alone on the porch, staring into the clear night sky. Carwyn had gone back to Isabel and Gustavo's house to watch a movie with Ben, so Beatrice sat, holding the printout of the e-mail from Giovanni in London.

Six more days.

It was the longest they had ever been apart since he had returned to her. Three weeks. Considering they could be together for hundreds, if not thousands of years, Beatrice knew she should probably be grateful for the solitude.

Six more days.

She sensed Isabel coming through the trees. Even though they could move swiftly, it was considered rude to just appear at someone's doorstep in the quiet valley commune. So even vampires usually approached at human speed unless there was an emergency, or they were expected.

Isabel said not a word as she sat next to Beatrice on the carved wooden bench that Gustavo had made for them as a wedding present.

"Deirdre and Ioan used to separate for months at a time when they were first together... well, after the first fifty years or so. They were both so independent. They once went a year and a half apart, totally by choice, just sending letters to each other. Ioan was at our brother's castle in Scotland and Deirdre was on some island in the North Sea."

"Really?" If Isabel intended her words to be some strange comfort, she wasn't successful. Beatrice felt even more feeble thinking about Deirdre and Ioan's resilient marriage.

"My Gustavo and I though..." Isabel smiled to herself. "We can't be without each other that long. It just doesn't suit us. He is my other half. I went a month without him once and almost went insane. I snapped at everyone. I was so cross."

Beatrice gripped Isabel's hand. "Thanks."

"It doesn't make us weak to need them."

"No?"

Isabel looked over with a smile. "If your right hand was lame, wouldn't your left miss its mate? You might get along without it, but you'd always be aware that something was missing. That's natural, not weak."

"I'm not used..." Beatrice struggled to articulate what had been bothering her for months. "I just feel so tied to him. And to my..."

"Your father. You miss the tie to your father."

"Yes," she whispered, blinking back tears. "I mean, even more than when I thought he had died when I was a girl. There's just this big, empty void in my chest. When Giovanni's here, it helps. Especially when we—" She broke off, suddenly reluctant to continue.

Isabel chuckled. "No need to be embarrassed. When you exchange blood, it's very intimate. It's a tie of another sort, and one that will eventually surpass the tie you felt with your father. It's natural. And it's natural that you feel this void from your father's loss." She put an arm around Beatrice's shoulders and pulled her into an embrace. "If I even think about losing Father... It's too horrible to contemplate. And I was sired over five hundred years ago. For you? You were a newborn when he was lost, his blood still fresh in your veins. I cannot imagine it, Beatrice. You should never feel weak. I believe you are one of the strongest young women I have had the privilege of knowing."

Beatrice sniffed. "So I'm not a big baby for missing my dad like this? Some days, I feel like I barely want to leave my room. And then when Giovanni left... Honestly, if Carwyn would leave me alone more, I would curl up under the covers and never come out."

"And that is why he pesters you so much."

She snorted. "Yeah, I kind of figured."

"You are loved, Beatrice De Novo. By so many. On your darkest days, don't forget that."

April

He woke in their bed, alone; her sheets were not even rumpled.

"Beatrice?"

There was no answer. He raced out to the living room, where all the windows had been blacked out and covered by curtains so she could have the freedom of the house during the daylight hours.

"Beatrice?"

She was sitting by the fire, staring into it with blank eyes. There was an open textbook on her lap.

"Tesoro?"

She finally blinked and turned to him.

He walked toward her slowly. "Did you sleep at all today? Have you been reading this whole time?"

Beatrice looked down to the book on her lap, then over at Giovanni, who sat down beside her.

"I can read Greek now." His heart sank when he saw the lost look she wore. "Do you think he knows?"

Giovanni reached over and closed the book, taking both her hands in his before he pulled her onto his lap. "Yes."

May

He teased her as she stood in the kitchen, warming the blood before she drank.

"Come outside. Swim with me. We'll go to the waterfall." He stood behind her, wrapping his arms around her waist and nipping at the hollow behind her earlobe.

She shrugged as she stirred the blood. "It's getting cold now."

"So I'll heat up the pool. You're married to a fire vampire; take advantage of me however you like. I'll make it a hot tub if that's what you want. Just come swimming. Go running. Leave the house."

"Gio, you're acting like I'm a hermit or something. I've just got a lot to read right now and I'm working on my Persian so I can read the journals, and—"

"And you haven't left the house in a week."

She frowned. "It hasn't... it's only been a couple of days." *Hadn't it?*

He turned her around so she was facing him. "The last night you left the house was the night Carwyn had to leave, and that was over a week ago."

Beatrice took a drink of the blood. It wasn't as fresh as she liked it, but they had to order blood from Puerto Montt or drink pig's blood, so she was willing to put up with the stale taste if it meant no pigs. "Fine. I'll go swimming."

Giovanni cocked an eyebrow. "Don't sound so excited."

She mustered up a giant, fake grin and plastered it on her face. "There," she said through gritted teeth, "see how excited I am?"

He narrowed his eyes, then pinched her waist and stuck his tongue out in her direction. Her jaw dropped. "Did you just stick your tongue out at me?"

"Yes," he said. "I've been wanting to do that for years."

She only looked at him, confused, before she burst into laughter. Beatrice laughed and laughed, bending over as bloody tears came to her eyes. She heard Giovanni chuckle a little, but knew he was only laughing at her own amusement.

It was the loudest she had laughed in months.

June

"Have you bitten anyone yet?"

She cleared her throat. *Well, Ben, just your uncle, but you really don't need to know about that, do you?* Beatrice took a pencil, pressing on the button on the front of the radio phone to reply. "Nope. I'm clean so far."

"Good." She heard Ben reply. "Just remember, if you do need to drain someone, make sure it's someone really evil or really annoying. Or my geometry teacher, though that would be a pretty long way to travel for a meal."

"Got it. And, of course, there's the whole 'killing an innocent human being' thing, too."

"Oh, he's not innocent; he gives pop quizzes."

Beatrice laughed. "Ben, I'm not going to kill your math teacher."

"I'm just saying, when we get home, keep it in mind. I'm pretty sure no one would miss him."

"Right." She played with the edge of her book, trying not to notice Giovanni hovering in the corner. He wore a small, satisfied smirk that she was interacting with the outside world again. "So, how's school? How's everything going?"

"Can Gio hear us?"

She muffled a laugh and pressed the respond button again. "Yes."

"Oh, well then, it's going magnificently. I'm so fortunate to have a knowledgeable and patient teacher like my uncle, who is imparting his centuries of wisdom into my eager young mind."

Beatrice was rolling on the couch, laughing, when Giovanni walked over and pressed the respond button. "Tell me more, oh eager young nephew, who will be translating an extra passage of Virgil tomorrow afternoon."

"Dude!" Ben protested. "Gio, that's not cool. Hear her laughing? When was the last time you made her laugh like that?"

Giovanni cocked his head at Beatrice and let an evil grin cross his face.

Beatrice stopped laughing and leaped on him. "You better not!" she hissed as they tumbled to the floor, breaking one of the dining room chairs as they rolled.

"Whatever could you be talking about?" He laughed as he trapped her legs between his own and rolled on top of her. "I was simply going to tell him how much you like it when I—"

Beatrice cut him off with a kiss, rolling them over so that she was lying on his chest. She pinned him at the shoulders as the speakerphone squawked in the background.

"Guys? Gio? Did you short out the phone again?" Giovanni and Beatrice continued to roll across the dining room and into the living room, taking out another chair as each tried to best the other in their playful wrestling match.

"B? Can you hear me?"

Giovanni gripped her hips and rocked against her, ignoring the voice in the background.

"You guys are fooling around, aren't you?" Ben sighed over the line. "That's so gross."

They didn't notice when the phone clicked.

July

"What were you thinking?" He patted her face with cool cloths, more for his own peace of mind than anything else. She was already healing.

"I just wanted to see a glimpse of it," she said sullenly. "Just a... sliver. I didn't think I would burn that fast."

He fought back the scream he wanted to level at her. "You're too young, Tesoro. You just—" He broke off and clutched her to his chest, frightened beyond words. "Do you realize what would have happened if I hadn't been quick enough?"

"Crispy critter," she said as she pulled away from him. "I'm fine."

"Do not make light of this."

"Don't order me around."

He clutched her shoulders again and spoke in a hard voice, holding fast when she tried to squirm away. "Do you realize what it would do to me? To Benjamin?"

"Not fair."

"To Isadora? To Caspar? How about Carwyn?"

"Shut up!" She shoved him away and tried to stand, but her eyes were still blinded from the seconds of sun she had felt on her face.

"How about Dez? Matt? Isabel? Gustavo? Tenzin?"

"Tenzin does not give two shits about me, Gio!" She rose to her feet and grabbed the back of the couch.

He grabbed her hand. "You know that's not true."

"Then where the hell is she?"

August

He was playing again. He often did right before dawn. Relaxing things. Slow melodies by Bach or Satie or Chopin. Things he knew she loved. She wondered if it was an attempt to quiet her and let her rest, even though she rarely took comfort in sleep anymore. There were only a few hours a day that she was able to sleep. She didn't tire, but she did envy the peaceful oblivion that slumber had once provided.

And dreaming. She missed dreaming.

Beatrice approached the piano, sliding next to Giovanni on the narrow bench he had pushed back to fit his long legs. He didn't cease playing the Nocturne when he leaned over and kissed her.

"Hello."

"Hey."

"Want me to show you a few things?"

"Nope."

"A little Mozart melody?" His fingers tripped up the keys. "You'll be amazed by how fast you pick it up."

"Still nope."

September

"How could you?" She threw him into the face of the cliff, tossing him as if he weighed nothing when he finally caught up with her on the road back to the valley.

"He was old. He was going to die within a few weeks, Beatrice."

She paced back and forth in the small clearing. "But *I* didn't need to be the one to kill him." Streaks of crimson tears marred her perfect white skin. The rain beat down on them and the wind whipped through the small pass.

He tried to speak in a low, calming voice. "You broke out of the bloodlust much quicker than I had imagined. You're doing very well."

"But I still killed him, Gio! I did. And you stood there and let me. You stood by and let me kill that old man doing nothing more than sitting in his garden."

Giovanni slowly stood, still keeping his distance. "If he had been in good health, you would not have killed him. But he was sick, Tesoro. Surely, you must have tasted it in his blood. He was in pain. Your amnis calmed him as you drank. He didn't feel anything."

She screamed and pulled at her hair. "How could you let me kill him?"

"It was a mercy."

"No!" she yelled and rushed him, knocking him over and pummeling his face. She loosed her rage on her mate until he grabbed her hands. He could barely contain her; Beatrice had become almost immeasurably strong. "Why? Why did you let me murder him?"

With a surge, he rolled over until she was lying under him, sobbing in the rain as the bloody tears ran down her face and into the mud.

"This is why! Do you understand? Look at me, Beatrice." He finally caught her narrowed eye and she bared her teeth at him. "Look at me and listen right now. Did I let you kill that old man? Yes, and I'll tell you why."

He took a softer hand and brushed at the tears that stained her cheeks. "Because one day, very soon, it's not going to be a sick stranger in a garden that tempts you." He sat back and pulled her to sit in front of him, the rain still beating on their backs.

"Someday very soon, it's going to be Benjamin. Or your grandmother. Or Caspar or Dez or Matt. It's going to be someone you love. An innocent stranger on a train or walking down the street at night. And the temptation is going to knock you over and every instinct in you is going to be screaming to take and drink and not to stop because there is *nothing* in the human world more powerful than you. Do you understand what I'm saying?" He grabbed the collar of her soaked overcoat and pulled her closer. She still stared at him with sullen, tear-filled eyes as he continued.

"And when that moment comes, I want you to remember how you feel right now. I want you to remember this moment for the rest of your existence because that is what will keep the humans around you safe from the monster that lives inside you. That lives inside all of us."

Her eyes were dull as she stared at him. Her hands limp and lying at her sides.

"I hate you."

"I love you."

October

"Beatrice?"

She glanced at him, but didn't speak.

"Have you fed tonight?"

He looked so calm as he wrapped his needless scarf around his neck and prepared to go down to the lodge for Ben's lessons.

She nodded.

"Call if you need anything."

She shrugged and turned back to the fire. They hadn't exchanged blood since she had killed the old man. Her logical brain understood why Giovanni had allowed her to do it, but the gaping void in her chest, the hollow that never seemed to be filled, was only growing deeper the longer she let her anger fester.

And she couldn't see a way to bridge the gap that had opened between them.

An hour later, there was a knock at the door. So focused on the fire, she failed to register the approaching energy. A storm system had moved into the valley, bringing thunder, lightning, and causing her senses to go haywire in the charged air.

Beatrice rose and went to the door, gasping when she recognized the smell of cardamom on the other side. She flung it open and Tenzin was there, silent and soaked from the rain. Her shorn hair hung in thick chunks around her face as she waited on the porch.

Simultaneous rage and love reared up in Beatrice. She raised her hand to strike, but Tenzin only reached out and caught her fist before it made contact. Beatrice shook, then she crumbled to the ground, sobbing out her grief, anger, and heartbreak as her father's mate knelt down and gathered her in an embrace. Tenzin kicked the door closed and tucked Beatrice's head under her chin, rocking her back and forth as Beatrice clutched at her dirty white robes.

"I'm here, my girl. I'm back."

November

"It's normal to feel that, you know."

Tenzin and Beatrice were sparring on the edge of a clearing as one of Gustavo's men looked on. A human, one of the guides that worked in the valley during the summer months, sat at his feet. While Beatrice had very good control around humans most of the time, Tenzin had emphasized the importance of learning how to fight while the distraction was nearby. Considering Lorenzo had used the scent of human blood to pin her and kill her father, Beatrice was quick to agree to the practice, no matter how much her throat burned.

"Feel what?"

"That void from Stephen's loss. It will fade with time, but there will always be a trace. You were sired from his blood; it would be unnatural to not feel the lack of him."

They moved in a dancing fight, Beatrice's style having developed into something uniquely her own in the year since she had turned. It was a melding of the martial arts that she had practiced as a human, Gemma's vicious street-fighting, and Tenzin's flowing, but lethal, ballet. Though Tenzin was still faster, Beatrice was more than able to keep up.

"Do you still feel it?" Tenzin cut her eyes toward Beatrice before she punched out in a swift uppercut.

"Sorry," Beatrice muttered through her fractured jaw. "Stupid question."

"Have you talked to Giovanni about it?"

"Why?"

Tenzin smacked the back of her head. "Are you stupid, girl? Do you forget that he lost his father, too?"

"Oh, well..." Beatrice had no idea how much Tenzin knew about Andros's death, but she wasn't going to say. Giovanni had told her that no one could ever know that he had a hand in the death of his sire. She would not reveal his secrets, not even to Tenzin.

"And however that came about—" Tenzin looked down at the ground. "And I have always had my suspicions—your husband understands the loss you feel. He has felt it himself. If you need to talk to someone, he's the one vampire here that would understand. If you haven't talked to him about it, you're stupid."

Beatrice held a hand up and paused. "Are you coming back with us to L.A.?"

Tenzin frowned. "I suppose I am. Why?"

"Because apparently, I need you to tell me when I'm being stupid."

December

She was glowing. Her face may not have blushed anymore, but his wife had been glowing as she sat next to Ben and opened presents earlier that evening. They had gathered at Isabel and Gustavo's house, Beatrice and Giovanni, Tenzin, Carwyn, and Ben. All together, and she had not struggled to control her bloodlust once.

Giovanni imagined that he was glowing, too.

She lay on the couch, stretched out and listening to him play bits and pieces from the Nutcracker Suite as dawn approached. She hummed along, horribly out of tune, as always, but he didn't care. He heard her stand and walk toward him. She placed her hand on his shoulder and he leaned into her arm, rubbing his cheek against her flesh and enjoying the crackling, excited energy that filled the house.

They would go back to Los Angeles soon.

"Gio?"

"Hmm?"

She sat next to him for a moment before she ducked under his arms and straddled his lap. He pulled his hands away to grab her waist, but she winked and placed them back on the keyboard. "Keep playing."

Giovanni chuckled. "What game are you playing, woman?"

She put her arms around his neck, nipping at his ear and nuzzling into his neck. "I think..."

"Yes?" Despite his preternatural concentration, he was having trouble focusing on the Tchaikovsky.

"I think that maybe I do want to learn to play."

His eyes rolled back as she let her fangs scrape along his neck. "Oh, I think you're quite adept at playing already, Tesoro."

"No." She giggled. "An instrument."

"I'm allowing that joke to pass. To obvious."

She laughed and cuddled into him, wiggling on his lap as he struggled to concentrate on the keyboard. "Not piano though."

"No?"

"No, maybe... guitar. I could be a rock and roll chick. Not electric, obviously... well, maybe I could figure something out. I mean, if I really tried, I could probably figure out a way to make it work. Maybe an insulated case of some kind, but I'd have to make sure it didn't damage the guitar... What?"

He grinned and ceased playing, wrapping his arms around her and pressing his mouth to hers in a long kiss. His hands reached up, running through her hair and teasing the pins out that she had used to put it up earlier.

"I love you madly, Beatrice De Novo."

She smiled and nipped at his chin. "I love you, too."

"Welcome back."

CHAPTER ONE

Los Angeles, California
March 2012

Giovanni woke with a start, and Beatrice looked up from across the room. He sat up and swung his legs over the side of their large bed to stare at the photograph of the Ponte Vecchio, which hung on the wall of their bedroom.

"Hey."

He blinked before he looked over at her. Beatrice smiled. Her husband looked as if he was still halfway dreaming.

"Good evening. Did you rest at all today?" He rose and walked to her, bending down to kiss her bare shoulder. He still refused to wear any sort of clothing to bed. Since their room was blocked by a sturdy, reinforced door, multiple locks, and an electronic monitoring system that she'd had custom made for them, Beatrice just decided to enjoy the view. No one would be breaking in.

"I rested a few hours. You looked like you were dreaming. What was it about?"

He shrugged and walked to the small kitchen area, heating a bag of blood and leaning over to sniff the coffee pot she'd added in the corner of their room.

"Was it about your father again?"

He was silent for a few minutes, but she didn't try to fill the space. Giovanni finally turned with a frown on his face. "I don't know why I'm having so many dreams about him."

She cocked her head. "Because of me? Because I lost my dad? Because we've been talking about that?"

"Perhaps."

She had finally taken Tenzin's advice and confided in Giovanni about the gaping wound that Stephen's loss had left. As predicted, he understood completely. Just sharing the hurt had done more to lessen the grief than any of her own efforts.

"Gio... there's no chance that Andros could be alive, is there? I mean, you didn't actually see him die. He was just ash when you woke up. Lorenzo was the one who saw—"

"Beatrice, how did you feel when your father was killed?"

Tears sprang immediately to her eyes. "Like... something was ripped from my chest. Empty. Physical pain would have been a relief."

He only looked at her and nodded. "I felt the same. Despite how much I hated Andros, I loved him, too. And the pain of my father's death woke me from my day rest, even though it was practically impossible to wake me when I was that young. I know he is dead."

"Okay," she whispered. "I'm sorry. I just—"

"It's a valid question. Don't apologize."

He turned and picked up the bag of blood he had heated in warm water, drinking it quickly before he walked across the room. He picked her up and brought her back to the bed. Though she didn't need to sleep, his presence —the silent meditation of his touch—allowed Beatrice to rest her mind.

The sun still peeked through the edges of the windows, so they lay silently, curled together as her amnis wrapped around its mate. Though he didn't move, she could feel Giovanni's invisible energy stroking along her back and neck, fluttering over her skin and soothing her.

"What are you doing tonight?" she asked in a drowsy whisper.

"I'm introducing one of Gustavo's sons to Ernesto. Diego has some business in Los Angeles and he asked for an introduction."

"Oh, you get to play politics. Lucky you."

He pinched her side when she snickered. "Your grandfather asked for you to come, as well, but I made an excuse for you. I'm not going to next time."

She leaned over and kissed him. "Thank you. You're the best husband in the whole room." Beatrice squealed when he dug his fingers into her sides. Immortality had not lessened how ticklish she was. If anything, it had made it worse.

"Why? Why did I sign up for this abuse for eternity? What have I done to deserve this woman?" He chuckled as he continued to tickle her. Soon, she was gasping under him.

"Stop!" she panted. "Stop. I'll..."

An evil grin spread across his face. "You'll what?"

She brought an arm around and trailed her fingers down his back, teasing his spine as he shivered. Giovanni may not have been ticklish, but she knew exactly how to torment him.

"I'll... save some hot water for you!"

Beatrice darted out from under him and into the luxurious bathroom, locking the door behind her. She laughed and started the shower, only to hear the door splinter behind her. Giovanni tossed the broken wood to the side and strode into the room.

"We didn't need that door."

She drove the grey Mustang through the busy streets, pulling up to the old warehouse where Tenzin had set up a practice studio. The ancient wind vampire was already there, and Beatrice could hear her pounding on one of training dummies.

"You're coming later, right?" Ben grabbed his gym bag and opened the door.

"Yeah, I'm just meeting Dez for dinner, and then I'll come back and practice with you guys for a while."

"No rush. I think she's meaner to me when you're there."

Beatrice laughed and reached across to ruffle his hair as he tried to squirm away.

At fifteen, Ben Vecchio had all the marks of a boy on the verge of manhood. He had shot up the year they had been in Chile and was far taller than she was. Beatrice guessed he would rival Giovanni's height when he was full-grown. His chest was starting to fill out and lose its scrawny appearance, helped along by the intense physical training that Beatrice and Giovanni insisted on for his safety. His curling hair, deep brown eyes, and quick smile already attracted enough female attention to keep a grown man happy, much less a teenage boy.

Ben was well on the way to breaking a few hearts, and Beatrice absolutely adored him.

"Tell Dez I said 'Hi' and let her know I'm here when she gets tired of the old fart."

"She told the old fart she'd marry him, so I have a feeling you're out of luck."

He leaned down and winked. "Engaged is not married, B. There's hope until there's a ring on her finger."

She shook her head. "You're shameless."

"Yep. But I'm cute, too. See ya!" He slapped the top of the car and walked into the warehouse, whistling.

"Shameless," she said as she pulled away.

She turned at El Molina Avenue and parked on the street, glad to have found a parking spot so near the cafe where she and Dez met on Thursday nights. She could already hear a new band warming up inside, and no one was sitting on the patio, so she grabbed a table, glad for the clear night sky. Dez arrived a few minutes later, and Beatrice shoved down the instinctive hunger that tickled the back of her throat.

Though she was used to the scents of her family, close contact with other humans still awakened her instincts. She could easily control it, but that did require some concentration. Her best friend, for whatever reason, smelled particularly appealing that night.

"How are you, hon?" Dez chattered as they both settled into their seats. A waiter came out and they both ordered a coffee and dessert. "How was your week? Matt and Gio are both at that thing at your grandfather's tonight, right? What's Ben up to?"

"Other than still plotting how to steal you from Matt?"

She giggled. "Of course."

"He and Tenzin are practicing tonight."

"How's school going?"

Beatrice nodded. "Good, he seems to have swung right back into his classes since we've been back. Of course, Gio's way more demanding than his high school teachers, so that's not really a surprise."

"Of course."

"The boy could probably pass most college level classes at this point."

"Has he thought about early admission anywhere?"

Beatrice shrugged. "It's not a priority for him. He likes his friends the most now. He still does most of his learning at home with Gio. He only goes to school for girls, basketball, and to have something to do during the day."

They paused to let a group enter the cafe. The lively music spilled out as the door opened, quiet to Dez, but almost distractingly loud to Beatrice's immortal ears.

They chatted as they sipped their coffee, Dez happily filling Beatrice in on her wedding plans. She and Matt had been engaged the previous summer, but had waited until Giovanni and Beatrice had returned from Chile to get married. The wedding was only a few weeks away.

"—so the guests will have the option to eat either chicken or beef. I liked the idea. Of course, the cake looks amazing, but then, it's chocolate, so how it looks isn't all that important. B?"

"Huh?"

"You've been staring at my neck for the past couple minutes, hon."

She blinked. "Oh, sorry."

"No problem. Did you forget to eat before you came? You haven't touched your coffee."

Beatrice wrinkled her nose. "It's really strong. Are you wearing a new perfume or something?"

"No, nothing different."

"Are you..." Beatrice struggled, trying to determine what it was that was triggering her awareness. Scent had taken on an entirely new dimension for her since becoming a vampire. Everything smelled. She had quickly learned to block out as much as possible, so as not to become overwhelmed, but there was something about Dez that night...

"You're pregnant."

Her best friend's mouth gaped, just a little. "Uh... what?"

"I think that's it. You smell... more. I don't know what else it could be. You don't smell sick, and I know you went off birth control a while back, so—"

"How did you know that?" Dez almost looked offended.

Beatrice just shrugged. "Your scent changed. Matt liked it; I could tell."

Dez rolled her eyes. "And I thought being your friend was weird before... and I'm not pregnant. It's only been a couple months, and I haven't even missed my period."

"Well, you will. I'm pretty sure that's it."

Dez just shook her head. "How... I mean, what—"

"I told you, you smell different." Beatrice shrugged again and sipped at her coffee. It really did smell better than it tasted now. Unless she was at home and she could make it watered down, it was overwhelming. "You don't smell *bad*. You smell more... female, if that makes sense. I'm sure it's the hormones. Matt's probably been going nuts around you lately, huh? Humans react to that stuff even if they don't know what it is."

Dez cocked an eyebrow. "Humans, huh?"

"Yup." Beatrice smiled. "So you believe me?"

She shrugged. "Well, since you're a big, bad vampire with a super-strong nose, I guess I have to, though I think I'll still wait for the pathetic human doctor to confirm before I tell my fiancé."

She grinned. "Congratulations! So were you trying?"

Dez flushed. "We weren't *not* trying, if you know what I mean. Matt's older than me; he didn't want to wait. I was game for whatever. I knew I wanted kids and I'll be thirty next month. We're getting married in a couple weeks. No one will care we started a tiny bit backwards."

"I bet Matt's going to be really excited."

"I bet he'll be surprised. I don't think he thought it would happen this fast." She paused. "Heck, I didn't think it would happen this fast, but I suppose this is the logical result of all that sex."

Beatrice snorted. "You're so smart for a human."

Dez narrowed her eyes. "'For a human,' huh? I'm smart for a human?" She tossed her hair, picking up a menu and waving her scent toward Beatrice. "Oh, look at the poor, pathetic human tempting the big, bad vampire. Poor vampire. Hungry are we?"

Beatrice growled low in her throat, feeling her fangs descend, even though she knew she wasn't hungry. "Thtop it."

"Oh!" Dez gasped in mock surprise. "Are those your fangs? How embarrassing. Is there anything you can do about that little situation?"

"You fink you're tho funny."

"I *am* funny." Dez grinned. "Know what else is funny? Your lisp when you talk around your fangs."

Beatrice swallowed the burn in her throat and willed her teeth to ascend. "One of these days, I'm going to bite you. Then you won't think it's so funny."

"You better not. According to your accounts, I might like it a little *too* much."

"Haha."

Dez cackled. "It's hilarious, you look like you *should* be blushing, but you can't."

"Why am I still friends with you?"

"Because I'm awesome. And you're going to be an auntie."

Beatrice couldn't stop the smile that spread across her face and the tug at her heart. Though she had no desire for children, she was thrilled for her friend. "You're going to be an amazing mom, Dez."

"Oh…" Her face fell. "I'm going to get totally fat now. And you'll never get fat. I kind of hate you for that. I wonder if Matt's going to get totally grossed out."

Beatrice shook her head. "Please. Matt adores you. He's going to be thrilled—"

"B?"

She halted at the familiar voice of her ex-boyfriend.

"Beatrice?" She heard him again, but she didn't turn around. Beatrice looked across at Dez, who just looked panicked. "Dez, is that you?"

She could hear Mano approaching the table. Before he could get a good look at her, Beatrice reached out and grabbed his hand, clasping his bare skin in her cool palm and letting her amnis crawl up his arm. She stood and faced him, never easing her grip.

"Hi, Mano," she whispered. She looked over his shoulder, but he appeared to be alone. She looked back into the eyes of the man who had loved her. Who had seen her through one of the loneliest parts of her life with caring and self-sacrifice.

He blinked at her, his eyes already swimming with her influence. "You look different, baby."

"I know."

"You need some sun. Let's go out on the boat tomorrow."

She shook her head. "No, Mano. I'm fine."

"Where have you been? I've missed you."

She swallowed the lump in her throat, searching his face, pained at the loneliness she found. The longing. "I'm fine. And so are you."

"I am?"

"Yes. You saw me and you realized that you had moved on."

"But I love you."

Beatrice gripped his hand, stroking her thumb along the calluses on his palm "No, you've moved on. And you're ready to meet someone new. Someone who will love you as much as you love her."

"I am?" He blinked at her.

"Yep. You saw me, and we caught up. And you heard that Gio and I are married and really happy now, and you were happy, too. Because you realized that you don't love me anymore."

He shook his head, and she forced her influence further into his mind, pushing back the tears at his familiar scent. Mano still smelled like sunshine and the sea.

"Right," he finally said with a small smile. "You look great. I don't love you anymore."

"Nope," she choked out. "And you're going to meet someone great. And you're going to fall in love."

"I am?"

"Yes, you are."

"I've missed you, baby." He smiled at her again, the soft smile he wore when he was sleepy.

"I missed you, too." It wasn't a lie. She had missed Mano, even though she loved Giovanni with all her heart. She forced out a smile. "Bye, Mano. You're going to go home now."

He nodded and leaned down as if to kiss her, but she backed away. He still smiled.

"Bye, B."

She finally let go of his warm hand, and he turned and walked away down the dark street. Beatrice turned back to Dez, pulled her wallet out of her pocket, and threw down some cash. Dez reached over and squeezed her hand. "You okay?"

"Yeah. I need to go."

"That the first time?"

She nodded, forcing back the tears that threatened her eyes. "Yeah, it was just a surprise, you know? I was surprised."

"Well, you did great. And you were really kind to do that. He, um, he called Matt for months. He was worried about you. Will he remember anything?"

Beatrice waved her hand as Dez stood. "Just... vague stuff. He should remember he saw me, but the exact memories will be kind of cloudy. Hopefully, I did it right."

"Are you going to tell Gio you saw him?"

"Yeah, I wouldn't try to hide it. And he'll smell him anyway."

Dez just stared at her before she walked down the street, Beatrice following after. "Vampires are weird."

"I'll remind you of that when you have a giant human parasite sucking the life out of you and making you ill."

"Shut up, bloodsucker."

Beatrice walked into the kitchen behind Ben, who immediately ran upstairs to shower and call one of the girls who had been texting him during his practice.

"Ben," she called, "it's eleven o'clock, and you practiced hard. You better get some sleep."

"Sure thing, B!"

"Goodnight."

"'Night! Night, Isadora!"

She glanced at her grandmother, who was sitting at the kitchen table, reading a book. "Good night, Benjamin."

Beatrice leaned down and placed a soft kiss on her grandmother's delicate cheek. At age seventy-eight, Isadora Alvarez De Novo Davidson had lost none of the liveliness from her vivid green eyes; though her step was slower, her mind was not.

"And how is Dez?"

"Pregnant, but don't tell anyone. It's early."

"Oh!" Isadora smiled. "How wonderful. And the Kirbys will be thrilled."

"It's really early, so Matt doesn't even know. That's why you can't tell anyone."

Isadora frowned. "How early? Matt doesn't know?"

"Nope. I just told her tonight." Beatrice munched on an almond from the bowl her grandmother had out. "She smelled different. I got all fang-y."

Isadora was quiet for a minute. "You know, sometimes it's easy to forget you are a vampire, and sometimes, it's not."

Beatrice grinned and let her fangs run down. Isadora slapped at her shoulder. "Stop it, Mariposa!"

She giggled and took two almonds, sticking them on her fangs and muttering around them. "Yep, thcary, thcary vampire here."

They both broke into giggles, until Beatrice finally calmed down. "Where's Caspar?"

"He drove Matt and Gio to the meeting at Ernesto's."

"Ah."

"I'm going to go to sleep soon. I just thought I'd stay up to say hello. I missed you this afternoon."

"I was in the library."

"Looking at Geber's journals?"

"Yup." The journals, which her father had left in Tywyll's care, were all written in the alchemist's own strange code. In addition to learning Old Persian, Beatrice was also trying to decipher the peculiar phrases and code words the medieval scientist had used to disguise his research. If she could decode them, they might learn the identity of Geber's original test subjects and be that much closer to solving the mystery of the elixir. Though they hadn't heard a peep from Lorenzo, his presence lurked in her mind, teasing her that the book Stephen had taken was in his possession again.

"Mariposa?"

"Hmm?" She looked up at her grandmother.

"I said I'm going to bed now."

"Oh." She rose and kissed Isadora's cheek. "Night, Grandma."

"I'll see you in the morning."

"I'll probably be in the library around ten or so."

"Have a good night."

Isadora shuffled through the door and down the hall toward the ground floor rooms that Giovanni had converted into a suite for Caspar and Isadora. She could hear Ben walking around upstairs and felt the quiet hum of the electrical currents and waves of Wi-Fi that Matt had installed for Ben. The house may have been quiet, but it was never really still the way their house in Cochamó was, and Beatrice realized why Giovanni would get frustrated if he was surrounded by technology for too long. The modern world, to the senses of an immortal, was relentlessly noisy.

She was happily lost in a novel and curled up in the living room when the sound of the Mercedes broke through. She smiled at Caspar when he walked through the door. The clock on the wall pointed toward one and the old man bent down to kiss her cheek.

"Good night, my dear. I'll see you in the morning. This old man is exhausted."

"Night, Cas."

"What time did she turn in?"

"A few hours ago."

"I'll be joining her. Have fun with him."

"Oh?" She said, "What's that supposed to mean?"

Caspar shrugged. "Don't ask me. He's being terribly silent tonight."

"Huh, weird. He was fine earlier. Did everything go all right with Ernesto?"

"I believe so. He didn't seem upset. Just... quiet."

"Okay. I'll see you in the morning. Night."

He gave her a small salute and walked down the hall just as Giovanni walked through the door. He wore a strange expression and sat beside her. She stared at him as he looked off into the distance. Finally, he reached into his jacket and pulled out a thick, cream envelope with a broken wax seal. The interior was filigreed in gold leaf, and she could see a swirl of calligraphy peeking out from the letter inside.

"Hi. What's this? Caspar said you were doing the moody, silent thing. What's up?"

Giovanni tossed the envelope on her lap and leaned back, throwing an arm around her on the couch.

"Beatrice, how do you feel about Rome in the springtime?"

CHAPTER TWO

Crotone, Italy
1494

"Where am I?"

"Your new home."

Jacopo looked around the room, blinking. It looked nothing like the warm chambers of his uncle's villa in Ferrara or the bustling of Benevieni's house in Florence. The dim room where he woke was dark and damp. Though there were clean rushes that littered the floor, the chill of the air seemed to seep in through his bare feet and the smell of the ocean was everywhere. He sat on the edge of a small bed that smelled of sweet straw and herbs.

"This is not my home."

Signore Andros only smiled at him indulgently. The strange man had always bothered Jacopo, though never the same way as the teasing courtiers of Florence or Rome. He had learned at a young age to escape their stealthy hands and avoid their attention, but from the beginning, Niccolo Andros had seemed to be a different sort. Jacopo had never understood his uncle's fascination with the Greek, despite his wealth, knowledge, and connections.

"This *is* your home. And will be until I decide you are ready to move on."

"And when will that be?"

Andros only shrugged. "There is no rush. We must complete your education first. You are very young, even for a human. You have not yet reached your prime. That is why I have chosen you to be my student."

Jacopo may have been young, but he watched Andros with canny eyes. The boy had managed his uncle's servants for many years and had been an observer of human nature for far longer. Jacopo had never mingled with the other young men at court or even the servants his own age. He had always felt most comfortable among his uncle's books or in the company of Giovanni's friends.

He sat up a little straighter. "I am already well-educated. My uncle saw to my education. You know this, Signore."

"I do. That is why I chose you. You are extremely bright for a human." Andros stepped back, examining Jacopo as if he was an animal for sale. "Of fine form. Healthy. Yes, I'm very satisfied with my choice."

Jacopo cocked his head, and his mind began to spin. Andros had called him a "human," as if there was some other option, and there remained a faint, dull ache at the base of his skull. He felt as if he had woken from a strange fever, but his body did not ache, only his mind. His memory flashed to the strange preachers on the streets of Paris, raving about demons and spirits. His uncle had dismissed them as lunatics.

"You are young," Andros continued with a nod. "You will adapt nicely."

"What do you want from me?"

The odd man smiled. "It is not what I want *from* you. It is what I want to give to you.

Instinct caused Jacopo's stomach to churn, and his eyes darted around the room, searching for escape.

"Don't panic." Andros laughed. "I mean you no harm. Your uncle is dead. Florence continues its descent into madness." He came and sat next to Jacopo on the small bed, but kept a comfortable distance. "You will be safe with me. Cared for."

"Cared for?" The reality of his isolation hit him at last. Jacopo wondered what the servants thought had happened to him. His uncle had only been dead a few hours when the footman had announced that Signore Niccolo Andros had come to the villa. He remembered meeting the man in the study, but nothing else. "What has happened to my uncle?" Jacopo asked in a soft voice.

"Your uncle is dead," Andros said. "His family will bury him. The servants have sent for them already."

A slow ache twisted in his chest. "I am his family."

"No, you aren't."

Jacopo's eyes closed in pain. He was weary. He wanted nothing more than to curl up and go to sleep. If he woke, perhaps this would be revealed to be a strange nightmare. If he woke, his uncle might be alive. His warm feather bed would be beneath him. He would hear the maid singing a lilting song in the courtyard.

Andros's voice brought him back to reality. "As much as your uncle may have loved you, he was never *really* your family. Did he ever name you as his heir? Of course not. You were his brother's bastard. He would have married eventually and, if you were very fortunate, he would have made you steward of some house or property. You, my dear boy, were never his family."

Jacopo's eyes furrowed in pain. He knew in his heart that his uncle had cared for him, but the twisted words of his captor needled his insecurities. "I *was* his family. I was."

Andros rose, and Jacopo's eyes followed him. At first glance, Niccolo Andros did not look exceptionally strong or powerful. He was black-haired and bore the even, Mediterranean features shared by most men of Jacopo's acquaintance. He had a medium build, though his arms were thickly muscled, more like those of a laborer than a successful merchant. The only startling things about the man were his pale complexion and vivid blue gaze, which sparked with intelligence and calculation. When Jacopo looked into Andros's eyes, they radiated a quiet menace.

"No, my boy, you *weren't* his family, but you will be mine." Andros stepped closer in the small room, towering over the tall, young man as he sat on the edge of the bed.

"Do what I say, and I promise you I shall call you my son. In front of a far more powerful court than the piddling salons of the Medici, I will stand up and call you my child."

Jacopo frowned. "What do you speak of? What court is more powerful than the Medici? Are you a priest? Do you claim the Holy Father's favor?"

The older man chuckled. "Oh, my dear boy, how your eyes will be opened! Your world has been so small, even with all your uncle's travels. That which I speak of is beyond your comprehension. But you will understand. I promise, very soon, you will understand." Andros's voice grew gentle. "You have never truly had a home, a family. I will be your family. I will call you my son, and someday, all that I have will be yours, do you understand?"

Despite his fear, a strange kind of desire began to fill Jacopo. He had watched many men lie, and was more than proficient at the art himself, but Andros's eyes held none of the telltale signs of a deceiver. In fact, despite the ridiculous promise of the words he spoke, Jacopo almost believed him.

"You would call me your son?"

Andros smiled and stepped forward, placing a cool hand on Jacopo's cheek. "Trust me, my child. I am your family now."

Los Angeles, California
March 2012

He woke suddenly, twitching his nose at the memory of the salt air. Giovanni blinked the sleep from his eyes and immediately searched the bedroom. As was her habit, Beatrice sat in the large chair by the fireplace, reading a journal and taking notes in a small book. Her forehead crinkled in thought as she puzzled over some mystery. He took a silent moment to examine her.

She was stronger than he was now, though she lacked his experience, discipline, and control. For whatever reason, the cocktail of blood that had flooded her mortal body during her change had effected a truly spectacular transformation. In the year and a half since she had turned, Beatrice had grown in power and confidence. She rarely acted impulsively, and her grace was that of someone ten times her age.

Happily, she was still the same woman he had fallen in love with.

"Tesoro."

She looked up and a slow smile spread across her face.

"Hey, handsome."

He cocked a finger at her, squinting his eyes as he caught the teasing light in her own. She rose and sauntered toward him as he continued to beckon her. Once she was within arm's reach, he pounced. Beatrice laughed and rolled across the floor with him as they played.

"You're in a mood for just waking up." She laughed as they came to a stop halfway to the fireplace. Giovanni braced himself over her and looked down. "Do I dare ask what you were dreaming about?"

Sadly, not what you're thinking of. He kissed along her collar and nuzzled into her neck. "Have I told you tonight that I love you?"

"No."

"I do. I love you." His lips explored the nape of her neck, where her soft, honeysuckle scent was strongest.

"I love you, too."

He rolled to the side and let his hand trail along her shoulder. "And I love our home."

She laughed. "Okay."

"And our family."

She caught his chin and forced his eyes to hers. Giovanni met her gaze, bathing in the comfort of her energy as it wrapped them both. "Where are you tonight?"

He still marveled that she could read him so well. "Just... thinking about the past."

Beatrice's eyes held nothing but the soft light of understanding. "Anything you want to share?"

He shook his head. She paused for a minute, examining him before she leaned in for a gentle kiss. Giovanni kissed her back, letting his amnis spread over her skin to tease her senses. He could feel her desire twine with his, and he sat up, pulling her with him and pressing her mouth to his neck.

"Bite," he growled. "Feed from me."

"Thought you'd never ask."

"Since when have you ever waited for permission?"

Giovanni heard a low purr before her fangs pierced his skin.

"What is on your agenda tonight?" he asked as he dressed in his uniform of black slacks and a dress shirt. Beatrice lounged in the bath, enjoying the calm of the water before she left their room.

"I've got some translation to do on the journals. I already helped Ben with his homework today, but I'll drive him to Tenzin's later tonight and practice for a while."

"I wanted to talk to you about that. I asked Ernesto to call Baojia back from San Diego."

Beatrice raised her eyebrow. "Oh, really? Did Grandpa decide to let him out of time-out?"

Giovanni grimaced. "I asked Ernesto to bring him back so he could continue your training. I spoke to Baojia last week and he wanted to know how your weapons were progressing. He says Tenzin is not a good enough teacher."

She smiled. "It's going fine. I'm always grateful for help though. I was talking about it with Tenzin the other night. She says I'm more than proficient with the *dao,* and I'm fine with the *jian.* I never really liked using a *jian* much, to be honest, so I'm not too concerned—"

"Baojia says you're ready for the *shuang gou.*"

Her eyes lit up. "The hook-swords?"

"Yes."

"Wicked."

He smirked and walked over for a quick kiss. "Glad you agree. I'll probably be in the library most of the night. I want to go over some of my uncle's correspondence before we leave for Rome."

"This trip is going to be safe, right? I know you want to bring Ben, but it's not worth it if you think there's any danger of—"

"Nothing we can't handle, Tesoro." He leaned against the edge of the counter. "We'll see Livia, and I'll introduce you to her people. We'll play nice for a week or so, and then she'll lose interest. That's what she always does. She's always after the shiny new toy. Right now, she's curious, that's all. Honestly, I should have taken you to see her right after we got married, but we had a bit on the schedule."

"So no reason to worry?"

"No." He frowned. "Are you worried?"

Beatrice shrugged. "Well, she's the closest thing I have to a mother-in-law. From all reports, she's also an incredibly beautiful, two-thousand-year-old, Roman noblewoman. And she is, according to you, one of the most powerful vampires in Europe. Nope, nothing intimidating about her at all."

Giovanni bent down, ignoring the water soaking his knees. "Nothing to worry about. She'll love you."

"Yeah?" She couldn't hide the skepticism in her voice.

He grabbed her chin and laid a hard kiss on her mouth. "Since when is my woman afraid?"

Her eyes narrowed. "I'm not afraid."

"Good." He stood and straightened his collar. "You'll love Rome. And since Kirby and Desiree can come along with Benjamin, we'll all have a grand time. Tenzin will... she'll put up with it for your sake. Try to persuade her not to kill anyone."

"Hmm."

"What now?"

"Just thinking. We'll need to figure out something about accommodations. We're going to be there for three months and there's six of us, so—"

"We have a house in Rome. It has plenty of room."

Beatrice blinked. "We do?"

"I have a large house in Rome, an estate outside Florence, and a smaller flat in Milan. Didn't I tell you that?"

"Anything else?"

"That's all that I have in Italy. I have a few other places scattered around Europe."

Beatrice paused. "Was that on your husband profile right under your ability to burn pasta? Because, I'll be honest, anything after the description of your sexual skills I just skipped over."

He burst out laughing and tossed a hand towel at her. It hit her in the face.

"Hey!" She flicked her fingers and a spray of water crossed the room, soaking him.

"Thanks for that." He stripped off the wet shirt.

"Aha! My devious plan worked; you're naked again." She grabbed his hand as he walked past and pulled him into the tub.

"Tesoro?"

"Yes?"

"Are we going to accomplish anything tonight?"

"Probably not."

Hours later, he managed to pull himself away when Ben resorted to calling their room, threatening to steal the car to drive himself to practice. Though Giovanni was agreeable to that scenario, Beatrice was not. She muttered something about "stupid teenage drivers" as she pulled on her practice clothes and left the room, blowing him a kiss over her shoulder.

He wandered down to the library on the first floor, where he had shipped most of his uncle's collection of books, letters, and artwork. He had expanded the original library during the year they had been in Chile and added a pool house, as well. All the windows had lightproof shutters, which allowed Beatrice to have use of most of the house during the day. He had spared no expense making sure their home suited his wife's somewhat unusual needs.

Just as he was sitting down with a collection of letters between Girolamo Benivieni and his uncle, Giovanni Pico, the phone rang. Looking at the clock, he realized it was probably Carwyn calling before dawn.

Giovanni picked up the phone. "Hello, Father."

"That would have been awkward if it was Livia."

"You know she never uses the phone. She can barely stand using the postal service instead of uniformed messenger."

"And yet she does love her fancy lights and indoor plumbing."

"No one can ever claim she was anything but an aristocrat."

"So, speaking of your mummy—"

"Please, don't call her that," he said with a wince. Carwyn only chuckled. "Ever. I'm serious."

"Fine. Speaking of the Roman she-devil, when will you be there?"

He rolled his eyes. Carwyn had always had a clear disdain for anything having to do with Rome. The Welshman barely put up with his own friends at the Vatican, who had known about the priest's existence for centuries, and he delighted in making snide remarks about the arrogance of ecclesiastical and military empires.

"We'll be there at the beginning of May. Will you be joining us?"

"Will Tenzin be there? And the boy?"

"Of course."

"Well, I wouldn't want to miss out on the party. I'll see you there. I could use a visit with a few people in red bathrobes anyway."

That was unexpected. Carwyn usually avoided Vatican City if possible. "Oh? Anything I need to know about?"

"Just some... personal details. Collar-type things you'd have no interest in."

The priest was being uncharacteristically cagey, but Giovanni let it rest. He knew if his old friend wanted to share, he would. Carwyn had few secrets, but those he did have, he kept very close. Giovanni decided to change the subject.

"How's Deirdre?"

Carwyn paused. "She's doing well. As well as can be expected. She's keeping busy. Has quite a few projects she's juggling at the moment."

"Good."

"And how is your wife?"

"Doing extremely well. She's practicing with Ben and Tenzin tonight, though I believe she'll be training with Baojia again in the near future."

"Oh, you must be thrilled."

"I can... appreciate his usefulness."

Carwyn only laughed. "And the bloodlust? How's she doing with that? Any slips?"

He shrugged. "Doesn't seem to be a problem. She still feels it, from what she says, but her control is so good you wouldn't know it was ever a problem. She's extraordinary."

"Well, that's no surprise."

"I suppose not; she's always performed beyond expectations."

"Speaking of things I don't need to know about..."

Giovanni snorted. "Aren't you amusing?"

"Sometimes."

He frowned. Something was bothering his friend. "Are you sure you don't have things at home you need to take care of? We'd all love to see you in Rome, but it's not necessary if you're busy."

Carwyn paused. "I'm sure. I've been here too long as it is."

"Where are you? I thought you were calling from home."

"No, I'm in Ireland."

"Still looking through Ioan's library? If he's the doctor that Stephen mentioned in the journals, it's possible that they were in contact. Have you looked through his letters?"

"Deirdre has. I've been through his library, and so far, there's nothing. Nothing about the research that Lorenzo tortured him over, either. In fact, anything related to vampire blood seems to be gone, though I know he had at least one book that he wrote, detailing its uses in treating humans. Deirdre is quite certain that no one has been in their library except their immediate family and nothing seems disturbed. I've been writing letters to the rest of the family and his other colleagues to see if he lent his work to anyone, but as you can imagine, the list is fairly long."

"I hate to pull you away if you're needed there. Are you sure—"

"Yes, I need to get away from here for a bit." Carwyn sighed. "I'll see you in Rome the beginning of May, Gio. Keep out of trouble and say hello to B for me. I need to go."

"You're acting strange."

The priest laughed. "When do I not act strange?"

Giovanni scowled. "Fine. Keep your secrets."

"Just following your excellent example. I'll see you in a month or so."

"Good night, Carwyn."

"Good night."

He hung up, but couldn't shake the feeling that something was very wrong. Carwyn had lost much of his normally affable demeanor since Ioan's death, and Giovanni knew that witnessing his family's grief was even more wrenching than his own. Reminding himself that Lorenzo still walked the earth, free to hurt others, he dove back into research. He pulled out the letters and turned to one dated 1488, written from Benivieni to his uncle when they were in Paris.

"My dear Giovanni, I saw the odd Signore Andros in Rome last month. He was speaking with the Moor who is visiting with the governor on some trade issue. He really is a most strange gentleman. I cannot ascertain your preoccupation with him..."

CHAPTER THREE

Los Angeles, California
April 2012

In the four years since Ben Vecchio had lived with his adopted uncle, it wasn't unusual for him to pinch himself to make sure he was awake. It wasn't when he saw his uncle dart by so fast that his eyes blurred or noticed his aunt's new fangs peek out of her mouth. The fact that he had been adopted by vampires no longer fazed the young man. No, it was the mornings he woke in a warm bed, surrounded by the sounds of family and signs of comfort that he pinched himself.

But pinching was the last thing he needed to do to remind himself he wasn't dreaming when it came time for practice with Tenzin.

"I'm going to keep beating you up until you get this," Tenzin said as she punched his shoulder. "You're horrible today. Very distracted."

"Hey." He scowled and threw up an arm, instinctively blocking the strike she aimed at his face. "Can we take a break and watch them already? It's kinda hard to concentrate."

"What? Them?" Tenzin glanced over her shoulder at Baojia and Beatrice as they practiced with the new swords that Baojia had brought. Ben snuck in a quick jab to her knee while she was turned.

Tenzin's leg buckled and she looked back with a smile. "Good. Opportunistic is good. Fine, we can watch them for a while. I'd better make sure that vampire doesn't slice her up before Gio gets here anyway."

Tenzin walked over to the wall opposite the weapons training area in the industrial building. When she'd moved to Los Angeles, she had bought the nondescript complex off Allen Avenue and gutted it, turning the majority of the large area into her own personal training studio. She had shipped many of her own weapons over from somewhere in China, and now Giovanni, Beatrice, Tenzin, Ben, and currently, Baojia, used the large space to work out and train.

Beatrice and Baojia were sparring in the corner, Beatrice using the curved *dao* she usually trained with, while Baojia used the twin blades of the *shuang gou* he had brought to introduce into her training regimen.

"Why isn't she using them?" Ben asked. "I thought she was supposed to be learning."

"Watch and learn. He's showing her how to defend herself against them before he teaches her how to attack. Watching Baojia use them will be the most effective way for her to learn."

The longer Ben watched, the more he could see the wisdom of it. Initially, Beatrice was cautious, weaving and ducking away from the other vampire, darting in occasionally with a quick thrust of her saber, but mostly, dancing around him. He saw Baojia hook the swords together in one swift movement, sweeping the blades over his head and then down toward Beatrice's legs as she jumped to escape the broad reach of the wicked edge. He swung them around like a chain or rope, and the double-sided blades cut through the air, lethal from all angles as they sought their target.

Ben frowned. "He wouldn't actually hurt her, would he?"

Tenzin only shrugged. "He won't cut her head off. He's more careful than that. If he slices her up a bit, well... that's just part of training."

Ben had a feeling that his uncle might have a distinctly different attitude about the whole matter, but that was probably why Giovanni rarely joined them when Beatrice was fighting. As cultured and calm as his uncle usually was, Ben had witnessed his rare fury once when he thought Tenzin had attacked his wife too fiercely. The flames from his outburst had singed the hair off Ben's forearms from ten feet away. Beatrice was furious, but Giovanni only snarled and told Ben to run faster next time.

Secretly, Ben thought it was the coolest thing he'd ever seen.

"How long will it be before she's really good with them?"

"Watch her now," Tenzin murmured. "Watch, boy."

It irritated Ben that Tenzin always called him "boy," but he supposed he couldn't really say anything about it. Even if she only looked a few years older than him, he knew she was the oldest vampire he would probably ever meet. The funny thing about Tenzin was she still acted like a little kid at times. Beatrice said it was because she was so old and didn't get out in the modern world all that much, but Tenzin was still amazed by weird stuff like TV and cars. She hated cars, but she liked the television. She really loved going to the movies, and she and Ben had fallen into the habit of going to see one at least once a week. She liked 3D pictures the best.

Tenzin reached over and whacked his arm. "Boy, are you watching?"

"My name is *Ben*," he grumbled, but turned his attention back to Beatrice and Baojia. He could see what Tenzin meant. Beatrice was no longer simply reacting to Baojia's attacks, she was now actively attacking him, spotting tiny opportunities to throw the other vampire off balance, or make his grip on the *shuang gou* waver.

"Oh, wow," he whispered as they picked up speed. Soon, both vampires were whirling in an almost sickening blur, whipping around each other, jumping and leaping, while the blades caught the glint from the overhead lights. Finally, Ben had to look away. He was starting to get motion sick from the speed of their movements.

"Ah... ah..." From the corner of his eye, he saw Tenzin lean forward and laugh. Ben chanced a look up, only to see Beatrice standing in front of Baojia. She had taken one of the *shuang gou* from him and held it, along with her saber, at the other vampire's neck as he was pressed against the wall.

"And she's got him," Tenzin said. She turned to Ben with a grin. "Did you see? She's very good. No one will stab her again."

As soon as she said it, he saw the flicker of sadness in her grey eyes. Tenzin quickly looked away as Ben watched the expression drain from her face.

"Nope," he said, teasing. "That's my fake aunt, toughest vampire around."

Tenzin turned back to him with a smirk. "Now, you're just asking me to beat you up again."

"What?" he scoffed. "You're a little girl. What kind of—okay, ow!" Tenzin pounced on Ben and twisted his arm behind his back. "Ow, *ow*... Tenzin, I was joking."

"'Little girl?' You are an infant."

"I'm not going to be able to practice if you take my arm off. Ow!" His eyes rolled back until he heard a swift, whooshing sound. Suddenly, her grip loosened.

"Please don't damage the boy, bird-girl. He whines when he's in too much pain."

Ben rolled on his side to see his uncle's leather dress shoes by his face.

"Hey, Gio." He looked up at Giovanni's amused face.

"What did you say to piss her off?"

"I called her a little girl."

His eyebrow cocked, and Giovanni glanced at Tenzin, who had flown over to speak to Baojia and Beatrice as they were putting the weapons away.

"You're a brave fool, Benjamin."

Ben snickered and took the hand his uncle held out. "You should have seen B. She was awesome. She totally beat Baojia with the hook swords."

"Excellent." Giovanni smiled. "I am almost sorry I missed it."

"Yeah? Well, I'm glad I still have all my hair, so thanks for keeping away."

"What are you doing tonight?"

Ben's eyes darted away. "Oh... you know, just gonna head home and maybe hang out for a while. I got a history test on Monday. Stupid French Revolution stuff. Nothing major, but..."

"Ben, I can hear your heartbeat; I know you're lying."

He huffed. "I'm just... sheesh, man. I don't ask you what you're doing every hour of the day."

"Are you meeting a girl?"

"What?" Ben's face reddened. "No, I'm not." *This time.*

Luckily, Giovanni must have decided that Ben was lying about his true intentions because he just grunted and leaned toward the boy. "Be careful. Be respectful. That's all I require. And be in your bed by morning."

"I'm not—never mind." Let him think he was going out to meet Heather or Brianna. Ben walked over and picked up a towel, wiping the sweat from his forehead before he walked to the small locker room to wash up. "Whatever. I'll see you guys later."

Ben showered, grabbed his helmet, and walked out to his scooter. At fifteen, he was still breaking the law by riding it, but Giovanni and Beatrice both turned a blind eye since their schedules and his were so screwy, and Caspar was getting older. Besides, Ben just felt weird making Caspar drive him around when he was perfectly capable of doing it himself. With his height and his deep voice, Ben had never attracted attention riding the stripped-down Honda Ruckus, and he always kept it on surface streets. He couldn't wait till he was sixteen, and he could finally get Beatrice's old motorcycle.

Ben made a show of riding off, only to double back and wait in an alley, watching for his aunt and uncle to exit the building. He saw Baojia and Tenzin leave. Baojia walked toward a parked car with a driver in front, and Tenzin ducked toward the back of the building before he saw her small form take to the sky in a blur.

Still, he waited.

Ben didn't know why, but recently, the idea of how Beatrice and Giovanni were feeding was starting to bug him. Did they feed on random strangers? Criminals? He was starting to entertain crazy notions of them stalking gang members in dark alleys like modern day superheroes, and he knew he was being ridiculous. He felt awkward asking, so he decided that the easiest way to find out would be to trail them when they went out. It was Friday night, and he knew they would feed, because both of them always looked flushed on Saturday, and Beatrice usually slept a little during the day, which she rarely needed to do.

Ben waited in the shadows until he saw them walk out, hand in hand. They were on foot, so he left his scooter in the alley and prayed that no one would bother it. He followed behind them as they turned the corner and headed toward a clutch of storefronts. They must have walked a mile, both of them strolling at a human pace, chatting and laughing together like any other couple out for a date. Beatrice had her hand tucked around

Giovanni's waist, and his hand occasionally reached up to play with the ends of her hair. Ben envied the easy love he saw between them and wondered if he would ever find someone that loved him like that.

No matter, he thought with a grin. There was plenty of time for that and plenty of interested girls in the meantime.

Ben saw them turn a corner and walk toward a bar where a loud group of what looked like college kids gathered on the patio outside, drinking and smoking. They paused across the street, then looked at each other. Giovanni gave Beatrice a small nod, and they crossed the road.

"What are you doing?"

Ben almost fell over when he heard the voice at his ear.

"Dammit, Tenzin!" he gasped and spun around. "You scared me to death!"

"Why are you following your aunt and uncle?"

"I'm... not. I'm not following them. I'm just..." He cleared his throat and stared into her skeptical grey eyes.

She looked across the street, then back at him. "Yes, you are. And you are a bad liar."

"You know, I'm actually a really good liar unless I'm talking to a vampire who can hear my heartbeat."

She shrugged. "Well, it's too bad that half of your family are vampires then. Why are you following Gio and B?"

"I'm just... I was just... worried."

"About?"

"Them. You know, with all the danger and... stuff." He was flailing. Ben could charm his way out of practically any situation imaginable. He could charm the harshest teacher at school with a flash of his smile. He could get any of the girls to do his boring homework for him by batting his long, dark lashes, but Tenzin...

He sighed. Tenzin was uncharmable.

She waited, standing with preternatural stillness that seemed to wrench the truth from his gut.

"I'm just curious, all right?"

"About?"

"How they... you know..."

She furrowed her brows. "Are you one of those strange boys who likes to watch people do personal things? A 'Peeping Tim?'"

"Tom! It's 'Peeping Tom,' Tenzin."

"Oh, and you are one of them?" She didn't look disgusted, just curious as she cocked her head to the side.

"No!"

"Then why are you following them?"

"I'm just curious about... the eating thing."

"About what?"

Ben flushed to the roots of his hair. "The eating—feeding thing, you know? Who do they eat from? What do they... I mean, do they kill people? Do they... I don't know!"

She scowled. "They don't kill people. Why do you think they kill people?"

"I don't think they kill people."

"But you just said—"

"I'm just curious, okay?"

"So why don't you ask them?"

He shrugged. "I don't know. It just seems rude."

Tenzin curled her lip. "It's rude to ask them, but following them is not? You are a very odd boy."

"I'm not—"

"Come on." She waved at him and started walking back down the street. "I'll walk back to your bicycle with you."

He frowned and started to follow her. "It's not a bicycle, Tenzin."

"It has two wheels, doesn't it? Bi. Cycle."

"You're so weird."

"I'm not the one following my aunt and uncle and being a Peeping Tim."

"Tom."

"Who?"

Ben reached over to tug at a chunk of her dark hair. "Never mind."

"Is he gone?" Beatrice sipped a glass of wine and peeked at Giovanni from the corner of her eye as he sat across from her at the small table.

"Yes, she grabbed him. They're walking back to the warehouse now."

"Why do you think he was he following us?"

Giovanni shrugged and picked up the glass of Jameson she had ordered for him. "I heard him asking Caspar—in what he probably thought was a subtle way—about what we're eating. He's probably curious. He knows we're not feeding from bagged blood anymore. Do you think he's worried we're draining the innocent and wreaking havoc on Southern California?"

Beatrice snorted. "Well, will you have a talk with him tomorrow, so we don't have a repeat of this?"

Giovanni curled his lip, but nodded. "I avoided the sex talk, so I suppose it's only fair."

She looked at her mate, amused by the uncomfortable expression on his face. It was the oddest things that seemed to be an issue for him. Teaching Ben how to kill someone silently and with minimal blood spray? No problem. Telling him about sex or feeding? Immediate squirm.

Beatrice laid a comforting hand on his shoulder, but her ears perked up when she heard the booming voice of the college boy at the table next to her. The young man was regaling his friends with some highly unlikely sexual exploit. He was also, apparently, familiar with a surprising number of professional athletes, Hollywood starlets, and at least one dangerous African warlord.

Her eyes lit up, and she looked at Giovanni. "Go ahead," he said with a smile. "He's your favorite flavor."

She grinned. "I do love the sweet taste of bragging liar."

Her husband chuckled, shaking his head and leaning back to watch her work. As soon as the bragging boy went back to the bar, she followed him. He was taking a long draw from his imported beer when Beatrice sidled up to him. His eyes raked over her breasts before he finally looked up to her eyes. She smiled, careful to conceal her fangs.

"Hi, how are you?"

She held him by the neck in the back alley. "And what are you doing in your classes?"

The boy's dazed eyes swam. "Well... not much."

"So you're wasting all the hard-earned money that your parents are putting into your education?"

"Yeah, I guess so."

"Do you think your mother's proud of you?"

The drunk boy shook his head sadly. "Probably not."

"But you're going to turn over a new leaf, right, Dave?"

"Oh, yeah." He nodded with a smile. "Totally."

"Good. Make your parents proud of you."

"Okay."

"And the next girlfriend you have, you're going to be respectful and faithful, right?"

"Right."

She heard the back door open and felt Giovanni's energy as he walked toward them.

"Are you being a guidance counselor again? Stop playing with your food."

She glanced over her shoulder. "I get blood; he gets some good advice."

"Can't you just drink him so we can do other, more *interesting*, things?" She heard the low growl in his voice and decided the college boy had been given enough advice for one night. She looked back at Dave, letting her amnis wash up his neck.

"Give me your wrist."

He lifted his wrist and she grabbed it, turning to stare at her mate as she bared her fangs and struck. She heard the boy give a low sigh of pleasure as she drank from him, but she kept a firm grip on his throat, monitoring his pulse as she locked her eyes with Giovanni's.

Her mate watched her with hungry eyes, pacing a short distance away, and she saw his fangs grow long in his mouth. His tongue darted out and licked his lips as he watched her drink, and Beatrice knew that she would not be the only one feeding that night. She took a few more deep swallows of the boy's blood before she sealed the wounds and whispered instructions in his ear, keeping her eyes on Giovanni the whole time.

The mindless boy wandered back into the bar, and Giovanni waited for the alley door to click before he sprung on her. He shoved Beatrice up against the wall, pushing her arms over her head as he attacked her mouth. One hand held her wrists against the sharp brick while the other slid down her side, dragging her hips to his as he pushed their bodies together.

Beatrice hissed and bared her fangs, reacting instinctively to his attack. Her hands fought against his iron grip, and she finally worked one free only to reach around and drag Giovanni even closer, pulling at his shirt and digging her fingers into the hot flesh at the small of his back. He whipped her around so that he was leaning against the wall and she climbed his body, locking her thighs around his hips as they moved together.

"Home," he snarled.

"Here. We'll hear anyone coming."

"Fine." Giovanni grabbed her hair, angling her neck to the side as she gasped. "You listen, I have other things to do."

Her eyes rolled back when his fangs struck. If anyone interrupted them after that, Beatrice just didn't notice.

"They're babies! It doesn't count!"

"Yes, it does."

Beatrice frowned when she heard Ben and Tenzin arguing from the living room as she and Giovanni walked through the kitchen door hours later.

"Babies can't help drooling, so it doesn't count."

She raised an eyebrow and looked at Giovanni, who only shrugged his shoulders.

"I think you're wrong." They heard Tenzin speak again. "And I am older, so I am right."

"Do you think that B and Gio will ever adopt a baby?"

"I certainly hope not. They're very messy, and they smell horrible."

Beatrice shook her head and walked toward the living room. Giovanni locked the door behind him before he followed her.

"If we do," she said as she entered the room, "you two will be last on the babysitting list, that's for sure."

"Hey!" Ben raised his hands. "I was defending the human babies. Tenzin is the barbarian here."

Tenzin rolled her eyes. "I was simply saying that once a human has reached the drooling stage, it is a valid question whether they should be considered a real human or not."

Ben just stared at her, shaking his head. "So not cool, Tenzin."

Giovanni sat in his favorite chair and pulled Beatrice to sit in his lap. "You two bicker more than old married people."

"Hey! You're the only old married people I see," Ben said.

Tenzin curled her lip at Giovanni. "We do not."

Beatrice shrugged. "Just be nice to Dez and Matt's baby when it gets here, that's all I'm asking."

Dez and Matt had been married the previous week, and the couple was vacationing on one of Ernesto's yachts before they returned to Los Angeles and accompanied Beatrice, Giovanni, and Ben to Rome. Beatrice had some concern about her friend traveling so early in her pregnancy, but Dez seemed nonchalant about the matter, so she was trying not to worry.

"Is Tenzin coming on the plane with us?"

"No," Tenzin said firmly. "I will meet you all within the week, but you will not get me on that flying contraption again. It's unnatural."

"Who's coming on the plane, then?"

Giovanni leaned back and closed his eyes. "Desiree, Kirby, and the three of us. Carwyn will meet us there."

"Cool," Ben said as he stood. "I'm going to bed."

"Good, it's late."

Tenzin piped up from the couch, "We are watching movies tomorrow night."

Beatrice asked, "What are we watching?"

"We're going to Rome." Ben shrugged. "*Gladiator. Spartacus.*"

"*Ben Hur. Cleopatra,*" Tenzin said.

Beatrice grinned. "*Roman Holiday*?"

"*The Life of Brian*?" Giovanni suggested.

"No," Tenzin and Ben said together.

Beatrice said, "You two are so predictable." She leaned back and laid her head on Giovanni's shoulder. She felt his hand comb through her hair, and she closed her eyes, content and sated in her lover's arms. Soon, Ben walked up to bed, and Tenzin retreated to the den with the television.

"Everything's going to be okay in Rome, right?"

"Yes. Whatever happens, we will handle it."

Beatrice still had the sneaking suspicion that their trip to the Eternal City was going to be far more interesting than Giovanni predicted, but she kept silent. They had to go, and they might find out more about her father's informant when they were there. Stephen De Novo had received too much valuable and accurate information on his hunt for Geber's elixir of life for it to be merely coincidence. The ancient city held secrets, and hopefully, a few answers as well.

For almost a year, she had been studying Geber's journals and jotting down characteristics the alchemist had noted from his immortal "donors" when she found them. With enough time, and with Giovanni's knowledge of the intricate immortal court in Rome, Beatrice might have a chance of identifying the original four vampires who had contributed to the elixir. If they could find those four, then they were one step closer to understanding the mystery, and just maybe, they would be a step ahead of Lorenzo.

She felt Giovanni's skin heat up, and he began to nose against her neck.

"More?" she murmured.

"More."

CHAPTER FOUR

Crotone, Italy
1494

Jacopo was starving.

He pulled himself up from the thin pallet on the floor and crawled to the door where a jar of water stood. He had eaten the four thin wafers that had been slipped under the door, but his stomach still growled. The flavorless bread was the only food he had been given in the previous week, though his water had been replenished on a daily basis.

Jacopo reached for the door, pulling on it again before he paced the room. Just then, a timid knock sounded. A few moments later, he heard the key turn, and the door cracked open. He saw the edge of a vivid-blue eye in the darkness of the corridor, and then a mop of shining blond hair poked though.

"Hello?" The boy was small, perhaps ten years of age, and he held a large loaf of bread in his hands. He was dressed in clean clothes, costly: the clothing of a servant in a fine house.

"Who are you?" Jacopo crouched in the corner, watching the small boy come closer. His stomach rumbled as the smell of the warm bread wafted toward him.

"It's morning, so the master is in his chamber," the boy said. "He won't come out until nightfall. I brought this for you."

Still, Jacopo eyed him warily. "Who are you?" he asked again.

"I'm Paulo." He smiled and held out the bread. "Master told the servants not to feed you, that you had to steal food for yourself, but no one had seen you, so I thought you might be sick."

Bits of information clicked into place. The week before, Andros had come to him and told Jacopo that he was strong enough to start his training. *You need to be taught self-reliance,* Andros had said with a strange glint in his eye. The next morning, there was water when he woke, but no food.

Jacopo frowned at the boy and ignored the gnawing in his stomach. "He wants me to steal food from him?"

Paulo nodded. "I heard him telling the cook. He told her if she found food missing, not to be alarmed, that he wanted you to learn how to escape your room and steal it."

"Crazy old man," Jacopo muttered. "Fine, he wants me to steal; I'll steal from him. And I will learn how to escape this wretched chamber, as well." Though he hadn't been forced to steal since his uncle had adopted him, he had once been adept at picking locks. If Andros wanted Jacopo to escape his room, it wouldn't be a problem.

"So"—Paulo held out the bread—"do you want it? I brought it for you."

Jacopo looked at the seemingly innocent boy with the wide, blue gaze. Why would he bring him bread and risk the anger of the master of the house? Was this boy a spy of some sort? Would Jacopo receive a beating for taking the bread from him? Perhaps it was a test.

"I want nothing from you," Jacopo said. "Why do you bring me bread when Andros wants me to steal it? Do you run to him and tell him of my weakness later?"

As soon as he said it, Jacopo knew it had not been the boy's intention. Paulo's face fell, and a hard mask slipped over his previously open features. Jacopo regretted that he had rebuffed the boy's kindness, but he had no desire to attract the wrath of Niccolo Andros by defying him.

The boy straightened his shoulders. "I brought it to tempt you," Paulo said with false bravado. "It's only a shame you can't taste it for yourself." The blond boy took a large bite from the fragrant loaf, and Jacopo could smell the herbs the cook had used in the bread. His mouth watered.

He leapt up, pouncing on the boy and knocking him to the ground. Jacopo slapped his face and grabbed the loaf from his hands. Paulo's eyes watered, but he twisted his mouth into a sneer as Jacopo tossed the bread to the corner.

"Go. Tell the cook I stole your bread and beat you. She will not blame you for the loss." He stood and held out a hand to the boy, but Paulo rolled away and stood on his own.

"You're a filthy animal." Paulo curled his lip. "I can smell you from here. Signore Andros will surely get rid of you when he smells you through the house."

"Oh?" Jacopo cocked his head. "Has he brought boys to his home before?" What was this madness Niccolo Andros had planned? Where there other boys like him hidden in this cold, stone castle?

"No," Paulo said. "Signore Andros is a most cultured and honorable man. When he sees you, I'm sure he will be displeased and send you away."

Jacopo smirked. "So, I am the only one he ordered the cook not to feed?"

"Yes," Paulo said with a shrug.

He wandered to the corner and grabbed the bread, tearing off a chunk and stuffing it in his mouth. It was the finest thing he had ever tasted. "So I am the only one he keeps like this? The only... prisoner."

"He calls you his student."

"Is that so?"

"Yes." Paulo was backing toward the door as Jacopo tore off another chunk of bread.

"And I am the only student?"

"Yes, but he will send you away when he smells you, *animal*."

A grim smile curled Jacopo's lips. "Paulo, how many servants does Signore Andros have?"

"Many." He sneered again. "He has many servants."

"And how many 'students' does he have?"

Paulo's eyes narrowed. "Just you."

Jacopo walked toward the haughty boy, towering over him. At seventeen years of age, he was taller than most grown men, as tall as the father he had never met. He stared down at the blond boy in his clean clothes and scrubbed face.

"Well, if I am your master's *only* student, and you are one of many servants, then I think we know the one who is expendable, no?"

En route to Rome
May 2012

Giovanni woke, brushing the dream from his mind and looking around the compartment for Beatrice. He could hear the low hum of the engines as they flew. He spotted her sitting in a chair in the corner, notebooks spread over her side of the bed.

"Where are we?"

She looked up with a smile. "Hey! You know, you're sleeping a lot less now, too."

"I don't find that surprising, considering how much blood we exchange." His wife's blood was powerful, more powerful than even he had predicted, and his waking hours were growing longer as a result. Though the phenomenon had its advantages, he did not envy her lack of rest.

"I've found something interesting in the journals."

"Oh?"

She nodded with a grin. "I think I've finally identified the four original donors."

He sat up and leaned over the spread notebooks. "How? You've been looking for months."

Beatrice opened her notebook and handed it to him. "I don't have them exactly, but I've been making notes every time he mentions them in his journals, and I finally found a reference to the one I'd been missing, the earth donor."

"What did you find?" He began paging through her notes, deciphering the strange shorthand she had developed since she had turned. Most vampires developed some sort of unique language for their thoughts over time. Since their minds moved more rapidly than mortals, it was the best way to record thoughts and had the added benefit of concealing their meaning from the casual reader. To anyone else, Beatrice's writing would have been gibberish; Giovanni alone could read it.

"What is this?" He pointed toward an unknown symbol. "This is new."

"It stands for '*Aethiop*.'"

"'Aethiop?' You mean the earth donor was Ethiopian?"

She nodded with a grin. "Yep, and she—"

"She?"

"Uh-huh, another surprise. The others were clearly male, but this one was definitely female because Geber notes that preliminary testing on her blood showed no discernible difference because of sex."

"Which would only be notable if her sex was different." Giovanni smiled. "Nicely done, Tesoro."

"So, we have his names for the four, which all indicate their origin... except for his friend."

Giovanni paged through the notebook. "The Greek, the Numidian, the Aethiop, and 'my dear friend.'"

Beatrice sighed. "I don't want to make assumptions, because medieval Kufa was so diverse."

He nodded. "It was in decline, in a political sense, during Geber's lifetime, but it was an active center of learning and scholarship, so it could have been a friend from any number of backgrounds. Arab and Persian are the most likely, but many vampires were drawn to the Middle East during that period because there was so much going on."

"He does use the medieval Persian word for 'friend' so that could be significant."

Giovanni shook his head. "It could just as easily *not* be significant. All his personal journals were written in Persian. And if we are looking for your father's contact in Rome, it could be less than helpful. Livia has always kept a very diverse court... well, diverse for a Roman."

She cocked her head. "What do you mean?"

"She takes pride in having tokens from all areas of the Roman Empire, thinks it adds to the 'imperial' quality. Shows how magnanimous she is. So, all of these, Greek, Numidian, Ethiopian, any of these would be common in the Roman court. Nothing particularly notable there. We'll have to wait and see who's been keeping her company the last few years. It changes all the time with a few notable exceptions. Rome is probably the most 'international' of the European immortal courts."

"But old. We're looking for older vampires, for sure."

He shrugged. "The experiments were conducted around 800 A.D.? We're looking for four vampires over a thousand years old. In Rome, it's not uncommon. Though the majority of the population is fairly young, there are so many older vampires who come and go that one of a thousand years would not stand out."

She scowled. "Well, thanks for raining on my parade, Captain Sunshine."

He chuckled and put the notebook down. "However, this is exceptional work, as always. I don't tell you enough how brilliant you are."

"No, you really don't."

Beatrice was still pretending to pout, so he pushed the notebooks aside to grab her hand and pull her toward him. "You're brilliant... beautiful."

"Yes, keep it coming," she said, waving her other hand.

"Smart, sexy." He pulled her to straddle his lap and began running his fingers along her spine, enjoying the shiver of excitement that rose between them. "Very sexy."

"More," she whispered, and Giovanni grinned, not sure whether she was talking about the compliments or the caresses.

"Thorough. Thoroughly lovely, that is..." His lips nibbled along her jawline as her hands tangled in his hair. "You're just so..." He breathed out along her skin, causing her to shiver. "*So...*"

"What?" She panted as his fingers teased her.

He pulled back and traced his tongue along her lower lip. "You're so... *meticulous.*" He drew the word out sensuously.

Finally, she giggled and tackled him to the bed.

"Giovanni Vecchio, you sure know how to seduce a woman."

"No." He rolled over and tucked her into his chest as his hands continued to tease. "I just know how to seduce you."

Rome, Italy

It was after ten o'clock when they landed in Rome. The plane had touched down without incident, but Matt and Giovanni were both wary in the foreign territory. Luckily, neither was unfamiliar with the city; Matt had spent plenty of time in Rome, and for Giovanni, Rome was like a second home. His knowledge of it was trumped only by his knowledge of Florence, which had a very low vampire population. Rome, on the other hand, was teeming with the creatures.

They exited the plane, only to be met by a dark car that Matt had ordered. As planned, Beatrice stood guard over Dez and Ben, her watchful gaze sweeping around as Giovanni and Matt thoroughly checked the vehicle for any listening devices or explosives. He knew their arrival was expected, and Giovanni would take no chances with his family's safety. Rome was a city with a long memory.

"Clear for bugs," Matt said quietly.

"And I don't sense any energy signatures or smell any explosives. Beatrice?" Beatrice, like most water vampires, had developed an extremely keen sense of smell.

"I don't smell anything suspicious."

"Excellent." Giovanni walked over to the driver, shaking his hand and quickly asking him a few questions that reassured him the man had been sent by the usual car service he used in Rome. The five passengers squeezed into the small car as Matt sat in the front, directing the driver to Giovanni's home near the Pantheon.

"How old is your house?" Ben asked as they sped through the streets. The driver swerved to avoid a horde of passing Vespas, and Giovanni could hear the man cursing under his breath. It was Friday night in Rome, and the streets were alive with activity.

"Wow," Beatrice said. "And I thought New York was busy at night."

"My home was built in the sixteenth century, Ben."

"Wow, that's old. It has bathrooms and stuff, right?"

He grinned. "Yes."

"And I have my own room?"

"Yes, Angela said she had prepared a room just for you."

"Sweet." Ben grinned and settled back into his seat as he watched the lights speed by. "Dude, I need a Vespa."

"I do, too!" Dez said.

"No, you don't," Giovanni and Matt said together, while Beatrice laughed.

"There's really no need for a scooter." Giovanni tried to reason with them. You will be within easy walking distance of most of the sites. My home is very centrally located."

"And, Honey," Matt protested, "the baby—"

"Likes going fast. He told me." Dez patted her still-flat belly and grinned at her husband. "Just like he told me that he hopes there's food at Gio's house 'cause he's starving."

Giovanni chuckled and turned back to watch the streets. They zipped through Rome, drawing closer to the neighborhood where he had kept a home for almost as long as he had been immortal. The area around the Pantheon was in the oldest part of Rome, and his unassuming home there took up half a small block. He kept it deliberately plain from the outside, but it was an excellent defensive position with many passageways and access points he had built over hundreds of years. He kept two staff members in residence, his housekeeper, Angela, and a butler, Bruno, who he saw waiting as they turned up the small, twisting street that bordered the house.

"Here we are."

Matt, who had visited before while on business for Giovanni, nodded at Bruno as he hopped out of the car and opened the back door for Dez and Ben to climb out. Bruno and the driver grabbed their bags and carried them through the green door that led to a small open courtyard paved by marble mosaics. A fountain almost identical to the one at the Houston house bubbled there, and he saw Beatrice walk in front of him, strangely nervous for her to see his oldest home.

"Gio, this is so beautiful," she murmured as she took in the arches that lined the lush courtyard and the climbing plants that Angela lovingly tended.

"Welcome home." He leaned over and brushed a kiss along her cheek before he spotted his housekeeper waiting in a corner by the front door. A smaller door leading to the kitchen and the servants' quarters was on the other side of the courtyard. Angela was wearing a simple blue dress and a warm smile, her dark eyes and silver hair shining.

"Giovanni!" She walked over, pulling him down with wrinkled hands to kiss him in greeting.

"*Ciao,* Angela," he said with a smile. Angela had grown up in his home. Her parents had been his housekeeper and butler, though Angela had never married. He had hired Bruno fifteen years before.

"And this is your beautiful bride," she said as she walked over to fuss over Beatrice. His wife squirmed in discomfort, but returned the friendly kisses Angela gave her in greeting. "I never thought I would see you married! My prayers finally are answered."

"Angela..." He didn't want to make Beatrice uncomfortable, but he knew that Angela had been thrilled when he'd sent her the letter that they were coming for a visit.

"And this is your boy," Angela said as she greeted Ben and introduced herself to his other guests. Soon, Dez and Angela were chattering away, his housekeeper thrilled to have so many people to look after. Giovanni spotted Bruno paying the driver and sorting their luggage. He was a stocky man, happily sliding into middle age, but he was efficient and an excellent handyman, which was vital when you owned a five-hundred-year-old building.

"Bruno," he called, and the man walked over. Giovanni shook his hand and patted his shoulder in greeting. "How is the house?"

They spent a few minutes going over details, Bruno describing the leaking in the first floor bathroom that had been repaired the week before while Giovanni held onto his hand.

"Bruno, I want you to take the rest of the month off. I will call you if necessary."

He could see the man's eyes swim under his influence. "But, the guests
—"

"I will call you if you are needed, but my wife is American and not
accustomed to so much domestic help. You understand, I am sure."

Bruno blinked rapidly. "Of course."

"And there will be no interruption in your salary."

"Yes, Signore Vecchio."

"Gather your things and take a holiday. Use the house outside of
Florence. I'll let them know you are coming."

"Thank you, Signore."

"Think nothing of it," he said. By the time Giovanni turned around,
Matt was the only one left in the courtyard.

"Did you get rid of him?"

Giovanni nodded. "As soon as he has left, we'll check the house."

Matt chuckled and the two men walked inside, both keeping quiet until
they heard the courtyard door close as Bruno left. He caught Angela's eye
and the old woman nodded before she herded Beatrice, Dez, and Ben into
the large kitchen.

"I'll take the top two floors," Giovanni said. "And the south
passageway."

Matt frowned. "Does Bruno know about the passageways?"

"I don't know." He shrugged. "It is better to be cautious. He always
seems to plant a few in places I haven't thought of before. He's
surprisingly resourceful."

The human and the vampire scoured the house for electronic bugs,
cameras, and any other surveillance equipment. They found a few, but it
was a half-hearted effort. Bruno had worked for Livia the entire time he
had been in Giovanni's employ, but he knew that the butler had gathered
little intelligence for his mistress. It was an expected game; one Giovanni
and Livia would both pretend to be shocked over if they ever spoke about
it. Which they wouldn't.

After another half an hour, Matt was satisfied that the house was clean,
but Giovanni still felt uneasy. He had a sudden thought.

"Benjamin!" he called down the hallway.

He heard a quick scuffling before the boy appeared. "Hey, you guys
done? Angela made some awesome food. It's like the best spaghetti I've
ever had. I can't believe how much Dez is eating. I bet she's—"

"Be quiet. If you wanted to hide a bug somewhere, where would you
put it?"

Giovanni had learned from experience never to underestimate the
instincts of his nephew. He also wanted to accustom the boy to thinking
defensively. He saw Ben cock his head to the side.

"You said Bruno's in charge of fixing stuff, right?"

He smiled. "He is."

"Well, has he fixed anything lately? That he mentioned? He'd mention it, right? So you wouldn't get suspicious if you noticed something."

"Good thinking. Yes, the first floor bathroom was just repaired." Giovanni and Ben climbed the stairs, and Giovanni led the boy to the recently repaired bathroom. Ben turned and looked at his uncle.

"Well?"

Giovanni opened his senses, searching for the faint buzz, almost like a vibrating thread, that he would usually pick up from a small electronic device. It was small, but appeared to come from just behind a patch of new plaster.

"Well, damn." He'd have to have it repaired again. He punched through and plucked the small bug that was hidden behind the wall, holding it up so that Ben could see it before he crushed it between his fingers.

"Cool! Got one."

"Excellent thinking, Benjamin. And I don't feel anything else in here. Go tell Matt it appears the house is clear."

Ben rushed downstairs while Giovanni brushed at the plaster dust on his hands. He felt Beatrice come to stand in the doorway behind him.

"How is Angela's cooking, Tesoro?"

"Fantastic. And tell me again why you don't just fire him?"

"Oh"—Giovanni chuckled as he walked past and squeezed her waist —"she'd be expecting that, and I'd just have to look for a new butler."

"Yep, Gio." He heard her call down the hall as he followed the scent of herb focaccia that Angela knew he loved. "I can't imagine why I'm nervous about meeting Livia!"

CHAPTER FIVE

Rome, Italy
May 2012

There were certain things about having gobs of money that Beatrice had become used to. She never worried about paying her bills. She liked being able to buy her own house when she was single. And she never went crazy with her money; in fact, she ended up giving a lot to charity just because she felt guilty for robbing Lorenzo. She had pretty simple tastes, but liked being able to buy what she wanted, when she wanted.

Which, that morning, happened to be another computer keyboard.

"Damn it!" she yelled, tossing the keyboard on the floor where it shattered.

Ben rushed into the small library, which had been light-proofed like most of the rest of the house. "What's up?" He looked down. "Oh."

She sighed. "Bring me another one. This time with the rubber keyboard cover and see if Angela has any of those big freezer bags that the keyboard might fit in. I think moisture in the air is becoming a problem."

"If you need help looking for something—"

"No!" She shut her eyes. "Sorry, Ben. I appreciate it, I just..."

"It's okay." He nodded and backed out of the room. "I get it."

"Thanks." Beatrice bent and picked up the pieces of the keyboard, tossing them in the waste bin before she sat down at the desk again. She took a pencil and manipulated the roller ball attached to the computer at the desk. They had learned their lesson in Chile about Beatrice and laptops, but she still had hope that she would find some way to use a desktop computer, since she had less contact while operating it. So far, she was only on her second monitor, though the keyboard was proving a challenge.

Yes, she decided, money did have its privileges.

She smiled at Angela as the housekeeper passed in the hall, still giving her a slightly wary look. Beatrice knew the fact that she could be awake and alert during the day freaked the woman out. Despite that, Angela was so sweet that Beatrice could hardly blame her for it. She knew she was an oddity. She had the strength of an ancient vampire wrapped in the coordination and attitude of a baby. She had never fit in during her human life, why start now?

"B, got it!"

Ben barreled into the library and dropped off a new computer keyboard, a neoprene case she had cut out to fit it, and a large plastic bag that looked like a large version of the bags they received when they bought donated blood.

Speaking of blood...

Her fangs popped out when Dez entered the room. Beatrice had no idea why it was still happening. She had absolutely no desire to drink from Dez, but the longer her friend was pregnant, the more Beatrice reacted when she was near. Tenzin had speculated that, far from bloodlust, it was a latent protective instinct for Dez and her unborn child.

"Hey, I think we're going to take Ben to the Colosseum this afternoon. He keeps asking to see where the lions ate the Christians. Think we should worry?"

"I doubt it. And you know that there's no specific historical accounts of —"

"Yes, yes." Dez rolled her eyes. "I know. Next you're going to tell me Russell Crowe never really fought there, either."

Beatrice snorted. "Well, you guys have fun. Want to meet somewhere for dinner later?"

"Don't you and Gio have the meeting with the mother-in-law of doom later?"

She shrugged. "There's some sort of cocktail party at her place later tonight, but not until one or two in the morning, so we could meet you guys for dinner."

"Okay, cool! We'll call the house after the sun sets. Also, I'm very curious what a Roman aristocrat serves at a cocktail party."

"Um, I'm going to guess... cocktails."

Dez narrowed her eyes. "And the blood of her enemies."

"Oh, well that too, of course."

"Of course!" Dez skipped out of the room and Beatrice wondered when the fabled exhaustion of pregnant women would hit her friend. So far, Dez seemed to have *more* energy, not less. Though apparently, from the agonized whining she heard from their room every day, the morning sickness was in full swing. Angela just clucked her tongue at Dez and fed her grapefruit for some reason.

Beatrice was reading through the journals again when she heard Giovanni start to wake. She set them down and slipped upstairs. She was trying to be better about being next to him when he woke because she knew he liked it. She was also worried about him. He seemed to be dreaming more, though when he woke, she suspected the dreams were more like nightmares. His eyes held a lean, haunted look that was only growing worse.

She slid under the covers next to him just as he began to move, tucking herself under his arm as he pulled her tight, even as he slumbered.

"Mmm," he began to murmur something in Italian. His accent, she noticed with pleasure, was heavier since they'd arrived. He slipped into his native language more, and she was grateful that understanding him was no longer a problem. Beatrice had already been able to speak English, Spanish, and Latin before she turned. But now she could speak Italian and a lot of Mandarin, too. She could also read classical Greek, Persian, and Arabic. She was still working on her Hebrew.

Giovanni stopped speaking and nuzzled into her neck as he began to tease her clothes off even before he was fully awake. Now that, she decided, was talent.

"You move differently here."

"I what?" Giovanni blinked and looked around as they walked up the Via dei Condotti, past the luxury shops, headed toward the *ristorante* where Matt had chosen to meet them after their walking tour with Ben.

"You move differently." She slid an arm around his waist, keeping pace with easy strides. "I don't know, you're more... Italian, I guess."

"Beatrice, I am a Florentine. I will always be a Florentine."

"But see"—she poked his side—"Like that. In L.A. you would just say you're Italian. But here, you're *Florentine*."

"So?" He frowned. "I'm in Rome. There is a difference. Is there something wrong with this?"

"No, it's cute."

"Cute?"

"And you walk different, too. You're not in as much of a hurry here."

He just grunted at her, no doubt thinking she was imagining it, but she wasn't. He looked... lighter, somehow. Comfortable. In California, she often thought Giovanni seemed more British than Italian, but here, he gestured more. His accent was stronger. His shoulders were more expressive, and his eyes more languorous.

"Whatever it is, it's hot. So go with it."

"Oh?" He grinned. "Is that so?"

"Yes."

He leaned down and whispered something very dirty in her ear. If she could have blushed, she would have. Then he nipped at her ear and murmured, "Does it sound better in Italian?"

"Yes."

He pinched her waist and kept walking. "I'll keep that in mind."

They spotted Matt waiting outside the restaurant. He waved at them and jogged over.

"Hey, guys. Dez and Ben are inside. I just wanted to catch you before you went in. Gio, Emil Conti's inside."

Giovanni only raised an eyebrow. "Interesting."

Matt shrugged. "He does live around here, so it's not that unexpected."

Beatrice looked between them. "Emil Conti? Who's that again?" The name sounded vaguely familiar.

"Old Roman," Giovanni said. "Water vampire, very old family from the Republic. He's older than Livia, but has never enjoyed her popularity. He's not the attention-seeking kind."

"Brilliant guy, though," Matt added. "He could easily take Rome if he really tried."

Giovanni hummed. "That's debatable. I'm not certain what his support would be like. He and Livia have entertained a low-key rivalry for a few centuries, so I know she considers him a threat, but I'm not sure he has the ambition. Is Donatella with him?"

Matt shook his head. "No, a female companion. No one I recognize."

"Probably just out for a meal." Giovanni tugged on her waist and walked forward. "Tesoro, nothing to worry about. Let's say hello, then we'll join you, Matt. Thank you for the notice."

"No problem. He nodded at me. Recognized me, so I'm sure he's expecting you."

"Oh my, Kirby," Giovanni said. "Don't tell me we've become predictable. I might have to fire you."

"Eh." Matt shrugged. "I'm not worried. Who else would keep the secret of your embarrassing pro-wrestling addiction?"

Beatrice laughed and squeezed her husband's waist. "He's got a point."

Giovanni scowled, but she could see the smile flirting at the corner of his mouth. "Blackmail is an ugly business."

"But so lucrative." Matt held the door open and a mustached host, who nodded toward Matt and Giovanni, greeted them. She saw her mate scan the restaurant, but her own senses had already located the energy signature in the corner. They walked toward the vampire, who rose to greet them when they were a few feet away.

Like everything else in immortal society, Beatrice had discovered that greetings usually mirrored the culture and time where the vampire originated. She briefly wondered what the form of greeting had been in the Roman Republic, but was surprised when Emil Conti simply held out a hand to Giovanni. The two men shook before Beatrice was introduced.

"Emil, I would introduce my wife, Beatrice De Novo."

"A pleasure." Emil bowed slightly over her hand as he took it. Emil Conti looked nothing like an ancient Roman. He looked like a very formal, very successful, Italian businessman. He was handsome and wore clothes straight out of a fashion magazine. His dark hair was trimmed neatly, and his broad smile was gleaming white. Beatrice wondered whether dental care was really that good in ancient Rome, or whether he'd had work done.

"Beatrice, this is Emil Conti, a very old acquaintance of mine."

"May I call you Beatrice?" the vampire asked politely. "A beautiful name."

"Sure." She couldn't help but smile back. "It's nice to meet you, Signore Conti."

"But you must call me Emil, of course." He turned to Giovanni. "May I congratulate you on your marriage? I cannot deny I was surprised by the news, but very happy for your fortune. It is a blessing to find one's true mate."

Giovanni glanced at the blond woman still sitting at the table silently. "And where is Donatella this evening?"

Emil gave a careless shrug. "Shopping, probably. I think she's in town, but she's getting ready to leave for the lakes for the summer. You know how the city can be."

"Of course."

"I don't want to keep you; I saw your friends waiting for you, but thank you for introducing me to your lovely wife."

"Will you be at Livia's later?"

"Of course," he said. "Who would miss it?"

"You, Emil." Giovanni chuckled. "If you could avoid it graciously."

Emil gave another shrug and waved them off. "Go, enjoy your meal. I'll see you at the circus later. The squid-ink capellini with lemon and caviar is excellent tonight."

"Thank you."

Beatrice smiled. "Very nice to meet you."

He gave her a little bow and a wink. "And you as well, Beatrice De Novo. *Benvenuto a Roma*. May you have a pleasant visit in our beautiful city."

They walked back to the table and she could feel Giovanni's fingers in the small of her back.

"Benvenuto a Roma," he muttered. "Welcome to the shark pool, Tesoro."

Castello Furio, Lazio

"So, this is a *castle*?"

"Yes." He looked out the window as they twisted through the country roads northeast of the city. "Livia keeps a rather lavish apartment in the city during the winter, but she leaves the city in the summer when it starts getting warm and there are more tourists."

"Well, that makes sense."

"And she likes to make people come to her."

"That kind of makes sense, too."

He laughed and draped an arm around her in the dark car he had ordered. They were seated in the back with the privacy shield raised so they were not disturbed. Livia had offered to send a car for them, but Giovanni had demurred, stating that he didn't know how long they would be able to stay. He had done the polite dance over the phone the evening before with Livia's social secretary, the secretary pressing Giovanni to spend a few days at the castle, while Giovanni insisted that they could not neglect their own guests in the city. In the end, her husband's polite stubbornness had prevailed.

"So, we will go. We will introduce you to everyone. She will try to persuade you to persuade *me* to stay for a few days at the country house—"

"You mean, the castle."

"Why are you stuck on the 'castle' bit? This is Europe. There are castles everywhere."

"But not all of them are owned by my mother-in-law."

He frowned. "Livia is not my mother."

"But you said she kind of acts like it."

Giovanni shrugged. "She tries to."

Beatrice sighed and leaned into his shoulder. "This is so damn complicated. I thought my family was dysfunctional."

"Tesoro, you don't know the meaning of dysfunctional until you have spent time in an ancient Greek or Roman family."

"I'm starting to get that idea."

They turned into a small lane leading to an elaborate gate that didn't open by electronics, but by two uniformed servants who swung the gates out when Giovanni rolled the window down to identify himself. She saw the quick look of deference on the servants' faces before she caught the sheepish expression on Giovanni's face.

She narrowed her eyes. "You're kind of a big deal here, aren't you? Even more than your usual bad-assedness."

He cleared his throat and squirmed a little. "That is not a word, and I am somewhat well-known."

"Kind of how Tenzin is well-known at Penglai Island?"

He actually tugged at his collar. "Perhaps. Have I told you how beautiful you look tonight? That dress suits you. The color is... appropriate."

"Nice try, handsome. And what do you mean, 'appropriate?'"

"Really, there is nothing to worry about. They will all be dazzled by you."

"Right."

They pulled into a long, circular driveway in front of the biggest house Beatrice had ever contemplated entering. It was, as advertised, a castle. Round, stone towers marked the corners and huge walls rose between them. A massive iron gate was swung open as women in glittering dresses and formally-dressed men walked or darted across the lush green lawn in front. She gripped Giovanni's hand harder and wished, for some reason, that she had her *shuang gou* strapped to the back of her plum-colored cocktail dress.

"Missing your swords?"

"What?" She looked at him, amazed by his perception, until she realized that she was reaching over her shoulder as if to draw a weapon. Her husband only wore a sexy smirk. Well, that and a very nicely cut jacket and shirt over a pair of slim-cut black slacks. He looked...

"Like a prince."

He cocked his head at her as if she was crazy. "What?"

Beatrice took a deep, unnecessary breath. "Nothing. Let's go."

They left the car and walked along the pebbled pathway leading to the iron gate. They crossed under the arch and found themselves at the beginning of a long path that led over a lush green park dotted with olive trees and classical statuary. The paths were lined by immaculately cut boxwoods and the gravel paths were raked. The house itself lay spread across the back of the park, pure white, with red, terra cotta tile roofs. The arches and pillars of the facade welcomed them, but the dark hills that rose behind the castle cast an ominous shadow over the grand home.

The party was already in full swing, and tables and chairs were gathered in small groups in front of the house. The trees were lit by tiny lights that provided more than enough illumination for the vampire guests, though she doubted the humans could see very well. Small torches also lined the paths. She saw Giovanni glance at them with interest.

"Nothing to be afraid of," he murmured as he put an arm around her, nodding to the odd passerby. All the humans or vampires they passed seemed to glance at her husband with wide eyes. She saw their lips moving, heard the soft whispers, and knew that they were the subject of speculation.

"I think you may have downplayed how big a deal this was," she whispered.

"I think that Livia has gone to more trouble than I would have liked to 'welcome' us. I do apologize, but we seem to be the main attraction for the evening."

"Yeah, no kidding."

Just then, the glittering crowds seemed to part, and an immortal appeared at the end of a long pathway. She was stunning. Her dark curls were piled high on her head, and Beatrice saw diamonds glittering in the waves. She wore a vivid amethyst-colored goddess dress, one shoulder was bare, and her pale, luminous skin glowed in the moonlight and the flaming torches. Her almond shaped eyes were lined with kohl, and her lips were full and smiling.

"Oh... wow," Beatrice murmured.

"Livia," Giovanni called, tugging on her waist. She was rooted in place for only a second before she forced her feet to move toward the regal woman who lifted a hand in greeting.

"*Mio caro Giovanni,*" Livia said with a smile, approaching Giovanni. She reached up and kissed him in greeting, murmuring endearments and pinching his chin. Beatrice raised an eyebrow. Either Livia was a *very* affectionate maternal-type person, or there were some Greek myth dynamics going on in her mind. Giovanni, for his part, seemed to be barely putting up with her affections, and he never let go of Beatrice's hand.

"Livia, let me introduce you to my wife."

She threw up her hands in apparent delight. "Of course, the beautiful Beatrice!" Livia turned to her, the picture of welcome. "Let me greet you, my daughter." She kissed her cheeks, embraced her, and Beatrice felt the cool stroke of amnis gently run down her arms. Livia stepped back and looked into her eyes. "So, you are the woman who has finally captured my Giovanni's heart. I thought it would never happen, but I see the love between you. The devotion. And it fills my own heart with joy. Welcome to *Castello Furio*, Beatrice De Novo. Let my home be yours. You are most welcome here."

If Beatrice's breath could have been stolen, it would have been. Livia was vibrant. Magnetic. Beatrice had the almost uncontrollable urge to hug her, just to get closer to the warm hum that seemed to emanate from the beautiful woman.

"Thank you." She breathed out. "I'm so happy to finally meet you."

Somehow, Livia appeared to blush. "You flatter me, my dear. It is my honor to meet you. And I simply adore your dress. Come, let me introduce you to my people." She pulled her away from Giovanni and linked their arms as she guided Beatrice through the clutches of eager vampires and humans at the party. Beatrice panicked for a moment until she felt Giovanni's fingers reach out and his amnis caressed her arm, holding her even as they were separated.

Beatrice felt like a celebrity. Everyone wanted to meet her. Everyone complimented her dress. Everyone hung on her every word. It was strange. It was terrifying. Giovanni fared no better. Though he hung behind them, he had his fingers twined with hers while they greeted more people than Beatrice could ever remember, even with her improved memory.

"And you are sired from water, too. As all in our family are. What more could I ask from a daughter?" The group around them seemed to titter at Livia's quip. Beatrice glanced over her shoulder to see Giovanni roll his eyes slightly. She hadn't thought about it before, but unlike the hum of energy at Penglai, Livia's party had a very low energy signature except for a few bright spots. As they moved through the party, Beatrice began to take note of the strongest signatures, noting whom they belonged to and who was gathered around them.

There was a tall woman with strong Germanic features that held court with a group of tall vampires around her. She was stronger than most, but not as vibrant as Livia.

A regal man with ebony skin and a booming laugh caught her attention from one corner. His signature was very strong, but he didn't feel very old. He also had an entourage gathered around him.

Another, quieter immortal drifted around the edges of the party. He stopped to talk to others every now and then before quickly moving on. He looked North African, his features a fascinating blend of Arab and African. His face was scarred, and he didn't seem to attract much attention, but his energy swirled and drifted in a fascinating way. The vampire felt old. Very old. She noticed Giovanni hadn't acknowledged him before her attention was drawn to a familiar voice.

"Signora De Novo, how did you like the restaurant?"

"Signore Conti," Beatrice smiled. "It was lovely. How nice to see you again." Beatrice could tell her familiarity with Livia's rival came as a surprise to her hostess, but Livia's eyes flickered for only a second before the happy mask descended again.

"You are acquainted, then? How lovely. Signore Conti is from one of the oldest families in Rome. Our people have known each other for centuries."

"It is a pleasure to see you again, Beatrice." Emil bowed again, this time kissing the back of her hand, a gesture common among the immortal men she had met. Every time it happened, she stifled a snicker as Giovanni's amnis tightened around her waist as if he was a second away from pulling her back into his arms.

They continued to circulate for hours, and it was growing late when Giovanni finally pulled Beatrice from Livia's company. He promptly gathered her under his arm and found a quiet corner.

"Are you ready to go? Please say yes."

"I think we better if we're going to make it back to the house before dawn."

He nodded. "Stay here. She'll draw you into another round of socializing until we're forced to stay here at the castle. She keeps rooms for me here, but I don't want to stay unless you do."

"No." She shook her head. "I want to go home."

"Excellent. I'll be right back."

Beatrice watched him cross the party to speak to Livia, and the conversation of gestures began. She watched for only a moment before her eyes scanned the crowd again. She was hiding in the shadows, trying to avoid notice, but one set of eyes caught hers. It was the North African vampire with the pockmarked face. He gave her a deep, respectful nod before he seemed to disappear into the shadows on the other side. She searched for him, but did not see him again.

"All right. We're free." Giovanni pulled her under his arm, shuffling them along the edges of the party-goers and out the grand iron gate toward the car.

"So, when do we have to come back?"

He grimaced. "Wednesday. She's hosting a concert here, and I somehow agreed that we would come."

Beatrice chuckled. Something about Livia definitely bothered her, but at the same time, it was kind of funny to see Giovanni put at a disadvantage. Usually, he was unbending.

"I see you laughing at me, Tesoro. Watch out"— he pinched her thigh —"or I'll be forced to assert my 'bad-assedness.'"

She winked as he opened the door for her. "Promise?"

Beatrice heard him tap on the driver's window. The window rolled down and Giovanni threw two hundred Euro notes at the man. "Drive fast."

CHAPTER SIX

Rome, Italy
May 2012

Giovanni almost missed telling the driver the last turn to the house, he was so distracted by his wife's attentions. They had both discovered the benefits of having a lover with shared blood. As long as they maintained skin contact, they could send their energy over each other to tease their mate's senses. It had become a kind of game for Beatrice, and she enjoyed trying to break his concentration in public. The car was almost as fun.

He was ready to tear her beautiful new dress by the time they got back to the house, and he almost snarled when they exited the car and heard the telltale skid of the football in the courtyard along with the low laugh of his old friend.

Beatrice blinked, as lust-hazed as he was. "Wha—who's that?"

"Carwyn's here." He glanced at her red, swollen lips, knowing they'd have to pretend to be polite for at least a few minutes.

Damn priest.

Beatrice sighed and pushed the courtyard door open, only to immediately dodge the football that came in her direction.

"B, kick it back!"

She glared at Ben. "In these shoes? I don't think so."

"So fancy, you two." Carwyn stepped from the shadows with a grin. "You didn't really need to get so dressed up for me." He walked over and embraced Beatrice. "You look lovely, though. I appreciate the effort. Oh, and you smell nice, too." He only grinned when Giovanni growled at him. "You ready to run away with me yet?"

Giovanni picked up the football and tossed it at his friend's head. "No, she's not."

Carwyn only batted it away, not letting Beatrice out of his embrace. "And *you* definitely didn't need to get fancied up, Gio. I've told you a thousand times, I'm not interested."

"Haha. Why are you playing football with my nephew at four in the morning?"

He saw Ben begin to speak, but Giovanni only raised a finger to silence him. The boy was smarter than the priest.

"Well..." Carwyn placed a kiss on Beatrice's forehead before he ran after the ball and kicked it toward Ben again. "I'm playing football with *my* nephew because I just got here, and I am the cool uncle. You are the boring one."

He heard Beatrice and Ben both snicker, but Beatrice said, "Honestly, Ben, how long have you been up?"

"Just an hour or so." He kicked the ball back to Carwyn. "We were talking."

"Well, it's time for you to sleep."

"No." The boy whined. "You're going to talk about interesting things, and I'll miss it all."

Beatrice grabbed him around the collar and shoved him toward the door. "Say goodnight. I promise we won't plot murder and mayhem without you."

"Promise?"

"Promise. And you..." she turned back to Giovanni. "Don't be too long. I'm going to bed."

Ben made gagging noises as Carwyn let out a wolf-whistle. Giovanni grinned and gave her a wink. "Goodnight, Benjamin," he said, then whispered something suggestive in Italian that made Beatrice bite her lip and Carwyn roar with laughter.

"What?" He heard Ben say as they walked up the stairs. "Oh, I don't want to know, do I?"

"Nope."

Giovanni's ears tracked for a few more minutes until he heard the door to Ben's room shut. He turned to Carwyn, who kicked him the football. "Well?"

"Well, what?"

"What's going on with you?"

Carwyn shrugged. "It's nothing for you to be concerned about. And my trip here was nicely boring, thanks. I caught one of Jean's boats to Genoa and came from there. That Frenchman's not half bad, after all. Fantastic food—"

"Why were you so eager to come here?"

"Aren't you happy to see me?"

The two old friends kicked the ball back and forth in the low light of the courtyard, the skidding and bouncing the only sound in the still morning air. Giovanni could smell the scent of bread baking at the *paneterria* on the corner.

"Of course I am. And you know how happy Beatrice is to see you. I just wonder—"

"She looks amazing, by the way."

"I know. That dress does suit her."

Carwyn shook his head. "I'm not talking about her damn dress. You probably don't notice because you see her every day, but she looks extraordinary. She's very comfortable in her skin. Doesn't have that awkward, hungry look the new ones usually do."

"Ah. Yes, she's doing extremely well."

"If I didn't know her, I'd think she was twenty years immortal, at least."

"That old?"

Carwyn nodded, still kicking the ball back and forth, dribbling around the courtyard to amuse himself. He was dressed in black. Black pants, black T-shirt, black leather jacket, but no collar, which he often wore when in Rome.

"So, the meeting with the empress went well?"

"Yes." Giovanni said. "Livia's fine. We're going back on Wednesday for a concert. It's supposed to be good. Care to come along? I know Beatrice would like some company she didn't have to perform for."

Only a careful observer would have noticed the slight hitch in Carwyn's step. "Wednesday? Can't."

"Oh?"

"Meeting with the men in bathrobes on Wednesday night."

"Oh?" Giovanni chuckled at his friend's pet name for some of the Vatican staff he usually met with if he came to Rome, which wasn't often.

"Yes, one red bathrobe in particular."

"A cardinal?"

"A friend."

Carwyn passed him the ball, but Giovanni stopped it and held it under his foot, waiting for his friend to meet his eye. "What's going on, Father?"

Carwyn took a deep breath and frowned. "I'm not sure yet. Something... maybe long overdue. I'll let you know. It's nothing to be concerned about." He walked over and placed a hand on Giovanni's shoulder before he grinned and kicked the ball out from under his foot. "If there's something to worry about, I'll tell you. Now, go shag your wife like you were planning before I interrupted you with my arrival."

"Fine." He turned toward the door. "You'll let me know?"

"Of course I will. Go away."

He walked through the door, calling back, "You're room is ready for you when you get tired. Don't damage any of Angela's plants."

"Go away!"

When Giovanni walked through his bedroom door, he was greeted by the sight of his wife, naked, sitting in a chair and draped over the cello he kept in the closet of the Rome house.

"You've never played this one for me."

He fastened the series of locks on the door and walked toward her slowly. "No?"

"Nope." She looked up with hooded eyes. "You should. It would be..."

He took a finger, running it down her spine as she curled over the body of the instrument.

"What would it be?"

He heard her heart begin to pulse. "Relaxing."

"Do you need to be relaxed?" He knelt beside her, placing soft kisses along her side. Her shoulder, the crook of her arm. Her hip. Her knee. His fingers trailed up from her ankle.

"Maybe," she gasped. "But not just yet."

His hand gripped her knee as he pulled the instrument from her, propping it against the wall before he lifted her and sat in the chair, letting her naked body straddle him as he sat fully clothed.

"I love you," she said as his mouth began exploring her skin. He rubbed his lips along the rise of her breasts and let his fangs scrape her delicate collarbones. His fingers trailed down her spine, over her hips and down her thighs.

She gripped his hair hard, but Giovanni remained silent, watching her in the low light as his fingers slowly brought her to release. She gasped his name into the silence of their bedroom before he bent his head and let his fangs pierce her skin, just above the delicate scars on her breast.

"More." She panted as her back arched and he drew harder on the small wound.

More? It would never be enough.

He did play for her, hours later as the sun rose in the sky and Beatrice drifted in a haze, awake, but sated and quiet. He could feel her energy level out to a hum that told him she was meditating in the way that allowed her mind to rest, even if her body could not.

Giovanni did not envy her waking days. Even though his recent dreams had plagued him, he still took comfort in the sweet oblivion that rest brought. Though he needed less now that they shared blood, he fervently hoped that sleep would never abandon him completely.

The next evening, Beatrice and Giovanni, Matt and Dez, Carwyn, Ben, and even Angela gathered in the large kitchen of the house. Ben had slept until past noon before wandering out of the house with Dez as they explored the neighborhood and ate copious amounts of gelato. Angela was feeding them another full dinner. Giovanni smiled as he watched her enjoy the humans in the house with normal appetites.

"I can't believe how much I'm eating," Dez said, as she shoveled more pasta in her mouth.

"Neither can I." Beatrice stared at her in amazement.

"Hey." Dez glared. "I'm growing a human here. What's your superpower?"

"Speed. Strength. Night vision. Lightning fast reflexes. Water manipulation—"

"Okay, stupid question."

Ben piped up, "Don't forget allergy to electronics and sunlight."

Carwyn looked amused. "How have you managed to remain unbitten, boy?"

"It's been close a couple times with Tenzin."

Giovanni examined Dez, knowing that Beatrice worried about her friend. He knew she had been experiencing some morning sickness. "Dez, how are you? Did Angela point you toward a pharmacy? I know you're not very familiar with the city."

Dez smiled. "I'm great! And Ben gets around in Italy a lot better than me. We found a drug store the other day that has the stuff I forgot at home. But thanks for that basket in my room, too. That make-up is so nice."

He waved a hand. "Thank Livia. She has some sort of cosmetics company that makes all those things. She always sends over baskets when she knows I'm bringing guests.

"Well, please tell her I said thank you. B, did you get one, too?"

Beatrice looked up. "Get what?"

"The basket of make-up, perfume, lotions..." Dez rolled her eyes when Beatrice looked back in confusion. "Am I the only girl here? I swear, you and Tenzin are hopeless."

The priest looked around the house. "Where is she, by the way?"

Beatrice shrugged. "Not here yet. You know Tenzin."

"Okay," Giovanni said. "We met with Livia last night and met many vampires. Beatrice, who do you want to know about? Matt, this might be beneficial to you, too."

She leaned forward. "First off, why isn't that place humming the way Penglai does?"

Carwyn burst into laughter, but Beatrice shook her head. "Really, it's so weird! There were at least as many vampires at Livia's little party last night, but it didn't have half the energy of a 'low hum' day at Penglai."

Giovanni nodded. "I'm glad you noticed. Did you notice what else is missing from Castello Furio?"

She thought for a minute before her eyes lit up. "Water."

Dez looked around. "What? She doesn't have plumbing there? Even the Romans had aqueducts, right?"

Giovanni shook his head. "No, what Beatrice noticed, and I'm glad she did, is that for a water vampire, Livia does not surround herself with her element. It's an odd quirk for an immortal, because most of us draw strength from our elements. In Penglai, there's a careful balance of the elements. Many fountains and streams, gardens and rocks, most of the palace complex is open air, they even have torches lit at all times for those of the fire element. The idea being a kind of balanced threat."

"Ah." Dez nodded. "Got it. So if everyone has easy access to their element, no one's going to go crazy and try to take over."

"Like mutually assured destruction," Ben said with a full mouth. "I learned about that in school."

Matt said, "You learned something in school that you didn't already know?"

"Haha."

"The point is," Beatrice continued, "Livia's place should have all sorts of water around her house, but she doesn't. And all the vampires in her court seem really weak."

Carwyn said, "Tenzin would say it's because most of them drink donated blood and live in such a modern environment. The longer I live, the more I think she may be on to something."

"If anything," Beatrice said, "her house would favor earth and wind vampires, with all the open ground and the stone castle."

"She has a castle?" Ben asked. "Cool."

"Maybe that's why Matilda has always seemed so haughty," Giovanni mused.

"Who's Matilda?" three voices asked at once.

Carwyn spoke. "Tall. Blond. She's German. About my age. Very powerful wind vampire. She and Livia hate each other."

"Too many queen bees." Dez nodded. "There can be only one."

Matt snorted. "You watch too much T.V."

"Okay, so that's the blonde I noticed," Beatrice said. "Yeah, she felt strong. Who's the huge guy? Really tall. Big laugh. He looked African? His energy was strong, too."

Giovanni nodded. "He is. That's Bomeni. He's Ethiopian, but he's not as old, maybe my age."

"Who's his sire?" Beatrice leaned forward with interest. He suspected she was thinking about Geber's four blood donors. The Ethiopian he had written about was an earth vampire and a female.

"I don't know. It's a possibility we should investigate. He *is* an earth vampire from the right part of the world."

"Okay, so the most powerful vampires I noticed were Matilde, Bomeni, and Emil Conti, who is... water?"

"Yes."

"And then the weird guy."

He frowned. "What weird guy?"

"You didn't notice him?"

Giovanni shook his head. "Notice who?"

"There was this old vampire. He didn't just feel old—he *looked* it. Scarred face. Maybe North African? He was wearing these long robes. He looked out of place, to be honest. His amnis was weird. Kind of swirling around him, almost visible in some strange way. If I had to guess, I'd say he was a wind vampire, but I'm just guessing. Something about him reminded me of Tenzin."

Carwyn looked at Giovanni. "That sounds like Ziri."

"If Ziri was there, how could I have missed him?"

Beatrice looked between them. "Who's Ziri?"

Carwyn shrugged. "You hear strange stories about Ziri. With his age and power, it's hard to say what's true. I know one vampire, who is not an imaginative sort, say that Ziri melted into the air in front of him."

Giovanni scowled. "Impossible."

Matt piped up. "Hey, they say that at some point transporter technology may be feasible. We *are* creatures made up of mostly empty space at an atomic level. Maybe Ziri has just taken a leap."

Giovanni said, "Be that as it may, it sounds like Beatrice saw him last night. He's the only one that fits her description, and he does visit Rome on occasion."

"He doesn't live here?" Ben asked. "In Rome?"

"He doesn't really live anywhere that I know of," Giovanni said. "He was probably a nomad in his human life—he's very old—and couple that with a wind element... He roams."

"And right now, he's roaming in Rome." Ben snorted, looking around when no one laughed. He slumped in his seat. "Tenzin would have laughed."

They quickly finished their meal and cleaned up the kitchen before they went to the living room for drinks.

"So," Beatrice asked, "no fire vampires in Livia's court?"

"No." He shook his head. "Just me. She doesn't like them."

"Just you."

He shrugged. "Just me."

Carwyn said, "Oh, she loves Gio, all right."

Beatrice raised her eyebrows. "Okay, so it's not just me that was getting the incest vibe. Good to know."

"She's not my mother!"

"Still, Sparky." Carwyn leaned against the fireplace. "You have to admit she's always been very... affectionate with you."

"Ew," Ben said as he sat on the couch and began to nibble at the dish of dry, sugared fruit that Angela set out. "That's so gross."

Matt grinned. "You probably wouldn't say that if you saw her."

Dez elbowed him. "What's that supposed to mean?"

"It means she's incredibly beautiful," Beatrice said. "Really, stunningly beautiful. She looks like she should be a model, or something."

Giovanni cleared his throat. "Let's get back to business. Now that Carwyn's here, we have enough people to start getting some information. Matt, your main job is still going to be security, but Ben is old enough that he can do some, as well."

"Really?" Ben sat up straighter.

"Yes, Matt will get a firearm for you. Carry it with you when you go out, especially if Dez goes with you. And your knives. Carry those, as well."

The boy suddenly looked nervous. "Am I going to get in all sorts of trouble if I get caught with them, though?"

"On the slight chance you have to use them, we'll worry about getting you out of police custody after you've defended yourself. Priorities, Benjamin."

Matt elbowed the boy. "Hey, I've got some friends in the police here. Don't worry about it. Just keep yourself safe and remember: money and amnis erase criminal records."

Giovanni continued, "Matt will be our day man if we need information or investigation during the day. Our main objective on this trip is identifying Geber's four vampires, which will mainly be up to Beatrice and me. Chances are that Stephen's contact is a member of Livia's court, or a frequent visitor, and since we believe he is one of Geber's four, finding him is our starting point."

Carwyn said, "I'll be looking into finding more about what Ioan was researching. I have some avenues here since he had colleagues in the city that I know he corresponded with, and I'll be looking into private pharmaceutical labs in Eastern Europe, as well."

Dez frowned. "Why pharmaceutical labs?"

Beatrice said, "Lorenzo has the formula. He's going to want to produce it. It may be in production already."

"Speaking of Lorenzo," Matt said. "What are we doing there? Have we had any word?"

Giovanni spoke quietly. "Tenzin has requested we leave locating Lorenzo to her."

"By herself?" Ben asked.

"It is her mate that was killed, Benjamin."

"But no one's going to help her?"

Beatrice leaned toward the boy. "If she finds him, she won't need help."

Dez was sitting silently with narrowed eyes. "But would modern labs even have what you needed for a medieval alchemic formula? We're talking about plant ingredients, mainly. Produced in Persia in the early ninth century..."

Beatrice smiled. "I always forget your thesis was on medieval science, Dez."

"I'm just doubting that your modern chemistry labs are going to have the kind of ingredients you would need. And for the formula to work as intended, they would have to be organic..."

Giovanni began pacing the room. It was an angle he hadn't considered. The woman was right. Modern chemistry labs wouldn't have access to traditional plant ingredients like Geber had used in the formula. Though he didn't know the exact preparation, Stephen remembered the majority of the ingredients were plant-based and Zhang Guo confirmed it before they left China.

"So," Carwyn said, "who would have access to those kind of ingredients, if not a chemistry lab? What should I be looking for? Are we still talking about Eastern Europe? Stephen's contact in Rome—"

"Botanicals!" Dez stood and looked at him with a look of triumph in her eyes. "The baskets, Gio!"

Beatrice looked up. "What?"

"Of course." Giovanni breathed out before he strode over to Dez, placed two hands on her shoulders, and kissed her full on the mouth. "Dez, you brilliant, beautiful genius. I think you're right."

She grinned. "They're organic. Plant based! The packages even say, 'Using Traditional Botanical Ingredients,' also..." She took a deep breath and brought a hand to her lips. "Wow, I mean, B said, but... wow."

Giovanni smirked at her and both of them turned back to the rest of the room, all of whom were looking at the two of them in frank confusion.

Ben spoke first. "That was... weird."

Beatrice had her head cocked to the side. "I'm missing something. What about botanicals?"

Dez was still blinking a little. Matt narrowed his eyes. "Are you swooning?"

She shot him a look. "Hey! There's this tingly kind of... thing with the amnis that just kind of... you know, when the lips touch, just... shut up."

Beatrice smiled as Dez moved back to sit next to Matt on the couch. "B, if you were more of a girly-girl, you would have figured it out ages ago." Dez pulled a tube of lip balm from her pocket and tossed it to Beatrice. "Finally, my make-up addiction has been put to good use. This is the lip gloss from the basket Livia sent over. Botanical ingredients. Read the label. It's the trendy thing right now; no one would question it. Organic plant extracts in beauty products. It's super popular. A chemistry lab isn't going to have a ready supply of botanical ingredients or suppliers, but—"

"A cosmetics company might." Carwyn grinned. "I want to kiss you myself. Good thinking, Dez."

Matt put an arm around his wife. "No, really, I got this." He leaned over to place a long kiss on her mouth. "Way to go, honey. You're brilliant."

Dez was glowing. "It's perfect. Nothing out of the ordinary. They would have labs, suppliers, packaging, even a distribution network..."

"Wait," Beatrice raised a hand. "What are we talking about here? Or rather, *who* are we talking about? Dez, are you saying what I think you're saying?" Her eyes sought out Giovanni's.

He shook his head. "Beatrice, I don't know."

Was it possible? As conflicted as his feelings toward Livia were, as complicated as their relationship had always been... would she betray him that way? Would his father's wife even consider it a betrayal?

Beatrice turned the tube of lip gloss in her fingers, shaking her head. "There are many cosmetics manufacturers in the world. Lots of companies produce this kind of thing. There are many—"

Matt broke in. "How many of those companies are owned by vampires?"

Carwyn walked toward him. "We knew that Lorenzo was supported by someone with far more money and power than just Zhongli Quan. We guessed that it was someone in Europe because of the vampires Lorenzo brought to the monastery. You have to consider it, my friend."

"It's... possible." Giovanni nodded. "It's possible that Livia might be behind it all."

CHAPTER SEVEN

Residenza di Spada
Rome, Italy
May 2012

"Ah... ahahaha!" Beatrice stood and danced around the library. "I did it. I did it," she chanted, wishing Ben or Dez were there to witness her triumph.

Through a combination of plastic bags, keyboard covers, and rubber kitchen gloves, Beatrice had finally managed to type on the computer without starting a fire or shorting it out. She was dancing around the library and singing "We Are the Champions" at the top of her lungs when she heard a commotion in the hall.

"You know, you forget that I don't sleep as soundly as your husband, and my room is right down the hall," Carwyn muttered as he stumbled in the library and collapsed on the sofa. "Why am I awake?"

"Because I..." She continued to strut, a smile plastered on her face, as she sat down and hugged him. "Figured out how to work the computer by myself."

"Well, aren't you the big girl?"

"Cranky, cranky."

Carwyn glanced at the clock on the mantle, draped his arm across the back of the sofa, and gave Beatrice a squeeze. "It's twelve o'clock in the afternoon. Of course I'm cranky. But congratulations anyway."

Beatrice couldn't stop grinning, and she leaned into her friend's shoulder as he sat at her side, blinking. As silly as it may have seemed to Carwyn, being able to use a computer again felt like a huge victory.

"I should wake your husband up, just for spite. I'll pound on the door. Threaten to harm his piano. Flush his first-edition Gatsby. Something horrible like that."

She snickered. "Don't. And don't even think about the Gatsby. He hasn't been resting well lately."

"Hmph," he said and pinched her neck. "Been drinking too much daywalker."

He took a deep breath and relaxed, drifting in a hazy state as she leaned against him. Beatrice knew that, at over a thousand years old, Carwyn would often wake during the day, but unlike Tenzin or her father, he was groggy and slow. Still, it was nice to not be alone like she usually was.

"Carwyn?"

"Hmm?"

"How did your meeting go last night?"

"With the cardinal?"

"Mmmhmm."

"It was fine. About how I expected."

"Were you in trouble or anything?"

He said, "Not exactly. I'm the second oldest priest in the church. They don't really reprimand me anymore. They leave me to myself."

"*Second* oldest?"

Carwyn simply cocked an eyebrow before he closed his eyes again.

"Are there a lot of immortal priests?"

"There are a few. It's not unheard of. The church has known about vampires for hundreds of years. Perhaps longer."

Beatrice really didn't know what to think of that, except that it wasn't as surprising as it should have been. "But everything's okay?"

He squeezed her shoulders again and leaned over to kiss the top of her head. "Everything's fine, darling girl. Or it will be soon. Why is your man not resting well?"

"Dreams. He's been dreaming."

"Ah."

"He won't talk about it, though."

"Gio's always been a quiet one about things like that."

"I think he loves it and hates it here."

Carwyn chuckled. "I think you know him very well."

"I think I feel the same way."

"Well, you're both ahead of me. I just hate it."

"So why were you so eager to come here?"

He gave her a side-eye and clammed up again.

Interesting.

"Come with us to this crazy party she's throwing next week."

Carwyn groaned. "Oh, don't use the pitiful voice on me, B."

"Please." She hugged his waist. "Please. Everyone is so..."

"What?"

"Fake."

Carwyn let out a snort.

"And weird."

"You always have been a perceptive girl."

"And they all look at me like I'm some sort of cross between a celebrity and a sideshow freak. I don't care. I really don't, but it'd be nice to have someone to talk to while Gio has to play the dutiful... whatever."

"Son? Ward? Strange and inappropriate escort for his stepmother?"

"Yes, exactly."

Carwyn groaned again, but Beatrice knew she was wearing him down. "Please. Come with us. You can help me make sense of all the players in this crazy game."

"I'll tell you now. Who do you want to know about?"

"Nice subject change."

"I thought so." He sniffed and sat up, rubbing his eyes a little.

Beatrice searched her mind. "Emil Conti."

"Not a bad sort for a Roman. Far better than Livia. He's a Republican, of the ancient Roman variety, and a fairly solid businessman. He's got diverse interests. Lots of shipping, since he's a water vamp. Most of his business is run out of Genoa, and he has ties with Jean Demarais, but like most aristocrats, he farms out most of the day-to-day and stays here to dabble in politics."

"Matt said he could rule Rome if he wanted."

Carwyn frowned. "I think it would be more accurate to say that he could rule Rome if he wanted to, and Livia didn't. He's not as ambitious as she is and, as much as he dislikes her, he's not willing to go to war with her over the city, though some would like him to. The Vatican likes him. Would back him in a conflict, for what it's worth."

"How much influence do they have?"

He shrugged. "Now? Not much. In the past? Enormous. Livia courted whoever the Holy Father happened to be when it suited her in the past, but the Vatican isn't the political power that it once was. Thank heavens."

"That sounds kind of funny coming from a priest."

"Why? When I became a priest, the church wasn't a global power. It was a church. Its purpose was to shepherd the faithful, not influence worldly governments."

"This sounds like a much longer discussion than we want to have at twelve thirty in the afternoon."

"Very true." He patted her head. "What other gossip do you want? I know most of it."

She laughed. "Okay, Livia. Honestly, is she that bad? Do you actually think she could be the one behind Lorenzo?"

"Yes," he said immediately. "If it suited her purposes and enriched her holdings, yes. Gio is sentimental, but she is completely self-serving, and she's very, very greedy."

"You think—"

"I think I don't trust her to fetch my boots. She'd most likely put a scorpion in them."

She smiled. "So... good friend of yours, then?"

"Oh yes," he said. "We correspond regularly. Plus, she hates me because she blames Ioan and me for Gio retreating from public life, as she sees it."

"Oh?"

"She rather liked being the stepmother to one of the most feared vampires in Europe and Asia. Gave her a certain cache. She's been trying to convince him to move back and be her personal enforcer for centuries."

"'Personal enforcer.' Is that what they're calling it now?"

Carwyn's laughed cracked the still air. "Oh, B, I can tell you've bonded with her already."

"I'm pretty sure the feeling's mutual. She has that bitchy 'I'm pretending to like you, but I'd actually like to stab you in the eye' look I remember from high school."

Carwyn shook his head. "Heaven help me." He was silent for a few moments, drifting in the warm afternoon air. "Women are... gloriously tangled creatures, aren't they, Beatrice?"

She looked up with a smile. "You having woman problems, Father?"

Carwyn didn't answer, and Beatrice leaned back, studying his still face. She didn't know whether he had drifted off, or was just avoiding her question. "Carwyn?"

He sighed and let out a string of soft Welsh, his eyes still closed.

"Carwyn, you awake?"

"Shh." He put a heavy arm around her shoulders and pulled her a little closer. "Shh, love. Rest now, Brigid."

Beatrice's eyes flew open, and her mouth dropped. "Who's Brigid?"

At the sound of the name, Carwyn's eyes popped open. "Hmm?"

"Who's Brigid?"

He only frowned and cleared his throat. "Sixth century Irish bishop. Patron saint of Ireland. Who else do you want to know about? Matilda? Bomeni?"

"You're *so* not getting out of that question!"

He shifted and scooted forward, as if to go. "I should go back to sleep. Keep your celebrating down, B."

She pulled on his arm. "No fair."

He stood and turned back to her. "If I recall, once upon a time, you weren't quite so forthcoming about a certain vampire and *your* feelings, so leave it be."

"Carwyn, what—"

"Leave it be." His voice was rough, and a light flared in his eyes.

She sat, looking up at him. He didn't look angry, or even irritated. He looked... peaceful. And maybe a little resigned. "You'll tell me someday?"

A smile crept across his face. "I'll tell you when there's something to tell."

Beatrice couldn't help meeting his smile with one of her own. "Yeah?"

"Yes."

"Okay." She rose from the couch and gave him a quick hug. "Do you really need to sleep?"

He shook his head. "I can stay awake for you, if you've a need for company."

"'Night of the Living Dead?'"

"Romero?" He slowly walked toward the doorway.

"Of course."

"Well"—Carwyn raised his arms and stumbled down the hall—"Zombies do seem strangely appropriate at the moment."

"You try to eat my brain, and I'll get the swords out."

"Oooh, scary."

Fontana del Pantheon, Rome

"I can't believe how much gelato I'm eating."

Ben eyed Dez as she scooped up another spoonful. "It is pretty amazing. But then, I think we just need to accept that we are no longer eating lunch while we're in Rome."

"Yep, gelato is its own food group here."

Dez leaned back against the cool pillar as they sat in the shade in front of the Pantheon. They had woken that morning as they did most mornings since they had come to Rome. Late. Angela fed them breakfast before Dez and Ben struck out to explore the Temple of Hadrian, which was fairly close to the house. Every day, they would take in some site that the guidebooks recommended before they found a suitable *gelateria* and a shady place to people-watch.

Even though Ben made a game of flirting with Dez, she and Matt were two of his favorite people, and the three were having a great time exploring the city. If he was free, Matt came along, but most times, he was running an errand for Beatrice or Giovanni. That morning, he happened to be meeting with some of his "friends" to procure a suitable weapon for Ben to carry when he was in Rome. Ben slipped a hand into his pocket and felt the cool grip of the knife his uncle had given him the night before.

"Carry it whenever you go out. Particularly if you're with Dez. Get to know the neighborhood. Learn the streets. We're relying on you. Be smart, Benjamin."

His eyes darted around the square, watching the bustling crowd. Tourist season had already started, but Ben knew enough about cities to be able to spot the locals. He may have spent the previous few years taking it easy in Houston and L.A., but he had been born in New York and raised himself on the streets. And big cities, he knew, were remarkably similar in a lot of ways.

He could still spot the tourists with the fattest wallets. He could spot the savvy local girls. And he could definitely spot the guy with the shiny forehead wearing the unseasonably warm jacket who was trying a little too hard to be inconspicuous.

"Okay, I'm stuffed." Dez stood and stretched, shoving her sunglasses up her nose and looking around. Ben could hear the trickle of the fountain in the background, and the murmur of the crowd, but he kept an eye on the suspicious man out of the corner of his eye. The guy was definitely eyeing Dez, and Ben didn't think it was because of her California-girl looks.

"Ben?"

"Huh?"

"Let's head back to the house. I'm getting sleepy. Do you mind?"

Ben stood and casually slung his backpack over his shoulder. "Nah, that's cool." He slipped his hand into his pocket and started toward the street that would lead them to Giovanni's house. Very subtly, he noticed the man shift in their direction before he looked down at the newspaper he was reading. As Dez and Ben left the shade of the temple, they turned right and Ben caught the man following them at a distance.

"Hey, Dez?"

"Yeah?"

Ben grabbed her hand and hustled down a side street he had mapped out the week before. It looked like an alleyway, but led to a triangular-shaped piazza surrounded by office buildings. Also headed in that direction was a blond girl who was similar to Dez in height.

Perfect. "Let's go this way, okay?"

"What?" She followed Ben, her pace matching his as they turned left into the cobblestone piazza. Ben hurried to catch up with the blonde, glancing over his shoulder. The man was definitely following them.

The triangle-shaped piazza opened up before narrowing down into a driveway leading out to a larger thoroughfare. Though that was the direction most of the pedestrian traffic was flowing; there was also a twisting walkway past a parking lot leading through the houses and to the primary school behind the Pantheon. Ben had found it when he was scoping out the neighborhood. It was roundabout, but the best way he could think of to lose whomever it was that seemed to be tailing them. The blond girl went straight; Ben tugged Dez's hand and turned left.

"Ben? Where are we going?"

"I think I saw a bookshop that had English books in the window."

Dez perked up immediately. Though Giovanni had a full library at the house, his selection of books in English was somewhat limited, so Ben and Dez had been on a hunt to expand it. He glanced over his shoulder as they turned the corner. He could see the man following the blond girl to the main road. Ben pulled Dez into a small shop that sold postcards and cigarettes. The man behind the counter, with the universal wisdom of all convenience store owners, eyed Ben with suspicion, only relaxing when he saw Dez walk in behind him.

"Signore, uno... uno cappelo, per favore?" Ben motioned to Dez. "Per la signora?"

The older man shrugged and pointed to the back of the shop where a few rows of tacky caps with pictures of the Colosseum were lined up. Ben grabbed a navy blue cap and tugged it on Dez's head.

"Ben, I don't see any books here. I think you—hey!" She was looking around and jerked back when Ben pushed the hat on her head. "Ew! I'm not wearing this."

"You should." He kept hold of her hand and pulled a few euros from his pocket, handing them to the shopkeeper on the way out of the store. "It's getting warm and you don't want to overheat." He peeked his head out, but couldn't see the man anywhere. "I think I was remembering a shop on the other side of the Pantheon. Where we were this morning."

"Oh." Dez looked around. "Yeah, that was a big triangle like this one. Ben, I'm not wearing this hat. It's ugly. Why did you waste the money?"

He pulled her out into the parking lot and to the left toward the alley that led to the school.

"Oh, just humor me until we get home, will you?" His eyes never stopped glancing around, looking for the shiny forehead of the man who had been watching them before. He was nowhere in Ben's sight, and he allowed himself to relax a little.

"Ben?" He finally turned and looked at Dez. She was no longer smiling. "Who was following us?"

Ben was moments away from denying it, not wanting to seem paranoid or worry her, but he stopped himself. Dez was too smart to buy the quick lie.

"I'm not sure. I remember his face. I'll try to draw it when I get home."

She just nodded and squeezed his hand. "Okay. Which way should we go back?"

Ben let out the breath he was holding. He knew he wasn't overreacting, but he'd been afraid that Dez would think so. He let her hand go, reaching back into his pocket to grasp the knife. "Down here. I checked it out last week."

She smirked and tugged the cap lower on her head. "Lead the way."

Residenza di Spada

"And he hadn't seen him before?" Beatrice questioned Dez as they stood in the enormous walk-in closet in the guest room where Beatrice kept her wardrobe. She had acquired more clothes in the past month than she had in the previous three years, thanks to Dez's shopping habits, her suddenly active social calendar, and Giovanni's habit of losing his patience with buttons and zippers when the mood struck.

"No, he drew a pretty good sketch, though. He gave it to Matt as soon as he got home. Matt, Gio, and Ben are talking in the library right now."

Beatrice sighed and glanced longingly toward the door.

"Nope, not on your life. You have to figure something out to wear to this party next week, and if you're serious about not wearing that... grand occasion of a dress that Livia sent, then you better stay here." Dez pointed toward the magnificent Renaissance era gown that Livia had sent by uniformed courier the day before. It was a sixteenth century style, rich with priceless fabric and stunning detail. The wine-colored brocade would set off Beatrice's pale, luminous complexion. The gold cording around the collar would make her brown eyes and hair glow. It was stunning.

"It has a hoop skirt. Are you kidding me?"

"Technically, it's called a..." Dez looked over to the laptop on the desk. "Farthingale."

"Well, farthingale or hoop skirt, I'm not wearing this thing. It's ridiculous."

Dez grinned. "The corset's kind of hot, though."

Beatrice gave her most ladylike snort. "Okay, I'll wear the corset with a nice pair of black jeans and some kick-ass boots."

"Have you seen what Gio's wearing? Is it tights? Please tell me it's tights."

"Should it weird me out that you want to ogle my husband's ass in a pair of tights?"

Dez just shook her head. "Not appreciating that ass would be like walking through the Sistine Chapel and not looking up. No, really, what's he wearing?"

Beatrice laughed. "It's pretty simple. She probably knew she couldn't get away with anything too elaborate. And no tights. There are these kind of fitted leggings, but they go just above his knee. The jacket looks similar to mine, but plainer. Mostly, he was grumbling because she's doing this whole party in his honor. She has this party every year, but usually people just dress up in whatever costumes they want. Livia made it a Renaissance theme for Gio."

Dez stood, blinking at her. "There are some serious issues going on there, B."

"You're not joking. And his outfit is right here. Take a look."

Dez unzipped the garment bag that contained the sleeveless leather jerkin and black leggings that Giovanni would wear to the party.

"Okay, not gonna lie, that's kind of hot."

"It's going to be *really* hot. This party is outdoors in June. Thank goodness it's at night."

"Haha. Seriously, that leather..."

"I'm definitely not complaining about the leather. So, what am I going to wear to this? You think I can I get away with wearing my Docs?"

Dez laughed for a few minutes before she looked back at Giovanni's clothes. Then she looked at Beatrice's dress, then back to Giovanni's. She narrowed her eyes and smiled.

"No Docs, Beatrice De Novo di Spada Vecchio whatever the heck your name is now. But I may have an idea."

CHAPTER EIGHT

Crotone, Italy
1497

The lash struck again, and Jacopo could feel it cut into his flesh. Still, he did not cry out, steeling himself against the pain that had become part of his daily life. His flesh, though dripping and bloody, would be healed shortly. Andros always made sure to preserve the perfect body he had created by healing him with his demon blood.

"Good. You are no longer even flinching."

Jacopo made the mistake of letting his shoulders relax slightly, only to be struck on the back of the thighs with Andros's staff. He grunted and his knees buckled, but he did not cry out.

"Cato may have been a Roman, but he was correct in one thing: The first virtue is to restrain the tongue. Do you know why, my son? You may speak now."

Jacopo took a deep breath and flexed his arms and shoulders. He could feel Paulo wiping at the blood on his back so Andros could heal the open wounds. The muscles, unfortunately, could not be as easily mended and would ache for days.

"Why is silence the first virtue, Father?"

"Because words can be twisted. And they should be. I will teach you how. Words are to manipulate and fool, but when you hand them to your enemies, they will be used against you. Your Bible may not be worth much, but Solomon did speak some wisdom. 'Even a fool is counted wise when he holds his tongue.'"

"Yes, Father."

He felt the cool lick of Andros's blood as he pierced his finger and began to seal the lashes. Giovanni could feel the strange tingling sensation of the wounds closing.

"Nothing will inflame your enemies more than your silence. Give them nothing. Nothing to accuse you with. Nothing to condemn you. Let your actions speak for themselves. Never talk to an enemy, but listen always."

"Yes, Father."

"And let your actions be your words. Is it better to reason with an enemy or kill him?"

"If I could reason with him, he would not be an enemy."

Andros stepped in front of him and looked up. He smiled and patted Jacopo's cheek. "Excellent. You have done well. You had your music class today. Do you like your new instructor?"

"Yes, Father."

Andros scowled. "I said you could speak, my son."

Jacopo's face, as always, was impassive. It was the only defense against the mercurial moods of the ancient Greek. The monster would be as loving as his uncle some nights, then turn in an instant and beat him. Always, Andros said, for his own good. For his education. His training. Jacopo examined the man's eyes. They were relaxed. Amused even, and his mouth may have been turned down, but his fangs were not descended. It appeared that Andros wanted a debate instead of rote answers.

"The music teacher is a heathen, Father. He teaches me profane songs. I do not care for them."

Andros smirked. "There is no profane music. Only music. Some is good. Some is bad. Sometimes the coarsest peasant tune is the one most pleasing to the ear."

Jacopo blinked. He had been exposed to the finest composers of the Basilica di San Lorenzo; and while he had heard beautiful madrigals sung in Paris, nothing could compare to the breathtaking experience of the holy mass.

"I would prefer learning music that edifies the spirit, Father."

"That is your pathetic uncle talking, boy."

His temper flared, as it always did when Andros criticized Giovanni Pico.

"You are a heathen demon," Jacopo spit out. "And God will condemn you for your madness."

Andros curled his lip and picked up his staff again. "I wonder about you sometimes." Walking behind Jacopo, he struck the back of his thighs again. "Don't you know? There is no god. The Greeks stole their gods from the Minoans. The Romans stole their gods from the Greeks. It's all nonsense, and your Hebrew god is no different."

Jacopo remembered the gentle instruction of his uncle, reflecting on the common strands of faith that wove through the ancient world. "You're wrong."

"I'm not, and you know it. You know more now, more than your pitiful uncle and his friends. More than the deluded mortals who plot and plan." Andros came to stand in front of him and looked up into Jacopo's defiant eyes. "They build cathedrals for their immortality. But you will have no need for buildings made of stone."

Jacopo bit his tongue and decided to take Andros's earlier advice. In the three years he had been with the strange man, he had learned the lesson of silence. The vampire reached up and grabbed Giovanni by the ear, pulling him down to his face.

"You know the truth, my son," Andros whispered. Jacopo could feel the creature's vicious fangs scrape his skin. "You know who the ancients saw that made them believe that the gods were among them, don't you?"

Jacopo forced his jaws to part. "Yes, Father."

"They saw *us*, my boy. They saw the water vampire move the ocean, and Poseidon was born. They saw the wind immortal fly on the night storm and draw the lightning to his hands, and Zeus came to be."

"Yes, Father."

"Never forget." Andros patted Jacopo's cheek and gently stroked the dark curls on his head. He looked up into the young man's vivid green eyes and smiled. "I *am* god."

Castello Furio, Italy
June 2012

Giovanni leaned back in the plush seat of the sedan and eyed Beatrice in the slim leggings and fitted bodice. The black boots she wore rose over her knees and hugged her calves, flaring just below the tight muscles of her thighs as she sat across from him.

"Tesoro," he murmured, "if the women of the court dressed anything like that, I would have had a much harder time keeping my reputation unsullied."

She only grinned and glanced at his lap. "You're not having a hard time right now?"

"Oh, I knew I should have taken my own transport." Carwyn groaned and closed his eyes. "Or better yet, avoided this fiasco all together. Why? Why did I let her sway me with the pitiful voice?"

Beatrice bumped Carwyn's shoulder. "You love me, and you know it."

Giovanni smiled at his old friend and his wife. They bantered back and forth as they made their way to Livia's party, and he reflected on how different this trip was than the last time he had been in Rome. Then, he had been desperate and pleading. He'd had no time for parties or pleasure when his every waking moment had been focused on manipulating different parties at court—Livia most of all—to negotiate for Beatrice's release from Lorenzo.

After all that, could Livia had taken up supporting Giovanni's own estranged son? It was something they would have to determine. He frowned and shook his head, contemplating the idea of staying in Rome longer than their original plan of three months. If the answers were there, they would need to stay as long as necessary.

"Hey, Professor." Beatrice nudged his knee with the toe of her boot, which he grabbed and pulled into his lap. "Stop brooding. We're going to a party."

"And one in your honor, Sparky. You should be grateful."

"Why do I like either of you? Please, remind me."

"Aww." She teased him, slipping across the seats to cuddle into his side. "Poor Gio. Forced to play nice with the empress for the night."

He rolled his eyes. "Not you, too. It's bad enough that the priest calls her that." He sighed and waved a hand. "Fine, get it out of your systems now, so you can both behave."

For the next twenty minutes, Carwyn and Beatrice thought of every needling joke about royalty, Romans, and incest that they could. By the time they pulled into the park, all three of them were laughing.

"B, I swear, if you call her a cougar to her face, I will buy you a car." Carwyn snickered. "A house. Maybe an island. Something ridiculously extravagant, just so long as I can see the look on her face."

"Hush!" She giggled and turned to Giovanni. She cleared her throat. "Okay, we're done."

"Are you sure?" He cocked an eyebrow at them, which threw both of them into fits of laughter again.

"Okay, okay, we're really done." She gasped and grabbed his hand, pulling him toward the iron gates, lit by a thousand tiny lights.

"Yes." Carwyn coughed. "And I promise not to mention any Greek plays."

"*How* many times must I state that she is not my mother?"

Beatrice and Carwyn barely controlled themselves by the time they entered the main hall. While more casual gatherings were held in the gardens, Livia had decorated the main hall of the castle for the party that evening. Candles and torches were everywhere. The room was draped in rich tapestries, and demure human servants darted about, offering wine or blood from their wrists.

Part of the way that Livia controlled the huge Roman population of immortals was her decree that feeding from live donors was only allowed at her parties or festivals. While most of the more prominent vampires ignored her, she had enough influence over the younger and weaker of the court that she was rarely defied. It kept the majority of the population under her thumb and relatively weak compared to the older minority. It also ensured her parties were very well attended, which fed her already gargantuan ego.

He heard Carwyn mutter under his breath. "Heaven help us, she actually has a throne now."

Giovanni looked down the length of the room. Livia's table had been set up to look very much like the head table at a fifteenth century feast. She was dressed in a burgundy dress that would have far outshone his wife's—that is, if Beatrice had not paid a seamstress top dollar to butcher Livia's gown and make her a costume that was more fitting for her personality.

"She does put on a good show—I'll give her that." Beatrice looked around the room, seemingly oblivious to the stares her costume drew. Giovanni knew better. His wife, in her own way, was making a statement to Livia and the entire Roman court.

She bowed to no one.

Grinning, he tucked her hand under his arm and walked toward the front of the room. The crowd parted automatically. Livia rose, all smiles as they approached. Only Giovanni caught the acid glint to her eye as she examined the remains of the priceless gown she had sent.

"Beatrice!" Livia smiled, her fangs peeking from the edge of her mouth. "What an... interesting ensemble. I'm so glad you both could make it."

"Thanks, Livia. I just love my new corset." Beatrice glanced down at her black leggings and leather boots. "I hope you don't mind. I don't really do hoop skirts."

Livia forced a smile. "How American of you."

Beatrice feigned naiveté. "Thanks!"

"And, Giovanni, your priest friend came as well, how amusing."

"Always a pleasure, Livia." Carwyn stepped forward, snagging a passing glass of champagne. "I do love spending time in your incredibly ancient and imperial presence."

She only lifted an eyebrow at the dig.

"Not that you really have an empire, anymore. Thank heaven and the Gauls."

Giovanni cleared his throat, but Carwyn only continued.

"And the Goths. The Vandals, too, I suppose. You *have* been sacked a lot, haven't you?"

Giovanni broke in. "Beautiful party, Livia. Do excuse us while we say hello." He dragged Carwyn away with Beatrice following. They both wore smiles.

"You just can't help yourself, can you?"

Carwyn only laughed, drained the champagne and looked around. "Where's the bar?"

An hour or so later, they had greeted all the appropriate people and left Carwyn chatting with Emil Conti, who he did get along with, surprisingly enough. The priest had also been instructed to keep an eye out for the presence of Ziri, the ancient wind vampire, in case he decided to make an appearance. Giovanni approached Beatrice from behind as she chatted with a younger group of immortals who had congregated near the fountain in the massive entry hall.

He snuck behind her and grabbed her around the waist.

"Tesoro mio," he bent down and murmured in her ear. "What have you been doing without me for so long?"

She turned and winked at him. "Everyone likes my boots."

He slipped his hand along the stays of the bodice she wore and over her smooth backside, teasing the back of her thigh. "I'm rather fond of them myself."

He felt the frisson of energy rise between them and drew her away from the gaping vampires she'd been talking to, throwing them a wink before he tucked Beatrice under his arm. "Come with me; I want to show you something."

"Come on, you can think of a better line than that."

He chuckled, shuffling them past the guards, who nodded at him respectfully as they made their way through the labyrinth of a castle. Finally, he reached the tower rooms he called his own on the rare occasions he stayed with Livia. He opened the door, slipping the latch closed behind them. A tall, circular staircase ran around up the sides and he pulled her upstairs.

"Where are we?"

He grinned. "This, Beatrice, is the vampire equivalent of my childhood room."

"What?" She laughed. "You stayed here?"

"Yes, after my sire's death, I stayed here with Livia for around ten years or so, getting my bearings, meeting the right people. She wanted me to stay longer, but..."

"I'm surprised she kept it for you."

They reached the top of the stairs, which opened onto a richly appointed library with curved bookcases that lined the walls. Narrow windows looked out over the park and the full moon shone through.

He left her in the center of the room and walked around, tracing a hand along the bookcases, which had not a hint of dust.

"She wants me to move back, you know?"

"I know."

He laughed low in his throat. "As if anything here could tempt me." He looked over his shoulder to see her looking around in wonder. The room looked like the fairytale version of a tower library, complete with dark oak cabinetry, velvet armchairs, and a fireplace he took a moment to light.

"It's sure beautiful. This whole place is."

He turned to her, watching as she took it all in. The gold leaf picture frames and jeweled clocks. There was a Faberge egg on a side table and a Lalique decanter with the finest whiskey. He had seen it all before, and he only had eyes for his wife.

"Beautiful."

He circled her, slowly drawing closer as her busy eyes memorized the room. "Yeah, everything's gor—"

He darted in and stopped her mouth with a kiss. "Beautiful."

She smiled, strangely shy in the opulent surroundings. "Gio, this is still so—"

"Fake." He looked around, then placed his hands around her waist and looked into her eyes. "Real."

She nodded in understanding, and Giovanni leaned down, drawing her mouth into a leisurely kiss. They stood in the center of the tower as the moonlight streamed in the windows and the faint sounds of the party drifted to their ears. He nipped at her lips, tasting them and enjoying the sweet wine that lingered.

His hands roamed down to cup her bottom, and he lifted her against his body. Their kisses grew heated, and Giovanni felt her heart begin to beat against his chest. Her hands tugged at his neck and he could scent her arousal as it filled the room. It was heady, intoxicating. He wanted nothing more than to feel her skin on his and her flesh against his tongue.

"You were right," he murmured in between soft bites of her swollen mouth.

"About?"

He backed her up against the nearest bookcase, propping her on the edge of one deep shelf as his hands stroked down her legs, fingers teasing under the edge of her boots to tickle the sensitive skin behind her knee.

"Hoop skirts would make this problematic."

"I think ahead that way," she panted.

"Beatrice..." He hissed as his hands clutched at her thighs. Beatrice's fingers tugged at the laces of his pants, as her other hand stroked him through the thick fabric. He bit back a groan when her hand closed around him. Desire? He had never known desire until he had known her.

"Now," she whispered. "Gio, I need you."

One hand reached up to the nape of her neck, angling Beatrice's mouth to his as the other pulled at the drawstring that held her leggings tight. His hand slipped under the fabric and searched for her heat as she bit down on his lower lip.

Feeling how ready she was, he freed himself and drove into her with one swift stroke. Her satisfied cry echoed off the cold stone of the tower library, but Giovanni didn't care who heard them. He pulled back and gave her a wicked smile. He'd dreamt about taking her in this room for years.

A few books fell to the floor as they moved faster, and his hand reached back to cradle her head so it wasn't bashed against the hard oak shelves. He dove back toward her mouth, swallowing the cries of pleasure as he drove her toward the edge.

"I love you," he whispered as she clenched around him. "*I love you so much.*"

Beatrice's fingers dug into his shoulders. He could feel the painful dig of her nails, but he stared into her eyes as the pleasure blinded her. His hand gripped her bare thigh. If she hadn't have been a vampire, they would have left bruises.

He felt his own climax approaching and slowed, pressing his mouth to hers and pouring his pleasure into their kiss as his amnis flooded her body. He felt her hands reach up to frame his face, and her own energy flowed over his skin in a soft wave. He closed his eyes and came with a groan.

Giovanni laid his head on her shoulder and put his arms around her waist, pulling Beatrice closer as their hearts beat in unison. He could feel her stroke his hair, running her fingers along his neck where she drew the moisture against his skin, cooling him as he relaxed into her touch.

"I love you, Jacopo," she whispered.

He matched her breaths and laid soft kisses along her neck.

"I wish I could write as my uncle did." He pulled away and looked into her eyes, sparkling with love and satisfaction. "I don't have the words, Tesoro mio."

She smiled at him anyway and pulled him down for one more quick kiss before he set her down on the floor. They righted their clothing, smiling and sneaking glances toward the stairs and the sounds of the party.

"Do we have to go back?" she asked.

Giovanni grinned. "Unfortunately, yes." He pulled up his pants and quickly tied the strings that held them in place, shaking his head the whole time. "I hated wearing these clothes when they were in fashion."

She giggled and snuck a hand around to pinch his backside. "I kind of like them. And don't you like my boots?"

He eyed the curve of her calf, the smooth line of her waist, and her breasts riding high in the stiff bodice. "I like your costume far better than mine, that is no question."

She only laughed, and he watched her struggle to get the drawstring tight enough. He finally reached over and grabbed her waist, drawing them tight with a smirk.

"I'm going to have to dance."

"What?" She laughed.

"Dance. Move in a regular pattern to the rhythm of music. Surely you're familiar with the concept." He pulled her hand and led her down the stairs, in no rush to rejoin the party.

"We have to dance?"

He chuckled. "You certainly may, if you like, but listen to the music."

Giovanni paused and cocked his head. He heard the strains of the violin and the guitar. "Unless you are well-acquainted with the *galliard*, feel free to sit this one out."

"The gall-what?"

He pulled her down the hall. "The galliard. It's a dance Livia was particularly fond of, and she'll want me to dance one with her."

"I'm biting my tongue here..."

He snorted. "It's not exactly the tango, Beatrice. It's all very formal."

85

"I'm just trying to imagine you dancing."

"Me?" He raised his eyebrows in shock. "My wife, I am an excellent dancer."

"Oh, really?"

"Really. I had a dance instructor from the time I was a boy."

She snickered. "This, I can't wait to see."

"So happy to amuse you."

"Also, you better teach me the tango."

He reached down and pinched her as they passed two of the solemn guards. "That, my love, will be my pleasure."

Giovanni bowed toward Livia, pleased that they had been joined by a group of twenty or so other immortals as they danced. He looked at the edge of the crowd, where Beatrice leaned against a pillar, watching him with an amused smile. He winked at her before he turned his attention to his partner. He saw Livia's gaze flick toward his wife, then she lifted a hand, and the musicians paused.

"We should dance *la volta!*" The other dancers smiled with delight, pleased to take part in the vigorous, but more intimate, dance. He smiled stiffly and bowed toward her again as the music resumed.

They began the intricate steps. At the first turn, Livia sprang, and he lifted her, waiting the few beats of the music before he turned and set her down again. They repeated the steps, weaving among the other dancers as they moved in formation.

"Are you enjoying the party?" she asked during one lift.

"Quite. I can't remember the last time I danced."

They separated for one turn, then were back next to each other.

"And how is your wife liking Rome?"

"Very well. Thank you."

"And your guests? You should bring them to the house one evening. We'll have a quiet dinner in their honor."

Giovanni suspected that a "quiet dinner" could easily involve forty or more people.

"I'll keep that in mind." He spotted his opportunity. "Speaking of guests, Beatrice's friend wanted me to thank you for the cosmetics you sent over. She was quite taken with them. How is your business?"

She smiled and her eyebrow lifted slightly. "Business has been very rewarding lately. Thank you for asking. And how is your search?"

He was about to answer when he saw a flash of gold hair at the edge of the crowd. Giovanni was swept into another turn, and when he spun back, the gold was nowhere to be found. His eyes searched for Beatrice. He could not find her.

"Giovanni?"

He frowned down at Livia. He had lost step in the dance. She laughed.

"It *has* been some time since you've danced."

Giovanni picked her up into another turn. When he set her down, he spotted Carwyn leaning against the bar, flirting with a redhead in a brilliant blue dress. His friend was grinning, not paying attention to anything but his conversation.

"You seem distracted. Am I boring you?"

"I... no, Livia, of course not." There it was again! A flash of golden curls under a brocade hood.

"You never answered my question."

"What question?"

He finally heard the music drawing to an end.

"How goes your search for your son?"

Had he told Livia he was searching for Lorenzo? She knew he was searching for Andros's books. The music stopped. The crowd clapped. And he looked down into her scheming brown eyes. Giovanni's heart began to pound.

"I don't know, Livia. Perhaps *you* might be able to tell me."

Just then, he heard Beatrice gasp. He recognized her sharp inhale from across the room, and his hand reached down to grasp the dagger tucked into his boot. The fire flared along his collar. He looked up to see Lorenzo smiling at Beatrice with bared fangs while two of Livia's guards held his wife back.

Giovanni hissed and flung the dagger across the room, aiming straight for Lorenzo's neck, only to have it intercepted by the chest of another guard. The vampire grunted and turned to look for the source of the blade.

Within seconds, Giovanni's fire burst out, lighting his arms, though the thick leather jerkin Livia had sent for him prevented the fire from spreading over his torso. His arms reached out and grabbed the two guards who approached him, immediately engulfing them in flames while the crowd ran screaming and the guards turned to ash. He heard Carwyn shout, and the marble beneath his feet shifted. Another swarm of guards ran for him as he looked for Beatrice.

"Stop now, *Papà*!"

Lorenzo held a sword to her throat as Beatrice snarled and Livia's guards restrained her. Giovanni stilled immediately. The ground beneath him grew still. Everyone froze exactly where they were.

"I'll cut her head off given the word."

"Hold, Lorenzo," Livia said as she stepped between them. "I have no reason to harm the girl."

His eyes darted to Beatrice, who was held by four guards, arms twisted behind her back. The water of the fountain has risen behind her, but it did nothing but spill over the sides, drenching the floor and trickling down the stairs. Giovanni growled, but forced the fire back. He looked for Carwyn, who was surrounded by more guards, though they did not touch him. His old friend was watching the scene with a calculating blue stare.

"Livia!" Emil Conti pushed forward. "What is the meaning of this? What kind of violence have you allowed in your own home? And toward your guests?"

Giovanni could tell the crowd was as confused as Conti was. A low murmur began to rumble and a frantic energy filled the air, causing his heart to beat faster.

"Emil, thank you for asking." Livia raised her voice, the small woman speaking with authority as she continued to stare at him. "I am taking Giovanni di Spada as my prisoner. It is my right."

Conti sputtered. "What? What ri—"

"I accuse him here as the murderer of my husband, Niccolo Andros, his own sire."

The murmur grew. Emil Conti drew back, a horrified look on his usually placid face. Livia stepped closer, standing in front of Giovanni and looking up as the fire coursed along his collar and the guards held onto his leather-clad torso and legs.

"You foolish boy!" Livia spat out and slapped him. "Don't you know? No secret stays hidden forever."

A red haze fell over his eyes, and Giovanni opened his mouth to speak, but a breath of air whispered in his ear.

"Silence, Jacopo."

His eyes darted around the room, stunned by the sound of the name only one other knew. The glittering immortals of Rome were tittering like panicked birds as Livia and Emil argued. The whisper came again.

"Say nothing to her."

Giovanni blinked and looked again. Carwyn was staring at him in shock. Beatrice was standing by the fountain, but the sword had been lowered from her neck. Everyone around them was frozen, as if waiting for a command. He was sure that no one else had heard the ghostly whisper.

He looked to Beatrice and her eyes met his, pleading with him. She was furious. Frightened. He mouthed, *'Ti amo'* at her, frowning when she began to struggle again. Just then, an apparition took shape behind her; a man appeared from the shadows of the room.

He was dressed in long, flowing robes, and he held a finger up to his lips. He glanced at Beatrice, and his mouth moved in a silent murmur. A moment later, the whisper came to Giovanni's ear.

"Do not worry for your woman, Jacopo. Be still. Be silent. Give your enemy nothing."

Giovanni stopped struggling, and a strange calm stole over him.

Because when an immortal as ancient as Ziri spoke, he listened.

CHAPTER NINE

Castello Furio
June 2012

She wanted to scream. She wanted to cry. Everything seemed to move in slow motion around her, as if the castle had been plunged to the bottom of the sea. Silent. Why was it so silent?

Beatrice stood frozen as Livia's guards pulled Giovanni away into the twisted maze of the castle. Finally, what felt like dozens of hands released her, and she lifted her arms with an unspoken scream. A roaring filled her mind, like a river rushing over a cliff, and she felt the pulse of energy behind her.

The water in the fountain rose, trembling and quivering at her command. Beatrice narrowed her gaze on Lorenzo and Livia, who stood next to each other. The vampires of the hall seemed to drift like lost as sheep in the confusion.

Her rage driving her, she stepped toward her enemies, only to be tackled from the side. When she realized it was Carwyn, the scream died in her throat, but she still struggled.

"Stop," he whispered fiercely. "Contain yourself for now."

"Can't."

"You must."

In the safety of his arms, the roaring began to clear and sound filtered back to her. The confused murmur of the crowd. Emil Conti's voice arguing with Livia. Lorenzo's arrogant laugh.

The laugh caused her rage to bubble up again, and Carwyn's grip on her grew even tighter as he pushed her to a small alcove.

"Lord in Heaven, you are strong, B."

"Let me go." Her voice sounded foreign to her ears. Quiet. Feral.

"That's really not the best move right now. If you were in your right mind, you'd know that."

"Let me go."

"We have to find out more. She won't harm him. Look around the room. Everyone's in shock. She's going to feel out the crowd before she makes a move. I have a feeling she's not pleased. I somehow doubt Lorenzo was supposed to show up tonight. She's not happy with him."

His arms embraced her, but they were not Giovanni's arms. She began to shake again.

"My dad... Ioan. They took Gio. They took him."

"Christ, we've got to get you out of here. Now. You're going to collapse or explode. Possibly both."

She felt wind at her feet, and a sharp longing for Tenzin rose in her. Tenzin. She needed Tenzin now. Where was Tenzin?

"Come with me, priest. Bring the woman."

Who did that voice belong to? It was cold and comforting at the same time. And... familiar. Her eyes flicked to the silhouette at the entrance of the alcove. Amnis swirled around the voice, filling the small niche.

"Ziri." Carwyn's voice was cautious, but she recognized the hint of optimism.

"This is a surprise. I did not see her making a move for weeks. Lorenzo has not pleased her by appearing like this."

"What are you—"

"We must get her out of here. Her rage will not be contained for long. Come, Mariposa."

Her eyes darted to his when he spoke her childhood name. Ziri stepped toward her, and she could finally make out his eyes. The whites shone in his dark face. Despite her shock and anger, she blinked. The vampire's irises were a pure, deep black.

"Who are you?"

He held out a hand, and she felt the whisper of air stroke across her cheek.

"I am Ziri, and if you allow it, I will call you my friend."

Carwyn had darted out of the alcove to go look for Emil Conti. Ziri swept Beatrice down a dark hall that led outside. Once out of the suffocating walls of the castle, the wind vampire picked her up and flew her to the car. He tucked her into the backseat and waited outside for the priest.

Beatrice blinked, as if coming out of a dream. What was she doing? They had taken her husband! She was just about to shove her way out of the car when the door opened and Carwyn slipped in, grasping her wrists the minute they raised to shove him back.

"Ah-ah. Calm yourself, Beatrice De Novo. Now is the time to listen."

She had found her voice. "They took him. Let me go!"

"No." He let go of one arm to pound on the divider, and the car jerked forward. Beatrice reached over and punched him in the jaw.

"Let go of me, damn you!"

He grabbed her wrists again. "Beatrice, look at me."

She was shaking with anger.

"Beatrice, you need to understand that Gio is in no mortal danger right now."

Her fangs descended and she tasted blood in her mouth. "You say that when he was taken by that *bitch*? By that backstabbing bitch? With Lorenzo there? With—"

"With hundreds of witnesses watching her take him. He is, right now, a political prisoner. And no one knows anything. There are factions within factions that will all try to manipulate this situation to their own advantage. She has accused him, but everyone knows that she'll lie if it suits her purposes."

Her face fell. "But—"

"Whatever you're about to tell me, don't. Right now, your husband is a bargaining piece to Livia. He is safe." Carwyn locked his eyes with hers. "Do you understand? He is safe. No harm will come to him as her prisoner. At least not right now. She won't make any rash moves; she's too smart for that."

The reality of the situation began to take hold, and Beatrice felt the rage slipping away. In its place was a bone-deep pain. Carwyn must have caught the shift, because he let go of her wrists and pulled her into his arms. She shook with suppressed grief as the dark car made the twisted journey back to Rome.

When they pulled up to the house by the Pantheon, Ziri was already waiting by the gate. Carwyn paid the driver and the black car sped away. They stepped through the green door and the smell of cardamom hit Beatrice's nose.

"Tenzin!" she cried into the courtyard and felt the rush of wind as Tenzin sped to her.

"What has happened?" Small arms encircled her, embracing and lifting her when she stumbled. "What has happened tonight? Where is Gio?"

Ziri stepped into the courtyard. "Livia arrested him. It was unexpected."

Beatrice felt Carwyn on one side, holding her, when Tenzin dropped her arms. Her hiss was vicious. "What? That arrogant dog took my boy? I will kill her!"

"Lorenzo," Beatrice muttered as they made their way into the silent house. "She's the one helping Lorenzo."

Tenzin said, "I know."

"How?"

"What do you think I've been doing for the past few weeks? It doesn't actually take me that long to get across the ocean."

Beatrice heard Ziri's low chuckle as they made their way up the stairs, careful to keep silent as they walked to the library so they wouldn't wake Ben.

"What am I going to tell Ben?" she whispered. As tough as Ben pretended to be, she knew he adored Giovanni. Depended on him. Giovanni was the constant. Nothing could harm him. She felt frozen by grief and confusion.

"Shh, my girl," Tenzin whispered. "I will get him back. Do you hear me?"

"They took him. How could they take him?"

"With trickery and surprise. That is how." Tenzin's arm slipped around her waist. "But they have lost the surprise, and no one will hold him for long."

Dawn was close when the four of them settled into the library. Beatrice collapsed on the couch. Carwyn sat next to her. Ziri and Tenzin both stood by the cold fireplace. Beatrice was reminded of the fireplace in the tower that Giovanni had lit. Other memories assaulted her. The warm grasp of his hands. His burning kiss. Would that be her last memory of him? The last time he touched her?

"Whatever dark, depressing thoughts you are entertaining, B, snap out of them." Carwyn's voice was brusque and, surprisingly, exactly what she needed to hear. "Taking political prisoners is commonplace in our world. She won't hurt him. She might torture him, but it won't be anything he hasn't endured before.

A glass of water she'd been watching on the coffee table shattered. Water scattered over the table, but the pieces of glass were swept up in a gust and immediately tossed into the fire. She looked up to see Ziri smirking at her with his terrifying black gaze.

"Who are you?" she asked.

His dark head bowed, and he swept back the striped robes he wore. "I am Ziri."

"I know that. Who are you?"

Ziri said, "You are very much like your father, do you know?"

She felt Tenzin's tension from across the room. Beatrice's eyes darted to her father's mate, who was watching her fellow wind vampire with suspicion. Tenzin remained silent and let Beatrice question him.

"I am. How did you know my father?"

The ancient vampire looked thoughtful for a moment, tilting his head while Beatrice examined him. He was definitely the ancient immortal she'd seen at Livia's garden party. His skin was pockmarked and looked dusky from the sun. His features were a curious blend of Middle Eastern and African. Beatrice was reminded of a library exhibit she had helped curate about the Berber people of Morocco. But Ziri looked old, far older than the

Berber people. He was ancient and curiously regal. Not a Berber, but then, North Africa had not always had the same names. She remembered Geber's journals.

"Are you the Numidian?"

Ziri smiled again. The swirling amnis that surrounded him reached out to her hand, but she did not flinch when she felt the press of his ghostly greeting.

"I am Ziri. I am the Numidian of Jabir's journals, and I was your father's guardian... for as long as I was able."

A few hours later, Matt stumbled into the library and looked around in confusion.

"Who's the vampire sleeping in the second floor guest room? Hi, Tenzin. Who are you?" He looked at Ziri, then around the room with sharper eyes. "And where the hell is Gio?"

Beatrice sighed. "Sit down, Matt. I'll explain."

Tenzin spoke, "The vampire isn't awake, is he?"

"No."

"Good, he needs to rest."

Carwyn and Beatrice both looked at her in confusion.

"What's that?" the priest said.

Beatrice asked, "What are you talking about?"

Even though most vampires rested during the day, they didn't 'need' to. Beatrice had never grown tired in a bodily sense, even though she rarely slept. She would weary, exhausted by her own thoughts, but that was why she meditated. Tenzin, she knew, was the same way.

"I'll let him explain, but Lucien... He is…" Tenzin stammered, looking disturbed. "It's difficult to say exactly. He is not... well."

"Lucien Thrax?" Carwyn asked. He looked confused. Tenzin looked strangely nervous. Beatrice looked to Ziri. The old wind vampire looked like... nothing. She had never seen a face so carefully blank.

"Who's Lucien?" Beatrice asked.

"Lucien Thrax—an old friend of mine. A very old friend. And he was a friend of—"

"Ioan's." Carwyn interrupted. "Lucien and Ioan were close correspondents. Lucien is a doctor, B. The son of the greatest healer the immortal world has ever known."

"She's also the oldest," Tenzin said.

Carwyn nodded. "Lucien and Ioan were friends for many years. He's one of the contacts that I was going to look for while I was here. He's often in Eastern Europe."

"He was in Bulgaria when I found him. I'd heard rumors." Tenzin frowned. "He hadn't heard about Ioan."

Matt spoke up. "Bulgaria?"

Tenzin nodded.

Beatrice said, "Why do you ask, Matt?"

"Dez was doing research into Livia's businesses. One of her companies owns a very small plant in Bulgaria. From what she could find out, it was pretty busy until about three years ago; then it was shut down. But not exactly. It was kept in operation, but with a skeleton staff and no product being shipped out, then a little over a year ago, they put out a hiring notice again. Nothing's been shipped out yet, but the plant is in operation."

Tenzin nodded. "That fits the timeline I've been thinking of. If Livia is using this plant to produce the elixir, that means they started just few months after Stephen was killed and Lorenzo took the manuscript."

Beatrice asked Matt, "What was the cosmetics company making? Before it was shut down, what did they produce?"

Matt scowled. "High-end cosmetics for the European market. Using traditional, botanical ingredients."

"That's it." Beatrice sighed. "It has to be."

"B, I need to talk to Gio, there was something else—"

"Gio's not here, Matt," Beatrice said quietly.

She had never seen the man look more shocked. "What? It's past dawn. He stayed at Livia's? What the—"

"He stayed at Livia's, but it wasn't his choice," Carwyn said. "She accused him of murdering Andros in front of the Roman vampires. She's taken him prisoner."

Matt's mouth gaped. He looked at Beatrice. "B, is it—"

"Shut up!" Tenzin walked over and stood in front of Matt. The small woman looked up into the human's shocked face. "Whatever you were about to ask, don't."

"But—"

"Does it matter to you? If Giovanni killed his sire? If he didn't? Does it matter to you? Does it change your opinion of him or your loyalty to him?"

Matt just blinked. "No, of course not. I know what a good man he is."

"Then don't even ask. If you ask B, you're forcing her to reveal information she holds in confidence or lie to you. Do you understand?"

Matt paused before he spoke. "Yes, Tenzin."

"Good. Now, go get your wife. I want to know more about this company."

Matt looked abashed when he was dismissed, and Beatrice tried to catch his eye, but she could tell the man was already focused on the task at hand. The thought of Matt and Dez working with them almost brought tears to her eyes. Part of her wanted to force them to return to Los Angeles with Ben, but the other part knew that she needed them more than ever.

"Hey." She heard Ben's voice at the door and turned. "What's going on?" Ben yawned and rubbed his eyes. "And who's the weird guy?"

Ziri smiled. "My name is Ziri, boy. And I am a friend of your aunt's."

"What's going on? Matt looked really upset. Is everything alright?"

Beatrice waved him over, and Ben came to sit next to her. She blurted it out, knowing that nothing she said would soften the loss of his uncle. "Gio's been taken prisoner, but he's going to be fine."

All the bravado fell from Ben's face, and he looked like the insecure child she'd first laid eyes on in the bushes outside the Huntington Library years ago.

"What? He... he's—"

Carwyn stepped in and put a hand on Ben's shoulder. "He'll be fine. We're going to get him out. It'll just be—"

Ben shot out of his seat; anger spread across his face. He stalked over to Tenzin. "Where the hell have you been, Tenzin? If you were here, this wouldn't have happened!"

Beatrice rose. "Ben, she was working on—"

"What does it matter if you find Lorenzo if Gio gets killed? Don't you care about him?"

Tenzin said nothing, staring at the boy through her dark curtain of hair.

Ziri spoke quietly from the other side of the library. "Lorenzo is here, Benjamin. He's working with Livia. He's the reason your uncle was taken."

Ben eyes darted between Ziri and Beatrice. He looked back at Tenzin. Beatrice could see his anger flee. "Is it true?"

Tenzin only nodded; she stiffened when Ben threw his arms around her. Tenzin waited for a moment, but finally lifted her small arms and hugged the young man back. Beatrice could hear Ben whisper, "Get him back, Tenzin. Please, get him back." Then he spun on his heel and rushed out of the library. Beatrice could hear him climb the stairs to his room.

They spoke about details for a few more hours. Ziri asked for the use of a bedroom with a desk and some paper to write a few letters. Beatrice was still confused about what, exactly, his part in all this was. She got the impression that there was a lot that Ziri wasn't telling them. She also got the impression he was waiting for the mysterious Lucien Thrax, who Tenzin thought would wake a few hours after dark. Beatrice was still confused why such an old vampire needed so much sleep.

Matt had already been on the phone with Emil Conti's people, arranging a meeting with Carwyn and their boss for the following night. Dez and Tenzin were talking about the details of the Bulgarian cosmetics company.

And Beatrice felt lost.

Finally, she realized she would be useless for anything until she could spend some time alone. She climbed the stairs to their room, only to find Ben sitting outside on the floor by the door. He looked up with red eyes.

"I know you usually don't let anyone in your room, but—"

"Come in."

Beatrice unlocked the door and she and Ben entered. She fought back the tears when she saw the rumpled bed Giovanni hadn't made because they were rushing to get ready for the party the night before. A damp towel was tossed on the floor by the couch. She picked it up and inhaled the distinctive smoky smell of her mate's skin a moment before she crumpled to the floor.

She felt Ben's hands lifting her and pulling her to the couch. He grabbed a linen handkerchief from his pocket. He had taken to always carrying them, just like his uncle. He joked that it impressed the girls.

"I need to calm down," she whispered, patting the bloody tears from her eyes. "He needs me to be thinking straight. To be calm and smart and —"

"It's okay, B. It's just us, okay?" She could hear the hitch in his voice. "For right now, it's okay. It's just me."

She sniffed and tried to remember when Ben had grown up. It had happened without her even realizing it. The young man threw an arm around her shoulders, and Beatrice allowed herself to lean into him. Ben rocked back and forth, comforting his aunt and sniffing back his own tears.

Beatrice looked over to their bed and knew that she would not lay in it again until her husband returned to her. Ben was murmuring comforting words in her ear, his arms tight around her shoulders. Beatrice finally let herself close her eyes and let go of the sorrow that she'd held back for hours.

Ben was right. It was just them.

CHAPTER TEN

Crotone
1504

He heard Andros's heavy step in the hall. Jacopo looked up for a moment, but quickly returned to the translation of the Arabic manuscript he was working on. It was one that his father had rescued from the destruction of the Mongols in Baghdad.

The door swept open and Andros walked over and patted his shoulder. Jacopo heard Paulo follow, carrying a heavy trunk.

"Son, it is good to be home."

"How was Rome?"

"As expected," Andros said. "She grows more pompous every century. I can't imagine why Livia thinks so much of herself when this detestable country is run by thieves, mad priests, and inbreeds."

Jacopo glanced at Paulo, but the young man only rolled his eyes. Jacopo had been with Andros for almost ten years, Paulo even longer, and both the men were used to the unpredictable moods of the vampire.

A visit to Rome, however, only ever raised Andros's ire.

"But the trip to Florence was a pleasure. The ugly sculptor finished his statue of David, and it was installed in front of the civic house while we were there. A true masterwork. A pity the human is so detestable in his form. Otherwise, he might be worth turning for his talent."

Jacopo's ears perked up. "You went to Florence?"

Andros only glanced at him. "We did."

Jacopo waited. He had known for years that his uncle's friend, Poliziano, had died only a few months after Giovanni Pico. Savaranola had met a gruesome end, along with most of his uncle's collection of books and papers, during Florence's descent into madness six years before. The only survivor of the four men who had raised him was the poet, Benivieni. But

Andros was always careful to dole out only the information he wanted Jacopo to have.

"Benivieni is in good health, from what I heard."

Jacopo kept his face carefully blank. "Thank you."

"Of course."

Andros began to unpack books and papers from the trunk Paulo had carried in.

"I have more translations for you to do if your current work is up to standard."

"It is."

He heard Andros chuckle. "Your confidence pleases me. And your Arabic is quite good. After you have turned, you will start your study of Sanskrit."

Jacopo's head jerked up. "After I have turned?"

Though Jacopo had known of his father's intentions for years, he rarely mentioned it and never referred to it directly. It was implied—an eternal sentence that hung over Jacopo's shoulders.

"Yes, you have been with me for ten years now. I have started to note some mild deterioration of your physical form. It is time."

Jacopo's heart raced, and he cursed internally, knowing that Andros could hear it. The old vampire looked up.

"Have you changed your mind? Would you prefer that I kill you, instead?"

Jacopo looked over Andros's shoulder and saw the pathetic hope flair on Paulo's face. He knew the young man wanted immortality in a desperate and hungry way. He also knew that Andros would never turn the young man, whom he considered "defective." Jacopo forced himself to smile.

"And waste the fine education you have given me, Father? That would be a mistake, would it not?"

Andros watched him with careful eyes. "It would. But, I suppose, I could always find another student."

Jacopo rose to his feet. In his late twenties, he was taller than his uncle had been, taller than Andros, and far taller than was common for most men of fifteenth century Italy. His shoulders had filled out, and the strict exercise regimen that Andros had forced on him had molded his body into perfect form. Jacopo looked at the ancient statues of demigods that Andros used to decorate the stone fortress where he resided, and he saw a mirror image of himself.

He gave his father an arrogant smile. "You could find another student, Father?" A cold smirk flicked across Andros's lips as Jacopo continued, "You would never find another like me."

Castello Furio
Rome, 2012

Giovanni's eyes opened. For a moment, he was in his father's fortress in Crotone, the cold, stone walls echoing the damp room he had woken in his last days as a human. He sat up into a crouch and eyed his surroundings.

The room where Livia's guards had thrown him was surrounded by a thin fall of water, an effective counter to any of his elemental power, which also filled the underground chamber with a pervasive chill. He could heat his skin, but could do nothing to create a spark. The door had no handle, and the walls mimicked the diameter and shape of the tower where he had slept in apparent safety so many years before. In the back of his mind, he wondered if his current prison was built under the very tower that had sheltered him in Livia's castle. He did not find it hard to imagine.

Though he could not use fire to escape the chamber, he had immediately tested the walls when he had been thrown in the night before. He sensed no weakness and no nearby energy signatures. Giovanni was completely isolated in the cold room. He could hear the rushing of an underground river somewhere close. No doubt, it fed the waterfall that trickled down the walls.

He wished he had fed the night before. He and Beatrice had planned to feed once they returned to Rome after the party, not trusting any of the blood that Livia would provide. Thinking about his wife made his blood rush, and he was more grateful than ever that Carwyn had accompanied them the night before. His friend would protect Beatrice. His mate would be safe.

He detected a familiar signature approaching, so he stood and braced himself against a stone pillar.

The door opened, and Livia strode in, tailed by two guards dressed in the same clothing that he remembered the vampires at the monastery wearing on the night they had slaughtered the monks and ransacked the library with Lorenzo. At least Giovanni finally knew who was backing his son.

She stood in front of him. Gone was any pleasant facade; her disgust lay plain on her face.

"I suppose you think you are quite safe because I was forced to take you in front of witnesses."

He said nothing, but a small smile touched his lips.

"Your son changed my plans, but did not ruin them, you know. I will still kill you."

Giovanni still said nothing. Livia smiled back at him and approached.

"You see, Giovanni, I will be very, very fair." She reached up and ran a finger along his jaw. "I have spent two thousand years manipulating this city into thinking of me as its queen. I know exactly the words to use." Her hand ran back and tangled in the hair at the nape of his neck.

"There may be some objections, at first. You have plenty of your own allies and a very honorable reputation. But by the time I cut your head off and throw it in the river that flows under this castle, all will think of you as a murderer and a liar. A thief of one of the greatest collections of knowledge our world has ever seen. A greedy vampire who would keep the best interest of our kind for his own profit."

He opened his mouth to speak and saw her pause, waiting for the words of protest to leave his lips. She was waiting for him to object or defend himself.

Giovanni asked, "How is my wife?"

The flash of fury confirmed that Beatrice was, as he suspected, quite safe from the she-demon in front of him. Giovanni's smile grew.

"I have no interest in your common wife. She may be seen by some as extraordinary, but it is not evident to me. A human of questionable breeding with little to no grace? I'm still wondering what you see in her."

The impassive expression blanketed his face again.

"Lorenzo has expressed an interest in using her as a plaything once our plans are complete. I'll most likely give her to him. She won't be any use to me."

Still, he let no expression flicker over his face.

Livia forced his head down and whispered in his ear.

"Let this all be a misunderstanding, my darling boy. Show me your contrition and I will let you live." He felt her fangs flick along his earlobe. Giovanni reached back to his earliest memories and emptied himself of all emotion, as he had under his father's sword.

"I would bear you no ill will. I, of all people, understood his temperament. His particular foibles were my friends for a thousand years. Let me free you of him once and for all. Confess to me, my Giovanni."

He closed his eyes and pulled away, opening them to meet her gaze. Finally, he spoke in a soft voice. "Livia?"

"Yes?"

"Do you know what my father called you?"

Her eyes frosted over. Livia stepped back and pulled the sword from the belt of one of her guards. She ran it into Giovanni's gut, but he only smiled. Even as the blood spilled out, he smiled.

"He called you the Roman whore, Livia."

She reached back and pulled the other guard's sword from his waist. He felt it pierce higher, closer to his heart as she ran the thin blade between his ribs. As his father taught him, he did not even flinch.

"The Roman whore," he said again, feeling the pull of the blades against his skin and muscle. "That is what your dear husband called you in the privacy of our home."

"I will kill you, Giovanni di Spada."

He smiled. "My name is Giovanni Vecchio, son of Niccolo Andros. Mate of Beatrice De Novo. And you will not kill me."

"Dead man."

"Whore."

She raised her hand and slapped him before grabbing a blade from his body and ramming it in again. Giovanni smiled, but said nothing more. She turned on her heel and strode from the room. The silent guards walked over, drew their weapons from his body, and left behind her.

He heard the heavy clanks of metal as the unseen locks fell into place. Livia knew almost as well as his father how easily he could escape most places. As he looked around the room, Giovanni realized that she had constructed this dungeon with him in mind. He also noted it did not look new.

He reassessed his options. He would not underestimate Livia's intelligence; he would not be able to escape on his own. Luckily, he was not alone. Carwyn was in Rome. Beatrice was stronger by the day. Tenzin would arrive soon, if she hadn't already.

Giovanni tore off strips of cloth to stuff into the stab wounds. With no blood and no ability to manifest his fire, he knew he would heal slowly. He took a deep breath of the damp air, pictured his wife's laughing face in his mind, and closed his eyes to wait.

CHAPTER ELEVEN

Residenza di Spada, Rome
June 2012

Beatrice was meditating to the strains of a Bach concerto when Tenzin came in her room. The wind vampire looked at Ben, stretched out at Beatrice's feet, sleeping in the late afternoon. The boy had refused to leave his aunt, even when he needed to rest.

"Get up. Get dressed. We're going to Livia's castle."

Hope flared in Beatrice's eyes. "We're going to get him?"

"No. Not yet, anyway. But she doesn't know I'm here, and she needs to."

"Why?"

The small vampire smiled. "Because I scare the shit out of Livia. I always have. She hates me." Then the smile fell. "Plus, she has Lorenzo with her. I have a few things to say."

Beatrice stood and looked over her wrinkled clothes. She was still wearing the loose shirt and leggings from the party. "What should I wear?"

"Whatever you want. Whatever you think she'll hate. And bring your *shuang gou*. If we're lucky, we'll get to kill something."

She hopped to her feet. "Hell, yes."

Beatrice ran to the bathroom to take a shower. As she reached down to untie the drawstring on her leggings, her fingers twisted in the knot. For a moment, she clutched it, remembering Giovanni's hands tugging at the drawstring in the tower room. She lifted the front of her shirt and inhaled the sweet and heady fragrance of their combined scents. Then she stripped off her clothes, stepping into the shower as she locked her sorrow away.

A few minutes later, she poked her head out the door. Ben was gone, and Tenzin sat at the desk in the corner of the room, poking through Geber's journals.

"We should give these to Lucien to look through. He'll be able to read them."

Beatrice went to the closet and began to dress in a pair of black jeans and a skin-tight black T-shirt. She slipped on the leather boots she'd worn to the party. "I doubt it. It took me months to wrap my head around Geber's writing."

"Trust me, he'll be able to read them."

"Is he awake yet?"

Tenzin shook her head. "He probably won't wake until well after sundown, and we'll already be in the air."

"Oh, right, you can fly us. Much better," Beatrice muttered as she tied her hair back and strapped on the scabbard Baojia had made for her to carry the twin hook-swords that had become her weapon of choice. She slid the two blades into the black leather sheaths and stretched back over her shoulders to make sure she could draw them easily. She thanked her vampire strength and flexibility that she was able to wield them at all.

"Ready?"

Beatrice nodded. "We have a few minutes before sundown. What are we expecting to happen?"

"We'll fly up there. Scare her. If we're lucky, some of her guards will attack us and we'll get to kill some of them."

Beatrice hesitated as she remembered Carwyn's admonition to be patient. "As much as I'm looking forward to killing something, are you sure this is a good idea?"

"If they attack us, we can defend ourselves. No one will question it, particularly since you have been put on the defensive, and I am a known ally of Giovanni's."

"And you're sure going there is the right move?"

"It's the only move. Currently, Livia has all the bargaining power. We need to shift the balance and throw her off her plan. Making her appear weak is our main objective."

They left the bedroom and walked down the stairs.

Beatrice asked, "So how are we going to do that?"

"When we get there, let me do the talking. I may hate politics, but I know how to play the game when I must."

"What do I do?"

"You'll stand behind me and look pissed off and menacing. Like I said, if anyone threatens you, kill them."

"Even Lorenzo?"

Tenzin cut her eyes to the side. "He's not that stupid. He might not even be there. It depends on how much attention he's looking for."

Beatrice paused at the base of the stairs. "Tenzin, why are we *really* going?"

The small woman looked up at Beatrice with furious eyes. "For almost a thousand years, the Eastern immortals have left her to her pretense of an empire. She kept to herself. We had no interest in her. Lorenzo changed that. Livia needs to realize that as long as she harbors a vampire who killed my mate and defied my father's court, she has lost any pretense of disinterest."

"She's powerful."

Tenzin gave a wicked smile, baring her curved fangs. "Never forget, Livia has tasted defeat in the past. She's vicious, but she's become soft on her cushioned throne."

Beatrice nodded, feeling nervous and elated at the same time. She watched as Tenzin strapped her ancient scimitar to her waist and opened the door to the garden. Twilight had fallen.

Tenzin held out her hand for Beatrice to grasp as they took to the air with a quick jerk. "My girl," she called out. "I believe we should remind her what it is to fear."

A few minutes later, they landed with a soft thud at the gates of Castello Furio. Beatrice could hear the sounds of a party going on in the house.

Tenzin's eyes swept the grounds. "She's thinking more defensively."

As soon as the words left her mouth, two guards rushed them. They came to a halt a few meters away, but Tenzin kept walking at a steady and determined pace.

A guard spoke. "Stop, both of you! You may not enter the castle with weapons."

Tenzin drew her sword in the space of a heartbeat, sliced off the head of the guard who spoke, and kept walking as the body crumbled to the ground. "Oh, really?"

The other guard immediately snarled and drew his weapon, but Beatrice reached back for the *shuang gou*, drew them, and cut off the head of the vampire in one smooth movement. She hooked the swords in front of her and kept walking.

Four guards came at them next. Tenzin took to the air and swiftly killed two as Beatrice reached out to either side and hooked her blades around the necks of her attackers. She pulled both of them toward her, feeling the cold blood spatter on her face as their spines were severed and their heads fell at her feet.

By the time they were halfway across the garden, more guards had gathered but had stopped attacking them. They walked up the stairs, and Tenzin sent a great gust of wind to slam against the doors, pushing them open.

The two vampires entered the grand entryway and halted as every eye in the room turned toward them. Beatrice walked to the fountain and tore off a sleeve, flicking her fingers to spray a sheen of water over her blood-splattered face. She patted it dry, staring at the gaping immortals in formal wear that watched them. The music had died, and a path opened through the crowd, guiding them forward.

Beatrice bared her gleaming white fangs and let her amnis churn the water in the fountain until it splashed over the edges of the stone basin.

"Sorry about that." She sniffed and flicked the water back in. "We left a bit of a mess on the front lawn, too."

Tenzin hushed her as they walked to the right and into the great banquet hall of Castello Furio. It looked like the party the night before had not stopped with Giovanni's arrest. Beatrice could see Livia sitting on a plush chaise with a group of admirers in one corner. The noblewoman was dressed in another rich amethyst gown, her hair piled in a tower of curls. She looked up, and the smile fell from her face. She stood as Tenzin came to a halt and sniffed the air.

Out of the corner of her eye, Beatrice saw Lorenzo emerge from a doorway to the right with a company of guards. The guards spread along the edges of the room and Lorenzo stood behind Livia. His smiling eyes never left Beatrice. She glanced at him, then turned back to Tenzin, who stood quietly in front of the Roman. No one spoke until Tenzin opened her mouth.

"Livia."

"Tenzin."

"Give me Giovanni Vecchio."

Livia curled a red-painted lip. "Don't be ridiculous."

"In thousands of years, I've been called many things, but 'ridiculous' is not one of them, Roman dog."

Livia narrowed her eyes and scanned the two vampires, noting their bloody clothes. "Why do you come to my house to insult me, barbarian? To kill my guards? What kind of civilized person comes to a party with bloody weapons?"

"You will give me my friend."

"Why? Giovanni di Spada killed my husband and mate, Niccolo Andros, his own sire. I have every right to keep him as my prisoner. He is a murderer, a liar, and a thief. His own son confirms it."

Even though the accusation had been made before, Beatrice could still feel the shock roll through the room, and her own rage mount. She glanced around at the crowd, all of whom were keeping a safe distance. No one seemed to be able to take their eyes off of Tenzin and Livia.

"I do not know the truth of this accusation, nor do I care." Tenzin lifted her bloody saber and pointed it toward Lorenzo. "I know that *you* harbor a vampire who has defied a judgment of the immortal elders of Penglai Island. What have you to say to that?"

Livia shrugged. "I have received no official correspondence from that court. Who are you to speak for them?"

Beatrice could hear a few gasps around the room. Apparently, Livia was surprising even the jaded Roman population with her arrogance. From the corner of her eye, she saw Emil Conti approach with watchful eyes.

"Who am *I*?" Tenzin bared her fangs. Beatrice could hear the rustle of alarm spread through the room, but Livia remained still. "I am Tenzin. That is all the explanation you require."

Livia lifted an eyebrow. "Oh? And who makes these ridiculous accusations of my associate?"

Beatrice forced back the angry words that wanted to burst from her mouth. Her fangs grew long, and she tasted blood. She glanced over at Tenzin, but the small vampire looked eerily calm as she turned her back on Livia and addressed the Roman crowd.

"This vampire who Livia favors, Lorenzo, defied an official judgment of the Eight Immortals when he stole a manuscript from their scribe, Beatrice De Novo. Further, he and his vampires slaughtered the learned monks of Elder Lu Dongbin in the Wuyi Mountains. They killed humans under immortal aegis, none of whom had provoked such an attack."

A growing wind built in the room, lifting Tenzin as she surveyed the crowd. Beatrice looked on, unable to tear her eyes from the frightening specter of her friend wielding her power. Tenzin turned to Livia, but her voice echoed off the stone walls.

"The vampire *you* shelter defied the Elders, slaughtered the monks, and then..." Tenzin swooped down and grabbed Lorenzo by the throat, lifting him in the air and beyond the reach of his patroness. "Then, this bastard killed *my* mate."

The reaction was instantaneous. The Roman vampires, still even in the face of Tenzin's frightening power, began to whisper and scuttle to the edges of the room. The black-clad guards stepped forward, surrounding Beatrice, but keeping their distance from her drawn weapons.

Livia calmly walked down the steps and came to stand in front of Beatrice. She looked up with haughty eyes. "And what immortal accuses Lorenzo of this murder?"

Beatrice made sure she spoke loud enough to be heard over the rushing wind.

"I do. He killed my father and my sire, Stephen De Novo."

Livia was silent for a moment before she burst into laughter. "Lorenzo killed your father? How predictable. And why should we believe the accusations of an angry child?"

Beatrice let a satisfied smile curve her lips when she realized the trap that Tenzin had so carefully laid. Lorenzo dropped from Tenzin's grasp a moment before the wind vampire landed next to Beatrice. Tenzin kicked the blond vampire to the corner and stepped between Beatrice and Livia.

"Quite right, Livia." The Roman inched back as Tenzin crowded her. "You are *quite* right. Who would believe the angry accusations of a grieving child? Even more"—Tenzin aimed a glare at Lorenzo—"who would believe the accusations of a *spiteful* child? One who has always coveted his father's wealth? Why, to believe something like that without question, would be... madness."

The air was suddenly still and not a whisper could be heard. Livia took a step back. Anger churned in her eyes, but her face was otherwise placid. Finally, she turned and sat on the brocade sofa where she had been holding court. Lorenzo brushed his clothes off and came to sit next to her. She placed her hand in his.

"So, Tenzin, what do you want? We all know your power, but you are in *my* court now, not an island in the sea. You know I will not release your friend, and you cannot have Lorenzo. There is obviously some investigation to be done in this matter, which I trust you will allow me to pursue. I'm a very fair person. Are you?"

"Not particularly."

Beatrice heard a few laughs in the crowd. One of them, she was almost certain, belonged to Emil Conti. Tenzin continued watching Livia with cold, calculating eyes.

"You know what I want, Livia. I want Giovanni Vecchio returned to his wife, the daughter of my mate. I want the head of the vampire on your left. I've considered killing you, as well, but I'm willing to let you live as long as you meet my demands."

"I could kill Giovanni with a snap of my fingers." Livia raised a hand and Beatrice could not stop the snarl that left her lips. Livia smirked. "But I won't, of course. Some of us aren't barbarians."

"And some of us are." Tenzin stepped closer and pointed at Lorenzo. "He exists at my pleasure. I could kill him quite easily; I'm sure you know this. If any harm comes to my friend, I will."

"As I said, I'm not—"

"And if that is not enough incentive to keep Giovanni Vecchio safe..." Tenzin again raised a swirling wind that lifted her in the air as she faced the Roman immortals. She lifted her arms, raising her bloody sword. "Vampires of Rome, I am the only child of Zhuang Guo, warrior king of the ancient steppes. I am the daughter of the Northern Wind. It has been many years since the hordes from the East have descended on your land, but make no mistake, we can and will raise them again."

Faster than the eye could follow, Tenzin darted down to twist the neck from the guard who stood next to Livia, splattering blood across her purple gown. A group of guards rushed toward them, but Beatrice raised her swords, twisting them in a razor-sharp whirl until they fell back.

Tenzin snatched the head of the guard and flew to the top of the room, then dropped to the ground in a crouch and tossed the guard's head at Livia's feet. Then she stood up, smearing the blood across her cheek as she tucked her hair behind her ear.

"Make no mistake, Roman. I am not civilized. Giovanni Vecchio remains safe, or I will call the Golden Horde. And remember, no ancient power remains to guard your Eastern gate."

Then Tenzin grasped Beatrice's arm, and the two vampires flew from the room in a rush of wind.

A few miles outside of Rome, they suddenly dropped to the ground. Beatrice looked around at the small, deserted piazza with a fountain in the middle. Judging by the position of the moon, it was probably around ten o'clock.

Tenzin pointed toward the fountain. "Wash up. You don't want to scare Dez or Ben. And you did well back there."

"You know, I always thought you were scary, but if I were Livia, I'd be metaphorically shitting my pants right now." Beatrice walked over and began washing. She was grateful for the deserted fountain and the moment to gather her thoughts. She took a calming breath and lay as much of her body in the water as she could, wrapping herself in the soft comfort of her element. Tenzin sat on the stone ledge.

After a few silent minutes, Beatrice spoke. "How did you leave him alive?"

She saw Tenzin look up at the moon. "I can be patient."

"You'll kill him soon enough."

"Or you will."

Beatrice shook her head. "He killed your mate. If it was Gio—"

"My girl, he killed your father. Your sire." Tenzin blinked a few times. "If you have your opportunity, take it. I will not be angry."

"Are you sure?"

Tenzin stood and held a hand out to Beatrice, lifting her out of the water. "There are more important things than my vengeance. That is why I could leave him alive. That is why you will kill him one day."

Beatrice frowned. "But, Tenzin—"

"Come, we need to get back to Rome. Lucien will be awake now. You need to talk to him."

Giovanni heard her approach. Livia swept into the room and shoved the guard back that tried to follow her. She paced, and he could see the water in the air drawn to her as her amnis swirled.

For a moment, Giovanni felt fear. He had not fed and was still weak from the injuries she had inflicted on him earlier in the night. But he braced himself against the stone pillar and remained silent, watching her stomp around the room.

Suddenly, Livia turned to him and screamed at the top of her lungs. Then she flew at him, stabbing him in the gut with a dagger she pulled from her bodice. She kicked his knees and slapped his face. She loosed her rage on Giovanni as he stood utterly still, not understanding what had caused the usually composed vampire to lose her temper.

Livia stabbed him over and over, until his leather jerkin hung in bloody strips, and he began to blink, lightheaded from the blood loss. Still, he said not a word and barely flinched, determined not to give her the reaction he knew she was looking for.

"Say something!" she screamed in his face, her fangs cutting her lips. He felt a spatter of her blood touch his face and she eyed his neck.

She paused, then a sick smile twisted her lips. She sprung on him and tried to latch onto his neck to drink, but Giovanni raised his arms and batted her away, throwing her as far across the room as his weakened body would allow.

He said only one word. "No."

Livia stood again and screamed, stamping her foot. Giovanni began to think she would finally kill him, but as soon as he thought it, she took a deep breath, pushed the mangled hair from her face, and looked at him with her typical look of contempt. Then she turned her nose up and walked from the room.

Only when he heard her steps retreating down the hall did he allow his shoulders to slump. If he did not get blood soon, he would fall into sleep, his body shutting down to protect his mind.

A few moments later, Giovanni scrambled to his feet when he heard footsteps in the hall. The locks twisted and a human servant entered the room. The young man raised an arm, clearly indicating that Giovanni was allowed to drink. His fangs slid down and he grasped the man's throat. Then he took a deep breath and backed away, clamping down his control so he did not drain the donor. He could see the fear evident in the young man's frightened gaze.

Keeping one hand on the man's throat and letting his amnis flow to calm him, Giovanni pressed his lips to the offered wrist. He took deep, slow draughts of the fresh blood until he felt his wounds begin to heal. Finally, he sealed up the man's wrist and released him.

"Thank you."

The young donor blinked, then said, "The mistress says to tell you another will be sent tomorrow."

Giovanni narrowed his eyes. "What?"

"Another will come to feed you, Master."

He nodded slowly, then waved the man away. The guard opened the stone door and let the donor out before the locks clicked in place again. Giovanni took a deep breath as the strength began to flow through his limbs and his wounds began to knit together.

He thought about Livia's strange fury as he healed. Her violence. Her attempts to drink from him. She had looked...

"What was that, Livia?" He paced his stone cell. "What was that in your eyes? What was—" He halted when the answer occurred to him. She hadn't been angry. Livia had been... frustrated. Like a child whose mischief had been thwarted.

Giovanni began to smile. Then laugh. Soon, his deep laughter echoed off the stone walls that held him. Someone had spoiled Livia's plans.

It appeared Tenzin was back in Rome.

CHAPTER TWELVE

Residenza di Spada
Rome, Italy
June 2012

When Tenzin and Beatrice reached the house in Rome, they dropped into the courtyard to see an unfamiliar vampire sitting near the fountain talking to Carwyn and drinking a glass of golden wine. The immortal may have appeared to be young, but his long, angular face and deep-set eyes gave him an ancient stare.

Carwyn smiled and waved them over.

"Beatrice, meet Lucien Thrax."

"Finally." She smiled and held out a hand.

The vampire rose. He was lean and weathered. His shaggy brown hair fell over his forehead when he bent over Beatrice's hand and clasped it with both his own. "Many thanks for your hospitality, Beatrice De Novo. I am sorry I retired before we could be introduced last night. Your household has been gracious to me."

She found herself clasping his fingers, which were unusually warm for a vampire. His energy felt different from any she had ever sensed, but his eyes were open and honest.

"You're very welcome. I understand you're a friend of the family, in a manner of speaking."

Lucien closed his eyes and smiled slightly. "I was honored to call Ioan ap Carwyn one of my dearest friends. Carwyn and I were taking a moment to catch up on news. I met your lovely friends Desiree and Ben earlier this evening while you were..." His smile broadened. "Otherwise engaged."

Carwyn snorted as he rose, motioning Beatrice to his seat while he and Tenzin gathered more chairs from the other side of the courtyard. "Speaking of that," Carwyn said, "I don't suppose you saw Gio?"

Tenzin shook her head. "No, but we did get to kill some guards."

Carwyn patted her small shoulder. "That's my small, ferocious girl."

Beatrice smiled. "You missed it, Father. She scared the proverbial shit out of Livia."

"I miss *all* the fun."

Tenzin only looked him up and down. "If you weren't such a behemoth, I'd fly you, too."

Carwyn just shuddered while Beatrice and Lucien laughed.

"We earth vampires," Lucien said, "aren't terribly fond of air travel, if you haven't noticed yet, Ms. De Novo."

"Please, call me Beatrice. And yes, I've noticed."

"Horrid, unnatural way to travel," Carwyn muttered.

"Yes, it's far more pleasant to tunnel underground like a giant rat."

Beatrice shook her head. "You two really do bicker like siblings."

Lucien burst out laughing. "Beatrice, you haven't seen half of it!"

"Both of you, stop." Carwyn waved a hand at them and looked back to Tenzin, suddenly serious. "Really though, what is the mood in the court?"

"Livia knows she's backed into a corner, which means anything is possible. We need to get him out of there. She's become more unstable than the last time I saw her. She's still frightened by me, but she's keeping Lorenzo at her side like a favorite pet, which means that he's valuable to her right now. We have to assume it's because of the elixir."

"Or something to do with Geber's book," Carwyn said.

"No doubt, but that's not the point. We need to get Gio out, and we need to do it in a way that she'll not be able to point to us. My introduction should be arriving any night now."

Beatrice said, "Your introduction?"

"Yes. Despite the way I charged in today, I will be very properly received the next time we're there. It should drive her crazy." Tenzin grinned. "One of Elder Lu's children is coming in the next week to discuss mutual textile interests in Southern China, and Livia will be forced to acknowledge him as they have business. He's naming me as a member of his retinue as a favor."

"What?" Beatrice looked around. "Really? And she'll just have to welcome you back? Even after the stunt we pulled tonight?"

"You mean the stunt *I* pulled? Remember, B, you did nothing but defend yourself. She'll have no excuse to keep you out of court. With their natural sympathy for Gio and the Roman fascination with the new girl, you might be our most valuable asset."

She just shook her head. "This makes no sense."

Carwyn said, "You have to remember, as powerful as Livia is, she's not the only member of the Roman court. There are many others with their own interests, and she has to placate them, too. She can't piss everyone off and remain in power. Tenzin, what did you think of Conti?"

Tenzin paused for a moment to think and Beatrice thought about the quietly confident water vampire. Like Carwyn, she was curious what Tenzin would think of him.

"Conti may be poised. With the right push, he could take power. He'd be far better than Livia and his connections are more consistent."

Beatrice asked, "More consistent? What does that mean?"

Carwyn leaned forward. "Emil Conti is a bit older than Livia. He was born during the Republic, not the Empire, so he has more... democratic ideals. He's an elitist, but he tends to keep the same friends over the years, unlike our favorite empress. He's also a much better businessman, which means he likes stability and avoids drama. If Livia was pushed out of power, it would be best for everyone if someone was poised to take her place so there wasn't a vacuum."

Beatrice said, "And, Tenzin, you think he's ready?"

She nodded. "He's positioning himself in all this. He senses an opportunity. He could be an ally, so you should get to know him."

Beatrice said, "But does that help us get Gio out?"

"Oh," Tenzin said, "none of *us* can get Gio out. We'll need to be in her presence when he escapes. That way, Livia can't point to any of us."

"But then how—"

Carwyn broke in. "Leave that to me." He gave her a quick wink. "Just a few days and I'll have something worked out."

Beatrice looked over to Tenzin, who was exchanging some kind of wordless communication with the priest. All of a sudden, her friend nodded. "Ah, yes. Send him to me when he gets here, and I'll fill him in on what I know about the castle."

"Good."

Beatrice felt her anger spike. "Will someone clue me in, please? It *is* my husband we're talking about."

Carwyn reached over and patted her hand. "Not just now. I'll fill you in, but I have a feeling our friend here is tiring."

Beatrice looked at the sky, which was still pitch black. Then she looked at Lucien, who had been listening silently to their conversation while leaning his head back and letting his fingers brush through the tangled ferns that lined the edge of the fountain.

"Oh," he murmured, "don't mind me. I'm quite comfortable and quite happy to stay out of all of it."

"Lucien," Tenzin said, "you're neck-deep in all this, and you know it."

He opened his eyes, looking around the courtyard for a moment before he locked his eyes on Beatrice. Eyes that could never belong to a mortal man. They were stone-grey and ringed by a deep brown. Like bits of rock emerging from the earth. Despite the lack of lines on his face, she knew Lucien Thrax had seen many centuries.

As if guessing her thoughts, he said, "I'm almost as old as this one." He winked at Tenzin.

"Where—"

"I come from the mountains, like my mother. But farther north. Not all that far from here, as the crow flies."

Beatrice took a deep breath. "Not that you're unwelcome, but *why* are you here? I know you're not one of Geber's four if you're an earth vampire. You're old enough, but Geber's earth immortal was a woman."

"What a wonderful mind you have, Beatrice." He smiled and drifted in the cool night air. "And you ask an excellent question. Ever since Tenzin found me near my home, I've been hoping I might be able to help you. You see, in addition to being a good friend, Ioan and I were colleagues, as you would say now."

"Colleagues?"

"Yes, though we trained centuries apart, the healing of vampires and humans was our shared interest, and we often corresponded. I've brought some letters and papers that might be of use to you."

"Letters? From Ioan?"

"Yes, there were number of books and papers he sent some time ago that he asked me to look over. They concerned his research into vampiric blood and his theories on what might alter it. His ideas were interesting, even going back to our origins, as mysterious as those are."

Beatrice sat forward, enthralled by Lucien's quiet voice. "What do you mean?"

"Why do we live as we do? Why do we have an affinity for the elements? Why must we drink from the blood of living humans or beasts to remain as we are? Why do we heal from injury?"

"And why," Carwyn asked in a quiet voice, "is our blood unable to heal humans as it heals others of our kind?"

Lucien nodded. "Ioan and I both researched this question over the years. We both had our own theories. He was convinced that there must be some way that we could harness the power of our blood to make humanity stronger. A trade, if you will. That we might drink from them, but that we could offer something good in return."

"Just like Geber."

Lucien offered her a sad smile. "You speak of the elixir."

Beatrice blinked. "Yes! How do you—"

"Oh, my dear Beatrice." Lucien nodded and slumped in his chair, staring into the burbling fountain. "I'm very well acquainted with Geber's elixir. You see..." He looked back to meet her eyes. "I've taken it."

By the time Beatrice noticed Ziri had joined them, she was immersed in Lucien's story. The old wind vampire drifted around the edge of the courtyard, watching Lucien as he spoke.

"I looked over her charts, spoke to her doctors, but there was nothing more that I could do. Pancreatic cancer is one of the most vicious, you see.

And very fast moving. By the time Rada was able to reach me, she was almost gone. Her family was devastated. And I knew that she would never accept immortality. We had discussed it many years before, but she..."

Beatrice spoke softly. "She was a friend?"

Lucien smiled wistfully. "A research assistant. For many years. And a... a dear friend, as well. She left me to go to medical school, marry, have children. It was good. It was what she wanted. But we kept in contact over the years, though her family never understood, as she did, what I truly was."

"And she died?"

For a moment, a gleam of joy lit Lucien's face. "No, she didn't."

Beatrice frowned, "But—"

"I was sitting in a cafe in Plovdiv, sipping a glass of wine and mourning her. You see, I thought that I had seen her for the last time that evening. I felt sure she would not last the next day. Her body was ravaged. Then, Lorenzo walked through the door."

"Lorenzo?" Beatrice whispered, her fangs dropping in instinctive alarm. She could feel a brush of air soothing her shoulder, but didn't know if it came from Ziri or Tenzin.

Lucien shook his head. "I remember thinking later that it was as if an angel appeared. Oh, I knew his reputation, of course, but you never know exactly how much of anything is true in this world. We started to chat. He was sympathetic when he heard of Rada's illness. Who among us has not lost a multitude of human friends?"

Beatrice was willing to bet that there were no humans Lorenzo mourned, but she didn't interrupt.

Lucien continued, "He seemed to sense that Rada was special to me. And then, he made his offer."

A creeping suspicion took root in Beatrice's mind. "When was this?"

"Eight months ago. October of last year."

She whispered. "Almost a year after he took it."

Lucien smiled bitterly. "As Tenzin informed me a few weeks ago."

"He had the elixir."

He nodded. "A form of it, anyway. He said that he was developing it for the pharmaceutical industry. That it was experimental, but would have miraculous effects." Lucien shrugged. "What could it hurt? I thought. She is dying already. Practically a ghost in my arms. I took the elixir for Rada without hesitation. I gave it to her within hours of talking to Lorenzo."

"And?"

"It was just before dawn on a Monday morning. I went to my home to rest and meditate, trying not to retain too much hope. I didn't *really* think it would work, despite the gold I'd paid for it." Lucien paused and brought a hand up to rest on his chin before he spoke again. "But that night, when the sun set, I still ran to the hospital. To her room, and there she was."

Beatrice could see his red-rimmed eyes, and her heart ached.

"She had cheated death! She was still thin, but the color had returned to her face. The doctors called it a miracle. The cancer was completely gone. Her blood tests showed normal results." He sighed and looked up at Beatrice. "I was convinced. How could I not be? It *was* a miracle. Lorenzo had developed the elixir of life."

"Tell them," Tenzin said gently. "Tell them the rest, Lucien."

"I stayed at my home nearby for a few months. Rada seemed to be thriving, and I met with Lorenzo again to learn more about this medicine he had developed. He told me about Geber and the four vampires, though he did not tell me who they were. My instincts are always to be skeptical, but how could I be? I had seen the results with my own eyes. And it fit with much of what Ioan and I had theorized over the years. That blood had always been the key. The combination of elemental blood which linked to the four elements present in human blood—"

Beatrice broke in. "What do you mean? What do you mean the four elements in *human* blood?"

"Ioan and I had always speculated that there was something about human blood that fed the elemental energy in all vampires, which was why we must have it. Human blood, in a way, *contains* all four elements. The cells are made up of matter, as earth is. There is water, of course."

"And then the oxygen it carries is the air," she nodded. "I get those. But what about—"

"Fire?" Lucien grinned, and she saw the spark of the scientist in his eyes. "More elusive. But blood carries heat, does it not? It carries the energy of the entire human body, an energy grid of far more ancient design than the ones humans have developed."

"So, what Lorenzo told you fit with what you and Ioan already speculated, so you bought into the elixir?"

He shrugged again. "As I said, how could I not? I had seen Rada's results. And it wasn't until later that he told me of its other benefits." Lucien took a deep breath and let it out, slumping into his seat. "I cannot tell you what it felt like to hear, after *thousands* of years, that I might be free from the demands of bloodlust, Beatrice De Novo."

"I don't understand. Did you feel guilty? Truly? After *thousands* of years being who you are?"

Lucien smirked. "You live in a very luxurious time, my dear. A time where there is donated blood for the newborn. A time when you can carry a reserve, if you will. You never had to conquer bloodlust while feeding from an innocent. An innocent who looked you in the eye. Talk to me after a few thousand years and let me know if feeding from humanity still holds no shame for you."

She bowed her head, humbled by Lucien's words. Beatrice knew she was young, though she often forgot it when she was in her friends' company. "So, you drank from Rada?" she said. "After you'd heard?"

He took a deep breath and nodded. "I discussed it with her. She was a scientist herself, after all. She offered." Lucien's eyes drifted away. "I kissed her, as I had so many years ago, and then I bit. It was only a few drops. She was still recovering, and... we were not as we once were."

The vampire fell silent. His eyes seemed to glaze over, and he stared at the flowing water in complete stillness until Tenzin leaned over and touched his shoulder. "Lucien?"

He blinked and came back. His eyes narrowed on Tenzin. "How long?"

"Just a few moments this time."

He nodded. "I finally left the city and went to my home in the mountains earlier this year. Just after Christmas. It was then that I began noticing odd things happening."

Carwyn leaned forward. "What things?" Beatrice noticed that Ziri had come closer, as well.

"I needed to sleep. Much more than just a few hours in the afternoon as had been my custom. I thought, perhaps, it was the consequence of the lack of bloodlust. Truly, I felt none. I *still* feel none, though I try to drink. I never feel the burn in my throat, nor the ache in my belly from the lack of it. I have no hunger."

"None?" Beatrice asked.

"None. So I decided, for lack of bloodlust, more rest is surely not so great a sacrifice. If I need no food but a bit of bread, now and again, I am willing to pay that price."

Beatrice had a suspicion that more rest was not the only problem. "What else? It was more than just the bloodlust, wasn't it?"

Lucien nodded. "I began losing time. I would wake in a room that I had no memory of entering. I woke once, thinking it was the next evening, to find that I had no memory of three days past."

Carwyn gaped. "Three days?"

He nodded. "Three days had passed. I don't know if I sleepwalked. If I simply slept? I have no memory of it at all."

Beatrice asked, "And you live alone?"

"I had. I can no longer. I have a fear that I would simply wander out of the house and lose time, meeting the dawn without any knowledge of it. I have lived the past five months in fear, my friends." Lucien ran a hand through his shaggy hair, pushing it off his forehead in a frustrated gesture. "I have no idea what has happened to me. I must assume that it is the result of drinking Rada's blood, but I have no idea why. I force myself to drink now, but it is difficult. I have no taste for it, and I'm not sure my body is drawing any strength from the blood I ingest, no matter how fresh it is."

"And it's getting worse?" Beatrice whispered.

Lucien paused, looking around the courtyard. "Yes. And I have no idea how much worse my condition will grow. I tried to find Lorenzo when I started noticing symptoms, but I heard he was in Rome. He did not answer my letters. In truth, I did not expect him to."

"What about Saba?" Carwyn asked. "Have you written to her?"

"I have sent a messenger to my mother, but, as you know, she is difficult to find. I do have hope that some of my sire's own blood might heal me. But even if the messenger finds her in the mountains, it would be some time. I have no idea how fast this illness might take me. And the distance from Ethiopia to Rome—"

"Ethiopia?" Beatrice sat up straight. "Did you say—"

"It might not matter." Ziri's quiet voice came from the edge of the courtyard. He drifted over and stood next to Lucien, running a hand along the man's cheek in a tender gesture. "Even if you found my old friend, dear Lucien, I don't know if your mother's blood would heal you."

"Uncle..." Lucien took a deep breath. "You have knowledge of this, I think. But not knowledge that will comfort me."

Ziri nodded. "I have knowledge about the elixir, yes. We were foolish to keep it a secret. We truly thought it had been lost, that our children were safe from our folly. We should have known better."

Beatrice murmured, "No secret stays hidden forever."

Ziri nodded. "You speak truth, Beatrice De Novo."

Lucien gripped Ziri's fingers. "Uncle, am I dying?"

"I don't know." Ziri's eyes furrowed in pain. "But I know that something is wrong. Something that can even hurt the most ancient among us. Something that I and my closest friends are responsible for creating."

CHAPTER THIRTEEN

Crotone
1507

Jacopo was crouched in the corner, his throat aching and his eyes glued to the small, lit candle. He reached a finger out, and the flickering flame reached toward him. For a moment, he held it, then it began to spread as if by its own will, up his finger, quickly engulfing his hand. The sharp bite of pain caused him to wince, and he quickly reached for the basin of water Andros had left for him.

For the first time in ten years, he was grateful for the damp air of the craggy castle his father called home. The wet soothed his aching skin and helped him to tame the blue fire that wanted to rush over his body.

Andros had told stories of those fabled immortals who could control fire. His education in both mortal and immortal history had been exemplary. But he had never expected to carry the burden of it. He closed his eyes again and tried to forget the terror of the flames bursting out on his aching body and the quick flash of water his father had used to douse him. Every hair on his body had been burned away within seconds after he first woke, and he rubbed a hand along the bare skin on his scalp.

He heard a commotion in the hall, and a sweet scent reached his nose, causing his new fangs to drop in his mouth. They pierced his lip and the pain caused his skin to heat. Steam rose from his arms as the door opened. Andros entered, dragging one of the servant girls.

She smelled like food.

It was the smell of an orchard when the fruit was ready to drop. The tantalizing aroma of new bread and freshly pressed olives. It was everything. He heard the rush of her blood, rich and sweeter than new wine, as a low growl built in his throat.

He spoke around his long fangs. "Why is she here?"

Andros held the girl up like a prize. "For you. My blood is gone from your system and you need sustenance."

Her name was Serafina, and she was Paulo's lover. Jacopo struggled to look into her eyes, forcing himself to look at her and remember her voice, her laugh, and her smile before she became nothing more than blood to him. He had known he would need to feed from one of the servants, but he had not known which it would be.

He closed his eyes and tried to block her scent.

"I don't want—"

"You will not drain her. That only exhibits a lack of control. Though you are young, you must never be without self-control, do you understand me?"

"Yes, Father."

Jacopo rose to his feet and approached, a small fire burst out on his shoulder, causing the once-friendly girl to look at him in horror. Though Andros quickly doused the flame, another pain twisted his heart. Serafina had once sung and laughed while she cleaned his room.

He held a hand out toward her, trying to calm the terrified girl who had reminded him of his uncle's lover, Giuliana. She had the same dark brown hair and fair skin. The same sweet disposition. Tears streamed down her face, though she bit her lip and smothered her cries.

Andros tossed her toward him and he caught her in his arms. She slumped against him and he heard her whispering under her breath. *"Per piacere, Signore. Abbi pieta. Per favore, per favore."*

Andros's voice slipped over her cries. "Now feed."

Jacopo tried to soothe the burn in his throat. He embraced Serafina, running a hand through her long hair. He could do this. The iron control that enabled him to stand the harshest beating from his sire would let him drink from the girl without killing her.

It had to.

"Shhh," he whispered. He nosed against her neck, forcing himself to become accustomed to her scent before he bit. "Be still. I will try not to hurt you."

As if by its own volition, he felt the energy flow from his fingertips, soothing the girl who ceased her struggles. Serafina lay limp in his arms as he put his mouth to her neck, felt for her pulse, and bit.

Heaven.

He moaned against her neck, pulling her closer as her blood poured down his throat. He pressed her body to his, feeling his flesh rouse as he drank the girl's blood. For a few moments, he was lost in lust. Blood. Body. Desire for both wound him in iron coils until the girl's cries broke through.

She was praying.

So Jacopo pulled his fangs from her neck, forcing back the monster inside that wanted to take her. He willed down his arousal and let his fangs pierce his own lips, pushing her away while he dug burning fingers into his arms.

The girl stumbled before she fell to the floor. He backed away from her and into the corner of the room. The scent of her open wound called to him. Her dress was torn at the neck. He swallowed the lingering burn in his throat and closed his eyes, licking the last of her sweet blood from his mouth. He stopped breathing. Anything to keep from killing the helpless girl.

"Nicely done. Your control is impressive. Exactly what I would expect of my son."

Jacopo's voice was a hoarse growl. "Thank you, Father."

"Do you need another?"

Another? He needed thousands. A vision of the Arno River came to him. If the Arno was a never-ending stream of blood, he would swallow it whole. But that was not what Andros wanted to hear.

"I am fine."

The old water vampire smirked as if he knew the truth, but appreciated Jacopo's lie anyway. Then he walked over and picked up the girl by her arm.

"Grazie, Signore Andros," she gasped. "Grazie per—"

Her words stopped when Andros twisted her neck. Jacopo heard the tiny snap before she fell to the ground, lifeless.

"No!" He started toward her, his heart breaking as he looked into the girl's lifeless eyes, but Andros intercepted him. "Stop." He put a hand on Jacopo's chest and shoved him into the wall. "This will not do. She was human. You are a god. We do not control ourselves to have mercy, but to conquer our own lusts. To be master of them."

"But she was an innocent."

"She was a whore. She had no honor. The girl lay with anyone who paid her attention."

A vision of Serafina and Paulo came to his mind as he stared at her body. They were whispering in the kitchen at night while Paulo snuck some bread and a few kisses from the pretty servant. It was the only time Jacopo ever saw the young man truly smile.

"She wouldn't have been useful much longer, anyway. She was carrying Paulo's bastard in her womb." Andros curled his lip and shook his head, patting Jacopo's cheek in a friendly gesture. "Remember, never keep the same woman for too long. They begin to have expectations."

He couldn't take his eyes from her. Andros walked to the door and opened it.

"Paulo!"

Jacopo heard the steps approaching. Had Paulo known that the girl carried his child? The young man stepped into the room and his fangs dropped again. Jacopo bared them viciously when the scent of the human's blood reached his nose. He heard the faint intake of breath when Paulo spotted his lover's body, but he made no protest.

"Clean this up. Take it out to the sea and dispose of it."

The young man was frozen, his eyes fixed on Serafina's body. For a moment, Jacopo saw his fists clench, then the young man deliberately relaxed them and bent down, kneeling beside his lover. His eyes darted to Jacopo's in the corner of the room, and his lip curled in disgust.

Andros brought a basin and a rag over and began to wash the blood from Jacopo's chin, neck, and chest where it had dripped down. "There, my son. Let me help you. You did well. I am proud of you, so very proud."

Jacopo watched as Paulo closed Serafina's eyes and smoothed her crumpled dress behind Andros's back. For a moment, the young man's hand halted over the girl's belly where his unborn child had grown, then he lifted her slight frame in his arms and walked from the room.

Jacopo felt his fangs retract, and the taste of her blood was bitter in his mouth.

Castello Furio
June 2012

Giovanni stared into the hateful eyes of his son as Lorenzo accompanied Emil Conti and Ziri into his dungeon. He knew, from all outward appearances, that he was being treated well. Though he refused to speak, the two men would have seen the simple, comfortable furnishings that Livia had brought to his cell the previous evening.

He was being fed every evening. He needed it; otherwise the nightly rage that Livia loosed upon him would have been far more evident. Luckily for her, his freshly washed clothes hid the red slashes across his chest, back, and thighs from where she tortured him.

"As you can see, signores, Signore Vecchio is being treated well, despite his refusal to speak or confess his crimes. Livia provides him with plentiful meals and all the necessary comforts, and she will continue to do so until a determination of his guilt can be provided to the court's satisfaction."

Emil nodded. "I do see, Lorenzo. And while I am satisfied that Giovanni is well—"

The canny water vampire drew Lorenzo into a detailed discussion of Giovanni's "case" leaving Ziri to mouth his ghostly whispers from across the room.

'Is she feeding you? Blink once for 'yes.''

Giovanni blinked.

'Is she torturing you?'

Giovanni did not blink.

'You are lying. I can see a mark on your chest. But I will not tell your wife.'

Giovanni mouthed, *Thank you.*

'She is well, and your friends are working toward your release. Do you understand?'

He blinked once.

'Keep strong. You will be in your mate's arms soon. And remain silent, as much as you can.'

He blinked again.

'Your grandsire would be very proud of you, if he could see your strength.'

When Giovanni blinked, it was not in response to anything the old wind vampire had asked. A frown spread across his face.

'Keep silent. I knew your grandsire well. We will speak—truly speak—soon, Jacopo.'

"—and so I am satisfied for now, but this matter must be resolved quickly. I do not care for this drawn-out process. It disrupts business and becomes an unnecessary distraction for the younger members of the court."

Lorenzo nodded at Emil with respect. "I will make mention of your concerns to Livia, Signore Conti. And Ziri?"

The old vampire glanced toward Lorenzo, seemingly disinterested in his surroundings. "Yes?"

"Are you satisfied that the prisoner is being taken care of in a proper way? Do we have your testimony to this? Your opinion would go very far in assuaging some of the more squeamish members of the court."

Ziri waved a hand. "Oh, yes. He's fine. I was simply curious. The design of this chamber..." He looked around in an academic way. "It is most unusual. Will it hold him, do you think?"

"I cannot go into the specifics, of course. But be assured, it is very secure." Lorenzo's lip curled as he eyed Giovanni in the corner. "Even against a vampire as ruthless and cunning as my father."

When Giovanni woke the next night, Livia was in his chamber, staring at him.

"I told him to kill you," she said.

Giovanni only shrugged.

"When Andros wrote to say he had sired you to fire, I told him then that he should spare himself the trouble and kill you."

He blinked and felt along his bare chest to see if the new wounds she had opened the previous night had already closed. They had.

"He didn't listen to me, of course. He rarely did."

She walked over to the side of his bed and sat on it. He lay still and silent, stretching his arms up and knitting his fingers together behind his head. Livia's eyes roamed his chest, and she reached down to trace along the red marks she had made the night before.

"I understood, of course. You were always so beautiful. He was so proud of you. Bright. Strong." She dug her small hands into the defined muscles along his abdomen. "So strong. Stronger than him, as it turned out."

He still said nothing, letting her voice whatever tormented thoughts crowded her mind.

"And I once thought he was the strongest being I would ever meet. I adored him, you know. The first time Andros snuck into my bedchamber, my husband was snoring in my bed, the fat pig. But Andros..."

A wistful smile touched her lips as she gazed into the past. "I had seen him at the banquet that night. He was so handsome. *Strong*. His dark hair was thick and his belly was flat. And no matter how much wine touched his lips, he did not grow drunk. I saw him looking at me, so I encouraged him. Why not?"

Her fingers stroked his skin, drawing damp circles as she reminisced.

"He snuck into our villa that night and fucked me against a wall as my husband snored beside us. It was magnificent."

Though his stomach churned, Giovanni remained motionless and silent. At least she wasn't stabbing him.

"When he finally brought a vampire to turn me, Andros tied my husband up and made him watch. That was even better. Andros fucked me and drained my blood, then my sire gave me his before Andros killed him so he would not interfere. He was nothing. A pawn. I was Andros's *mate*. From the first night of my immortality, I belonged to him."

Livia smiled and ran a finger across his throat.

"My first meal was my stupid, fat husband. I can still taste his blood. It tasted like revenge. While it wasn't cold, thank the gods..." She bent down and whispered into his ear. "It was very, *very* sweet."

Livia took both hands and traced along Giovanni's arms.

"But you, Giovanni... Andros loved you. He adored you. Almost as much as me, I think."

Far more, you stupid cow. Giovanni rolled his eyes.

She curled her lip and slapped him. "If only he had listened to me and killed you."

Livia rose and stepped away from him. "Do you know who built this chamber? Your father did. I told him if he was determined to keep you, then he must build a chamber here that could contain you. I never trusted you, do you understand that? In five hundred years. Never."

Giovanni sat up and looked around. So, this chamber was of his father's design?

"He could be such a genius. Turning me. Using my human connections and my dead husband's gold. Finding the book. We were made to rule, he and I. We *would* have ruled, if you hadn't killed him, you stupid boy."

He swung his legs over the side of the bed and sat silently, examining her. Finally, he opened his mouth to speak.

"The. Roman. Whore."

She pulled a dagger from between her breasts, walked over, and stabbed him in the neck. Bending down, she whispered, "I will enjoy killing you. Then I will drink your blood and the blood of your little wife, you bastard."

Livia spun and left the room as Giovanni sat stunned and blinking.

So, his father had built this chamber.

Giovanni pulled the dagger from his neck and pressed a sheet to the wound.

And Livia had left him a blade.

How generous.

CHAPTER FOURTEEN

Residenza di Spada
Rome, Italy
June 2012

It was late afternoon, and the house was buzzing with activity.

Ben and Dez were doing research into Bulgarian cosmetics companies and their not-exactly-public financial information. They were trying to determine who else might be funding Livia's enterprise, or if she was in it on her own. So far, Elder Zhongli was the only other immortal they'd found any evidence of and, according to Tenzin, he was most decidedly dead.

Matt seemed to be making phone call after phone call in the downstairs study. She couldn't tell whom exactly he was talking to, but Beatrice thought he was speaking French.

She could hear Carwyn and Ziri making plans downstairs in the library. Carwyn had an appointment to speak to someone at the Vatican about unrelated church business, and Ziri was speaking with Emil Conti about a visit to see Giovanni wherever Livia was holding him. Apparently, no one knew of Ziri's connection to Beatrice or Stephen, so he could be presented as an impartial observer and gain access to the dungeons. Emil Conti was willing to play along.

Angela had been cooking all day. The whole house was suffused with the smell of herb bread, lemon, and fresh basil from the pesto she made.

If she listened closely, Beatrice could hear the soft rise and fall of Lucien's breaths in the second floor guest room. He had been at the house for over a week and Beatrice was still surprised by how weary the simplest tasks seemed to make him.

Tenzin left just before dawn, saying she had some business to take care of and would take shelter with the Chinese delegation she would be joining with Elder Lu's son.

So Beatrice sat in her empty bedroom, wearing one of Giovanni's shirts she'd stolen from the laundry, and going quietly mad as another day passed without her husband resting in their bed.

Finally, she picked up the phone and called Los Angeles.

"Hello?"

"Caspar?"

"Beatrice, darling—Isadora, B's on the phone." She heard the quick shuffle of feet and her grandmother picked up the other line.

"Mariposa?"

Beatrice smiled just hearing her voice. "Hey, Grandma."

"How are you, dear? Matt called us a few days ago, and Dez called us yesterday, but they didn't seem to know much."

"No change, really."

"But it's been over a week now! Has anyone been to see him? Does he get a—a lawyer? A doctor? Is there anyone that you can call or petition?"

"It's not really that kind of arrest, Grandma."

She heard Caspar soothing her grandmother in the background.

"Beatrice." His calm voice soothed her, as well. "I know Tenzin and Carwyn are there. Are there any other vampires who have publicly voiced support for Giovanni?"

"Not publicly. At least not right now. She's really powerful, Cas. These Roman vampires are like sheep or something. There are a few who seem to stand up to her, but for the most part, they all just follow along."

"She's still being careful. Gio has enough of a reputation for her to be very cautious about all of this. I expect she's quite angry about having to arrest him as she did. It doesn't sound as if that was her plan. Please be patient, my dear."

Beatrice knew all of it. She had heard the arguments for patience and prudence. She had listened and followed the instructions of those far older and more experienced than she, vampires she knew loved Giovanni, too. Still, she could feel the tears well up in her eyes, and she cleared her throat. Caspar trailed off.

"How are you holding up, dear girl?"

Her voice caught. "Um... can I... can I just talk to my grandma for a little bit, Caspar?"

"Of course." She heard him put the phone down, followed by a few murmurs in the background and a closing door before Isadora came back on the line.

"Beatrice?"

At the sound of her name, silent tears began to stream down her face. Soon, she was choking on her cries as Isadora made soothing noises in the background.

"Oh, my girl. If I could only be there for you now."

"I can't do this, Grandma. I can't be who I'm supposed to be without him here."

"Yes, you can."

"No! Everything's wrong. I can't think straight. I don't feel like myself. I have to force myself to eat, and I know it's not good for me. I can usually sleep a little bit when he's here, but now, it's just… *nothing*. And everything is wrong, and I can't do this."

"Beatrice, you can. And according to what everyone says, this is upsetting, but—"

"It's not upsetting! It's infuriating!" She stood and tried pacing the room, but the rotary phone wouldn't let her get far. She gripped the back of the chair so hard that the wood splintered. "I'm so angry, I want to kill something, Grandma. I want to kill *her*. I want to tear her heart out. I want to rip Lorenzo's head off his body and toss it to a pack of dogs. I want to round up all the spineless weaklings that follow her orders and tear every last one of them apart. I want to burn this damn city to the ground and spit in its ashes. And there is nothing—*nothing*—I can do except sit here and wait for ridiculous protocol and negotiations!"

By the time she had vented her anger, her grandmother was speechless.

"Well…"

"Grandma?"

"Beatrice, this is one of those times when I am reminded that you are a vampire now."

A harsh laugh broke from her throat, but it quickly turned to tears again. She brushed at her tears. "I'm pretty sure I'd feel this way if I was still human, too."

"Possibly, but the potential to carry out the bloodshed would not be as likely."

She grabbed another of Giovanni's handkerchiefs and cleaned her blood-streaked face.

"Beatrice, you must be strong. For him. For yourself. For Ben. Control your anger. Nothing good can come from losing control. I'm sure they're probably expecting you to be foolish and out of your mind with your Gio in prison, so prove them wrong."

"I know you're right."

"Of course I am. I'm your grandmother."

She couldn't help the smile. "Thanks, Grandma." There was silence over the phone as both women seemed to catch their breath.

"Hey, Grandma?"

"Yes, dear?"

"Distract me, okay? Tell me what trouble you and Caspar have been up to lately."

Isadora's tinkling laugh did more to soothe her weary heart than all the kind words from her friends.

"Well, I went to a wonderful painting workshop at the Huntington the other day. Did you know that Caspar has started volunteering in the gardens there? All those little old women just adore him. I'd be jealous, but it's too adorable how he preens for them. It's rose season now, and you know how he loves his roses. Oh! And I should tell you about the art opening that Ernesto took us to the other night. It was wonderful, the girl who was featured..."

As Isadora chattered about roses and art galleries, Beatrice closed her eyes. The familiar voice of her grandmother and the everyday news she spoke of was its own kind of meditation. A reminder that, past the blood and the intrigue, beyond the danger and the heartache, another kind of life waited for her and Giovanni. A life filled with family and love. With their own pursuits and challenges.

If only they could get there.

Finally, she broke into her grandmother's news, anxious to rest her mind on one more subject.

"Grandma, I know Matt usually keeps an eye on things if we're not there—"

"Don't worry about us, Beatrice. We have quite a bit of company, if you know what I mean. Baojia is usually here in the evenings and then there's a lovely woman and a gentleman that Ernesto introduced us to that help with the driving and taking care of this and that around the house during the day. They're quite understanding of us old people!" Isadora laughed, but the keen edge to her voice let Beatrice know she was well aware of the security that Ernesto had arranged.

"Well good. I hope you don't give them too many problems. The two of you are troublemakers, I know."

"But only the best kind of trouble!" Isadora laughed.

By the time she hung up the phone an hour later, Beatrice thought she could just about make it through a few more nights without killing anything.

Unless a good opportunity presented itself, of course.

She was studying some of Geber's journals later that evening and watching Ziri and Lucien from the corner of the library. The old vampire patted Lucien's gaunt cheek as he rose. He walked over to Beatrice.

"I will be visiting your mate later this evening with Emil Conti. It has all been arranged. I will be able to send my voice to him without anyone else hearing. Did you have a message?"

I love you. I miss you. Don't die. You cannot leave me alone in this world. I will kill anything that harms you. I will raze a thousand castles to get you back.

"Tell him," she said, "I will see him soon."

Ziri smiled as if he could read her thoughts, but only nodded and walked out of the library.

"He admires you."

She turned toward Lucien's voice. "Oh?"

"He admires your resolve and control. It is unusual in one so young."

Beatrice closed the journal. She hadn't really read anything anyway. "What is he to you? Ziri? You call him 'Uncle.'"

"He's not an uncle, not in the human sense. But he is one of my mother's dearest friends."

"Your mother is the earth vampire who worked with Geber, isn't she?"

Lucien smiled and rose. He walked toward Beatrice and settled into the chair across from her. They were sitting in the corner of the library closest to the fire. As always, Beatrice found the sound, scent, and presence of the flames soothing.

"She is. There is more to the story, but Ziri says he will fill us all in when Giovanni is back. He doesn't like telling stories twice."

"Okay. I suppose. Since I don't seem to have any choice in the matter, I'll be patient. How are you feeling?"

"As well as I have been." He cocked an eyebrow. "Ziri keeps telling me that he will explain more soon, but he is being irritatingly close-mouthed about it. He has always been like that. Maybe that is why he and my mother get along so well. They can sit in a cave and not speak for fifty years and be totally content." He closed his eyes and sighed. "I am not sure... well, I am not sure." He looked up and shrugged. "I suppose that sums up my life, lately. I am not sure of much."

Her own curiosity burned, but Beatrice forced herself to remain calm and strove for the patience she knew her husband would expect. "Who's your mother? Will you tell me about her?"

He smiled fondly. "Her name is Saba. And I may complain about her, but she is wonderful. She is a phenomenal healer and is very wise. She lives in the highlands of Ethiopia."

"You're pretty old. She must be ancient."

He smiled. "She is the oldest of our kind I have known."

"Truly?"

"Truly. I have never met her equal in power."

"How old is she?"

He shrugged. "I doubt even she knows. She says that she simply was. She no longer remembers being human."

It was impossible to fathom. "Does she have a big family?"

"She did at one time, but she stopped siring children many years ago. I am one of the youngest of her direct clan, and one of the last still living. But most vampires, if they looked back far enough, would hold some relation to her."

"Interesting." Beatrice contemplated the idea. Some of the oldest traces of human life had been found in Africa. Why would vampire life be any different? Then another thought struck, and she smiled. "She's kind of like Eve."

Lucien nodded and smiled. "The comparison is probably quite apt. In a way, I suppose she is our own Eve. A common mother from the times when elemental affinities were far more fluid."

"What do you mean? I thought we always inherited the element of our sire, unless you become a fire vampire."

"Now this is true. It is very uncommon for a vampire to sire out of their own element. It occasionally happens, but it's quite rare. But many years ago, it wasn't as uncommon, especially if the sire was mated to one of a different element and they shared blood. Saba's mate, when she made me, was a wind vampire. His blood is probably the reason I am not nearly as established as most earth immortals. I like to travel and do so frequently."

"Until recently."

"Yes," Lucien said. "Until recently."

"I'm not going to lie, Lucien, I'm having a hard time being patient with all this. I need to know what all of this means. If this elixir is so dangerous, why did they keep it a secret? Why didn't they destroy the book to begin with?"

"Well…" He leaned back and closed his eyes. "We have many strengths, our kind, but the longer we live, the more weaknesses become evident, too. We're not very good at sharing. Part of this is a survival mechanism, of course, but part of it is simply habit. We get so accustomed to hiding from the human world, we tend to hide things from each other, as well. And we're quite greedy for information. Art, ideas, philosophy… these are the things that make immortal life interesting for those that live for centuries, because they are the only things that change. Humanity"—he grinned—"really does not change that much, you will learn. But stories, the ebb and flow of ideas, creativity, all of these things are always changing. It's why we tend to congregate in certain places when there is an explosion of art or science. Anything new, really."

"Like Italy? During the Renaissance when Gio was born."

Lucien leaned forward, his eyes lit. "Exactly. Giovanni probably had no idea at the time, but Renaissance Florence was teeming with vampires. Ziri was there. Even I was there for a time, though I'm not very fond of cities."

"That's interesting. Any other times?"

He folded his hands and relaxed, a wistful smile crossing his face. "Hmm, Greece, for a time. Baghdad, before the libraries burned, of course. Egypt, on and off for centuries. India in the fifth century. I am quite fond of Russia, but not many are."

"Rome?"

"Yes and no. Some, like Andros, were attracted to Rome during the Republic and later, of course, but it was not my favorite time. It was wonderful during the Renaissance. Japan in the sixteenth century. The American colonies during the Revolution."

"What about the times of conflict? Wars? Do vampires like wars?"

He shook his head. "Not usually. We're very self-interested, and wars are not interesting. Plus, we've all seen so many of them that they become repetitive, I suppose."

She shook her head. "Lucien, you're one interesting guy."

He shrugged. "I am, and I am not. I like talking about the past more than most immortals. I don't mind reminiscing. Most older vampires won't."

"I've noticed that. Both Carwyn and Tenzin don't talk about the past. They hardly even mention it."

"It's survival. You'll probably become the same way, after a time. Dwelling in the past can be very depressing. You should always be looking ahead." He smiled. "Look forward. Where is the next great idea or invention? That is what makes immortal life interesting."

"And family. Friends."

He nodded. "Yes, those are the most important. It has always been so. And it will remain. Another constant."

"Constant... right." She bit her lip and tried not to let the overwhelming loneliness envelop her.

"You are thinking about your mate."

"Of course."

"He is your constant. As, I'm sure, you are for him."

"I hope so."

Lucien grinned. "He was always so formal and distant, your Giovanni. I never knew him very well, but he was always so..."

"What?"

He grimaced. "Polite."

Beatrice burst out laughing. "Yes, he is."

Lucien laughed along and shook his head. "But irritatingly so. It was like he was saying, 'Nice to meet you' and 'You're beneath my notice' all at the same time."

"You can't accuse him of being a humble man, no."

"That's good." Lucien nodded. "Good. That means that he'll be fine. Even if she tortures him, he'll be fine. He is above her."

Beatrice fell silent. "Yes, I suppose so."

"I have no doubt he's dealt with worse."

Thinking of some of the more horrible stories she'd managed to pry out of him, and some of the other things that Beatrice had inferred, she had to agree. "Yes, he has."

Lucien only nodded. "He'll be fine."

Beatrice smiled when she heard Carwyn barrel into the house. He walked into the kitchen to bark at Ben about doing his homework, charm a plate of food from Angela, and then she heard him stomp up the stairs.

"Ah! There's my favorite girl. Oh, and, Beatrice, you're here, too."

Lucien chuckled and flipped up a surprisingly modern hand gesture at the noisy vampire. Carwyn put a plate of food on the library table and started eating. "So, what did I miss while I was meeting with the bathrobes?"

"How did the meeting go?"

"Fine. *Great*, actually." He grinned and took a drink from the bottle of beer he'd brought.

"Yeah?"

"Yes. I'm feeling like a new vampire. Fangs are sharper. Growl is scarier. And still, just as good-looking. Watch out, Livia."

Beatrice and Lucien exchanged amused looks.

"What's gotten into you, Father?"

For some reason, that question made Carwyn burst into laughter. Finally, he calmed down and said, "Enough about me. What kind of mischief can we make? I feel like causing some trouble."

"Well, Ziri and Emil went to the castle to make sure that Giovanni is healthy and being kept safe. Beatrice and I were reminiscing about history and talking about how polite her husband is. And then you interrupted us."

Carwyn darted over to them both and smacked the backs of their heads.

"Hey!"

"What kind of evening fun is that? You two are boring."

She stuck out a foot and tripped him before could make it back to the table. "Well, some of us are trying to be patient and not kill anything."

"Oh ho!" Carwyn grinned from the ground. "I know what you need, B."

"What?"

He cocked an eyebrow and smirked.

She rolled her eyes. "Other than that."

Lucien and Carwyn both laughed. Beatrice started for the door, only to feel Carwyn tackle her from behind. He picked her up and ran down the stairs.

"What are you doing? Put me down!"

"Nope. Your husband isn't around for you to shag. You're being a good girl and not killing things. So..." He opened a door she hadn't been through before and tossed her down the stairs. She bounced and tumbled until she came to a small landing.

Beatrice scowled and looked around before gasping in pleasure. "Oh!"

It was a stone basement. Damp and gloomy. Stacked with odds and ends, it looked like the catch-all room for a very large, very old house. But along with old furniture, boxes, and chairs were a rather startling number of weapons mounted on one wall and a large mat that looked like it was used for training.

"You"—Carwyn marched down the stairs and went over to the mat —"need to beat something up. So let's go. We haven't fought in months and your husband isn't around to kill me if I punch you, so have at it, my dear."

Beatrice could have cried; she was so happy. "You're the most awesome friend in the world, Carwyn!"

"I know. Stop gushing like a little girl and hit me already."

She pounced.

Despite his larger size, Beatrice was much faster, so they were evenly matched as they fought. They kept it to hands, fists, and elbows, for the most part, and they laughed and joked as they both tried to beat each other within an inch of their immortal lives. It was exactly what she needed.

Three hours later, she was still not tired, but the soul-crushing tension had been partly relieved. They finally stopped, neither one really winning, and Carwyn leaned against the wall while Beatrice slumped against his shoulder.

"Thanks."

"No problem. Happy to help."

"I miss him so damn much."

"You're just like him, you know."

"How do you mean?"

He patted her head. "Remember when Lorenzo took you the first time? Gio had to dance this dance for almost a month while you were gone. Remember that?"

"Oh, yeah. I'd almost forgotten. That seems like so long ago."

"I think we came down here every day while we were in Rome, and he did the exact same thing. We'd beat each other up just so he didn't go mad. It was the only thing I could do for him."

She blinked back tears. "You're a damn good friend, you know that?"

"I do." He put an arm around her and pulled her close. She wrapped her arm around his waist and let him hold her up for a little while. "He never gave me a cuddle afterward, though, so you've definitely got him beat in the 'thank you' department."

She pinched his waist. "You need to find yourself a woman, Carwyn. If you don't, I'll be too tempted to run away with you."

"I've been telling you for years what a catch I am."

They laughed quietly, and Beatrice found that, for a few minutes, she could rest. They sat silent until she was distracted by a faint noise. A low rumble seemed to be coming from behind another door in the basement, and she sat up straight.

"What was that?"

"Hmm?" Carwyn sat up and looked around. "Oh, the noise. What day is it again?"

"It's—what? What day is it? It's Friday. Why?"

"Ah! They're a bit early. Excellent."

She scowled at him. "Who?"

Just then, she heard familiar voices behind the door. They were raised in irritation and she heard a scuffling sound before the door cracked open. Beatrice couldn't contain her grin.

Gavin Wallace stumbled through the door. "I don't care how you try to pretty it up, woman. It's a strange and unnatural way to travel. The fact that we had to go underground is bad enough, but then water? Do you have any idea how—"

"Shut up, you whining Scot. Do you think I enjoyed having you carry me across the Channel? It's not like you're very practiced at the whole flying bit anyway. I'm surprised you didn't drop me in the sea."

Gavin and Deirdre continued to bicker at each other as Jean Desmarais swept into the room. Beatrice rose and rushed toward them. "What are you doing here? Why—"

"My Beatrice," Jean grabbed her hand and kissed her cheek. "The reports do not do you justice. You are stunning, *ma cherie*."

Deirdre grabbed her shoulders and embraced her. "We're here to help, B. You're looking well. How are you holding up?"

"I'm..." *Stunned. Happy. Relieved.* A smile broke across her face, and she turned to a very sour-looking Gavin.

"I can't believe the red-headed demon pulled me into this. I'm *not* glad to be here. I'm positive this is going to end badly for me, and I've never liked Gio all that much to begin with. He's an arrogant bastard, who has horrible taste in whiskey." A reluctant smile quirked his lips. "He does, however, have rather fantastic taste in women. You're looking well, Beatrice."

"It's good to see you, too, Gav."

Gavin sighed and crossed his arms. "Fine. Now that we're here, what kind of trouble are we in for?"

Carwyn stepped forward and slapped his hands together. "The best kind, of course. And the kind that needs your area of expertise."

Gavin cocked an eyebrow. "Breaking and entering, then. Excellent."

CHAPTER FIFTEEN

Castello Furio
June 2012

When he woke, Beatrice was sitting on the edge of the bed, playing with the ends of his hair, as she knew he loved. Giovanni blinked once.

"I'm dreaming."

"Yes."

He reached a hand up and let it ghost down her arm. "This is much better than most of the dreams I've been having lately."

She smiled. "I'm sure it is."

He lay quiet, reveling in the vision of her beside him. He was afraid to move. Afraid that the dream would shatter, and he'd be back in the cold cell alone. She had no such worries and angled herself toward him, leaning over his chest to look into his face.

"Why do you let him haunt you?"

"Andros does not haunt me."

"Not Andros."

"Lorenzo does not haunt me."

"Not Lorenzo."

He frowned and chanced a single finger to trail along her cheek. "Who then?"

"You. You let the memory of who you were haunt you."

He paused. "I did many things wrong."

"You look back at the actions of a child and expect the wisdom of five hundred years."

"It is far easier to forgive others than to forgive yourself."

She sighed and laid her head on his chest. "I forgive you."

"I am dreaming?"

"Yes."

He fell silent, the protest dying on his lips as he enjoyed the weight of her body pressing against his unbeating heart.

"I love you, Beatrice."

"I know."

"Loving you has been the finest thing I have done in five hundred years."

"You have done many good things."

"I do not tell you enough."

She looked up and smiled. "You tell me every night."

"It is not enough." He rose and twisted her in his arms, flipping her so that she lay under him. Desperation colored his words. "It is *never* enough."

"It is enough."

"No." His lips touched the swell of her cheek. They whispered down to her jaw and explored the delicate line that led to the tip of her chin. "Never enough. It should be the unceasing prayer on my lips. The echo in every breath I take."

"It is enough."

He drew back and looked into her dark eyes. "I would level empires to be with you again. It is never enough."

"Mine is not the only love you have."

"It is the only one that matters."

"You know that is untrue."

He ignored her quiet voice and kissed her again. His mouth met hers in growing hunger, his lips and teeth and tongue fighting to hold on to the vision of her. He could feel himself waking.

"I love you, Beatrice. *I love you.* I thank God for bringing you into my life."

She grinned then, the mischievous smile Giovanni had fallen in love with when she was a lonely girl in a library, and he was frozen in time. "You don't believe in God. Not really."

He narrowed his eyes. "I do."

"You don't."

He scanned her face. Her luminous skin. Her dark eyes and hair. The slight bump on the bridge of her nose. The tiny scars and imperfections that marked her as the only woman in the world. The only woman. For him.

"I believed in God when He brought you to me."

"You don't believe in coincidence."

He could see her fading. The fall of water in the room grew louder, and she began to melt away. Her eyes drifted around the room, but she was the only thing he saw. "Don't leave," he whispered. "Don't leave me."

Her eyes were filled with tears and her hand lifted to his face, holding his cheek in her soothing hand.

"*Ubi amo; ibi patria.* Come home to me, Jacopo."

"Don't leave me." He blinked to suppress the tears that came to his own eyes. "Please."

When he opened them, she was gone, and Giovanni lay silent in his cold cell, the sound of rushing water surrounding him.

He might have lain still for hours; he did not know. He waited to hear the unseen lock turn in the stone door, signaling Livia's entrance. No sound came, only the falling water that dripped down the walls. His fingers played along the edge of the dagger she had left. It had been over a week and yet his keen senses had detected no weakness in the room. It was round, and the water was fed through some channel that coated the walls with a constant stream and filled the air with a swirling dampness. There was a slight opening where the water flowed, but it was far past his reach. Though he could jump, he could not suspend himself long enough to take advantage of the weakness and because it was round, it contained no corner that he might brace himself.

Giovanni could hear the rushing of some underground stream that flowed beneath the room. The chamber was probably set on a pile foundation of some kind, as had been used to build Venice. Between the river below him, and the water flowing around, it was as if he was floating in a stone bubble. If he was an earth or water vampire, an enviable prison. For a fire vampire... a very effective one. His father always had done quality work.

He stared at the ceiling, trying to determine what lay beyond it. It was impossible to sense past the stone. He was concentrating so intently, he almost missed the scratching sound coming from the floor. Suddenly, he felt the floor buckle beneath him and a shock of red hair pushed through. He sat up, and his heart raced when he saw his visitor.

Muddy. Disheveled. The cloud of red hair fell into her face, but she pushed it back, and Giovanni grinned when he saw the wicked gleam in Deirdre's eyes. She put a finger to her lips and reached down, pulling a very annoyed looking Gavin up behind her. The wind vampire looked about as happy as a drenched cat.

"This is the most humiliating, most—"

Deirdre slapped a hand over his mouth and pulled Gavin away from the hole that was starting to crumble along the edges. Giovanni saw another hand reach up and Jean Desmarais lifted himself gracefully out of the river. Unfortunately, as soon as Jean entered the room, the force he had been using to push the water back faltered and the room began filling with water. Rapidly.

"Oh, for fuck's sake! Can this get any worse? I thought I was going to be able to dry off for a bit."

Deirdre curled her lip. "Thank you so much for alerting the entire castle to our presence, Gavin."

Giovanni could already hear shouts coming from past the door. "Whatever stealth you had was lost when the water started leaking under the door, so whine away as long as you have some plan to get us out."

"Well, in that case—"

"Yes, feel free to continue," Jean said as he looked around the room. "Especially if you're keen for Livia to know exactly who is breaking out her favorite prisoner."

That thought seemed to shut Gavin up, and he also began to look around.

Deirdre said, "It's exactly as he described. Gavin, I know you're wet, but you're going to have to fly me up there. Can you do it?"

Gavin scoffed and lifted Deirdre in his arms. The two vampires flew to the top of the chamber as Giovanni turned to Jean. "Why can't we go out the way you came?"

Jean shook his head. "Very strong current and a nasty drop off somewhere just past this chamber. I have no idea where it leads. I could drag one person, but not three and none of you are strong enough to swim back upstream without my help. No, our contact said there is a large, empty chamber above this. He felt it."

"Who—ah, I see." Giovanni nodded. Ziri must have been able to get a feel for the surrounding space when he visited the chamber to see him. "And so Deirdre will break through the ceiling..." His eyes looked up to see Deirdre pushing against the stone, tossing pieces away and digging her hands into the solid chamber walls.

"If she and Gavin don't kill each other. They've been bickering ever since they showed up in Le Havre."

Deirdre had dug about a foot and a half into the rock when she motioned for Gavin to fly her down. The water was almost up to their knees.

"It's very thick. I think I have another foot and a half to go. It's dry set and mostly solid. Very few joints and very tight. There's no soil here, so it makes it more difficult." She was paler than normal, and Giovanni could tell tunneling into the river, then through the floor of the prison had tired her. She needed blood, but no humans were available.

Giovanni nodded and tried to push back the impatience that wanted to grab hold of him. "Deirdre, do you need—"

"Here." Gavin stuck out his wrist, baring it to her face. Giovanni could see her fangs descend, and Deirdre almost skittered back. He knew without asking that she had not drunk from another immortal since her husband had died. Giovanni frowned at Gavin. For him to even offer...

"Here, woman." The gruff Scot huffed and pushed his wrist closer to her face. "Don't be stubborn, unless you want to die. I don't, and neither do I plan on failing a job this simple."

Deirdre hesitated another moment before she grabbed his wrist and dug in. Giovanni glanced at Jean, who was watching with interest, one eyebrow cocked at the pair. Gavin's face was carefully impassive, but Giovanni saw him swallow once. After a few deep draws, Deirdre pulled back and Giovanni could feel her amnis flex in the air around them. She grabbed onto Gavin's shoulders and the two wordlessly flew up to the top of the room again.

After a few more moments and a few more pieces of stone, the marble came crashing down, and Giovanni could scent the stale air as it rushed into the room. He and Jean were floating in the water. Someone was trying to push the door open, but they had tossed the loose stones against it. Between that and the press of water against the door, they were secure.

Finally, Gavin pushed Deirdre up through the passage she had made. Then, he flew down and pulled on Giovanni's arm first and flew him to the top of the cell. He crawled through and lifted himself into an empty chamber that was even higher than the first.

"How deep was that room?" He looked at Deirdre as she walked around the second stone-lined room.

Deirdre said, "I'd estimate twelve meters? It was about three stories down. And it looks like I'm going to have to break through another—"

"No." Giovanni's eyes had spotted something up in the corner of the vaulted ceiling. He heard Jean and Gavin climb through the floor, but his eyes were glued to a tiny ledge and small door he had spotted. "My sire built this room, and Andros didn't believe in one way out. There would always be an escape hatch. Always another way out. Look." He pointed up and turned to Gavin. "Nice flying, by the way. When did that happen?"

Gavin only gave a roguish grin and a wink. "Handy, no?"

"Very. Can you fly up to that corner? I believe there is a door up there."

Gavin nodded and flew up quickly before he dropped back down. "Well, yes, there's a door, but it's rather thick—maybe a foot or more of solid oak. Can you burn through?"

He frowned. "It's locked?"

"Yes. Odd kind of thing. Not one I've seen before. Almost looks like a sundial with a—"

"Starburst along the outer edges and a kind of rippling channel that runs around it?"

"Not unfamiliar, then?"

Giovanni shook his head. Trust his father to use his most difficult lock to secure the door. He pulled the dagger from the small of his back. "Andros loved designing locks I would have difficulty breaking. He tried for years to find some design I could not master."

Deirdre cocked an eyebrow. "And did he?"

Giovanni walked over to stand by Gavin and flicked the end of his blade. "No."

Jean's low chuckle echoed in the empty room. Giovanni held a hand out. "Gavin, if you please?"

"Well, you're not as pretty as the last one that asked for a ride, but I suppose you'll do." Giovanni heard Deirdre snort. The wind vampire flew up to the corner of the room and held him, hovering while Giovanni carefully picked the lock. It occurred to him that while Livia had never trusted Giovanni, Andros had never trusted her. Why else would he create a way for him—only him—to escape? No other being he knew of could pick the lock in front of him. He couldn't have escaped without help, but perhaps Andros had more faith in him than he'd thought.

After a few tense moments, he pulled the starburst from the thin channel and pushed the door open, revealing a dark, earthen passageway. Gavin, who must have been tiring, tossed him through. Then he flew back. Giovanni waited only a few moments before Jean entered the tunnel behind him. They both waited longer—much longer—before Gavin and Deirdre entered. Gavin, Giovanni noted with some amusement, looked decidedly more energetic.

"I can smell fresh air," Gavin said. "Deirdre, can you tell where it leads?"

She held her hands out and ran both along the walls as she walked forward. "Southwest. It's long and sloping. If it keeps at this angle it would exit... past the castle wall, I imagine."

Jean said, "Let's keep to the plan. The party must still be going on, which means that Carwyn, Tenzin, and Beatrice are still upstairs."

His heart leapt. "Beatrice?"

Gavin held a hand out. "You'll see your woman soon, but not here. Livia has to find you missing and discover that none of them—"

"Fuck Livia," he almost shouted. "I want to see my wife."

Deirdre stepped in front of him and put a hand on his chest. "Calm down, Gio. She's the one that came up with this plan."

"Hey!" Gavin looked rather offended, but Deirdre only rolled her eyes.

"With input from our resident thief, of course."

"Retired," Gavin said. "Mostly."

Giovanni could still feel his skin heating in anticipation. The smell of smoke was sweet in his nose, and he imagined Livia's skin turning black as she screamed. The steam began to rise from his wet arms.

"Gio, listen." Deirdre spoke more urgently, sensing his growing tension. "Jean and I will tunnel back down to the river and escape that way. Gavin is going to fly you to his house... somewhere. No one knows but he and Beatrice. Your wife has spent days planning this with my father and Tenzin to orchestrate some particular outcome, so don't spoil this plan by losing your head."

Giovanni took a deep breath and tried to shove back the fire that wanted to burst out. He smothered the desire for Livia's blood for the moment. She would still burn, he vowed, but he would respect his wife's wisdom in this and wait to hear her plan. "Fine. Gavin, take me out of this damned place."

"Don't order me around. You already owe me one. More than that if we're—"

"Be quiet. This is not the time to argue," Deirdre cut in. She gave Giovanni a quick hug before she turned to Gavin and halted. The two stood in awkward silence until she said, "Don't drop him." Then she turned to the wall of the tunnel, lifted her hands, and the earth moved in front of her. Jean gave Gavin and Giovanni a smile and a small salute before following.

"Well..." Gavin cleared his throat. "Let's get going. I'm starting to hear voices below."

Giovanni could hear both voices and water as the large, empty room they had flown through began to fill from the chamber and the river below. The two men rushed up the passageway; the walls and floors were smooth, even if the air was stale and ancient. When the smell of fresh air became more evident, they slowed and listened. Gavin shook his head and whispered, "I hear nothing."

"Agreed." Giovanni pushed through a loose pile of rocks that blocked the passage and peeked out. They were on the side of a hill, and he could see the lights of the castle in the distance. They had wound south and then west to a slope that overlooked Livia's stronghold. He swallowed, imagining his wife sitting in the glittering salons of Livia's court. So close, yet still past his reach. He swallowed the growl and turned back to Gavin. "Get me out of here. If I can't see her, take me to where I can."

"Orders, orders. Why must he always issue orders?" Gavin shook his head. "I'm not one of your minions, you know. And I'll be more than happy to be done with my part in all this."

"Fine. Then get me out of here."

Gavin picked him up under the shoulders and lifted into the air. "You try to do a favor for someone—"

"How much are you getting paid, Gav?"

He could feel, rather than hear, Gavin laugh as they cut through the air, heading north. "A rather princely sum, of course."

"Carwyn or my wife?"

"Your wife drives a hard bargain, Dr. Vecchio. And she's cute. It's deceiving really, hardly fair."

Giovanni felt the smile curve his lips. His wife. He would see her soon. Within hours, hopefully. As if anticipating the question, Gavin said, "I'll drop you off and then go back for her. I should be able to get her to you by dawn."

"Good."

"And yes, you will be somewhere very secluded."

"Good."

"Do me a favor, though, and try not to break any *retaining* walls, please."

He smirked. "I'll try my best, but I can't make any promises."

"You know what? You're just going to buy this house from me. It's sure to sustain damage, and I'll never get the mental pictures out of my mind."

"Done."

"It's not her, mind you. Picturing *her*—"

"It's very important that you shut up now, Gavin."

They were whipping over the Italian countryside, flying well out of range of human eyes. The air was cold, but the anticipation of seeing Beatrice warmed him to his soul. They flew over the rolling hills of Tuscany, past the lights that illuminated Milan, finally climbing the foothills, then the mountains of Northern Italy and into the Alps. They passed high above the water, and the lights from the homes along the lake's edge glowed in the darkness. The long, uninterrupted line slowly scattered as they approached a large inlet where a single home was nestled between the hills and the water.

"Home, sweet home." He heard Gavin sigh.

"You don't actually have to sell me the house, if you don't want to."

"No, it's for the best. I've been here too long, as it is."

Giovanni thought for a moment, then smiled. "You mean you've slept with all the attractive women nearby?"

"Exactly. I've ruined them for all others, so it's perfect for an old married man like you."

"Thank you so much."

Gavin dropped him off on the sloping dock that stretched into the water and flew into the house. He emerged a few minutes later with a bag of blood for himself and tossed another to Giovanni. He bit, ignoring the stale taste of the refrigerated blood and enjoying the peace of mind that came with not worrying about whether his meal was poisoned or not.

His reluctant host tossed him the empty bag and then took to the air without further ado as Giovanni paced the dock and tried to imagine how he would pass the hours until he saw Beatrice again. Deciding that he needed to cool down and wash the stink of Livia's prison from him, he stripped off his tattered clothes and dove into the lake.

Giovanni swam for what might have been hours, up and down the lake. He went in the house and drank another bag of blood. He swam to the bottom of the lake and watched the moon track across the sky. The minutes dragged into hours while he waited for her.

He was floating on the surface of the water and staring up at the stars when he heard the splash. Startled, he sat up, only to be tackled from behind by two familiar arms.

"You're here!" she cried, wrapping herself around him. "You're really here."

"Tesoro." He groaned a moment before their mouths met in a furious kiss.

Her legs tangled with his. The force of her embrace took his breath away. He held her close, aching to feel her amnis spread over his skin. Giovanni tore his mouth from her kiss and stripped the clothes from her body until they were pressed together and their energy combined again. His hands raced over her and held her in an iron grasp.

Beatrice's hand tugged at his arms, his back, pulling him close. Closer. Not close enough. In the blink of an eye, he grasped her hips and slid into her. She bit into his shoulder as they sank beneath the surface of the water.

And suddenly, he was home.

CHAPTER SIXTEEN

Lake Maggiore
Switzerland
June 2012

Water. Blood. Warm blood running down her throat. The grasp of hands. His hands. Her mate's hands. Her mate's blood.

He was back.

Beatrice felt his feet hit the lakebed a moment before Giovanni's long legs began striding toward the shore. She remained wrapped around his body, clutching him tightly. He held her as they rose from the water only to kneel in the long grass at the lake's edge. Steam rose from his body as he began moving in her again. Her hands dug into the earth around them and she arched her back, desperate for his touch.

Her first climax hit like a sudden wave, and she cried into the night. Her mate said nothing, only growling as his arm reached behind her, lifting her body as her head fell back. His fangs struck hard and deep in her throat, and he drank from her. The sharp bite threw her over another crest, but he did not halt feasting from her neck as she sobbed in relief and pulled him even closer. Her nails dug into his shoulders until he reared back, blood dripping from his lips and fangs gleaming white in the moonlight.

Blue fire swirled across his body, illuminating his arms and chest. His hands gripped Beatrice's hips and she lifted her body to move with him. Fast. Faster. Every layer of civilization burned away in their desperate need. She could feel the water drawn to her skin, protecting it from the scorch of Giovanni's hands, but nothing could protect her from the passionate assault of her mate's body. She didn't want it to. His eyes held hers as he moved, pinning her to the ground as effectively as his touch.

He finally pulled her up and pressed her against his chest. His hands tangled in her dripping hair and she felt him pull at the nape of her neck, angling her face up to his. Her skin hissed and a cloud of steam enveloped them. His hands and hips set a punishing rhythm, but his mouth was tender as it explored her face. He kissed her forehead, the swell of her cheeks, the arch of her brows. She felt his lips burn across the line of her jaw before his mouth dipped down and his fangs pierced the other side of her neck. She came again, and he clutched her closer as he drank. A low growl grew in his chest until he threw his head back and roared his release into the night.

Beatrice collapsed in his arms as the fire covering his skin waned, and the cloud of steam drifted away on the night breeze. His movement slowed. The iron cage of his arms softened, and his hands began to stroke down her back as Giovanni murmured in a hoarse voice. She sobbed in pleasure and relief, but he only pressed her closer.

"*Ubi amo; ibi patria. Calma, Tesoro. Ti amo, Beatrice. Calma.*"

She blinked away the tears and buried her face in his neck, inhaling the rich smoke of his skin. She could feel her blood leaping within him, and his amnis pulsed and swirled around her. Beatrice felt Giovanni tilt his neck to the side and press her mouth closer.

"Drink from me, Beatrice. Please, drink."

Beatrice gave a small cry before she bit into the thick vein at his neck. His blood burned down her throat, inflaming her desire again. She reached down and felt him grow hard in her hand as the muscles of his chest tensed.

She pulled away from his vein with a contented sigh, licking his rich blood from her lips and letting her fangs scrape over his chest.

"More," she whispered.

He laid her down in the long grass and stretched out next to her. This time, they were slow. Languorous and lazy with soft hands and long strokes. She pressed her mouth to his and inhaled his breath when he entered her. Tears ran down her cheeks, but he kissed them away. They moved together as the night birds sang to warn of the dawn.

Hours later, Beatrice still felt like she could not stop touching him. They had finally taken shelter in the house when the morning chased away the stars. The bedroom lay at the very center of the home, surrounded by winding hallways that shielded it from the sun. They had laughed and joked as they wandered through the labyrinth of a house, turning first into the kitchen, then an office, a sitting room, and a library before they finally discovered a room with a bed.

"I hope you like this house, Beatrice, because I believe we're buying it from Gavin. He said something about mental pictures."

"Well, seeing as we... *enjoyed* his kitchen—"

"And his library."

"I think you punched a hole in one of the walls in the hall."

"You tore up some of the carpet in the study."

"Then I can't blame him." She laughed. "And I like it. It's like a maze. Only, instead of a minotaur at the middle, you finally get to the bedroom."

"And a comfortable bed is far better than being gored to death."

She snorted. "Is that supposed to be a joke about your sexual performance?"

He barked out a laugh, but then grew very quiet. He pulled down the sheets to inspect her. "I wasn't too rough was I? Did I hurt you?"

"Don't be silly." She stroked along his shoulders, running her fingers through his hair. "I needed that as much as you did. I was a mess without you."

He buried his face in her neck and took a deep breath. His skin was still warm, but comfortingly so. And his amnis wrapped around her tightly, curling and twisting as it met hers, binding them together as surely as their bodies were linked.

"I dreamt about you."

"In prison?"

"Yes." He paused and his fingers encircled her wrist. "I think it was the only thing that kept me sane."

"Did she hurt you?"

He was silent, and the fury ran hot within her. Beatrice gritted her teeth and hissed. "She will die."

"When we get back to Rome—" He broke off when he felt her tense up. "What is it?"

"I don't want to talk about Livia. You should get some sleep. There will be plenty of time to talk about this stuff later. Right now, I just want to lay with you and try to rest."

He pulled her chin around and forced her to look into his eyes. He was frowning, and Beatrice knew that he was not satisfied with her answer.

"Fine, but you're explaining that later."

"Okay."

He tucked her under his arm and pulled the sheets up to cover her.

"Do you want me to sing to you?" he asked softly.

"Just sleep. Having you here is enough."

"Try to rest, Tesoro."

She smiled and buried her face in his chest. She felt him drift away into a bone-deep, contented sleep. Beatrice watched him for hours, wiping at the tears that fell down her face and drinking in the sight of him, determined to make it last.

"Why does chamois blood taste so much better than other goats? It's not sour at all."

Giovanni shrugged and continued field-dressing the dark-skinned animal they had hunted the following night.

"The meat is very good. I know the right way to cook it. You will like it."

Though Gavin had the house stocked with blood and there were many towns nearby, Giovanni had wanted the exertion of the hunt, so they had slipped away from the balmy edge of the lake to run miles north into the mountains. Giovanni enjoyed the fresh, dry air of the Southern Alps and Beatrice enjoyed Giovanni. All she had to do was catch a glimpse of him from the corner of her eye, and she smiled.

He wore some of the clothes Gavin had at the house, small on him, but still better than the rags he'd worn away from the castle. One look at the shredded tunic he'd thrown on the dock, and her rage against Livia had bloomed again.

"Come." He held out his hand after washing his hands in a small stream. He made a small satchel from the shirt he had worn and carried the best cuts of meat down the mountain for them to share. She grinned at her shirtless husband carrying the game they had just killed. There was still a drop of blood at the corner of his mouth.

"You know, I feel very frontier woman right now."

He laughed. "This is how people got food for most of history. It is good to know these things."

Beatrice wrinkled her nose. "Well, when the coming zombie apocalypse hits and there aren't any more grocery stores, I'll just let you take care of the hunting and the gathering, all right?"

Giovanni laughed again and sped down the game trail they had followed. It was a clear night and the moon was full. She could see the distant lights of the town as they came down out of the hills, enjoying the stretch of her legs as she ran. As they approached the small road that led back to the house, Giovanni slowed to a human pace, so as not to attract attention. "Beatrice?"

"Mmhmm?"

"Why did you tense up when I talked about going back to Rome? Do you think she will be able to capture me again? Are you afraid?"

"No! No, I don't—"

"She surprised me last time." He halted on the path and narrowed his gaze. "I was not on my guard. You should not fear that I will be taken again. I do not make the same mistake twice."

Her eyes widened. "I'm not afraid that she'll take you again."

"No?" He frowned and started walking, muttering under his breath. "You have lost confidence in me. You fear—"

"Gio, you can't go back to Rome." She halted in the middle of the trail. "I mean… at least, not yet."

His nostrils flared in anger. "I am going back to Rome."

"No, you don't understand—"

"I understand that you no longer think I am strong enough to protect those under my aegis."

Her jaw dropped. "What? That's not—"

"But I will. Do you know what I have planned for that Roman bitch? Would you like to hear it?"

"Stop, Gio. That's not what I'm talking about! I know you're strong enough."

"Obviously you don't, if you think I'm going to hide from her."

She clutched at her hair, frustrated and angry that the argument had devolved into her husband thinking she lacked confidence in him. "Giovanni, it's not that we can't go back."

He picked up the bundle of meat he'd dropped and stalked down the trail ahead of her. "Damn right, it's not. I may live quietly now, but there's a reason—"

"*You* can't go back."

He halted again, slowly turning until he faced her. "What did you say?"

Her heart thundered, and she felt tears run down her cheeks. "I said, *you* can't go back. I have to, but you can't. Not yet."

His eyes flared, and he stepped toward her. "This is... what? Some plan you've come up with?"

She swallowed and nodded tentatively. "Yes. Me and Ziri."

"Ziri?"

"And Carwyn. And Tenzin, too."

"And this plan involves you going back to Rome and me... what? Staying here safely tucked away?"

"No." She walked toward him. "We need you to find someone. Two people, actually."

He stepped back, and a blank mask fell over his face. "So, you will return to Rome and I—"

"Carwyn, too. He's going to go with you."

"But you won't."

Beatrice shook her head, and her heart fell in her chest when he took another careful step back.

"So, we would separate again?"

Her throat felt frozen, but she nodded with effort.

Giovanni's eyes were glacial. "Unacceptable." He turned and sped back to the house.

"Gio!" She called after him, but he did not turn back. She walked at a human pace, knowing that he needed time to think.

When Beatrice got back the house, he had put some of the meat away and was cooking two thick fillets over the built-in grill in Gavin's kitchen. He must have heard her walk in, but he did not turn around. Her nose twitched at the scent of the savory meat.

"Do you know why I don't often care to eat roasted meat, my wife?"

She had always suspected, but it wasn't something they talked about. "Why?"

"Roasted meat has a distinctive aroma, doesn't it? Something about that combination of flesh and fire."

"Gio—"

"Strangely enough, the smell of human and vampire flesh is not that different. Well, not that most would notice. The essentials are the same. Flesh. Fire."

She cleared her throat and bit her lip. "I'll take your word on that."

He nodded. "Good. You *should* take my word on that. Do you know why?"

Beatrice whispered. "Because you've killed many—"

"Hundreds, Beatrice." He threw a bloody knife across the room where it lodged in a wall. "I have killed *hundreds*. Yet, apparently, my wife and my closest friends only think that I am capable of fetching someone for their little plan."

"You're the only one who can do it."

He sneered and shut off the grill, tossing the meat onto a plate. "That's bullshit, and you know it. Carwyn or Tenzin could easily deal with finding —"

"Arosh."

His eyes widened. "Wh—what did you say?"

"Arosh," she whispered. "We need you to find Arosh."

He shook his head, anger forsaken for confusion. "He is dead, Beatrice. The fire king has been dead for centuries."

"He's not."

He crossed his arms and leaned back against the counter. "I think you had better explain."

"Arosh was one of Geber's four. It was Ziri, the Numidian. Saba, the Aethiop, Arosh, the Persian, and... Kato, the Greek."

Giovanni shrank back when he heard the last name. "Kato?"

"Yes, Kato."

He rushed over and clutched her shoulders. "Kato, the ruler of Minos. King of the ancient sea. *Kato* is the Greek? You are telling me that the water vampire that Geber used... is my own father's sire?"

"Yes."

"He is not dead as I was told?"

"No. Ziri will explain it to you. There's still a lot I don't understand."

He let out a harsh breath. "And you want *me* to go find two of the most ancient and deadly vampires to ever walk the earth? Two unopposed rulers of the ancient world, thought to be dead for centuries?"

"They're not dead," she whispered. "And we're pretty sure we know where you and Carwyn need to look. Ziri will be here in two days to explain it all."

The harsh expression fell from his face. "Two days?"

She nodded, and he pulled her to his chest.

"Two *days*, Tesoro?"

"It's all we can afford."

"I just got you back. You cannot ask me to—"

"Tenzin and I need to be back in court in that time. Livia won't be able to prove anything, and Ziri will vouch that I spent the last few days at his estate examining some books, but any longer than that…" He wrapped his arms around her and she buried her face in his chest. "I don't want to leave you," she whispered. "I don't ever want—"

"Shh." He stroked her face and rocked her as the tears slipped down her face. "We cannot do this." He framed her face and brushed back the hair that had fallen in her face. "You must come with me. If we are going to find these immortals, then at least we should be together."

"Someone has to stay back in Rome, Gio. We think she may already have the elixir. Rumors are starting to circulate, and I—"

"But *two days?*"

His lips began a frantic race as he held her tighter. Her eyes. Her cheeks. His hands tilted her face toward him before he attacked her mouth. He inhaled her gasp and lifted her in his arms, walking them to the counter where he set her on the edge. He paused and wove his fingers into her hair as he looked at her with a haunted stare. "How can I leave you again?"

"Gio—"

"How can I leave my heart?" He ducked down and pressed a kiss to her neck. "My love?" His hands drifted over her shoulders. "My life? Beatrice, how?" He buried his face in her neck and pulled her closer so she wrapped her legs around his waist.

"I don't want this either."

Their desire was a desperate, frantic call. He lifted her and walked to the bedroom where he slowly slipped off her clothes, letting his fingers memorize the texture of her skin. His mouth followed every dip and curve, and she held back tears when he lay down next to her and let his head rest on her abdomen, wrapping his arms around her hips as he whispered her name over and over.

She pulled him up and rolled them over, so she rested on his chest. "Some day," she whispered. "We will come here when things are peaceful. And we will swim in the lake every night."

"Yes?"

She sat up and spread her hands along his chest, tracing the line of his arms until her hands met his. She nodded and knit their fingers together.

"Yes. And we will buy a boat and you will teach me how to sail it." Her fingers were enveloped by his warm hands, and she felt his thumb stroke the back of her palm.

He whispered, "How do you know I can sail a boat?"

"You can do everything."

A sad smile crossed his lips for a second. "And you will show me the strange contraption you have created to use the computer."

"And you'll finally be able to check your own e-mail."

He twisted their arms around, so that Beatrice was curled on her side facing away from him and his arms encircled her. "And I will make love to you every night in our boat." He kissed along her shoulders, and his hand drifted over her hip.

"And you will read me Giuliana's sonnets and sing me beautiful songs," she whispered. The tears slipped down her face as he lifted her thigh and slid into her. He pressed her back to his chest and kissed the side of her neck. She leaned back into his embrace and turned her face to his, kissing his lips as he made love to her.

"And you will make me laugh." He smiled against her mouth and his hands stroked her breasts, her belly, the soft skin at the juncture of her thighs. "And tease me and remind me not to be so serious. And not to burn the food."

She laughed, but it turned into a sob as pleasure collided with the heartbreak of losing him, even for a little while. "And in a hundred years, when we get sick of each other—"

"I will never tire of you," he said frantically as he approached his own release. "Never."

"We'll take separate vacations." She knit their hands together again, wrapping his arms across her breast. "And then—"

"I will find you!" He gasped as the climax rolled through him and his arms banded around her. "I will find you, Beatrice. Wherever we go—"

"We will find each other," she cried out, and he turned her so that she was sheltered in his warm embrace. Beatrice felt him press a kiss to her hair.

"We will find each other."

CHAPTER SEVENTEEN

Lake Maggiore, Switzerland
June 2012

Giovanni spread his arms across the back of the couch in the lake house study. Beatrice sat next to him, nestled into his side, still reluctant to stray too far from the comfort of his presence. They had spent two days wrapped in each other, both avoiding what he was now beginning to suspect was their inevitable separation. The ancient wind immortal, Ziri, took a chair opposite him and his wife, and Carwyn sat near the fire, looking grim.

"Ziri, thank you for coming. Please, explain. Particularly about my grand-sire."

Ziri folded his hands in his lap. "Your grand-sire, Kato, is alive, as far as I know. My friends and I deliberately misled the immortal community regarding his death. I don't know his condition, and we don't know how the book came into *your* sire's possession, but that is why you must find Arosh. Only someone who rivals him in power will stand a chance of getting close enough. And Arosh will have Kato with him."

"I understood that Arosh is the one who killed my father's sire. He and Kato were legendary enemies."

"Yes, of course they were. For many years they battled each other for land, resources, power... that is why they became such close friends."

Beatrice leaned forward. "You're going to have to explain this part a little more clearly to me, Ziri."

The old vampire smiled. "You must understand that this was the age of empires. The pale shadows of empires that came later, the Greeks, the Romans, the Roman church, none of them *truly* understood empire as we did. Zhang, before he changed his name to be civilized, ruled the East with his Golden Horde of vicious immortals and their people. Arosh held Zhang back at the gates of the Western world. Saba, the most ancient of us, kept her peace in the flourishing African highlands. I ruled the deserts, and Kato... Kato ruled the waters. We were rivals. Enemies. Our power kept each other in check. There was death and conquest, but there was balance, as well."

Beatrice asked, "What changed?"

"We grew tired of empire. All of us had ruled for thousands of years, sometimes as gods, but humanity was growing stronger, more sophisticated. They were becoming more interesting to us, and the age of the immortal empire began to wane. Zhang was first. His hoard dispersed and he parted company with his child—your friend, Tenzin—and retreated to form the council of the Eight Immortals in Penglai Island. Saba... well, Saba hadn't ruled in any real sense for ages. She just retreated farther into the mountains. I gladly let my people fracture as they had wanted for years. Wind immortals never really take to any kind of central government."

"And what of Kato and Arosh?" Giovanni asked.

"They held out the longest, but finally, your grand-sire traveled to his great rival and they met. I don't know what they spoke of, but I think they both must have realized what we had was passing. Human thought and development had reached the point where they had become more than ragged bands of hunters and gatherers. Civilizations were beginning to flourish. Observing them had become more interesting than ruling them."

Giovanni cocked his head. "And you expect me to believe they just gave up this great power you speak of?"

"In a way, it was a relief. To give up the burden of rule and to sink into a more leisurely life. We all had our pursuits and, as centuries passed, the four of us came to a kind of understanding. A camaraderie of those who understood what it had once been to be a god." Ziri's black eyes twinkled. "Not many understand what that once meant. Arosh and Kato became very good friends, over the years. Their legends passed into our own peculiar history, but few remembered the particulars. None of us wanted to."

"But they were supposed to be dead. My father said that Arosh was the one who had killed Kato, and in doing so, killed himself. So how is it that you say they are living?"

Carwyn broke in. "Start at the beginning of the tale, Ziri. You must go back to Kufa."

Ziri nodded. "Of course. As I was saying, humanity had become interesting. There were periods of great enlightenment, often followed by periods of ignorance and destruction, but thoughts were changing. Kufa, in the eighth century, was in the heart of the Islamic Golden Age. There was a wonderful confluence of thought and technology. Theology and philosophy. Arosh had been living there for many years. He was Persian, but had been intrigued by the new ideas. Kato joined him. Eventually, we were all drawn there, and we spent a century watching the region flourish."

"When did you meet Geber? Was Arosh the "dear friend" he wrote of in his journals?"

Ziri smiled. "We knew him as Jabir, but yes, Arosh and the alchemist had become very good friends. They enjoyed debating science and faith. And Jabir was so bright for a human, eventually Kato joined them in their discussions and the three of them became very close. The idea of the elixir was born from their friendship."

"Who thought of it first?" Beatrice asked in a quiet voice.

"It was Jabir's idea, though we all latched onto it very quickly. He was fascinated by how we could heal, particularly if we shared blood, which the four of us did freely."

Carwyn smirked. "You must have been... very close."

Ziri shrugged. "As I said, there are few who understand each other as we did. It was, and still is, a kind of intimacy that extends beyond the understanding of most humans or even younger immortals. We gave no thought to sharing blood in order to nurture that."

"But Geber—*Jabir* noticed it?" Giovanni asked.

"He was fascinated by the science of us. By the properties of our blood and what it could mean. He was the one who wanted to stabilize it for human use."

Beatrice shook her head. "And you all agreed? Didn't you have any reservations?"

Ziri shrugged. "Not many. We all had our own reasons for wanting it. Saba thought it could be used to heal humans. She has always been a healer. Arosh thought that somehow it could be used to conquer bloodlust and grant him independence from needing humanity, even as food. Kato had taken a lover who refused to turn, though he was very attached to the young man. He hoped to make him immortal with it."

"And what of you?" Giovanni asked him. "What was your agenda, Ziri?"

"I was curious," he said.

Beatrice said, "Curious?"

The old wind vampire chuckled. "I believe that it is not a condition you are unfamiliar with, Beatrice De Novo."

Giovanni pinched her waist and smiled. "No, indeed not." He pulled her under his arm and turned his attention back to the story. "So, you all agreed to help Geber in his research. And you were successful?"

"That, I'm sure we can all agree, is debatable. Jabir *did* stabilize the blood. It took years, but the formula appeared to work. He had tried it on several servants who were diseased and it had proven to be useful for healing. As for the bloodlust, we weren't as certain. And we were all very cautious. It was your grand-sire"—Ziri nodded toward Giovanni—"who eventually tried it. His lover, a very kind and loving young man, was ill. A wasting disease, probably some kind of cancer. But it was spreading and Kato became... strangely emotional. He forced his lover to take the elixir, then drank from him. He said if the young man did not live, that he did not care to, either. It was shocking to us, to risk himself for a mortal, but it was his choice, after all."

All three vampires were riveted on the old immortal as he spoke. "And then what happened?" Beatrice said.

"We thought it was a success. The young man, Fadhil, grew strong again. Kato drank his blood and claimed to need no more. He claimed he was no longer thirsty. That he no longer felt the pull of hunger or the burn in his throat."

Carwyn asked, "So why didn't you all try it? If it appeared to be a success, why not?"

Ziri cocked an eyebrow. "Kato was in love with this human. In raptures over the possibility that his lover could live forever, and he would no longer have to feed from humans. The best of all worlds. No sacrifice. No trade-off. The rest of us... we were more cautious. I wanted to give it time. Perhaps, I thought, in one hundred years, if the human was still living, perhaps then I would try it. I left shortly after the initial tests. I was bored in Kufa and needed to travel."

Giovanni said, "But how did it end? Why did you deceive the world about Kato? What happened to him?"

"I received a message from Saba a few years later. She did not say much, only that Arosh and Kato had gone away. That she was taking Geber's research for further study and that I should not try to replicate it or drink from any human that had taken the elixir. She said—and this is how I know it is very dangerous—that she had *killed* all those who had been test subjects. There were dangers. She said that Arosh had asked her to spread the word that he and Kato had killed each other, and she wanted my help in spreading the rumors."

"And you agreed?" Giovanni was angry. "Without asking for more information? Without confirming—"

"What would I confirm?" Ziri broke in. "Who would I ask? Saba only tells you what she wants you to know. Arosh? I had no idea where he was at the time. And, most importantly, I trusted my friend. If Saba said this was necessary, then it was. We had been friends, the four of us, for thousands of years. If she asked me to spread this rumor, it was for Arosh and Kato's protection."

Giovanni stood and paced. He was angry with the vague picture that Ziri had painted. Angry that he knew so much... *but still not enough.* Why did Lorenzo and Livia want this elixir? No one even truly knew what it did.

Beatrice said, "Well, if it did to Kato what it's doing to Lucien—"

"Lucien?" He spun toward her. "Lucien who?"

"The Thracian, Gio," Carwyn said gently. "Tenzin found him in Bulgaria. He's drunk from an elixired human and there's something very wrong. Whatever is happening to him seems to be weakening him dangerously."

Giovanni looked at Beatrice. "What has happened while I was gone?"

She looked embarrassed. "Well, I was going to fill you in, but... two days, you know?"

He couldn't argue with her. Catching up on news hadn't even crossed his mind. He heard Carwyn snort as Giovanni sat next to her and pulled her onto his lap.

Carwyn muttered, "Haven't you two done anything besides shag this entire time?"

Giovanni shot him a look. "Two days."

"Fine, but yes, since you didn't know, Lucien Thrax is staying at the Rome house, and he's not well. Tenzin is with one of the Chinese delegations. You and I are going to go off looking for two supposedly dead vampires so we have some sort of proof that Livia is trying to... whatever she's trying to do. And your wife and Ziri are going back to Rome to keep an eye on the court and find out if Livia actually has any of the elixir like the rumors are claiming."

Giovanni could think of a dozen objections to that plan immediately, but there was one question his brain couldn't file away. He turned back to Ziri. "How did my father get this book? I thought Saba had taken it, so how did it come to be in Andros's possession?"

"Your guess is as good as mine. I had met your father a few times while I was spending time with Kato. They weren't close, you know. Kato regretted turning Andros, though he never said so directly. He thought Andros was too greedy for power and knowledge. Your father was a voracious book collector, but not out of any altruistic reasons. He was greedy for knowledge, but he stored it away like he was stealing secrets. And he had become obsessed with creating the perfect vampire. A foolish quest—what interest is there in perfection? The next time I saw him was during the Renaissance." He smiled at Giovanni. "You probably don't remember, Jacopo. You were quite young, but I met him in Rome during the Giovanni Pico debates. I was there to meet with your uncle, but I remember you, as well."

Carwyn bolted up. "What? That was your uncle? I always thought that was you!"

Beatrice said, "I figured that out when I was human, Carwyn. What makes you so slow?"

He sat back with a sulky look on his face. "I just don't choose to be nosey, unlike some people."

"Both of you, stop," Giovanni said. "So you were watching the debates in Rome and you met Andros there? I remember him being there. He was trailing after my uncle at the time, though I didn't understand why until later."

Ziri nodded. "Yes, I met him there. He had acquired the majority of your father's books after his 'death' and had some questions. He knew Kato and I were friends, so he was cautious. But I could tell from his questions that he had somehow laid his hands on Geber's research. He was too curious. He would not let the subject go. It was at that point that I knew I would have to kill him and get the books back. I left Rome and went to seek Saba. I needed to know what she did."

The air had left Giovanni's lungs. "So... you would have killed Andros? And taken the book?"

Ziri's eyes drifted to the fire. "By the time I returned from Africa, years had passed. I had met with Saba and we were both in agreement. Though she claimed to have no idea where Andros acquired the book, she did not tell me what she had done with it. She did tell me where I could find Arosh and Kato if I felt like I needed their permission to kill Andros. I did not go. From talking with her, I knew Andros could not live. This knowledge *had* to remain a secret." He looked up and met Giovanni's gaze. "Imagine my surprise when I returned to Italy to find that a young immortal had done the job for me."

Carwyn sighed. "So it's true?"

Giovanni turned to his friend. "My father was not who people thought he was. He was—"

"Hold, Gio." Carwyn held up his hands. "You don't have to explain yourself to me. I know it's not something you would have done lightly."

Giovanni turned back to Ziri. "How did you know? How did you know that it wasn't an accident? A robbery, as we claimed?"

Ziri smiled. "Because I recognized *you*, my friend. I recognized the boy who had grown into a man and then been transformed into one of us. I remembered the bright child and I heard about your uncle's death. I could guess what had happened. Andros had finally made himself the perfect child. And that child was so perfect, he knew that his sire needed to be burned from the earth. So I say, *well done*, Giovanni Vecchio."

Guilt still burned in Giovanni's chest and anger toward the placid immortal who seemed so detached, but Beatrice rubbed his thigh comfortingly. "And the book?" she asked. "Geber's research?"

"The fires," Giovanni murmured in understanding. "You thought as I did."

"Everyone knew that the library of Niccolo Andros had been scattered. Some books burned in Savonarola's fires. Others lost or destroyed... I had no reason to think that Andros had shared the information with anyone. Whom did he trust besides himself?"

Giovanni's mouth was a grim line. "No one."

"No one." Ziri nodded. "And until Stephen found the books, I doubt Lorenzo knew what he had, either. They were artifacts to him. But when Stephen found them, Lorenzo took a closer look. And, as your father learned, he found something quite unique."

Now, it was Beatrice who spoke. "You never told me how you found my father."

"Tywyll the water vampire is an old, old friend. I have used him for information many times in my travels. He is old as Arosh or Kato or any of us, though he's always preferred the solitude of his British rivers and his dirty pubs. When Stephen came to him to exchange gold for safe passage, he recognized what your father had. He did not know the whole of it, but he must have remembered our work in Kufa. I had told him about the time I'd spent there, though I never told him why. He put the pieces together and contacted me. I told him... enough. He wasn't very curious, but he wanted me to help Stephen."

Ziri turned to Beatrice. "I will not lie to you. My initial intention was to find your father, kill him, and destroy the book. But I became interested in his mind. In his research. I thought... why not another? Perhaps another could succeed where we had failed? Perhaps this search had not been in vain. So, instead of killing him, I watched him. I protected him." Ziri leaned back in his chair and crossed his arms over his chest. His face was carefully blank. "I suppose, in the end, I was still curious."

Giovanni sat, staring at Ziri for a moment as he tried to process the revelations the ancient had given them. Finally, he spoke. "Ziri, if you would leave us, please."

Ziri gave a regal bow. "Of course."

Beatrice sat next to him. Carwyn stood across the room. He could tell that some of the information had been new to his wife and friend, but not all.

He said, "I can see that much has been discovered and planned in my absence."

Beatrice tried to interrupt. "Gio, we—"

He cut her off. "You have all made your plans, but now I am back. And I will tell you what I will do."

CHAPTER EIGHTEEN

Lake Maggiore, Switzerland
June 2012

Beatrice opened her mouth again, but Carwyn caught her eye with a warning glare. He shook his head slightly, so she shut her mouth.

"I am going back to Rome. I am going to find Livia and kill her. Then, I am going to find my son and kill him. I will take the book back, destroy it, and see to it that any of the elixir that has been made is destroyed. I will maintain my reputation so that others who threaten my family will fear me. If that means that I have to kill half of Rome, so be it. If that means I have to travel to Greece and kill the council there, I will." His voice rose. "If that means that I have to spend the next hundred years killing, maiming, and burning the European immortal community to the ground, I will. I will not run and hide. I will not stand for others shielding me, and I will *not* stand for Livia to live while I walk the earth. Is that understood?"

Beatrice was speechless. She could handle Giovanni's fiery anger, but the cold rage that poured off her husband was something she rarely encountered. Again, she opened her mouth to speak, but Carwyn spoke first.

"Fine, Gio." Her eyes widened, but Carwyn glared her into silence before he continued. "You know you have my backing, as well as the support of Jean in France and Terry in London. The Germans may have a problem with it, but I have a feeling that you could make your case to Matilda. It's too bad you're married already. A political marriage could have solved that problem, but I'm sure you can work something out. Greece will be tricky, but they're not strong enough to really oppose you once you control Rome."

Beatrice's head began to swim, and she felt Giovanni stiffen beside her. Carwyn just continued on in a deadly quiet voice. "I can secure the support of the Vatican. Emil Conti would be your most likely rival for power. We had planned on cultivating him as an ally, but that is easily cured. You'll probably need to eliminate him and most of those under his aegis to avoid any future problems. A takeover in Rome is long overdue. Most of the other centers of power have switched to a new guard in the last hundred years or so. Rome was the only holdout. Once you're established, you'll need to start thinking about whom you want as a lieutenant. I have some ideas, but you might want to bring in entirely new people. After all, you are an outsider, so it wouldn't be nearly as simple as an internal coup. Still, it's manageable."

She wanted to protest. Her heart was racing, and the words were on the tip of her tongue, but Carwyn just kept talking in a steady voice. "You'll need to send Beatrice and Ben back to the States, of course. She's strong, but as she'd be targeted constantly, her presence would be a distraction for you. She'll be far safer in Los Angeles under Ernesto's protection until things are stable. If everything goes well, in fifty years she'll be by your side again, my friend."

Carwyn finally leaned back and crossed his arms over his chest. "Really, not all that long in the vast span of things. Excellent plan, Gio. Let me know when you want to leave."

Giovanni shot out of his seat and across the room, plowing his fist into the wall and shouting, "Damn it!"

Carwyn said, "You want to blaze into Rome and take out Livia. That's what you're looking at. You know I'm right."

She saw him glare. "I'll hand it over to Conti."

Carwyn snorted. "Brilliant plan. Conti will take it and then try to kill you. He'd have to, or no one would respect him, and he'd be battling rivals for the next hundred years."

"I'll…"

"What?" Carwyn rose and walked over to stand next to him. Beatrice was tempted to speak, but knew that Giovanni needed to reach the same conclusions they had weeks before.

Carwyn leaned closer and spoke softly. "What are you going to do, Gio? You want to kill Livia? You get Rome. That's the way it works. You'll be embroiled in politics for the next three hundred years, at least."

"I have no desire to rule Rome."

He took a deep breath. "Then you need to listen to Beatrice's plan."

Giovanni pulled his fist out of the wall and turned around. He leaned against it and crossed his arms. "Livia still needs to die."

Beatrice finally spoke. "She will. And hopefully, you'll be able to kill her, but this needs to come from someone in Rome, unless we want the city to descend into chaos that you'll be expected to clean up. In the long run, it's the easiest way. Emil Conti has been making moves to return the city to a more republican form of leadership for years. He's sensible. Stable.

Given the right circumstances, he could take over and we wouldn't be stuck with it. We just need to create the right opportunity for him."

Giovanni smirked. "You sound so very American right now, my dear."

"Hey." She shrugged. "We do love our revolutions. But this time, we'll try to make it slightly less bloody."

He took a deep breath and let it out slowly. "What's your plan?"

"Dez and Ben have discovered where she's been producing it. It's a cosmetics factory in Bulgaria. We need you and Carwyn to go shut it down. Find the humans she's been working with. Find out how much they know. From what Ziri remembers and looking at Lucien Thrax's condition, we know that this elixir is harmful to immortals, but she's been circulating rumors that she has some great revelation. A secret that will make Rome the center of the world again and make her even wealthier. We need to get people doubting her. Questioning her intentions. If we can make people distrust her—"

"We can try, but who will believe us?" Giovanni shrugged. "She's charismatic. Powerful. Even if we find out the elixir is poison, she could play it as if she was a victim. She's very good at manipulation."

Carwyn spoke up. "If we can find Arosh, Ziri's certain we'll find Kato. If we can find Kato, we'll know the truth about the effects."

"The truth doesn't matter," Giovanni shouted. "It only matters what people believe."

"Then we'll *make* them believe. Listen Gio, she either knows what the effects are, or we'll make it sound like she does and didn't care. Saba, the greatest healer in our history, killed everyone who had taken it. *Killed* them, Gio. Ziri thinks the truth will be damaging enough for her allies to abandon her. Once that has happened, Conti can step in with minimal conflict, because he is the obvious successor. There will be some bloodshed, of course, but we'll be able to let him take the lead so that he's the one stuck with the city. We'll be backing him up, instead of acting as usurpers. Jean and Terry will throw their support behind him. The Vatican likes him already, which will lend him further legitimacy with the younger Roman vampires, most of whom identify as Catholic. It's the easiest way."

"You're forgetting that we have nothing as proof. *Nothing*. We have guesses and the memories of one of the vampires involved. We have one sick vampire. Memories and suppositions. Even Lucien doesn't know what's really going on with his own health." Giovanni paced the room.

"And then you have Livia! She has a lost secret. The elixir of life. And no doubt she'll have mocked up some kind of lab results to make this elixir look legitimate. She'll make it sound like we're trying to stir things up against her, and no one is going to trust us."

Beatrice murmured, "Well... that's why you're going to have to bring Kato back."

She could have heard a pin drop.

"Oh, of course!" He threw up his hands. "So, not only are Carwyn and I supposed to *find* these two vampires—who aren't supposed to exist—but we need to bring them back to Rome, as well!"

Beatrice forced a smile. "Ziri's pretty sure Kato will like you."

Giovanni turned to Carwyn. "Tell me she's joking."

"She's not joking. Ziri says Kato would love you." Carwyn slapped him on the shoulder and moved across the room.

Giovanni's eyes darted between him. "Are we forgetting about the deadliest fire immortal in history? Are we forgetting about Arosh? If Arosh took Kato away for his own protection, then I'm fairly sure he's not going to be pleased about being found."

"Well, that's true." Beatrice nodded. "And that's why *you* need to go."

"Tesoro..." He rushed to her side and took her hands. "I'm very strong. I'm very powerful, Yes, I could probably hold my own against him in battle for longer than any other, but *no one* is as powerful as Arosh. He is the oldest fire vampire in immortal legend. He ruled Persia and Eastern Europe for thousands of years. I stand very little chance of actually making him listen to me!"

"But Ziri says he hated Andros."

His face was frozen. "That just means he'll kill me faster."

"But what if you tell him you killed him? We're pretty sure he'll listen then. Also, Ziri has a letter for you guys to take."

"Oh, of course. A letter!" Giovanni brushed a hand over his exasperated face. "Do we even have an idea where he might be after all this time?"

Carwyn said, "Ziri has the location that Saba gave him when he first decided to kill Andros. It's somewhere in the Caucasus."

Giovanni blinked. "So, we have the location that a notoriously vague immortal gave a friend over five hundred years ago to track down two vampires who have managed to remain hidden from the immortal community for a thousand years?"

Beatrice cleared her throat. "Well, if you're only going to look at the down side—"

"Forgive me if I am less than optimistic about our chances of finding them."

Carwyn said, "Do you really think that, once they'd found a good hiding place, they'd move? You know how the old ones are. Five hundred years is little to them. They're probably tucked into the Northern Caucasus, happily feeding on the local population and playing chess."

Giovanni stared at his friend.

"See that," Beatrice said. "That's his skeptical face, Carwyn."

"I'm familiar with it."

Her husband said, "I agree that I would probably have the best chance to find him. And you'd need a fire immortal to approach Arosh if you're going to get close enough to deliver any sort of message. A female would be better, but... it might work. We will need a letter from Ziri. And we trust him?" His eyes turned back to Beatrice.

She nodded. "We do. Tenzin vouches for him and so does Lucien."

Giovanni sat for a moment, thinking. Then he sat next to her on the couch. "The Thracian has always been trustworthy."

She could see him begin to really consider their plan, and she felt herself relax. "So?"

"So Carwyn and I will go shut down this factory in Bulgaria and then find Arosh and Kato, who are in..." He looked toward Carwyn.

"It sounds like the mountains in the Republic of Georgia."

"Lovely. And after we avoid being killed, we're going to convince Arosh and Kato to come out of hiding in order to go to Rome and testify that Livia knew about this elixir and whatever harm it can cause. Which we're still not sure of."

Carwyn said, "It would have to be damn serious for Saba to kill any human they had tested it on and for Arosh and Kato to fake their deaths."

"Agreed." Giovanni paused, and she could see his mind churning. "So while we're doing this, Beatrice and Tenzin will be stirring up revolution in Rome?"

She nodded. "I'll be getting closer to Emil Conti. He's already displeased with the actions Livia took against you. The population seems to be split, but given some encouragement, he could probably turn the tide against her. He's already becoming more popular. He senses an opportunity, and I'm surprisingly... well, I'm kind of popular in Rome."

Carwyn said, "Everyone is enamored of the new girl Livia doesn't like."

Beatrice grinned. "I'm driving her crazy. Tenzin and I killed a bunch of her guards and she couldn't really do anything about it."

Giovanni sighed and rubbed his temples. "So, I'm going to let you and Tenzin create havoc in Rome and destabilize a dangerous and powerful vampire even further while I go off on a dubious errand to find two legends who I'm still not entirely convinced even exist anymore."

Carwyn walked over and slapped him on the back. "Yes, you are. Tenzin and B are brilliant and between the two of them, along with some help from Lucien and Ziri, they're going to be fine."

Giovanni reached up and touched her cheek. "And we will have to say good-bye."

Beatrice blinked back tears. "For now."

"We have to say good-bye *tonight*."

Carwyn cleared his throat. "And I think that's my cue to go. Gio, I'm going to procure a car for us. Hopefully, something older that you won't break. I'll be back later. B, I'll see you later, darling girl." He leaned down, brushed a kiss across her cheek, and left the room.

As soon as they were alone, Giovanni pulled her into his lap.

"I still don't like this."

"It's either this, or we face you killing Livia in a bloody coup as an outsider and becoming even more tangled in politics for the next few hundred years. Do you want that?"

"No."

"Then..." She tucked her head into his neck. "This is the best way."

"Do you feel safe? Around Livia? Around Lorenzo? He's still there, isn't he?"

"Yes, and I don't like it, but I'll be fine. Tenzin is teaching me patience."

"Yes, she's good at that. I remember once we hid for over six months in a cave in Russia waiting for a target. She played this dice game against the wall of the cave constantly. Almost drove me mad."

She smiled and took a deep breath, drinking in the smell of his skin, trying to soak up enough of his presence to last her through the weeks, and maybe months, ahead. He held her, playing with her hair and letting his lips trail over her skin.

"Is Ben all right?"

"He's fine." She smiled a little. "He's been taking care of his aunt."

"He's a good boy."

"He's becoming a man through all of this. Keeping me company when I'm sad. Helping Dez with research. Helping Matt with security."

"Tell him I'm very proud of him."

She blinked back tears. "I will."

"And I'm proud of you, too. This is... as much as I do not like aspects of it, this is a good plan."

"It is?"

She felt him nod and press a kiss to her temple. "It is. If everything goes well, we'll be home by Christmas."

Beatrice smiled a little. "Yeah, maybe."

"Let's plan on it, shall we?"

"Okay."

They held each other for another hour. The fire in the grate crackled in the still night air. They could hear Ziri pacing out on the dock, though he did not interrupt them. Beatrice knew that they would need to leave soon if they were going to make it back to Rome before dawn.

"I love you so much it hurts sometimes," she whispered.

His arms tightened around her. "Love should never hurt."

A wave of panic flooded up, and she was suddenly overcome with doubts. Her heart began to pound. "This—this is stupid. You're right. We need to stay together. We'll go back to Rome. We'll just take everyone away and say to hell with them all. You and Tenzin can come back and kill Livia and Lorenzo later. I don't—"

"Beatrice—"

"I don't give a shit about the rest of the vampires! Let them kill themselves with this drug. We'll go back to the States. We'll—"

"Beatrice." He soothed her, pressing her face into the crook of his neck. He rocked her back and forth for a few moments as her heart evened out. "You know that we must put an end to this. If this elixir is as dangerous as everyone seems to think, it could spread through Europe. Asia. Africa. On the surface, it looks like a miracle. Imagine how many would be taken in. Eventually, it would reach our own home. It could endanger the people we care about. This secret has been in the shadows for too long. We need to uncover the truth—the whole of it—and it needs to come to light. Whatever the consequences. You know this."

She clutched his neck. "Why did it have to be us?"

"Who else could it be? This is the secret that brought us together, Tesoro mio. Some things have to happen—"

"Exactly as they do."

"Yes."

She only held him tighter, feeling his hands stroke her back. He hummed a song in her ear and she closed her eyes and took a calming breath. "You better come back to me, Giovanni Vecchio."

"I told you already. *Ubi amo; ibi patria.* Wherever you go, I will find you."

Giovanni watched her from the dock as Ziri grasped her hand and took off into the clear, dark night. They would have enough time to get back to the safety of the house in Rome before dawn. He felt Carwyn stand behind him.

"She'll be fine."

"That's not your wife flying off to go play politics in the viper's nest."

"No, you managed to fool her into thinking that you were the better choice. How did that happen?"

Giovanni smiled. "Natural charm, I guess."

"Keep telling yourself that if it makes you feel better, Sparky. I'm still betting you used amnis on her."

He couldn't stop the low chuckle that came to his throat. "Did you bring me any clothes that fit, by the way? I've been wearing Gavin's miniature wardrobe for the past few days."

"Don't lie. You haven't been wearing clothes at all."

They started toward the house. "I have a feeling you might not like that wardrobe option as much as Beatrice did."

"Good thing I brought you some clothes then."

"Hawaiian shirts?"

"Of course. We're being men of mystery."

"How are we going to find two vampires who are supposed to have been dead for centuries, Father?" Carwyn burst into laughter, and Giovanni turned to him, confused. "Did I miss the joke?"

"Oh…" Carwyn tried to calm his features, but couldn't seem to help himself. He was bent over, laughing and wiping tears from his eyes. "I suppose you *have* been gone for a while, haven't you?"

Giovanni shook his head, still confused. "What the hell are you laughing about?"

"It's a good thing we're taking a road trip. We need to catch up."

"I've been a bit busy."

"As have I, my friend, as have I. The joke, as you say, is on… well, everyone." Carwyn slapped him on the back and pulled open the door. "You see, strictly speaking, I'm not exactly a Father anymore."

Giovanni stopped in his tracks and his eyes widened. Carwyn was still chuckling.

"Come on. We'll talk in the car. Might as well get going; it's a long drive to Bulgaria."

CHAPTER NINETEEN

Residenza di Spada
July 2012

"You need to let him stab you."

"I'm not letting him stab me."

"He needs to learn."

"Forget it, you mad vampire. It's not going to be me."

"He has been raised to have too many manners. He won't stab a woman. Even me."

Ben's eyes darted between Tenzin and an angry Gavin. "For the record, I really don't want to stab anyone."

Tenzin's eyes swung toward him. "Too bad. We're practicing hand-to-hand combat with knives. That's what you need to do." Gavin just huffed and leaned against a wall in the basement.

"I'm not stabbing any of you guys. Forget it. We'll practice with…"

Tenzin crossed her arms. "What?"

"I don't know, but I'm not stabbing anyone!"

She rolled her eyes. "It's not like you can kill us."

"I agree with the boy," Gavin said. "Just pretend."

Tenzin said, "You have obviously never trained anyone to fight before."

Gavin looked indignant. "Yes, I have."

"Are they still alive?"

The two started bickering again and Ben sighed. For the past few weeks, ever since Gavin, Deirdre, and Jean had showed up in Rome, everyone had been stuck in Giovanni's house, trying to be inconspicuous. Deirdre spent most of the time on her phone or visiting with Dez and Angela. Jean was either talking on the phone or meeting with an assistant who ran errands for him. Gavin, Ben had decided, was the most fun to hang out with. And he let Ben drink. Well, he did until Beatrice caught them in the library and went ballistic.

The rest of the time, Gavin helped Tenzin with Ben's training. Matt had given him a handgun to carry, but Tenzin still insisted that knives were often more reliable and better because of their silence.

'Remember, boy. A knife never runs out of bullets. You can use it anywhere. And it doesn't announce its presence.'

Ben touched the grip of the hunting knife he carried. He had a simple sheath tucked into the inside of his waistband that made it invisible, even under summer clothes. It definitely beat the rusty old steak knife he'd carried with him on the streets when he was a kid. That one he'd found behind a restaurant in the Bowery when he was eight, but it had come in handy more than once.

Gavin and Tenzin were still arguing, so Ben spoke up. "Listen, both of you, I really don't think I need to stab either of you. I know you may find this hard to believe—"

Ben felt the cold slip of a hand at his neck a moment before the barrel of a gun hit the small of his back. In a heartbeat, Ben leaned back into his attacker, ducking down and to the left as he twisted his body under the arm that was reaching around his neck. In one smooth movement, he drew the hunting knife from his waist and turned so that he came behind his assailant. His arm reached around, slicing up the front of the man's shirt until it was poised at the neck.

The whole maneuver had taken just a few seconds.

Cocky vampires, Ben thought as his other arm braced itself against the rock hard back of Jean Desmarais.

Jean chuckled and patted the hand that held the knife at his throat. "Nicely done. See? Neither of you needs to bleed. The young man is well-trained already. Boy, if we were on the streets, would I be breathing?"

"You don't breathe." Ben's heart was racing, but he kept his voice in check. He let his hand fall and stepped from behind the Frenchman.

Jean merely shrugged. "You see? Tenzin, you have taught him well. The boy is very good with a knife already."

Tenzin eyed him with the guarded expression Ben had come to expect from her. "I can't teach reflexes like that."

Ben ignored her and tucked his knife back in his waistband. "Jean, sorry about the shirt."

"Think nothing of it. Perhaps you could procure one of your uncle's for me. My wardrobe is rather limited."

He slapped the Frenchman on the shoulder. "No problem, man. I'll go grab one. You sure you don't want one of Carwyn's?" Ben heard Jean laugh as he jogged up the stairs.

He walked through the kitchen where Lucien, Angela, and Dez were involved in a conversation about baking or something. He wandered up the stairs and past the library. Deirdre, Matt, and Ziri were there, speaking some language he thought might have been German. Or Russian. He couldn't really tell. All three sounded like they needed to gargle.

By the time he got to the third floor, Ben could hear the cello recording coming from Beatrice and Giovanni's room. He knocked lightly on the door and waited for her voice.

"Come on in, Ben."

He was the only one who ever disturbed her when she was up here. Not even Dez was really allowed. Tenzin came up sometimes, but she never knocked. He poked his head into the bedroom. Beatrice was sitting at the table in the living area of the suite and tapping her pencil against a notebook.

"What's up?"

"Can I borrow one of Gio's shirts for Jean? I kind of sliced his up in the basement."

She frowned. "Do I want to know?"

"Probably not."

A smile flickered across her face. She was better since his uncle had escaped from Livia's castle, but still not herself. She wouldn't be until Giovanni was back. He missed his uncle, too, but the thing they had? Ben thought he would probably never feel that way about anyone. His aunt and uncle were the center of each other's universe. Even he could see that.

"Yeah, there's a bunch that came from the cleaner's a few weeks ago. Pick any of those. Except the green one."

"I'll just grab a black one. That's what he was wearing."

Ben went to the closet and ignored the few crumbled Oxford shirts that lay on top of the dresser. Giovanni's clothes hadn't really been touched. Everything was still as it had been that first horrible night his uncle had been arrested. Ben shook his head and grabbed a random black shirt, hoping it would fit. Jean was a little smaller than his uncle, but not by much. He wandered back out to the bedroom.

"What are you working on?"

"Huh?" She looked up. "Oh, I'm just taking some notes. I'm going to that reception thing that Livia's hosting at this club in town later."

"Like a dance club?"

"Kinda. It's more like a social club. I'm not sure, but Emil Conti's going to be there along with most of the most influential vampires in the city. Ziri said that she's trying to be more visible since word got out that Gio escaped."

"That probably made her look pretty bad, huh?"

"Yes. But Emil requested another visit, so she had to admit he'd escaped. And she knows we were at the reception the night it happened." A satisfied grin spread over her face. "It's driving her crazy. And yes, it makes her look really bad."

He sat down. "Well, that's good, right? That's what you want."

"Yep, that's what we want. And that's why she's hanging out in the city more and having this reception. She's trying to show off and make sure people remember she's still the queen. But Emil's going to be there, along with his wife, who I haven't met yet."

"So you're gonna go make nice?"

"I'm going to go hang out and try to boost his ego and his reputation. The more people think of him, the more likely he's going to be to make the moves we want to get Livia out of power. Hopefully, flattery will get us everywhere."

Ben asked, "Anyone going with you?"

"Not this time." She glanced up into his worried eyes. "It's fine, Ben. Nothing's going to happen to me. It's a very public event. I'm not even going to be very far away from here."

"You sure? Maybe Matt—"

"This is a vampire thing, Ben."

"Tenzin?"

She dropped her pencil and reached a hand across the table. "Ben, honey, I'll be fine."

He shrugged and tried to act nonchalant. "Okay, whatever."

She smiled and patted his hand. "Now, go take that shirt to Jean. He's a little too proud of that hairy French chest. We don't want him scaring Angela."

Ben burst into laughter and stood. He walked out and looked back at his aunt. Beatrice was sitting at the table, looking pensive, and staring at the moon through the open window. He gently closed the door.

"My dear, if looks could kill, then you would be a splatter on the wall."

Beatrice glanced up to see Emil Conti standing over her with a martini and a cool smile. "Emil, I doubt you're complimenting my outfit, so I'm going to assume she was glaring at me again."

He chuckled as he sat next to her in the plush velvet chairs that lined the VIP section of the club.

She had been mistaken, Livia *was* entertaining them at a nightclub. It was one she owned, and Beatrice could feel the vibrations of the music from the dance floor below. The favored vampires who had received an invitation stood at the edge of the darkened glass, surveying the humans who crowded the club like their own, personal buffet.

Which, Beatrice thought, they kind of were. The few humans allowed upstairs were swimming in amnis and quickly taken to the private rooms. The grunts and moans of pleasure were dampened by the thick walls, but not completely drowned out.

"A vampire-owned nightclub," she said. "Kind of a cliché, isn't it?"

Emil smiled. "It's a cliché for a reason. It's a good business to be in and provides an excellent cover. She's had this one since the seventies. Thankfully, the decor has been updated."

"You own any?" They were somewhat isolated in their corner of the balcony. Beatrice had staked out a spot earlier where she could keep an eye on the whole party, but still be heard if she lifted her voice. It also had a great view of the table where Livia and Lorenzo had set up court.

"I don't. I have very boring businesses like shipping companies. Fishing. Though I do own several small cruise lines."

"That could be fun."

"If I had a taste for retiree blood, I'm sure I'd get my fill."

They laughed together, but both of them looked over to the head table.

Both Livia and Lorenzo had humans draped over them and made no disguise about taking a sip openly. The vampires surrounding them looked on like a hungry pack. Even Emil narrowed his eyes, but Beatrice had a feeling it wasn't in envy.

"Doesn't that piss people off?" she asked, her voice raised to allow the sensitive ears around them to hear. "I mean—I don't like to compare—but at my grandfather's parties in Los Angeles, everyone is allowed to bring their own company, if you know what I mean." Beatrice noticed the subtle attention that had shifted in their direction. So had Emil. A smile flickered across his mouth.

"In truth, Beatrice, most cities do not have the strict discipline about feeding that Rome has." His voice was very carefully neutral. "It is one thing that sets us apart."

You're definitely not saying that's a good thing, are you? His dark eyes were narrowed in calculation as she continued. "It's definitely unusual. I know I'm young, but I've traveled quite a bit. Other than the feeding thing, you're lucky to live here. I love Rome. The energy. The sights. It's an amazing city."

"I'm glad you're enjoying your stay. Despite the unpleasantness earlier this summer."

"I'm sure things will all be sorted out. I'm relieved that Gio is no longer confined, but then, no one contains my husband for long."

"And you have no idea where he is?"

She smiled. *Are you asking for me or the silent audience we've attracted?* "None at all."

Laughing eyes met hers. "Of course not. After all." Emil looked around the room. "I can scarcely keep track of my own wife, and she's never been arrested."

"Are you talking about me?" A graceful vampire slinked over and draped herself across the arm of Emil's red velvet chair. Donatella Conti was, according to Ziri, a very keen water vampire with very good instincts. She had been turned during the Renaissance, the same as Giovanni, but was a distant relative of the Borgia family. Her union with Emil Conti was a political manipulation of her sire, who had died shortly after the match. Beatrice couldn't quite figure Donatella out.

She was a gorgeous chestnut brunette who wore designer fashions like they were loungewear. She made no disguise of her disdain for Livia, but still seemed to live in a charmed bubble of popularity. She and Emil had both come with other dates, but gravitated toward each other throughout the evening.

Emil ran a possessive hand over her thigh. "Of course we are talking about you, my love. Who else?"

Beatrice said, "I love your dress. That color is amazing on you." It was a blood-red cocktail dress that Beatrice remembered some skinny actress in Hollywood wearing to an awards show the year before. The actress looked anemic in it. Donatella looked stunning.

"Thank you," Donatella said, as her gaze raked over Beatrice's uniform of black jeans and a skin-tight black shirt. She'd dressed it up for the night with satin top that Dez had picked out and her tall, black boots. "I like your boots, Beatrice De Novo."

Beatrice let her fangs run out and smiled. "Thanks. These are Gio's favorites. I'm pretty sure I don't match Livia's dress code, though." It was true. She was the only woman wearing jeans in the club, but no one dared turn her away at the door.

"And, I suppose, that is why Rome loves you." Donatella smirked. "And you are American. You can get away with it."

"Oh?" Beatrice said. "I think Roman women can get away with a lot more."

Emil smiled and ran a hand up the curve of his wife's calf. "You are quite right."

"Maybe it's time for a change," Beatrice said. She could hear the chatter around them drop off and she was fairly certain Livia, Lorenzo, or both were listening as well.

The smile fell from Emil's face and he glanced around. "Change can be dangerous. Disruptive."

"Change can also be healthy."

"If done for the right reasons, I suppose so."

Beatrice looked up at Donatella, who was watching her with narrowed eyes. "For instance, Donatella, I saw a similar dress on an actress last year. She looked like a little girl playing dress-up. You, however..." She trailed off, hoping that the vampire had picked up her cue.

As if she had orchestrated it, Donatella slid into Emil's lap. A smile flirted at the corner of her mouth. "It's all about finding the right person, isn't it, Beatrice? The right person can wear the boldest colors."

"They can. It's good to shake things up every now and then."

Emil stroked his wife's hair while Donatella and Beatrice exchanged a private smile. "You ladies," Emil murmured. "Always talking about the newest trends."

Beatrice cast her eyes around the club at their silent audience. "Emil, I am *all* about new trends."

She was on the street, waiting for her car to pick her up, when Emil caught up with her.

"Beatrice, please, allow me to offer you a ride home."

She looked around. Livia's guards watched them from the front of the club. Her driver pulled up, but she waved him away and turned back to Emil. "That would be nice, thanks. Where's Donatella?"

He shrugged. "I believe that she is seeing her companion home. Mine brought her own driver."

They slid into the dark blue luxury sedan, and Emil immediately raised the privacy screen, encasing them in silence. He swung his eyes toward her and bared his teeth.

"You play a dangerous game, Beatrice De Novo. No one is sure how you got him out, but we know that Giovanni did not escape on his own. There was no way it could have happened. I saw his cell myself. I don't know what he has planned, but—"

"Neither my husband nor I have any interest in ruling Rome." Her fangs had slid down in reaction to his aggressive stance, but Beatrice curbed her natural instincts and tried to relax. This was their potential ally, she reminded herself, and he had every reason to be suspicious.

"Then what are you insinuating? Surely you must have noticed that others were listening to you tonight."

"I think you know exactly what I'm insinuating."

"Assistance only?"

"Let's just say, we like to help our friends."

Emil sat back and relaxed his stance. "What you're talking about has many risks."

"Like I said, change always does."

"We're not talking about fashion crimes anymore, Beatrice."

"I never was, *Emil*." She tapped her finger on her knee and watched him. "She can't remain in power. It will not be allowed. If there is no other option, Giovanni will remove her. But we're hoping there are other options."

Emil watched her with a measuring stare. "Other options would prove to be far less trouble for you. But I don't know that you're aware of how much power she really has."

"You're talking about these rumors circulating. About her cure for bloodlust?"

He shifted in his seat. "It's never been stated quite that succinctly, but everyone knows she has ties to the pharmaceutical industry. If that is something she has attained, the cure could bring her immense wealth and influence. Every vampire in the world would pay to be free of the one thing that controls us. Only a shield against the sun would be more valuable." He cleared his throat. "Some of us may have tried to discover the truth of these claims, but so far it's been rather—"

"It's a cosmetics factory in Bulgaria." Beatrice took a chance. If Emil was going to risk his neck, she had to give him something. "They started production earlier this year."

He narrowed his eyes. "How do you know this?"

"Put it this way, I'm very good at research."

She saw him deflate in his seat, but still, his eyes flared. "So, it is true? She has discovered a cure?"

"Not exactly."

He frowned. "Please, continue."

"This formula was given to me by the Elders of Penglai Island. They wanted it protected. Not even their most skilled alchemists really understood it. And then Lorenzo stole it. And make no mistake, Emil. He *did* steal it. He *did* kill my father. He almost killed me."

Emil snorted. "I doubt he'd kill you. Have you seen the way he looks at you?"

"Please, he'd want anyone that Giovanni had. That has nothing to do with me."

"I wouldn't be too sure about that, but tell me more about this. As much as I dislike Livia, this does sound like something that could be good for our kind, Beatrice. Whatever our personal rivalries, we should think of the greater good of all—"

"See that!" she interrupted. "That right there? That's why *you're* the best person to lead Rome. You really do care about the city. You care about the vampires who live here. You feel a responsibility to them."

He drew himself up, almost as if she had insulted him. "It is my belief that those who have power have a responsibility to—"

"It's good! I'm not saying it isn't. It's nice to meet someone who's not completely self-interested. But the thing is, this formula is not safe. And she knows it." Actually, Beatrice had no idea whether Livia knew the effects of the elixir on amnis, but that didn't matter. Getting Livia out of power was more important. "We think it's a poison, Emil."

He looked skeptical. "Why would she want to poison her own people? I know she's not benevolent, but it's hardly in her best interests to kill all of them."

"We're not sure, but we're trying to find out what, *exactly*, it does."

He sighed. "Beatrice, I like you. I think Livia is a bad leader. And I believe your claims against Lorenzo. In fact, after Tenzin's speech, I'm fairly sure all of Rome knows that he murdered your father, but the fact remains that Livia has many allies. Allies here and abroad. She has done many favors for many people in her two thousand years. Unless those people decide to cut her off…"

"Well," Beatrice said quietly. "I guess we'll just have to make them realize that it's time for a change."

Emil crossed his legs and leaned back in the seat. He tapped his fingers restlessly on one knee as he glanced between Beatrice and the lights of the Eternal City that flashed past the car. He was silent until they pulled up to the Pantheon. Beatrice heard the driver get out and walk around to open her door. It opened, but Emil grabbed her hand as she was climbing out.

"You're right," he said. "You're right. Change is good. Change is… necessary."

She smiled and nodded. "I'll be in touch."

Beatrice whistled as she walked up the street and watched Emil's car turn the corner. She had just made her most important ally.

CHAPTER TWENTY

Plovdiv, Bulgaria
July 2012

Giovanni stepped out of the telegraph office tucked into a corner of the Kapana district and strolled up the cobbled streets. Summer nights were warm in Plovdiv, and pedestrians crowded the walkways of the neighborhood on their way to the clubs and restaurants of the graceful old town. Bulgaria's second largest city, and one of the oldest in Europe, had enjoyed a surge of prosperity since the last time Giovanni had visited. Like much of Eastern Europe, the city had always maintained a fairly high immortal population, with Lucien Thrax being one of its oldest inhabitants.

He and Carwyn had received a polite, if muted, reception from the vampire who ran the city after a letter of introduction from the old Thracian had paved the way. Their business in town was not questioned, which was all Giovanni wanted. If everything went as planned, they wouldn't be in Bulgaria long.

He caught the red of Carwyn's hair against the dark green wall of an outdoor cafe. The former priest was drinking a glass of plum *rakia* and writing a letter at a small table. A smile flirted at the corner of his mouth. Giovanni sat down next to him and Carwyn tucked the letter under the edge of his book.

"Who were you writing, Father?"

Carwyn smiled. "I told you—"

"I've been calling you that for three hundred years, Carwyn. I'm not going to just stop, you know."

"Fine, but I may stop answering."

Giovanni chuckled. "So?"

"What?"

"Who were you writing?"

"None of your business."

"You are quite the mystery lately."

The vampire shrugged and sipped the fruit wine. "What's so mysterious? I decided that a thousand years of service to the church was enough. After all, when I took my vows, I was only expecting to live forty or fifty."

"I'm not questioning your decision, my friend." Giovanni cocked an eyebrow. "Are *you*?"

Carwyn smiled and looked over at the fountain that trickled in the small square and the flow of young people that passed by. "No. I'm not going to deny it feels a bit odd, but I'm at peace about it. I'm... excited. It's a new chapter in life. There are going to be some changes for me."

Giovanni nodded. "So, is this the immortal version of a mid-life crisis?"

Carwyn snorted and waved over a young man to order two more glasses, then he turned back to Giovanni. "I blame the girls, you know."

"Why?"

"I'm warning you, never make daughters. You raise them. Give them hundreds of years of guidance and love, and then they think they know everything. Try to tell you what to do. Very irritating."

"What? All of them?"

"Not Carla, thank God, but then, she never speaks to anyone but me and Gus. No, it's the rest of them, Gio. They plot against me."

Giovanni smiled, thinking of the most likely culprits. Deirdre, Isabel, and Gemma may have been scattered around the globe, but he had no doubt the three sisters could gang up on their father if they put their minds to it.

"I'll keep that in mind. No daughters. Have you told anyone else yet?"

"Other than the cardinals? No."

"How did they take it?"

"How do you think? Officially, they weren't pleased. But they can't say anything when, *officially*, I've never existed in the first place. Besides, I've always been an oddity. Most immortal priests were turned from the Roman church and have far more respect for the Vatican."

Giovanni slapped his friend's shoulder and thanked the waiter, who set down the wine. "You'll be fine. This is good. You're right; it's a new life. I'm excited for you. So, who were you writing a letter to that you needed to hide it?"

Carwyn just grinned and took another drink. "Our friend is still inside with his wife. They look like a lovely couple, if I do say so. In no way does he resemble a minion of Satan."

"The best minions never do." Giovanni turned his eyes toward the large windows of the restaurant where Doctor Paskal Todorov was dining. It hadn't been difficult to track down the chemist or the cosmetics factory, but they had decided they needed to question the director to find out precisely what he knew before they destroyed the factory.

"He seems like a nice enough fellow. It's possible he has no idea who he's in business with."

"Considering that it's Livia, it's likely that he's completely unaware. She's never been very forthcoming."

"Particularly with humans."

"True."

Carwyn grimaced. "I'm beginning to feel bad about destroying the factory."

"Start another one and hire him to run it. It's not like you don't have the money."

"I'm not—"

"Don't lie." Giovanni shook his head. "You were always sketchy about that 'vow of poverty' thing. Don't even pretend you don't have the funds tucked away."

Carwyn's only response was a wicked grin. "Now, what kind of vampire would I be if I didn't tuck a bit away?"

"None. So, don't feel bad about the good doctor; you can always give him another job. Most likely, he'll find another on his own anyway."

"Fine."

The two vampires waited. Watched. The chemist ate a leisurely meal with his wife before they saw him finally stand and start toward the door. Carwyn threw a few euros on the table to pay for the wine before he and Giovanni stood and started following.

They allowed the humans to turn down the street leading to their home before they approached. It was late enough that most of the street was quiet, and Giovanni couldn't detect any observers.

"Doctor Todorov?" he called out. The doctor turned, frowning at the two casually dressed men who approached him. "Aren't you Paskal Todorov?"

"Yes? Can I help you?" the doctor replied in English.

Giovanni smiled warmly. "Forgive the intrusion, but I believe we have a mutual acquaintance in Rome."

"From Rome?" The human was clearly confused, but must have sensed no danger from their approach. He stood patiently as Carwyn and Giovanni walked toward them.

Carwyn immediately approached the doctor's wife and held out a hand in greeting. Giovanni held out his hand, as well. "Yes, I believe you know my associate, Lorenzo."

As soon as Giovanni's hand met Todorov's, the amnis flooded over him. He glanced to the left, and Carwyn was quietly engaging the wife in some pleasant chitchat she was completely oblivious to.

"Paskal Todorov, do you know a man named Lorenzo?"

"I know a Lorenzo Andros. He works for my company in Rome. He has inspected the factory."

Right on the first question, he thought. Giovanni curled his lip, annoyed that Lorenzo had used his father's name in his business dealings.

"And what are you producing at your factory, Dr. Todorov?"

"It is a cosmetics formula. A serum of some sort. I believe it is intended to combat aging."

"I see—"

"But it is dangerous." A frightened look came to the chemist's eyes, and Giovanni knew that he was tapping into the doctor's unconscious thoughts about the project. Possibly, thoughts he wouldn't even recognize.

"Why do you say it is dangerous?"

"I... I don't know."

"Did Lorenzo say it was dangerous?"

"He is not a trustworthy man."

So, not a minion after all. Giovanni wondered if, confronted with the truth, the doctor would voluntarily shut the factory down. Was it worth taking a chance to keep Livia in the dark about their actions? The minute the factory was destroyed, she would probably be aware that Giovanni was behind it. Could they shut it down without alerting her?

He looked over at Carwyn. "Keep the wife occupied, but don't make it obvious. I'm going to talk to him."

Carwyn nodded and began to ask the doctor's wife about local sightseeing while Giovanni lessened his influence over the chemist. Todorov blinked at him when Giovanni released his hand.

"Yes, Doctor, as I was saying, the health commission has some concerns about this cosmetic serum. And I'm sure you can understand our reluctance to make our concerns public. It's not an immediate health threat, but we do need your cooperation."

"Oh... of course." Todorov still looked confused, but amenable, and Giovanni knew that the doctor's human instincts, even as dull as they were, had picked up some danger from Lorenzo. "But... who did you say you were with?"

"It's a joint inquiry between our two countries. No one wants to make the concerns public as we do our investigation, but it is vital that we control the output."

"Oh... of course. I did understand that the trials had positive results. Were there problems I was unaware of?"

Giovanni thought back to Lucien's story that Carwyn had related on their drive to Bulgaria. "The immediate testing did have positive results, but there are some concerns about long-term use of the product."

"I see, I see." Todorov reeked of worry. "I do hope the commission knows that all proper procedures were followed by our labs. Our chemists are some of the finest, and I would hate if—"

"Your facility is not under scrutiny, Doctor Todorov. We know you manufactured the product in good faith."

The doctor looked sheepish. "In all honesty, the formula... well, it was unusual. But since all the components were botanical in nature—and Rome was very strict about quality—well, it was unusual, but not enough to worry me. Not really. Though..."

"Yes?"

"I did think it odd, Mr...."

"Rossi. Doctor Guiseppe Rossi." He took out his wallet and flipped it open, brushing Todorov's hand to create the illusion of impeccable credentials in the human's mind.

"Of course, Dr. Rossi. I did think it odd that the office in Rome was so insistent on security for the factory. Any time you have employees, there can be theft, but they were most persistent in their measures. I even had to hand count the first shipment to ensure that the product was completely accounted for."

A chill spread over his skin and he heard Carwyn's friendly voice falter.

"What shipment?"

"The first shipment of Elixir. It went out on the trucks last week, Doctor Rossi. It's on its way to Rome right now." Todorov frowned. "I... I thought you knew."

They stared over the boxes containing the blood-red liquid. It was packaged in frosted glass and deluxe, gold-trimmed boxes with ELIXIR stamped on the outside. The small vials held no more than half an ounce. According to Lucien, a few drops was all it took. A few drops to cure a human being of ravaging cancer. A few drops to weaken a three thousand-year-old immortal in a matter of months.

"We destroy it." Giovanni picked up a box, almost cringing just to touch the plain brown cardboard.

"We'll drive out to the country and you can burn it. Can you destroy it fast enough to eliminate flames and ash?"

"There will be ash, but we'll try to contain it."

Carwyn nodded. "And make sure we don't breathe any of the smoke."

"Agreed."

"Thank God they haven't made more than this."

"They made enough for one shipment, Carwyn. A shipment that's headed toward my wife and our friends."

"Do you suppose there's any way it's detectable?"

"I don't know." Suddenly the idea of destroying all the computers seemed less than ideal and he wished he had Dez or Benjamin available to hack into the mysterious technology and find out more about it. He felt sick and desperate. "This is a disaster."

Carwyn bent to help him and they began carting the small stack of brown boxes to the back of the Range Rover. "It's not a disaster. We just need to find the truck."

"And the boxes of Elixir. And make sure none of them went missing. Because that never happens at border crossings, does it?"

"Livia isn't going to produce something she can't detect, Gio. There has to be some way to detect it. Just calm down."

He exploded. "She doesn't know what the hell this does! None of us do! There is some sort of—of poison headed toward my wife and family, and I have no idea what it does or what danger it really poses, Carwyn. Do not tell me to calm down!"

The vampire's blue eyes flared. "Don't pretend you have any more at stake than the rest of us, Gio. We need to get in contact with Rome and let them handle it so we can keep going."

"We need to go after the—"

"Jean and Gavin are still in Rome and those two smugglers know more about tracking down shipments of dodgy goods than we ever will. You're right; we don't know what this does. The most important thing for us to do is find the answers."

Giovanni took a deep breath and nodded. Carwyn was right. "We need to find Arosh and Kato."

"If we find them, then we know what to worry about. If we find them, we find the truth."

They burned the boxes on an empty stretch of road outside the city a few hours before dawn. They stood downwind of the fire, blocking their mouths and watching as the smoke rose from the pit that Carwyn dug. When the flames were finally out, the earth vampire sunk the remnants and covered the ashes with dirt and rocks.

"There. It's gone."

"That bit is, anyway." Giovanni sighed and turned his face west.

The lights of the city glittered in the distance and he could still see smoke rising from the fire at the factory. Hopefully the small fire he'd set would conceal the destruction of the computers and the theft of the boxes and the computer that Dez told them she would try to access. There weren't many computers. Only seven. And they fed into an unassuming tower in Todorov's office. The metal box was swathed in blankets in the back of their vehicle. They would ship it to Rome as soon as they reached Istanbul.

Hopefully, the computer would give Beatrice and Tenzin a better idea of how the formula had been manufactured and what its effects were. They had tracked down the registration of the truck that had taken the small shipment to Rome and sent it to Matt. Giovanni only prayed that his friends could find the truck before it reached Livia.

"Come on, Sparky. We've got to get down the road a bit before dawn."

"What if they can't find the truck, Carwyn?"

"You can't think that way. You just can't. Besides, Jean and Gavin will track it down. When has Gavin ever failed to steal something he really wants?"

"I suppose that's true."

Carwyn slapped him on the shoulder. "Come, my friend. Let them do what they do best, and we'll get on with finding the legendary missing vampires in their mythological fortress in the Caucasus Mountains using only vague directions and landmarks that haven't held the same names for four hundred years. If we're very lucky, Arosh will burn us before Kato pulls the water from our bodies and leaves us shriveled husks of the vampires we once were."

Giovanni nodded. "But we have a letter."

Carwyn turned and walked to the car. "We do. And it better be a damn good one."

Giovanni followed him. "Speaking of letters..."

"I'm not going to tell you who I was writing, so stop asking."

CHAPTER TWENTY-ONE

Residenza di Spada
August 2012

"Yes," Ziri said, "that is the formula that I remember."

Lucien and Dez were sitting at the desk, going over the printouts from the hard drive that Giovanni and Carwyn had sent from Istanbul. Dez had spent the previous week going over the contents with a fine-tooth comb. Since Beatrice still had trouble accessing electronics, the printer had gotten a workout.

Dez had quickly pinpointed the shipping information of the single truck that had taken the first shipment from Bulgaria to Rome. There were only five boxes on the manifest. Apparently, someone hadn't wanted to wait. Jean and Gavin had immediately called contacts in the area, and the truck had been delayed in Serbia. They left the following night, hoping to intercept it before their favors were preempted by whomever Livia had in her pocket.

Ziri was still speaking. "It is amazing to me that they manufactured it so quickly. It took us months to put it together, even after Jabir perfected the formula."

Beatrice perked up from her chair by the fire. "Ziri?"

"Yes?"

"How *did* Jabir perfect it? Did he test it on humans before Fahdil and Kato tried it? What did he do?"

Ziri walked over and sat across from her. Beatrice could feel Lucien and Dez's eyes on them.

"He did test it on humans first. There was no shortage of ailing people in that part of the world, but he only tested it on the sickest of them. The first attempts did little. The human's metabolism destroyed any benefits our blood might have offered. But slowly, there were small improvements.

An extra hour before the blood was rejected. Then a day. It took over a year, but he finally found the exact formula to keep the human body from rejecting the blood. From there, the results were quite startling. One elderly woman in particular showed an amazing recovery."

"Yeah, I remember reading about her in the journals."

Ziri smiled. "He was always so careful with his language in those. Careful to conceal what we were and what we were doing. I'm very impressed you and your father figured them out."

"I doubt we would have had we not known about vampires already."

"True." Ziri sat back in his chair and stroked his chin in a thoughtful manner. "I do wonder how Livia and Lorenzo were able to interpret them so quickly."

"Gio thinks that there were notes that the monks made that Lorenzo stole when he ransacked the monastery. He said that Fu-Han had made progress."

"That was Zhang's old apprentice?"

"Yes. Giovanni said he had figured it out. Lorenzo must have taken his notes."

"Interesting."

"But Gio also said that Fu-han told him right before he died that there was something Lorenzo would not understand about the elixir."

Ziri cocked his head. "What? What wouldn't he understand?"

Beatrice shook her head. "He didn't say. He just said something about the fifth element. Not even Gio knew what the hell he was talking about. There are only four elements."

Dez piped up. "No, there's not. There's five."

Beatrice's head swung around. Dez was still sitting at the desk, and her eyes were glued to the monitor. Lucien was sitting to her left, studying the screen intently. He turned in his chair to address her.

"Dez is right," Lucien said. "The four elements are more philosophical than scientific. There are consistencies and variations across history. While four elements were named in ancient Western tradition, Aristotle added a fifth, *aether*."

"Aether?"

"The essence. The... *aether*. It's hard to explain. Aristotle described it as that which the heavens were made of. The eternal elements. All earthly elements are, in reality, unstable. They can be changed in many ways. Aether, the essence of the eternal, could not." Lucien smiled. "Call it what you will. The soul. The spark of God. Eternity. Aether is that which does not change."

"That's not science."

Lucien chuckled. "My child, God has existed long before science. He created it, after all."

"The fifth element was more prevalent in the East, Beatrice." Ziri broke in. "The ancient Babylonians had five elements, the sky being one, which you could relate to the Greek concept of aether."

Lucien continued, "Hindu philosophy and Bön have five elements as well. Bön has always held a fascination for Eastern vampires. Its study is what Tenzin's father is so well known for—well, that and bloodshed. Bön names five elements: fire, earth, wind, water, and space. The philosophy says that everything is related to these five elements. The four earthly elements influence everything about an individual, with the fifth, the space or aether, tying all things together."

"So, there *are* five elements." Beatrice nodded. "Okay, but how does that relate to the elixir of life? What could Fu-han have found?"

Ziri shrugged. "Who knows? The four earthly elements are all that truly pertain to our biology. There are no *aether* vampires. None possess a fifth power."

"What element is the most common?" Dez asked, looking up from the computer. "Just curious. Are there roughly the same number of all the different vampires around?"

Beatrice shook her head. "Not fire. Fire vampires are pretty rare, right Ziri?"

"Yes, I would say that there are roughly the same number of wind and water immortals. Earth vampires are more numerous."

Lucien said, "We do like our big families."

Dez patted Lucien's hand. "That must be why you guys are so easy to hang out with." She laid a hand on her swelling abdomen. "Family oriented."

Lucien watched Dez with a warm gaze. The human and the vampire had bonded over Dez's pregnancy, which was progressing with no complications. Matt had arranged an Italian midwife and hospital for his wife, but Dez also had the benefit of an immortal doctor on call. Lucien had been a healer for thousands of years and had grown very fond of Dez.

"How are you feeling, my dear?" He held a hand out. "May I?"

"Of course!"

Lucien placed a hand on Dez's stomach. Beatrice felt her fangs descend involuntarily and tried not to growl.

"Relax, Beatrice." Lucien glanced over his shoulder. "I'm not going to hurt her."

She took a deep breath. "I don't know why that keeps happening. You're her doctor, for goodness sake. I'm so sorry."

Ziri spoke. "It's instinct. It's natural for you because you consider Dez under your aegis. It's nothing to be concerned about. It just means that you will protect her and the baby."

"Aw." Dez winked at her. "I knew you were gonna be the best auntie."

Lucien smiled. "Have you felt the quickening?"

"Huh?"

"The baby. Have you felt the baby move?"

"Oh, yeah! Just a little. It kinda feels like bubbles."

"You'll feel more and more. He's very active."

Dez sat up straight. "It's a boy?"

"I'm not sure," Lucien said with a smile. "Extra strong senses, remember? No vampire ultrasound. And I can't smell the little one. He or she is very well protected in there." Lucien gave one last pat to Dez's little rounded belly. "Aren't you, *bebe*? Stay nice and snug until it's your time."

Dez melted. "Lucien, you are a big vampire sweetheart."

"Please don't let that get out. Well, you can tell my mother. She would laugh." He winked. "And this vampire sweetheart is exhausted, I better—"

Deirdre blew through the door in her typical, abrupt way. "I need to leave," she stated.

Beatrice sat up straight. "Everything all right?"

The redheaded vampire nodded. "Everything is fine. But there is nothing more I can do here. I need to return to my family."

"Oh." Dez stood and walked toward her. "I'm going to miss you!"

Lucien said, "You need to leave tonight?"

She nodded as she embraced Dez. "Matt has been looking for a ship that could carry me back. There is one leaving out of Genoa in the morning, but I'll need to leave tonight. Soon."

Beatrice glanced around the room. Ziri was unmoved. Dez was disappointed, but Lucien looked... lost.

"Deirdre," he said.

Deirdre's eyes swung toward him and she held out a hand. "Lucien."

And Beatrice suddenly recognized the anguish in his voice. The two friends had known each other for hundreds of years. Lucien and Deirdre's husband had been the closest of friends and colleagues. And Lucien didn't think he would see her again.

Deirdre walked over and embraced him. "You must not think this way, my friend. You must not."

"I do not know if I will see you again in this life."

Blood tears touched Deirdre's stoic face as Lucien enfolded her in his long arms. "Do not make me say good-bye to another loved one, Lucien. Whatever this is—"

"It is not goodbye. Not really, Deirdre. You and I both know this."

Beatrice just tried to hold herself together. At times, it was easy to see the mystery of Geber's manuscript as academic. It was a research project. A problem to be solved.

But it wasn't.

She watched the friends say good-bye, and her mind flashed back to her father's anguished face as he faced off against Lorenzo on the banks of the Nine-bend River. The scattered bodies of the monks in the Wuyi Mountains. The memory of the woman before her, wailing on the ground as she mourned the loss of her mate.

It would never be just academic.

The memories of loss were still fresh as Beatrice made the journey to Castello Furio later that night. Deirdre had left for Genoa. Dez and Matt had finally collapsed in exhaustion. They were both working day and night, trying to help solve the mystery and keep track of Ben while Giovanni was gone. Lucien had also taken to his bedroom. He'd had a bad spell after Deirdre left and drifted in a kind of fugue state he couldn't seem to wake from. It was happening more and more. Ziri and Beatrice had helped him to bed before Ziri flew ahead of her.

The last place in the world she wanted to be was Livia's castle, but there was a party that night in honor of the Chinese delegation that Tenzin told her she needed to be present for. After all, she had been named a scribe of Penglai, so she gritted her teeth, took a quick drink from the clueless driver, and headed out of Rome.

As they pulled up to the castle, she could see the glittering lights in the olive trees and the bevy of guards that only seemed to grow with each passing week. Whatever Livia was planning, she was gathering more and more guards. Beatrice debated, but left her shuang gou in the back of the car, tucking a few daggers into her boots, and another in her waistband before she walked through the gates.

The grounds were glittering with immortals and humans dressed in festive red outfits in honor of the Eastern guests. Beatrice was wearing her uniform of black jeans and a T-shirt. She still enjoyed flouting Livia's snobbish fashion sense. Plus, it was easier to hide knives in jeans and a T-shirt than a cocktail dress.

"Beatrice!" Donatella Conti called her name from across the lawn. Beatrice nodded and walked over. In the weeks since she and Emil had made their tentative alliance, Donatella had proven invaluable. Beatrice knew now that the seemingly frivolous manner of the immortal hid a very keen mind and a vicious loyalty to her husband and his interests. Donatella had cultivated Beatrice as her new pet in the Roman court, and most of Beatrice's communications to Emil were channeled through her.

"What are you wearing, my friend? What are you doing to me? Jeans?"

"I'm just not into dresses, Donatella." The Roman vampire leaned over and kissed her cheeks in greeting while Beatrice whispered, "The better to hide weapons, my dear."

"Oh, Beatrice." Donatella winked. "You just have to use your imagination." Scanning the woman's skin-tight designer gown, Beatrice had to really use her imagination to figure out where Donatella could be hiding anything.

"So, what's the gossip tonight?"

"Oh, she's saying she has some big announcement she wants to make."

"The Chinese delegation still playing nice with her?"

"As far as she knows, yes." Beatrice had learned through Tenzin that the small trade group, which was headed by Elder Lu's son, may have been there for business reasons, but quietly, they were supporting Beatrice and Giovanni's plan to destabilize Livia's power base. The Roman aristocrat had finally pissed off enough of the wrong people.

"Cool. We need to keep her happy until we hear more from Gio and Carwyn."

They strolled through the crowds arm in arm, whispering to each other. "Any news?"

Beatrice and Tenzin had told no one outside of their small circle where Giovanni and Carwyn were headed. And no one other than their closest allies really knew who they were looking for.

"We received some information from the factory in Bulgaria."

"Oh?"

"Which is shut down, by the way."

"Good to know."

"There was one shipment, which our sources do say contained a successful sample of the product."

"Coming to Rome?"

"Headed here, but hopefully it will be detained."

"Excellent."

"I'll keep you informed, but in the meantime—"

"Ladies."

Donatella and Beatrice both turned to look at the interruption.

The gall.

Lorenzo leaned casually against a stone pillar, watching them and holding two flutes of champagne. He held them both out. Donatella took one, but Beatrice only glared.

"Donatella, you are looking delicious this evening."

"Oh, Lorenzo." She let out a tinkling laugh. "You are too kind. And stupid. You are very, very stupid."

The vampire only cocked a blond eyebrow. "Oh?"

Donatella quickly covered the venom in her voice with a layer of honey. "To not have noticed my friend, of course! My beauty is nothing to her bold style. I am learning from our young American friend. She is so fearless."

When Lorenzo opened his mouth, Beatrice could see his fangs descended behind his full lips. "I'm well aware of Miss De Novo's fearlessness. She is a rare treasure, indeed."

"Your sire is a lucky man, Lorenzo."

That was bold. The disappearance of Giovanni Vecchio was the giant, blood-red elephant at all of Livia's parties. It seemed by mutual unspoken agreement that no one spoke of it. His name was not even mentioned except behind closed doors.

Or by his wife, of course.

She narrowed her eyes at the blond murderer who taunted her with his presence. "Oh, Lorenzo has always been jealous of Giovanni, haven't you, blondie? Giovanni's always had more class. More power. More... well, just more." She let a smile cross her lips.

"Are you sure of that? After all, you've never really explored your options, have you?"

"My grandma told me I don't need to taste piss to know I'm drinking wine."

Lorenzo only offered her a sympathetic look. "How is your family, Beatrice? I was so sorry to hear about Stephen's disappearance. Tragic."

The rage burst forth. "You fucking bastard! You know—" She cut herself off when she felt Donatella's arm restraining her.

"Come, my friend, let us find more pleasant company. I have a companion with me who would be to your liking, I think. His blood is very rich."

Beatrice relented at Donatella's touch. Lorenzo lifted his glass of champagne in a silent toast. As he brought it to his lips, Beatrice reached out and forced the liquid in the glass to expand, shattering the champagne flute at Lorenzo's lips and opening a small cut at the corner of his mouth. He smiled and reached up with an elegant finger, swiping at the cut and holding the finger out to her.

"Care for a taste?"

She turned her back on him and walked away.

The night wore on, and she managed to find Tenzin, who was crouched on a corner of one of the towers, pouting.

"Tenzin, come down."

The small wind vampire glared at her and floated to the ground.

"If I don't kill something soon, I'm going to go crazy."

"I thought you were supposed to be the patient one."

"I hate all this shit."

"You think I don't?"

The two friends leaned against the stone tower and watched the crowd, conscious of the numerous eyes that followed them constantly.

Tenzin said, "How much longer are we going to have to drag this out? I'm bored."

"Well, you're not the one that trying to avoid..." She looked around and lowered her voice. "Further complications, so to speak."

Tenzin switched to Mandarin, which Beatrice could speak passably well. "Would killing everyone really be that bad? I'm not saying it wouldn't be a pain in the ass to deal with the fallout, but at least you'd have some fun in the meantime."

"We're not really in the mood to rule a city, Tenzin."

"It would just be for a few hundred years."

"Do you know how crazy that sounds to my ears?"

"You'll get used to it, my girl."

Beatrice sighed. "Tenzin…"

"I know. I know."

They watched the party for a few more minutes, and Beatrice detected a strange energy building among the crowd.

"Tenzin, something—"

"I know. I feel it, too."

They both walked closer. There were murmurs of excitement. Whispers flew around and a strange buzz of energy enervated the immortals gathered. She felt the approach of a particularly strong energy signature and turned to see Emil Conti approaching her with Donatella hanging on his arm.

"Beatrice."

"What's happening, Emil?"

"You young people with your slang."

"No, really. What is *happening*?"

He blinked. "Oh. I believe our fair patroness has an announcement of some kind. I'm bubbling with excitement, can't you tell?"

Beatrice's eyes widened. "Not…"

Emil only cocked a lazy eyebrow, and Donatella smirked.

Livia mounted the stairs of a small stage where a string orchestra had been playing and tapped on her champagne flute to gather everyone's attention. It was completely unnecessary; the whole party was riveted to her before she even reached the top of the stairs. She was glowing with excitement when she started to speak.

"My friends, we are joined tonight by esteemed guests. We welcome them to the Eternal City. The Immortal City. Rome has long been a center of culture and learning. Of sophistication and enlightenment. I am happy to announce tonight that another achievement has been added to her crown."

"Pompous bitch," Tenzin muttered.

"As most of you know, I have been a patroness of the human sciences for hundreds of years. For in the prosperity of the human world, we find our own continued success. I am happy to announce that an ancient secret, a *stunning* discovery has, this past year, been recovered from the lost library of the great immortal, Niccolo Andros. It is in his honor that I announce a mystery of the ages has been solved. Long have humans and immortals sought the elixir of life. The unique formula that would offer our human friends the longevity and health that we immortals enjoy. Now, we have accomplished this." A buzz began to build among the crowd. "And in doing so, an even greater achievement has been made."

"She's going to do it." Beatrice shook her head. "She's going to announce—"

"My scientists have discovered not only the elixir of life, but the cure to bloodlust, as well." The buzzing stopped, and an eerie silence fell over the castle grounds as Livia continued. "And it will be available to all of you. This secret is a secret no longer. It belongs to us." Beatrice saw Livia's eyes light up. "It belongs to the world!"

The silence lasted only as long as it took for the first burst of applause to erupt from the excited crowd. It had to have been the humans in attendance who started it, Beatrice thought. Vampires weren't usually an enthusiastic crowd. But soon, everyone around them, including the immortals, was applauding and moving toward the stage. Livia was enveloped by vampires and humans vying for her attention.

Beatrice and Tenzin exchanged a grim look, and Emil said quietly, "Look how they gather around her now."

"Why?" she asked. "All of these vampires are blood drinkers from what I've seen. Why is it so important to find a cure for bloodlust? Are they all humanitarians? They can't all care about the good of mankind *that* much."

Donatella was the one who answered. "They're not being altruistic, Beatrice. And most of them enjoy blood as much as we do. But they *need* it. They don't just choose to drink, they *have* to. It controls us. Even the oldest vampire is a slave to hunger in the end. They all clamor for Livia's favor, but it's not a cure they are seeking. They crave control, and she offers it. So more will come." Donatella looked at Beatrice with a hard stare. "*Many* more will come."

CHAPTER TWENTY-TWO

Svaneti, Georgia
Caucasus Mountains
October 2012

Giovanni nodded at the old woman who refilled his wine glass and smiled at the young woman who set down the bread. The women left the room, retreating into the kitchen to whisper quietly about the foreign visitors and leaving the two vampires alone with the three humans gathered in the dark room. Giovanni's attention was drawn to the head of the family and leader of the small village in a remote mountain valley in Northern Georgia.

The man was seated in a richly decorated chair. Giovanni guessed that it was hundreds of years old, but had been lovingly oiled and tended, a mark of pride for the small village and the man who sat upon it that night. The head of the village, a Svan in his early fifties, was dressed in the curious blend of ancient and modern typical in the mountains. His jacket sported an American logo, but his head was topped by the grey felt hat typical of all men of the region high in the Caucasus Mountains. A long dagger hung at his belt and an icon of Saint George graced the wall. The cold wind whistled around the old house, and Giovanni was grateful not to be out in the wind, at least for a little while.

Carwyn was still exchanging stories with the man, laughing over ribald jokes in Russian, since neither of them spoke Georgian or the strange, old language of the Svans. Giovanni's Russian was passable, but not nearly as good as the priest's, so he sat back and listened.

"This region you speak of," the human said. "No one goes there." He waved a dismissive hand. "You want hiking or climbing, I will have my son, Otar, show you to some of the lower trails. It is too cold in that part of the mountains anyway."

Carwyn steered the conversation back toward the mountain pass they were now almost certain led to the forgotten fortress of Arosh that Saba had mentioned in her letters to Ziri. It had been first dark when Giovanni and Carwyn entered the village. They had taken shelter in a cave the earth vampire had carved out at dawn the day before. The tiny town was nestled at the base of several passes. They knew that Arosh's fortress lay in the mountains, but they weren't certain through which of the three gorges they needed to pass to get there.

Carwyn spoke. "This mountain we speak of is unique. And we will not need a guide for the hike. We ask only your permission to climb there and direction to the proper trail."

"Your horses will not make the journey this late in the year," the man continued to protest, as Giovanni's eyes scanned the room. The house was not a wealthy one, but the art and icons on the walls gave testament to the man's position of authority in the community. His son stood at the doorway, watching the two foreigners with cautious eyes.

"I appreciate your concern." Carwyn nodded respectfully. "But we must go there. It was recommended to us by a very dear friend. A climbing partner who insisted we must see the vistas from the peak."

The man's eyes narrowed. "I do not know who you might speak of. That mountain is not a good place; I am telling you, no one travels there."

Giovanni broke in. "Why? Why doesn't anyone go there?"

The Svan hesitated, glancing between Giovanni and Carwyn. "Bandits. There are bandits in that part of the mountains."

The man's son broke into the conversation, murmuring in their own tongue, as he and his father seemed to have a low-voiced debate. Finally, the father raised his hand and his son fell quiet. "If you want to go there. I will not stop you. But I must know that no one will come looking for you and causing us trouble."

Giovanni said, "No one will come after us. We do not wish to bring trouble to your home."

The older man nodded and sat back in his chair. "Otar will take you as far as the base of the trail, but that is all. He will not accompany you up the mountain."

Carwyn's eyes darted toward Giovanni's, and he nodded. Carwyn said, "That is more than we ask; we appreciate your hospitality."

"Tell me again," Giovanni said. "Why do you not want us to go there?"

Otar spoke from behind them, surprising Giovanni when he spoke in English. "That mountain is cursed. No one goes there. Or at least, no one comes back."

"Cursed by what?"

The younger man shrugged. "The old people tell legends. And sometimes, the girls disappear if they go too close."

"Only the girls?" Carwyn asked.

The young man was about to speak, but his father interrupted. "There are still robbers in the hills. It is better now than it was, but... we keep our children close to the village. Especially at night."

Giovanni turned to the father. "Tell me about the legends."

"They are nonsense."

He smiled. "I am curious. I am a literature professor in Italy. I love stories and myths."

The father shrugged. "The old people say that an angel appeared to Queen Tamar hundreds of years ago when she visited the mountains. He shone like fire and fell in love with our queen, so she gave him this mountain and let him build a stone tower. He stayed in the tower when she returned to the lowlands and her castle, but she returned here every summer to visit him. Many years passed in peace, but when the messengers came to the mountains, telling the people that the queen had died in her castle, the mountain she had given the angel was engulfed in flames. All the trees burned and none grew again. The angel continued to live there, but he grew angry with the Svan people. Hundreds of years passed, and the village that once thrived in the gorge beneath was deserted. Now, no one goes there. It is cursed."

An angel of fire.

Giovanni wondered what Arosh would think of the legend. He wondered if he would even get to ask or whether these dark hours in the small village would be his last before he was killed by the legendary immortal.

"You will stay in my son's house tonight, my friends. You may leave in the morning for your trek."

Carwyn smiled and demurred. "No, no. We must travel at night. My friend's skin condition makes it necessary to travel at night. And we only need your son to point us toward the trailhead. We will be happy to find our own way."

Giovanni was glad he was so pale. The men had been suspicious of his 'sunlight allergy,' but had been more than happy to take the money for their hospitality without too many questions. As they made their way out of the small home and toward the horses they had ridden into the remote village, Carwyn and Giovanni were careful to shake hands with the men, ensuring their cooperation through subtle amnis and removing any suspicion from their minds.

"You are sure you want to go there?" Otar asked Giovanni as he saddled his packhorse.

"Yes, very sure."

"I'm not sure what you're looking for, but if it's treasure, I don't think you will find any in those mountains."

"Do people come looking for treasure?"

The young man's eyes held a playful kind of mischief. "Many things have been hidden in these mountains over the years. Often, they are found. More often, they are not."

Giovanni's mouth lifted at the corner, wondering what treasure hunters had been disappointed. In the old man's house alone, he spotted several icons that any museum in Western Europe would love to have in their collection. Here, they hung on the walls, watching over humble families and simple meals.

"Truly, my friend"—Giovanni slapped the young man on the shoulder—"you must not worry about us. We are not here to look for anything that might bring harm to your family."

"I'm not worried about my family, but I'll be surprised if I see *you* again."

Carwyn left the small house with a bottle of wine and a wrapped package that smelled like the flat bread they had eaten earlier. An old woman patted the vampire's rough cheek and waved at them from the glowing door of the kitchen as they mounted their horses and followed the young man up to the trailhead.

"Leave it to you to think of your stomach, Carwyn." Giovanni spoke in Latin, hoping the young man didn't have any other surprises.

The vampire grinned. "If it's my last night on earth, and I'm not in the company of a beautiful woman, then wine is the next best choice. Well, beer would be better, but wine will do."

Giovanni chuckled and followed the soft padding of the horse in front of them. Otar led them up the western trail and into the hills. After a few miles, the young man stopped.

"This is as far as I will go with you. Keep to this trail and when you get to the dead tree line, you'll know you're at the right mountain. It will rise on the west side of the trail. Trust me; you won't miss it. I have been there only once. It was during the daytime, when it is safe."

Giovanni said, "I thought you said that no one went there."

The young man smiled. "Only brave little boys and unhappy girls go to this mountain. The boys go during the day. The girls, at night. The boys we see again."

Giovanni's eyes sought Carwyn's. What treachery was Arosh involved in? Was he feasting from the women of this small, mountain town?

Carwyn said, "Thank you, Otar."

The young man nodded and turned his horse around. "Good luck finding whatever you're after!"

"Thank you."

Giovanni and Carwyn continued up the trail. It became narrower, and thick stands of forest rose on either side. Despite the peaceful surroundings, Giovanni could feel the steady thrum of energy that grew stronger the farther they traveled up the mountain.

"Do you feel it?"

Carwyn nodded. "Oh yes. These hills are… different."

Eventually, the two vampires dismounted their horses, who were quickly becoming agitated by the crackling energy that permeated the air. Giovanni and Carwyn took their packs and strapped them on their backs before they turned the horses and shooed them away. The animals sped down the trail, and the two friends continued in silence until Carwyn started singing.

Giovanni smirked. "Really, Father? I'm trying not to think about the fact that I may never see my wife or family again, and you start a drinking song?"

"Well, it's no use meeting somewhat certain death in a bad mood, is it?"

"I suppose you may have a point."

"And why are you so certain that he's going to kill us, Gio? You've become so cynical in your old age."

"I've always been cynical. And tell me, my friend, have you ever seen two male fire vampires in the same room? The same building? The same city, for that matter?"

"Does Lan Caihe count?"

Giovanni snorted, thinking of the young, androgynous fire vampire of Penglai. "No, Lan doesn't count."

"Well then… no." His mouth twisted. "That's odd. I've never thought about it before. I haven't. Not that I know many fire vampires at all."

"There's a reason for that."

"Don't get along?"

"We tend to kill each other on sight. It's a very hard instinct to quell. Females do far better than males."

"Good to know." Carwyn paused, then took a long drink of the wine the old woman had given him before passing it to Giovanni. "Drink up."

Giovanni grabbed the bottle and took a drink. It didn't taste a fraction as sweet as his wife's mouth, but he tried not to think about that. He tried not to think about Beatrice at all. Otherwise, he'd be too tempted to turn himself around and abandon the whole crazy plan. The farther they traveled, the heavier the air seemed to grow. If he was human, he doubted he could have stood under the pressure. The air was thick with amnis when they spotted the first charred trees.

Otar had been right; there was no mistaking this mountain. Unlike the surrounding hills, the slope that rose up from the gorge was a vast, wasted ruin. Rocks tumbled down and sharp spires of blackened conifer trunks dotted the landscape that glowed grey under the full moon.

"Think this is it?"

Giovanni took his foot off the trail and stepped up. As soon as he touched the base of the mountain he caught a whiff of almond smoke. The unmistakable scent of another male fire vampire filled his nostrils, and a certain dread fell over him. "This is it."

They went slowly, not wanting to surprise whatever presence dwelled at the top of the mountain. Even Carwyn, who was usually at home in remote hills, seemed grim. Giovanni heard him praying under his breath as they climbed.

"Father?"

"Didn't I tell you to stop calling me that?"

Giovanni turned to him and held out a hand. "Thank you. For everything."

He saw Carwyn's eyes glow bright in the moonlight, and his voice was hoarse when he grasped Giovanni's hand. "Don't be so morbid, Sparky."

Just then, a rushing sound filled the air. The wind whipped by as if churned by some great flying beast. They turned, but nothing showed itself in the night. Giovanni took a deep breath and continued their silent climb.

They had just climbed over a scarred knoll when they heard the rushing wind again. This time, it was closer. Then, he felt a great rush of wind, as if the air around him was being sucked up toward the summit of the mountain. His heart faltered for a moment.

"Carwyn, duck."

They both dropped to the rocks before the wave of scarlet fire swept down the mountain. Carwyn's amnis pushed up, and a wall of rock rose before them. They pressed against it as the flames rolled down the slope. Giovanni could even feel the rock they sheltered behind begin to heat, and he struggled to rein in his own instinctive reaction. The fire bloomed on his skin and burned away his shirt and coat. His fangs ran out, but he bit his lip tried to control himself.

"Carwyn?"

"Yes?"

"I know you're not, strictly speaking, a priest anymore—"

"Trust me when I say I'm rethinking that decision just now!"

"Pray anyway."

The flames halted for a minute and Giovanni stepped out from behind their earthen shield, the blue flames swirling along his skin, but contained for the moment.

"Arosh!" he called.

He felt the slow suck of air again, and he darted back behind the rock as the flames swept down the mountain again. They were slower this time, creeping and testing, and Carwyn rolled the rocks and earth up around them to smother the flames before they reached their feet.

A whispering Persian voice came on the wind. "Who seeks Arosh?"

Giovanni took a deep breath and answered. "I am Giovanni, son of Nikolaos Andreas, sired by Kato of Minos."

The flames were no longer testing. They came in furious waves. Carwyn roared as one curled up his leg. He sank his foot in the rock to kill the burning tendril.

"I don't think that helped much, Sparky!"

"Apparently, I'm not the only one who hated my father."

The flames halted again, so Giovanni tried another name.

"We have been sent by Ziri, the Numidian. We come as friends!"

The deep voice came again, closer this time. "I have no quarrel with the holy man. Tell Saba's son to depart from this place. I have no wish to anger her or the immortal's god. But the son of Andreas is mine."

Carwyn looked confused. "Saba's son?"

"He must mean because you're an earth vampire. If you want to go, go."

Carwyn reached into his coat and pulled out the wine bottle, uncorking it and taking a long drink. "Tempting, but no."

Giovanni's heart was racing and he could no longer contain his own flames. He could feel them rushing over his body, and his heavy canvas pants were burning at the cuffs. "He's going to kill us."

Carwyn nodded. "That seems to be more likely by the moment, yes. I wonder if it would help if he knew you killed your sire."

Giovanni swallowed the growl that wanted to leap from his throat when he felt the heavy amnis press around them. He quelled the flames as much as he could before he stepped out from behind their rocky shelter, but the blue fire swirled as he held his arms out. He threw out a burst of flame when he saw the spear of fire heading toward him.

The battling flames met and burst high into the night sky, flooding the rocky slope with red light. Then they stopped, and a great roar erupted from the top of the mountain, as Giovanni's fire leapt forward. He fought the instinct telling him to strike back and called on every ounce of self-control as he forced himself to pull back. Then he stood bare and smoking on the rugged cliffs as he cried out:

"I am Giovanni Vecchio, murderer of my sire, Nikolaos Andreas! I am sent from Ziri, seeking his friends Arosh and Kato. I ask for an audience with the great kings. I mean *no harm* upon this mountain or the immortals here!"

A gaping silence followed his pronouncement. He could hear Carwyn's soft prayers coming from behind him and suddenly, Giovanni heard footsteps.

Emerging from the smoke, the ancient fire vampire approached, his black eyes raking Giovanni's blue fire and his amnis sparking in the air around him. Red flames licked along his ruddy brown skin, and long, black hair flew out behind him. His regal forehead needed no crown to speak its authority, and mysterious symbols were tattooed on the rise of his cheekbones. He wore brown leather leggings, but nothing else except an angry glare. He came to a halt a few meters above Giovanni, hands fisted on his hips as he examined the younger immortal in front of him.

"Did you really kill Andreas?"

Giovanni took a deep, calming breath and pulled his fire back further. "Yes."

The vampire arched a black eyebrow. "And Ziri sent you?"

He took a deep breath and nodded. "Are you Arosh?"

Giovanni felt a fluttering wind behind him, and a vampire came to light behind the ancient one. The silent immortal crouched down and eyed him with a feral gaze. The fire vampire reached down and petted the wind vampire's head as he would a beloved pet, and he calmed. Then the vampire looked at Giovanni, and his mouth turned up at the corner.

"Some have called me Arosh, but I am known by many names."

"I seek Arosh, ancient king of the East, friend of Ziri of Numidia, and friend of Geber, the alchemist."

There was a flicker in the old one's eyes. "Geber, you say?"

"Are you the Arosh I seek?"

"I am." Arosh craned his neck to look over Giovanni's shoulder. "You may come out, holy man."

Giovanni heard Carwyn call out, "Is the posturing done?"

Arosh looked amused. "Yes, for now."

"Good." Giovanni heard Carwyn stride toward them, packs clutched in his hands and wine tucked under his arm. "And, strictly speaking, I'm not a holy man anymore. But I do have wine."

A smile broke over Arosh's fearsome face. "Wine, my friend, is always welcome. I think I will like you. What is your name?"

"Carwyn ap Bryn. Son of Maelona of Gwynedd, daughter of Brennus the Celt."

"You are well met, Carwyn ap Bryn. And you, Giovanni Vecchio, if you are who you both say. Come with me, my son will follow us." He motioned to the wind vampire, who took to the air and circled above them. "I hope you brought no men with you," Arosh said, "or Samson will kill them."

Carwyn and Giovanni exchanged a cautious look. "We are alone."

"Good. He doesn't harm the girls, but he's been trained to kill the men."

"Understood. It's just us."

They walked up the mountain, their host skipping over rocks and rubble as he climbed. Arosh made no pretense of human speed, so they didn't either. As they crested the summit, Giovanni could see a house in the distance. As they approached, they were met with a square tower surrounded by a lavish estate. Lush trees surrounded the home, and Giovanni could hear laughter and music coming from inside. The grounds were lit with torches and gravel paths ran through neat gardens. He could hear a fountain burbling somewhere and a murmur of female voices.

Their host yelled out, "Nothing to fear, my jewels."

Suddenly, a bevy of women poured out of the fortress, tumbling and laughing over each other in their rush to greet Arosh. They gathered around him, nubile teenagers and lush women of all ages, all stroking his arms and hair as he walked into the house. He pulled them along, kissing their eager mouths and running his fingers through their hair as they made their way into the glowing home.

Giovanni and Carwyn both stood, gaping at the vicious fire vampire surrounded by the crowd of women. Samson, the silent wind vampire, landed behind them, cocking his head when they stared. He held out a hand and motioned them toward the house. They followed cautiously, and Giovanni's eyes roamed the lavish house and the girls who came out to greet them, grabbing their hands to lead them into the house with cheerful smiles.

"Gio?"

"I'm as confused as you are, Father."

"Why do I feel like we just found the vampire version of the Playboy Mansion?"

"Because I'm fairly sure we did."

CHAPTER TWENTY-THREE

Rome, Italy
October 2012

"Wow, look. It's another priceless and culturally significant work of art."

"Stop with your gushing enthusiasm. It's embarrassing to walk next to you."

"You're the one letting yourself go."

Dez turned and slapped Ben's shoulder as they strolled through the Galleria Borghese.

"Shut up, you brat. I'm pregnant."

"You may blame the baby, Dez, but I'm pretty sure the gelato has something to do with it, too."

He laughed and ducked away as she swung her purse at him. The gallery was mostly deserted that Thursday afternoon, the summer crowds had dissipated to nothing, and the damp weather was making their usual stroll through the villa gardens less than attractive, so they had decided to take in the collection of paintings.

"I'm kidding! Sheesh, I'm kidding. You know you're gorgeous. I'd still steal you from Matt if I thought I could get away with it." Ben winked and threw an arm around her slender shoulders as she pretended to pout.

"You're mean, Benjamin Vecchio."

"Yeah, but I'm cute, too." He kissed the top of her head as they continued to walk. "And you really are beautiful."

The smile spread across her face as she beamed.

"Are you missing school?"

He snorted. "What do you think?"

She laughed a little. "Are you missing your girlfriends?"

"Well, probably not as much as I should be. You know what I really miss?"

"Basketball?"

"Besides basketball, that's a given."

"What?"

"Getting my license." He groaned. "I can't believe I'm finally sixteen and in a foreign country where I can't even drive."

"Aw, Benny." She hugged his waist a little. "Maybe Gio will get you a Ferrari for all your hard work."

"Oh, that's *so* likely! Why don't you suggest that to him when he gets back?"

They both fell silent after that. It was a subject they tried not to bring up. After the last communication from Istanbul, no one had heard from his uncle or Carwyn in over three weeks. Ben's world felt like it was balanced on a very thin edge. He could only imagine how Beatrice felt.

"I will," Dez said quietly. "As soon as he's back, I'll tell him how helpful you've been. You're a first-rate hacker."

"Shhh. Don't tell B that I'm better than her now. It'll hurt her feelings."

"Your secret is safe with me."

Dez and Ben had spent weeks sifting through all the information on the hard drive from the Bulgarian plant. Then they'd systematically been going through all the public records of Livia's companies. It was a good thing that Italian seemed to come so easily to Ben. Between his knowledge of Spanish, which he'd taught himself to read as a child, and his Latin education with Giovanni, he had picked up a working knowledge of Italian within weeks of arriving in Rome. In the six months they'd been there, his fluency had only grown. He and Dez had been a vital part of discovering Livia's holdings and assets. They were still tracing the money that had funded the cosmetics factory, but so far, the Roman noblewoman seemed to be the only immortal with a concrete tie to the place, which was both frustrating and reassuring.

"You know," he said. "I was thinking about that German corporation we found that she funneled money through last April, if we could—"

"Hey, this is supposed to be our non-work time, mister."

"I know, I'm just…"

"What?"

He stopped in front of what looked like a Renaissance era oil painting on wood. "Bored," he said. "I'm really, *really* bored."

"I know the computer work isn't exactly the most thrilling, but—"

"Maybe if Matt would let me, you know, help with some other stuff."

Dez cocked a skeptical eyebrow in his direction. "Ben, not even *I* know most of what Matt does. He gets information in… slightly less orthodox ways, you know? I don't think you want to get mixed up in any of that."

But he did. He stared at the painting of the men carrying the body of Jesus to his tomb. He glanced at the small plaque. Rafael. Then he looked more closely at the painting.

"Hey, Dez?" He cocked his head and leaned forward. "Is that..."

Her eyes were narrowed at the painting, too. "Looks kind of like..."

"Emil Conti?"

"That's what I was thinking, too."

They exchanged a glance and stepped back.

"Dez, our lives are really weird."

"And you're bored anyway."

"What can I say? I have a high tolerance for weirdness."

They had detoured down a street near the train station to check out a bookstore that catered to English speaking tourists later that afternoon. Both were sorting through their finds when the scooter almost knocked Dez over.

"Hey!" Ben shouted at the driver in Italian. "Watch where you're going!" The driver didn't turn around or even notice them. Ben turned back to Dez. "You okay?"

She was staring at the retreating man on the scooter with a frown on her face. "Yeah... yeah, I'm fine."

"What's the look?"

"That driver."

"What about him? He was an asshole." Ben took the bag from her hand and helped her back onto the narrow sidewalk.

"No, not the driver, exactly. The uniform. I recognize—that's the service she uses!"

"What?" Ben shook his head and wondered how fast they could leave the somewhat rough streets of the Termini neighborhood. "Who?"

"Livia. I've been wondering—you know how Gio and Carwyn joke about how she'll only send stuff by uniformed messenger? Well, it's kind of true. Back when they were getting invitations and stuff from her—when we first got here—I noticed that they never came in the mail. They always came by delivery. Even that crazy dress she sent for B, it was the same uniform that guy had. That must be the company she uses."

Ben looked around, scanning the shops along the Via Marsala and wondering how fast they could walk back to the house. Even though the area was improving, Dez was still dressed far too nicely to go unnoticed by the dark, familiar eyes of the pickpockets and thieves that trolled the neighborhood. He looked around and wondered if he should just call for a cab.

"Let's go check out the shop!"

His head jerked around. "What?"

"The shop! Look." She pointed down the street. "I can see those same scooters, a whole bunch of them, down there in front of that shop. Let's just go hang out for a while. If we watch, maybe we'll recognize someone. Maybe she uses the same couriers and stuff. It sounds like something she'd do."

He felt a nervous twinge in the bottom of his stomach. "Dez, I don't really think—"

"Come on." She tugged his arm. "We're just going to go watch it for a while. Didn't you say you were bored?"

He was, but watching a messenger service that was used by Livia, all while Dez was with him, wasn't exactly what he had in mind. She was already walking toward the shop.

"Dez!"

She didn't turn around, and Ben had to hustle to catch up with the petite blonde, all the while cutting his eyes at the men who watched her as she passed. He strode quickly to catch up with her, but refused to run. Dez was already attracting too much attention. Finally, his long legs reached her and he pulled her arm, tucking her a little behind him while he slipped his hand in his pocket and hooked a finger in his waistband, flicking the handle of the knife he carried. He saw a scrawny thief's eyes dart to his, then down to his hand before he turned away, looking for an easier mark.

"Let's just walk a little slower, okay? Try not to shout, 'I'm a rich tourist' at the top of your lungs."

She just looked confused. "I wasn't saying anything."

"Yes, you were."

He took her arm and they walked closer to the shop. A group of men sat in chairs outside as young couriers darted in and out of the storefront. Judging from their posture, Ben thought they wore weapons. He sighed and looked farther up the street, spotting a small café that looked like it catered to backpackers. It had an outdoor seating area and a few tourists were sitting around, drinking coffee.

"Dez, if you're determined to watch the place, let's go up here."

"Where?"

"That café."

She squinted. "We won't be able to see much from—"

"We'll see enough."

The tension in his stomach was growing as they walked opposite the shop. Ben tried to distract her, but he could tell the men in front of the shop had noticed Dez's eyes on them. Still, he didn't want to draw more attention to either of them by telling her to not be so obviously curious. They took a seat at one of the small tables and Ben asked Dez to go grab two drinks.

"Big ones. American coffees so we'll be here a while."

"Okay!" She was so damn cheerful it almost killed him. He sat down in the chair that had the best angle to observe the shop. It seemed to do a brisk business, and he could hear the phone ringing from inside all the way up the narrow street. The men in front glanced over at them a few times before they returned to their coffees and papers. A few of them talked on cell phones and their eyes darted around the street. Dez finally came out carrying a plain, black coffee for him and some sweet concoction for herself. He wondered if she'd had to instruct the barista how to make the drink. No doubt she had, by the friendly wave she gave someone through the window.

"They have decaf here!"

He couldn't help but smile. "Cool."

"I know, right?"

"Good for the baby and less likely to get you completely wound up." Dez on a caffeine high was truly something to behold.

"Now, what can we—" She began to turn around to look at the shop, and Ben grabbed her arm.

"Don't."

"But I can't see."

"Well, I can, so you'll just have to put up with my eyes."

"But I'm the one that's seen the messengers! And if there's one I recognize, we could follow him or something."

"That sounds like a spectacularly bad idea that Matt would kill me for letting you do."

She grimaced. "He's not the boss of me, Ben. Come on. It's daylight! It's not like any of the really bad guys are even up."

"I'm not worried about the *really* bad guys. Just the normal, everyday ones are enough to handle, thanks."

He sipped his coffee and watched the shop. Ben had skirted the edge of violence for most of his childhood. When he was younger, he'd picked the pocket of the wrong type of mark more than once. He was good at running away; he was better at avoiding a fight in the first place. As he'd gotten older, he'd learned how to spot the bullies he could handle and the ones he wanted to avoid. Dez, apparently, had not. He cursed under his breath as she tried to sneak a surreptitious glance at the shop. Her eyes followed every scooter that went up the street.

"Okay, that's it." He stood and finished his coffee in one gulp. He grabbed the bag of books and held his hand out for Dez. "We're going."

"What?" She looked over her shoulder again, drawing the attention of the men in front of the shop. "But we—"

He pulled her up and tugged her close. "You're attracting too much attention," he muttered. "We need to *go*."

"Oh." She looked embarrassed, and Ben felt bad for the harsh whisper. "Sorry, I… sorry."

"It's fine." He scanned the street. *Damn.* He wasn't as familiar with this neighborhood, but the street they were on looked fairly busy. He didn't want to walk back past the shop and draw more attention, so he took Dez's hand and walked farther up, hoping to catch a cross street that would lead them back to something more familiar.

"Ben, I'm sorry."

He didn't stop. "It's fine."

"No, really, I—"

"We just need to get back to the..." He heard the heavy steps echo along the narrow road, but he kept walking.

"Should we go back to the train station?"

In retrospect, they probably should have. The street, which seemed busy near the café, was slowly growing more deserted. The few shops they passed seemed to be closed for the afternoon. The rain started picking up again and small puddles formed in between the cobblestones.

"Ben, should we..." Dez trailed off, and her eyes widened. Ben knew she was also hearing the steady footsteps behind them. He risked a glance over his shoulder to see who was following. It was two men from the front of the shop. Both were wearing loose jackets that blocked the rain and probably concealed guns, too.

Shit, shit, shit. They were following them for sure, and Ben wasn't familiar enough with the neighborhood to plan a good escape, especially considering that the street they were walking up was becoming narrower and more deserted with every block.

"Ben?" Her voice was frightened.

Not good, Dez. Don't sound scared when they can hear us.

He took a chance and turned right by a closed shop, only to find a dead end.

Shit.

"Hey!" He heard one of the men call from behind them in Italian. "Boy!"

Ben turned and plastered on his most innocent smile when he replied in English. "Hey, do you guys know how to get back to the train station? My friend and I got kind of lost."

Dez picked up the theme. "Yeah, we just stopped for coffee, and I told him this would be a short-cut." She forced out a laugh. "Oops! We're still getting to know the streets here, and..."

The men were still approaching, but one of them was speaking quietly on a mobile phone. His eyes narrowed at Ben and he pulled his partner closer.

"Il ragazzo Vecchio," one said in the other's ear.

"E la donna?"

"La amica di la Americana."

'A friend of the American woman.' Well, Ben thought, at least they knew it was definitely one of Livia's shops. Someone must have taken pictures, or there were cameras he hadn't seen. More troubling, they knew who he and Dez were. His eyes immediately scanned the narrow alley they found themselves in. There was a fence behind them, but there was no way Dez would be able to jump over it. The men were blocking the exit, and

they were still speaking and gesturing. Unfortunately, the one on the phone was also slipping his hand in his pocket.

His senses triggered, Ben quickly skimmed through his options. They didn't look like they wanted to kill them, but those fingers dancing in the man's pocket were making him nervous. Very nervous.

"Just scare them," he heard one say in quiet Italian. "He says to rough them up a little. Send a message to the American woman."

"*Si?*"

Ben whispered to Dez under his breath. "When you see an opening, run back to the train station as fast as you can. Do not argue with me. Just run straight to the police." The man had slipped his hand in his pocket again and was looking at Dez with a smirk.

She whispered frantically, "But Ben—"

Ben sprang on the unsuspecting man, looking at Dez before she could finish her protest.

"Dez, run!"

His fingers slipped in the man's pocket and pulled out the gun, tossing it as far as he could down the street before the man twisted around and slugged him in the gut. Ben stumbled back and the man kicked his knee, sending him to the ground.

"Ben!" Dez hesitated for only a second before she ran toward the mouth of the alley.

He saw the other man moving toward her; luckily, he didn't look like he was pulling out any weapons. Just as Dez was about to slip past him, her heel caught in one of the cracked cobblestones that lined the street and the other man caught her arm and dragged her closer as Ben watched helplessly from the ground. The thug drew his hand back, punched the small woman in the face, and Dez crumbled to the ground.

Ben barely registered the pain in his stomach when his attacker kicked him. His eyes were trained on Dez, the swell of her belly where the baby grew, and the man whose foot was drawing back to strike her. His uncle's voice whispered in the back of his mind.

'Protect Dez.'

He blinked once and rolled to the side as Dez curled her body to protect herself and her unborn child. Ben grunted when his attacker's foot met his knee; then he deflected the blow and reached into his waistband, pulling out his hunting knife. In one swift stroke, he reached up and sliced the back of the man's knee, severing the tendons and causing the man to fall over him in pain.

'Neutralize the immediate danger.'

Ben blinked and shoved the knife into the man's stomach as he pushed the heavy body to the side. He didn't hear the curses of the man he had stabbed. The wet suck of the blade was the only sound he heard as he came up to a crouch and rushed toward the other man who was kicking Dez as she lay helpless on the ground.

'Do not *hesitate.'*

He blinked again and reached around the man's heavy body with the knife. Just as Dez's attacker began to turn, he struck. Once. *Suck.* Twice. The blade entered the man's soft abdomen, angling up under his ribs between the muscles exactly where Giovanni had showed him. Ben gave a quick twist of the knife when his hand met flesh, and he could feel the spurt of warm blood as he severed the artery he'd aimed for.

'Never leave your weapon.'

Ben pulled the knife out and kicked the man to the side. The first man he had stabbed lay cursing on the ground. The man who had been kicking Dez and the baby said nothing. A growing pool of blood leaked out of him and into the cobblestones that paved the street. The rain fell harder, and a rivulet of blood joined the small stream that flowed down the middle of the alley. Ben blinked again and tucked the knife into his waistband before he knelt and picked up the wounded woman.

Dez was moaning and her face was bleeding.

"The baby," she mumbled. "He kicked the baby."

"Hang on. I'm going to get us out of here."

Ben had no idea how he carried her. He didn't remember leaving the dead-end street or which direction he turned. He paid no attention to the pain in his knee or the strain in his arms. But he felt the warm blood soak his arm when Dez began bleeding between her legs, and he felt the warm tears that fell from her bruised face to stain his shirt.

The moment he came within sight of the train station, he started yelling at the dark blue coats of the police who stood at attention near the doors.

"*Help her!* She needs a hospital! She's pregnant and she's bleeding!" He wasn't sure whether he was speaking English or Italian, but he could hear the sharp cries of the men who rushed toward them. They grabbed Dez from his arms and laid her gently on the ground. A radio began to squawk in the background as he knelt beside her.

"Hold on, Dez. It's gonna be okay."

She looked up at Ben, holding her stomach as tears fell from eyes that were quickly turning black from the bruising. "The baby…"

"They're calling for an ambulance right now, okay?" His hand stroked her cheek, and he cringed when he saw the smear of blood his fingers left.

"Call Matt. You need to call Matt right now."

He nodded and tried to reach for her fingers, but rough hands pulled him away.

"Ben?" Dez looked around in alarm, but Ben could see the paramedics running toward her as the police began shouting and searching his pockets.

"It's okay, Dez. It's gonna be okay. Just give the doctors Matt's number, okay?"

"What's going on?" She looked around and tried to grab the coat of one of the police who hovered over her. "Stop them! He's the one who saved me. He kept the men—"

"Dez!" She looked to Ben and he gave a sharp shake of his head. "Don't worry about me. Just call Matt!"

Tears continued to streak down her face, but she nodded. Ben could see the gentle hands of the paramedics lifting her up as they secured his wrists behind his back and shoved him into the small police car.

CHAPTER TWENTY-FOUR

Rome, Italy
October 2012

"And your friend, she is stable?" Beatrice could tell that Emil was trying to be soothing over the phone. She could also tell he was angry.

Not as angry as Beatrice.

She spoke around fully elongated fangs. "She appears to be. She is in the hospital right now. Her husband called just a few minutes ago. The bleeding has stopped and they have her under observation."

"That is welcome news."

She paced the library, barking at the speakerphone and willing the sun to set faster. "She's pregnant, Emil. She's *pregnant,* and they attacked her. Her husband said that they aimed kicks at her stomach. There was—" She choked on her own rage. "'Extensive bruising.'"

There was a grim silence. "But the baby is fine?"

"They're monitoring both of them."

She could hear him take a breath. "Beatrice, I am glad that your friend is being cared for. If you have any concerns about human doctors or the hospital, you need only call my people. It pains me that she was not able to walk the streets of my city in safety. I hope you know... this *will* be dealt with, I assure you."

She picked up a vase and threw it into the fireplace, reveling in the crash. "You bet your ass it's going to be dealt with, Emil!"

There was a long pause over the line before he spoke in a cool voice. "I'm going to ask something of you, and you're not going to like it."

Her fangs cut her lower lip. "What?"

"I want you to stay away from the castle tonight."

Her jaw dropped. *"What?"*

"I know what you are feeling now. I know someone has attacked a valued member of your household, but I am asking you to stay away." Beatrice tried to quell the roaring in her ears so she could listen to Emil's crisp voice. "I can turn this against her, Beatrice. Donatella is furious. I am in shock that she would go to this extreme. This was very foolish of Livia, and I can use this to paint her in a very bad light, but *not* if the court is focused on your reaction."

"I want that bitch to die!" Beatrice screamed across the room. "I will kill her for this!"

Emil's voice was suddenly hard and sharp. "And that would be very foolish. You know this."

She closed her eyes and tried to calm herself and focus on more than her own rage.

Matt had been frantic, but Angela had called from the hospital to let her know that Dez was awake and talking. She had told the police the details of the attack, which brought Beatrice back to the reason she had called Emil in the first place. He was still speaking.

"Stay in the city tonight. Take care of your friend. Let me bring this in front of the court without the distraction of your rivalry with Livia. The vampires of Rome know better than to attack tourists. It is bad for everyone and risks exposing us all."

"Do you think she even cares about that anymore?"

"I do not know. That, in itself, is disturbing." Emil paused again. "This will look very bad for her, but you must stay in the city and let the focus shift to her and her actions. Or Lorenzo's. I think this sounds more like him than her. He has proven himself to be quite rash. Let me take care of this. Do you agree?"

She took a deep breath and tried to think about taking care of her family. "Fine."

"Is there anything else I can do? Any help my human staff can give you right now?"

"Yes. My nephew was arrested. He speaks some Italian, but we've told him never to talk to the police. Matt would usually take care of it, but—"

"Your head of security must take care of his wife. Let me handle this. The police will be no problem. What is the boy's name?"

Her heart ached when she thought about Ben. Dez said she thought he might have killed one of the men. She said he had stabbed both to protect her. "His name is Ben. Benjamin Vecchio. He's only sixteen, Emil. He was protecting her, and he was... he was covered in blood, so the police thought—"

"Do not concern yourself. He will be out of police custody in a matter of hours at the most. I'll have my men take him to the hospital."

She closed her eyes in relief. "Thank you. I will—*we* will owe you a favor."

"And I'll be sure to collect when the time is appropriate, which is not now. This attack has the potential to expose all of us to scrutiny. Let my people take care of this. I will call you when I know more."

"Thank you."

"Good-bye, Beatrice. Be well."

She hung up the phone and sat on the couch. It was late afternoon and the house that was usually filled with life was utterly and completely silent. No Dez. No Ben. Matt was at the hospital with Angela. Tenzin was wherever the Chinese delegation was staying. Ziri was... somewhere. Lucien was sleeping, completely unaware of what had transpired only hours before. It would be hours before the sun set.

She took advantage of the empty house and screamed at the top of her lungs. Beatrice wanted her husband. She wanted her friends. And she was completely cut off from the outside world as she waited for a call back from Emil with news about Ben.

She was tempted to walk down to the basement so she could punch the stone walls, but there were no phone connections there.

So she sat. She paced. She glared at the thin line of light she could see around the heavy shutters that covered the windows. She ached with rage and frustration. She suddenly remembered something Lucien had talked about just the day before.

"I think I offended God."

Beatrice had frowned. "What? How?"

"By drinking from Rada. Trying to conquer the bloodlust."

"How would that offend God?"

"Perhaps we are meant to struggle against it. Perhaps..."

"What?"

"There is a price, isn't there? There has to be. Strength. Immortality. Wisdom... it must have a price."

"What kind of god would demand a price of blood?"

"It is not blood He demands. It is humility. The knowledge that even as powerful as we are, we will never be gods."

As powerful as they were...

Beatrice didn't feel powerful. She felt helpless.

The phone rang.

"Yes?"

"Your nephew will be on his way to the hospital shortly. They were trying to interrogate him, but he refused to speak. That is a very clever boy you have. And very skilled. It appears he took out two of Livia's human staff. They found one of the men dead at the scene. The other my people are attempting to track down. There was an impressive amount of blood in the alley. The police were trying to contact the U.S. Embassy when my contact intervened."

So, Ben *had* killed one of their attackers. Possibly both. The thought both satisfied and pained her at the same time. "Who do we need to pay, Emil? I want this to disappear."

She heard him give a quiet laugh. "Don't be absurd. It is my responsibility that the boy had to use force to defend himself on our streets. Do not think of repaying me with money."

"You're not responsible for everything that happens on the streets of Rome."

There was silence over the line. "Not yet, anyway."

"Thank you."

"Stay away from the castle tonight. Take care of your people. I will have my head of security coordinate with Mr. Kirby regarding his wife's protection."

"I won't forget this."

"Neither will I."

He hung up the phone and Beatrice immediately dialed the number Tenzin had given her weeks before. She hadn't wanted to call until she had more information. A polite voice answered in Mandarin, and she asked for her friend. She heard a rustling as the phone was switched to the echoing quality of the speakerphone.

"Who is calling me?"

"It's me, Tenzin."

There was a long pause. "What is wrong? What has happened?"

Beatrice blinked back tears. "Um... Dez and Ben were attacked today. Ben killed one, maybe both, of the men that attacked them, but Dez is in the hospital. The doctors say she's stable."

"What does that mean? Dez is all right? What about the baby?"

"Stable means she's not bleeding anymore. It looks like the baby's going to be okay. I don't know that much, but—"

"Where is Benjamin?"

She cleared her throat. "I contacted Emil Conti's people. He's out of police custody now and on the way to the hospital."

There was a long silence on the phone.

"He killed one of the men who attacked them?"

"Yes. Maybe... maybe both. There was a lot of blood at the scene and —"

"Where was it?"

She frowned. "Where?"

"Yes! Where did this happen?"

"Near the train station. Why—"

"I will take care of this. I'll find you at the hospital later."

And Tenzin hung up the phone.

Beatrice arrived at the hospital a half an hour after the sun set. She struggled to control her fangs amidst the smell of blood that permeated the building. The sour antiseptic smell helped. Dez had been put in a private room at Matt's insistence, and she could see two armed guards standing outside. They were probably Emil's men. They nodded at her respectfully as she entered the room.

There were lines and IVs and monitors beeping, but her friend was smiling and flowers filled the room. Matt was sitting next to her, looking quietly furious and Dez was patting his hand and speaking in a low voice. She turned when Beatrice entered.

"B, I'm fine. Look." She pointed to the monitors. "The baby's fine. Told you growing a human was my superpower. I must have a uterus of steel. And the doctors have been awesome. And both my heroes are with me now. No one is allowed to freak out."

Beatrice had barely noticed a pale Ben sitting in a corner of the room. He lifted his hand in a small wave, but didn't attempt a smile. He was staring at Dez like there was no one else in the room.

She halted and pushed back the bloody tears of relief she couldn't let herself cry. "You're awesome, Dez. I've told you a thousand times."

"Good." The small woman in the hospital bed looked around the room with a glare. "Now tell everyone to take a chill pill and let me sleep. And this is no one's fault but my own. Ben warned me it was a bad idea, and I went ahead anyway."

Matt growled at her. "Dez—"

"Don't even start again. I know you're pissed at me and everyone is freaked out, but I'm fine." She looked around the room at all of them. "I am fine. The baby's fine. And if I'm going to have to sit my ass in a hospital bed for the next month or so, at least I'm in Italy. I'm betting the hospital food is way better here."

"Dez, I just..." Beatrice gave up and walked over to her best friend, being careful not to jostle the network of wires and tubes that were attached to her. "I was so scared for you," she whispered.

Matt spoke in a low voice. "Beatrice, I want to talk to you."

She sniffed and wiped her eyes with the handkerchief in her pocket. "Right."

"In the hall. Ben?" Matt stood and pointed to the chair he was vacating. Ben jumped up and went to sit beside Dez. Matt patted Ben on the shoulder before he walked out of the room.

Dez looked at her with worried eyes. "Don't be mad at each other. He was really worried, B. He was pretty frantic."

"I deserve anything he throws at me." She patted Dez's hand and stood.

Matt was pacing in a small waiting room down the hall. He didn't even glance up when she entered.

"If she didn't have to be in the hospital for the next month, I'd have her ass on a plane and out of here so fast your head would spin, Beatrice De Novo."

"I know. I would, too."

"*Don't!*" He spun on her. "I know she's your friend, but that is my *wife*! Do you understand me? My wife and my child and no amount of money or friendship or loyalty is worth the kind of hell that she has been put through, no matter how much she's trying to play the cheerful fucking patient right now!"

"Matt, I know. I would never, *ever* put her or the baby in danger. You know this."

He kept pacing, glaring at the ground. "Conti's people are on her until the baby is born. After the baby is here and the doctor gives the okay to travel, we are out of here. I don't care what you need or where Giovanni is. Do you get that, B? We're out of here. She is my priority, and I will *not* have her in danger again. Thank God Ben was there. And just so you know, when we go, I'm taking him, too. He doesn't need to get mixed up in this any more than he is. He already... he had to—"

"*I know.*" She walked toward him. "You're not getting any arguments from me, Matt. I wish we'd sent all of you back weeks ago."

He was still pacing, but she could see his reason returning. "Conti knows what happened? I'm assuming, since his men brought Ben back and his people have been stationed out there for the last few hours. His human security guy left me a message, but I haven't called him back yet."

"He knows. And Tenzin knows. I called them both. They all know how much Dez means to me. How important she is."

Matt paused in his pacing and looked up at her. His arms were still crossed, but she saw the anguish in his eyes.

"She's my life, B. She's *everything*. I can't... Nothing can happen to her, do you get that?"

Beatrice nodded and walked over to him. Finally, he reached his arms out and embraced her.

"I get it, Matt. Trust me, I get it."

Ben watched over Dez as she drifted to sleep. The nurse had just come in to give her some medicine that was supposed to kill the pain. The goons at the door had checked over the nurse's badge like they were the Secret Service or something. He thought that was good.

The doctors all said she was going to be fine, but Ben still watched all the monitors and took note of any unusual jump or extra beep. He had liked hearing the tiny thrum of the baby's heartbeat when they brought in the machine to check. It sounded kind of fast to him, but it made Dez smile, so he thought that fast was probably okay. Her face was swollen and both of her eyes were black. She was all covered up, but he knew she had bruises on her legs, abdomen, and even her chest. It made him sick to even think about it.

He heard a rustling sound in the hall, then the goons started to block the door.

"Get away from me. I'm with them, you idiots."

It was Tenzin. He walked to the door and put a hand up on one of the guard's broad shoulders.

"It's okay, guys. She's with us."

They parted to let her pass, and Tenzin stomped in the room.

"Idiots."

"Calm down. They're just guarding Dez. That's what they're supposed to do."

She looked around with narrowed eyes. "I've never been in a hospital before."

"What, never?"

"No."

Tenzin walked over to the sleeping Dez and put her hand on her forehead. Then she pushed back the blanket that covered her and laid her ear against Dez's belly, dislodging some of the monitors. Ben rushed over.

"Hey! Tenzin, that's—"

"Shhh." She put both hands on Dez's belly and held them there for a minute, listening to whatever mysterious sounds the baby was making. Then she straightened and pulled the blanket up.

"I'll let the healers put the electrical equipment back. She's going to be fine. The baby sounds active and her heart is good. Does she have any cuts that need healing?"

"No. Matt said... well, she has to be here for a while, so it's probably not a good idea to heal anything they would really notice. None of her cuts were major. Just scrapes from the street and stuff." He fell silent and went back to his chair beside Dez. Tenzin pulled a chair over and sat next to him.

She said, "I went to the alley."

Ben couldn't say anything. The police had told him. They'd told him he'd killed a man. In his heart, he'd known it the second the knife plunged in the man's belly. He'd meant to kill him, and he knew exactly what he was aiming for.

"I tracked the other man who attacked you both. It's been taken care of."

He nodded. Was he a bad person for being relieved that Tenzin had finished off the other man instead of him? He felt frozen. He didn't know how to feel. He shouldn't have taken them into that alley. He shouldn't have done a lot of things. Dez might not have known better, but he should have. He stared at the monitors above Dez's head.

Tenzin's voice was uncharacteristically soft when she finally spoke. "Was this the first?"

The first person he'd ever killed? Ben nodded.

He was familiar with violence. It had been a constant, lurking shadow his whole life. Ben had seen a lot. He'd watched a man kick another to death and leave him broken in an alley. He'd seen a gloating man stabbed, his blood spilling out in the mud as the money was stolen from his body by greedy hands. But Ben had never killed anyone.

"Ben?"

He whispered, "Yeah?"

"Was the man attacking Dez?"

He nodded.

"Was he hurting the baby?"

"He..." He swallowed the lump in his throat. "He was kicking her. He had to see she was pregnant. Her shirt was up, and her belly... He couldn't have—"

"You were defending Dez. You were protecting the baby."

He blinked back the tears, but they fell down his face anyway.

Tenzin slipped her hand in his, and Ben gripped her small fingers.

"You did well, Benjamin. You did right."

Ben held on to Tenzin's hand, and the two sat in silence as Dez slept under their watch.

CHAPTER TWENTY-FIVE

Svaneti, Republic of Georgia
November 2012

Giovanni decided that the home of Arosh—which could only be described as a palace—was an odd, but not uncomfortable combination of museum and harem. Silks and tapestries hung from the windowless walls. The rooms were lit by golden oil lamps and heated by glowing braziers. The rooms they had been shown to when they arrived were equipped with luxurious baths and opulent furnishings. The only electricity in the palace seemed to be in the bedrooms, a nod to the humans who occupied most of the rooms.

And by humans, Giovanni meant women. Dozens of them. Hundreds, possibly. Women of every age, shape, and color ran laughing through the house. They cooked Giovanni and Carwyn rich meals and offered their willing wrists for the vampires to drink. They tended the house and the gardens. They read books in the vast library. Many were beautiful, but not all. Some bore the scars of past abuse or injury, but all seemed content. Most appeared to be between seventeen and forty, but a few older women passed them in the halls, as well.

And one woman, a regal beauty named Zarine, ruled the house.

Her accent was Armenian. Her long, black hair curled down her back and her brown eyes were warm and wise. She appeared to be in her fifties or sixties, and she was fiercely protective of her master.

"Doctor Vecchio, are you sure that you will not take sustenance from one of the girls? You have been here for several weeks now. Arosh would be most disappointed that you have not fed properly."

He leaned forward on the silk-wrapped chaise. "And where is our host this evening, if I may ask?"

Zarine's eyes lit with amusement. "He is... occupied this evening."

"He is occupied *every* evening."

"He does not deprive himself. It is not his nature."

Giovanni bit his tongue and glanced at Carwyn, who was sipping wine and frowning at a group of passing women.

As soon as they had arrived at the house, Carwyn had given Arosh the letter from Ziri. The ancient fire vampire had taken it, glanced at the unbroken seal, then promptly disappeared into the palace with a dozen girls.

They hadn't seen him since.

Giovanni and Carwyn had been fed and watered. They had been given luxurious rooms and a tour of the house, which was filled to the brim with ancient treasures from all over the world. Arosh was a collector of all sorts of beautiful things. Art and women just seemed to top the list. There were also many treasures that looked Greek or Minoan in origin, but there was no sign of Kato, the fabled water vampire.

"Zarine, I do not wish to seem ungrateful—"

"Then don't. You are being given the finest hospitality of my master's home. It would be most unfortunate if you were not satisfied with that."

Though her voice and pleasant expression never wavered, he could see the glint of steel in her eyes. Zarine, as much as the silent wind vampire, Samson, was Arosh's most fervent and devoted security.

Carwyn spoke up. "Zarine?"

She turned toward the friendly vampire. "Yes, Carwyn?"

"All the women here... they *do* come willingly, do they not?"

She smiled. "And leave when they wish to. Samson simply alters their memories depending on where they want to go. He's very gifted in that trait. Most are placed with one of my associates in the city if they want to work. Some desire husbands and families. They all receive what they wish. If they wish to leave."

"But many don't."

She shrugged. "These girls... most of them did not have good lives before they came here. Here, they are my master's treasures. His 'jewels.'" She turned as Samson swept silently through the room and toward the front door.

The wind vampire was an enigma. He never spoke, and the Eastern European man had wild, grey eyes. He had been sired young, but his head was covered by an alarming shock of pure silver hair. Arosh called him his child, Zarine looked at him with affection, but the vampire moved through the house like a ghost.

Samson stopped for a moment when a younger girl caught the edge of his cloak. She pulled him down and whispered in his ear. The bruises on her face were still healing and one arm was set in a brace. She had appeared in the house the week before and been enfolded by the women of Arosh's palace. The wounded girl placed a soft kiss on the vampire's pale cheek. Samson gave the girl a slight nod before he disappeared into the black night without a word.

Zarine turned back to her guests with a smile. "As you can see, the girls are not mistreated here. Though, I appreciate your concern."

The earth vampire only shrugged. "I have daughters of my own."

Giovanni broke in. "Why doesn't he speak?"

"Samson?"

He nodded.

"I do not know. He never has in all the time I've been here. He has a tongue." Her eyes danced in amusement. "Of that, I'm quite positive. But I've never heard him speak."

"And what about your master?" asked Carwyn. "Should we expect to see him soon? My friend here is trying to be polite, but that's never been an affliction of mine. I cannot complain about your hospitality, but we really do need to speak with him."

Zarine's eyes softened. "I understand your impatience. Truly. And I know that you have traveled a long way, but Arosh is a king." She shrugged. "He comes and goes as he pleases and currently, he is enjoying the pleasures of his women. He may not appear for days. Or weeks."

Giovanni's eyes widened. "Weeks?"

He tried not to think of his own woman waiting back in Rome. He missed his wife. He missed her teasing voice and her soft touch. He missed waking with her and falling asleep wrapped in her arms. He even missed their arguments. And, he was worried. He couldn't deny it.

A particularly sweet-smelling girl walked past and his fangs lengthened in his mouth. A low growl built at the back of his throat. Arosh carried no stored blood. Why would he? He had a walking, giggling supply running around his palace. Carwyn's voice broke through his hungry reverie.

"Gio, I'm going to hunt tonight. I already let Samson know. There are wolves and bears in the mountains around here. Would you join me?"

Unlike Carwyn, Giovanni's system was not accustomed to subsisting on animal blood alone. He could hunt, but he knew he wouldn't be as strong from animal blood as he would be from just a few drinks of one of the many willing women who surrounded him.

"I..." He looked toward his friend.

Carwyn looked back with understanding before he rose and patted Giovanni on the shoulder. He leaned down and whispered in Latin, "Drink. Make yourself strong. We both need to be strong. She will understand."

Giovanni blinked and pushed back his longing for Beatrice. He nodded to a girl who had offered herself to him the day before.

"Fine. Send her to my room."

Zarine's lips curled into a smile. "Excellent. I hope you enjoy your time with her."

"Just feeding, Zarine."

She shrugged. "The girl will be disappointed, but it is your choice, of course."

He returned to his room, pushing back the flames that danced at his collar. Giovanni wanted to leave this place. He had been battling aggression from the moment he stepped through the door. Arosh's distinctive smell was everywhere, and the scent of burning almond wood filled the rooms. He had never been under the roof of another fire vampire. The only males he had ever met, he had killed or avoided as much as possible. Being around another male triggered the worst of his natural aggression and territorial instincts. He had to constantly fight back the fire that wanted to erupt. Perhaps, as much as he disliked it, feeding would help.

The girl tapped at the door and he clenched his fists to control his hunger.

"Enter."

It was two days later when Arosh finally appeared. He stretched out on a low couch and drew Zarine to his chest, stroking her hair and feeding her an orange he had peeled.

"How has your stay been, my friends?"

Carwyn said, "Clearly not as pleasant as yours."

Arosh threw his head back and laughed. "You amuse me, holy man! I understand your own odd beliefs, but why has the son of Andreas not taken his pleasure with the beauties of my home? I'm sure Zarine has pointed out those who are acceptable."

Giovanni forced back the instinctive curl of his lip and banished the memory of the disappointed girl he had fed from. "I am mated, Arosh."

"And you are faithful?" Arosh's eyes lit in amusement. "How odd."

"Not odd. No woman is appealing when compared to my wife."

Arosh's eyes narrowed for a moment before he smiled. It was the most sincere smile he had seen from the ancient. "Kato would approve of you. He took a number of mates over the centuries and was always very faithful to them when he did."

"Where is my grand-sire?"

Arosh ignored the question. "Your sire, however, did not hold others in such esteem. He had little regard for family. He had little regard for anyone but himself."

"I am aware of this."

"You would be. Tell me, why did you kill him?"

"Wouldn't you have? He had plans for me. I'm sure you can imagine."

"And you wouldn't have defied him."

Giovanni cocked his head. "I'd like to think I would have, but probably not. Could you have ignored your sire?"

Arosh shrugged. "I do not know. My earliest memory is of a fire-scarred cave. There was no one."

Carwyn frowned. "What? No one at all?"

"If there was, the fire burned them." Arosh slipped another piece of orange between Zarine's lips and ran a finger along her cheek. "That is too long ago to matter. All of my children have been sired to wind, so that must have been my own origin. Perhaps he left me. Perhaps he had no interest in my future. Unlike your sire, Giovanni Vecchio. Am I correct?"

"Yes." Giovanni did not let his eyes wander from Arosh's keen gaze. "My father was very... involved."

"I can imagine he was." He sat up and pulled Zarine with him, whispering in her ear that she should leave them. She nodded silently and backed out of the room, closing the doors behind her. Arosh watched her leave, then turned back to them.

"I knew your sire, Giovanni. I did not like him. His own sire didn't like him. Ironically, you seem like the type of child that Kato *would* have wanted. He valued loyalty above all, but had the wisdom to appreciate others and respect them. Kato felt a deep responsibility toward those under his aegis. He was not only feared, but loved. A true ruler must have both."

"I do not want to rule anything. I want only to live my life in peace and protect those who are mine."

"Ah!" Arosh grinned. "You are a wise child. You have learned early what it took Kato and me thousands of years to learn. Peace is a treasure beyond earthly price."

Giovanni took a deep breath. "Where is my grand-sire, Arosh?"

Arosh pulled the letter from his cloak, fingering the broken seal and staring into the fire. "Do you know, Giovanni, I asked your sire for a favor once?"

He and Carwyn exchanged glances, and he threw a careful mask over his face to hide the shock. To most, Arosh's admission would be nothing remarkable, but for a king of legend to admit that he had once asked another immortal for a favor was shocking.

"No, I did not know this. You honored him by ask—"

"He refused."

Giovanni almost choked. To be asked for a favor from a legend like Arosh was awe-inspiring enough. To refuse? *Unthinkable.* Arosh would have owed Andros a favor of his own. A favor from the ancient king was not something to be dismissed. Or refused. Ever.

"I offer my apologies, Arosh. My sire's audacity—"

"Is not your fault!" Arosh only looked amused. "And you have killed him for me, so that is very pleasing." He held up the letter that Ziri had written. "But it appears that you did not kill him on your own. You sired a child. And now you have a problem, Giovanni Vecchio."

He nodded carefully. Now was the time for bargaining. "Yes, we have a problem."

"And Ziri asks me to expose myself and my dearest friend to this annoying vampire in Rome."

"Not for her. To keep the world safe from the—"

"Yes, the elixir." Arosh curled his lip. "I had hoped to never hear about that dreaded concoction again. What a mess."

Carwyn, ever fearless, piped up. "What were you thinking?"

Giovanni was tempted to muzzle the priest, but Arosh only laughed. "It seemed like a good idea at the time, holy man."

"Ah well." Carwyn sat up straighter and looked at the ancient fire vampire with suddenly keen eyes. "I'd very much like to kill the bastard that murdered my son. Or watch someone kill him, I'm not picky. So, if we could get on with it, please?"

"Yes, holy man, let us 'get on with it' as you say." Arosh cocked his head and looked at Giovanni. "I have read Ziri's letter. I know what my friend asks of me, but what about you, Giovanni, son of Andreas?"

The ancient fire vampire wanted something. And though Ziri had already asked for the favor, he wanted Giovanni to ask it as well. That way, a favor would be owed. He had no choice.

"Arosh, I would ask a favor of you."

The dark eyes of the old king lit up. "And I may grant it. We shall see."

Arosh led them down into the mountain and through a twisted maze of passageways that Giovanni couldn't help but think Beatrice would enjoy.

"Kato always liked mazes," Arosh called as he led them forward. "And this one keeps the more curious girls away. I only let a few attend to him, though he's not dangerous to human women."

To human women? Giovanni couldn't help but notice that he and Carwyn didn't fall under that particular category.

They finally exited the maze and were led toward a chamber that reminded Giovanni of an old tomb. The large, stone doors were intricately carved and painted, and a channel of water fell from a hidden stream.

"The cisterns feed the waterfall and the fountains. He can't reside near the sea, but I can keep enough water here to keep him content."

What the hell were they walking into? Arosh pushed the doors open and the three vampires stepped into a large open chamber. The tiled ceiling was held up by richly painted columns and fountains flowed through the room. The walls were bare stone. Cold, but painted with rich murals depicting beautiful scenes of the ocean and sea life. They walked along a bridge that led them toward the sound of soft voices. As they crossed over a long pool, Giovanni spied his father's sire and gasped.

Andros had been right. Ancient peoples had seen this immortal and the legends of Poseidon were born. Kato sat submerged to his chest in a large, Roman-style bath. He stared straight ahead and quiet women circled around him, pouring water over his thickly muscled chest, curling hair, and long beard. His eyes were a deep, sea blue. His hair was the color of bronze. The immortal didn't appear sickly or ill. Kato, the ancient water vampire, looked like a god.

Giovanni heard Arosh shift behind him a moment before Kato moved. It was infinitesimal, a twitch. But suddenly, he was looking into the eyes of his grand-sire and he realized that something was very, very wrong.

The brilliant blue eyes held nothing; they were vacant and wild.

Kato's mouth opened. Long, thick fangs speared behind his lips and in a blink, he had flown out of the water and toward the intruders. Arosh stepped back again, taking Carwyn's arm and pulling him behind his body. A snarl ripped from Kato's throat, and Giovanni could scarcely draw a breath before he was overtaken. Kato grabbed him by the throat and lifted him into the air.

"Gio!"

"Stay back, holy man."

At Kato's touch, the water was drawn from Giovanni's body. He could feel it wicking away as the water vampire drew it out of him. No shield or energy could stop it as Giovanni's skin dried. His lips cracked. It was as if he was a sponge being wrung out by the hands of the old king.

And he was choking. Kato held him up and Giovanni knew that with one squeeze, the hands of this vampire could end him. He had no fire in this watery tomb. The air was too thick with moisture. His dry hands reached up to the iron grip of his grand-sire, but did nothing. It was like pawing at solid rock.

However, just as quickly as Kato had lifted him, the water vampire froze, took a deep breath, and lowered Giovanni to the ground. A soft look stole over the immortal's face, and he pulled Giovanni closer. The iron hand tilted his chin up, and Kato leaned over, placed his face at Giovanni's throat, and inhaled. Then he smiled and lowered his chin. He placed soft hands on his grandchild's shoulders and kissed his forehead.

Giovanni remained motionless. He had no idea what had just happened. Arosh, as if reading his mind, strode over and placed a hand on his ancient rival's shoulder. Kato flinched under his touch, but turned a beatific smile on Arosh, as well.

"You have enough. Excellent. Otherwise you would be dead. Kato smells his blood. He reacts to most strangers like this, which is why your friend should not approach." Arosh was almost whispering, as he placed a hand on Kato's forehead and stroked his friend's hair back with the gentlest of touches. "But you are of his direct line, and he smells his blood in you. This is why you are not in danger. I carry his blood as well, though it is not as strong."

"What has happened to him? What is this?"

"This, son of Andreas, is the result of curing bloodlust. Your grand-sire's amnis is shattered. Barely functioning. His body is as vital as it ever was, but the brilliant mind that was nurtured by the fifth element is broken. He is a creature of instinct now."

Giovanni was reeling. "How is this possible?"

"Come with me, and I will tell you."

CHAPTER TWENTY-SIX

Svaneti, Republic of Georgia
November 2012

"Pride, my friends, is the deadliest of fires. While other flames burn the surface, pride burns from within. It works its way from the heart until it consumes you. And like any fire, it will eat its prey until it is smothered or quenched."

They were sitting in Arosh's private rooms. A low fire burned in an earthen fireplace, and silk-covered couches encircled it. The panels of the ceiling had been drawn back, and the night sky was cold and clear. Smoke drifted up to be carried away by a breeze as Giovanni, Arosh, and Carwyn sat around the fire, drinking the sweet red wine the ancient fire vampire poured.

"My three friends and I were more proud than any other immortals who walked the Earth. We had reason to be. We were kings and queens. Civilizations existed at our pleasure. And in our arrogance, perhaps we forgot..." A smile lifted the corner of Arosh's mouth. "We were not gods."

Giovanni stared at him. "How did it happen?"

"I will go back to the beginning. I do not know all that Ziri has told you. He only wrote that I should answer any questions you had about the elixir."

"How did it come to be? What has it done to my grand-sire?"

Arosh took a sip of wine. "I was the first to reach Kufa at the beginning of the eighth century as the Romans counted, but Kato followed soon after. The city was becoming rich with ideas. Innovation. An interesting atmosphere in a region that hadn't seen such enlightenment for too long. Years later, I was introduced to the alchemist. Jabir was from

Khorasan, a province in Persia where I had kept a home for hundreds of years. I was familiar with his people."

Arosh's dark eyes were amused. "Jabir was so bright for a human. Our discussions quickly progressed to the point where I confided in him my true nature. I suspected he was trustworthy. And if he proved not to be?" Arosh shrugged. "He was easily disposed of. Kato joined us in our discussions soon after I revealed myself. Jabir was enthralled with us both."

Giovanni asked, "What of Ziri and Saba?"

"They arrived years after we did. Ziri already had a home in the area with some distant members of his clan. Saba lived as my wife while we were there. She chafed at the ridiculous restrictions of that culture regarding their women, but tolerated it for us."

"So..." Carwyn cleared his throat. "You and Saba were..."

Arosh smiled. "Saba takes whatever lover she chooses. The four of us have always been close, but she only tolerates me for brief periods." His smile widened. "We are too much alike and value our independence too fiercely."

Giovanni said, "But you were all in Kufa with Geber—Jabir at the end of the eighth century?"

"Yes. The alchemist was doing fascinating experiments regarding the artificial creation of life. Ridiculous premise now, but at the time, it was a serious study. Jabir was the first who saw the possibilities that combining our blood could have."

Carwyn reached for the bottle of wine. "How did he get the idea to begin with?"

"He saw how we healed each other. Kato and Saba had been fighting with daggers one night—she has always had a fondness for them—and Ziri and I were sharing wine with the alchemist. Kato managed to put a slice in Saba's face." Arosh laughed. "She was so irritated with him! Of course, he simply bit his tongue and cleaned the wound for her without a thought. Jabir noticed it and became fascinated."

"With the healing properties?" Carwyn asked.

"Yes. He began interviewing us. Making many notes about us. Our blood. How we healed. How we fed. He asked so many questions. Jabir noted four unique properties of vampire blood. Our blood healed, sustained life, and sated hunger. But it could not be consumed by humans. He tried, and it made him quite ill."

Giovanni held his glass out for more wine, and Arosh filled it. "And he combined the blood?"

"Yes, we already knew that blood of the same element did little to heal a serious injury. The four of us had discovered that through the centuries, but we had never made the connection between that fact and our elemental affinity."

Carwyn's eyes narrowed on Arosh. "What do you mean?"

"Jabir concluded that the dominant element in immortal blood—fire for me, earth for you—is what gives us our strength. To feed our own strength does little to repair our bodies, but to strengthen the other elements within us? *That* is what gave further strength and healing."

Carwyn said, "I'm still not understanding this."

Arosh leaned toward the fire. "Think, holy man! Blood contains all four elements. My blood has the strongest heat, the fire. Yours has the strongest *substance*, that is what enables you to control the earth as you do. Samson's blood connects him to the air. Kato's to the water. I have no need to feed the fire within my blood—"

"Because you are strongest in fire," Giovanni said. "As I am. So to strengthen ourselves, the blood of a different element helps more."

"It is all about *balance*. As much as it may wound our pride, immortals are stronger together, sharing our strength, than we are in isolation."

"Four elements together," Giovanni murmured. "Fire, earth, air, and water. Arosh, Saba, Ziri, and Kato."

Arosh nodded toward him. "Giovanni, Carwyn, Tenzin, and Beatrice."

He was reminded of Zhang's cryptic statement months before. *'Balance, Giovanni Vecchio. Balance is the key.'*

Giovanni looked up. "So, you theorized it would work for healing and, according to Ziri, it did. He found a formula to stabilize the blood for human consumption. How did you make the connection to curing bloodlust?"

"It was my idea. I guessed that if a human was strengthened by this elixir, it was possible that their blood—treated blood—might cure our insatiable hunger."

Carwyn asked, "Did you really care at that point? None of you must have had to feed very often. As ancient as you all are, why did it matter?"

A grim smile crossed Arosh's lips. "Pride."

Giovanni nodded. "As strong as we are, we still need humans. Whatever disdain some may hold for humanity after hundreds or even thousands of years, we all still need them to survive."

"Yes." Arosh's shoulders seemed to droop. "Only a cure for the sun is more greatly desired, but there is no hope of that. Trust me, many have tried. And will continue to try. It will not happen. Whatever god created us designed us to be mortal. The very source of this world's energy will kill us within minutes. Even the oldest immortal cannot avoid this sentence."

Carwyn said, "But you thought you could cure bloodlust?"

Arosh smiled at him, but turned to Giovanni. "You waited long to feed from one of my women. Tell me, my friend, do you and your mate exchange blood?"

Giovanni frowned and answered, "We do."

"And you both feed from humans, as well."

"Yes, but…"

Arosh cocked an eyebrow. "Not as much as before, is it? While you may have needed to feed every week before you took your wife's immortal blood, now you can go several weeks, a month even. How does human blood taste to you now?"

He shrugged. "Pleasant, but weak."

"Not like your mate's blood."

"No, her blood..." Giovanni cleared his throat and tried to rid the longing from his voice. "It is the sweetest wine. Nothing compares to it."

Arosh's eyes danced. "Some of what you say is sentiment, but some is not. Your wife drinks the blood of humans. You drink blood from her. In her blood, both bloods sustain you. But what if that human blood was even more strengthened by this immortal elixir? What then? Could it sustain us even longer? Could it cure us, even?"

Giovanni's eyes narrowed and his energy snapped in the air. "Can it? Ziri said that Kato drank the blood of his human and look what it has done to him. *How did this happen, Arosh?* What did Geber miss? What did *you* miss?"

Arosh's nostrils flared, but just then, a gust of winter wind blew from outside and cooled the room. "We *all* missed it. The elixir worked. It cured the humans—unfortunately, its effects were short-lived."

Carwyn shook his head. "So, even the successful cases that Geber documented—"

"Died. Yes. The effects of the elixir lasted anywhere between two to five years by our best estimates. Then, whatever illness had afflicted the human came back. Stronger than ever."

"Kato's lover?"

Arosh sighed. "Kato had taken blood from Fahdil two years after the elixir was tested and appeared successful. As proud as we all were with ourselves, we were still hesitant to drink from one of the test subjects. But Kato was too attached to this human. When the young man grew ill, it affected him. He gave the elixir to Fahdil and then drank from him. But, though we had reservations, none of us thought it could *really* be harmful. After all, it was only a potion! And made from our own blood. Where could the real danger be?"

Giovanni tensed. "You said something in the room with Kato. You said something about the fifth element. What were you talking about?"

Arosh's dark eyes glistened in the fire. "Something our pride did not see. We were never meant to conquer the bloodlust, son of Andreas. We only looked at what was seen, not that which is unseen. By focusing on the earthly elements, we forget that which *truly* animates us. The energy that sustains our immortality."

It was a whisper on Giovanni's lips. "*Amnis.*"

Arosh's mouth lifted in the corner. "Energy. Current. It has been called many things. Magic. Aether. Your holy man would call it the soul. Others in the East would call it the void, that which is not there, but permeates all things." Arosh stared into the crackling fire. "Whatever you call it, in immortals, it manifests as the energy that animates our bodies." He reached out a hand and tossed the flames higher. "It lets us control our element. It lets us manipulate the thoughts and memories of humankind. It is our weapon. Our shield. And, as I have learned, it preserves our mind. This 'amnis,' as you call it, is the fifth element that we all share. And no elixir can replace it."

"So blood sustains not just our bodies, but our minds and our souls, as well," Carwyn murmured. "And we must draw it from humanity."

Arosh nodded. "Or animals. As many, including you, have learned, the wild things of this world do carry a spark, but it is not as strong. You must drink more often."

"And preservation kills it," Giovanni added. "That is why we grow weak if we drink too much preserved or stored blood."

Arosh nodded again. "We must feed on the *living* to sustain our bodies, but even more importantly, our minds and energy."

"So by killing the bloodlust—"

"We found a way to preserve the body, but the elixir of life cannot preserve or sustain the mind. Though Kato does not grow physically weak, his amnis is almost gone. And that is why he operates on instinct."

Carwyn sat up and leaned forward. "So, when Kato drank from his lover it... what? It *broke* him? It damaged his amnis past the point of repair? Why couldn't he just start drinking human blood again? Wouldn't that have fixed it?"

Arosh shrugged. "He has no desire for it. Any blood he drinks I must force on him. And I do not know why it no longer feeds his amnis when he drinks human blood. Perhaps we may never know, but yes, it has broken his amnis somehow."

Giovanni said, "But his mind isn't completely gone. He did recognize me. He does still have some consciousness."

"He does *now*." Arosh took a deep breath and refilled his glass. "When I first found him, it was not so." He took another sip of wine. "Kato stayed in Kufa with Fahdil long after the rest of us had left. Ziri was the first to leave the city. Saba left. Eventually, I did, as well. I went north to my home in Persia. I did not know about Kato's decline for several years. His energy —his amnis, as you call it—was very strong. It sustained him, but it could not maintain his mind forever. When Fahdil finally contacted me, it was because his own health was failing. The human had protected Kato as well as he could, but he knew he was dying. When I arrived back in Kufa, Fahdil was dead, and Kato had been locked in a windowless room." Arosh frowned at the memory. "I was confused. Why was my friend confined? What chamber could even hold him? When I opened the door, I understood."

Carwyn asked, "What had happened to him?"

Arosh's eyes furrowed in pain. "Kato was crouched in a corner of the room. He *growled* at me, his oldest friend, but then cringed from the sound of his voice. He flew at me like an animal, but fell back in pain when I touched him. It was when I touched him that I realized... His amnis was almost gone. He had no shield from his senses. The slightest gust of air frayed his skin. A whisper hurt his ears. He was as a newborn vampire without any shield. Water was the only thing that soothed him."

"So his blood still connected him to his element..."

"But he had no control of it. Not as he had before."

Carwyn said, "So that is why he stays in the bath."

"Yes. The water still protects him from some of his senses, so he is most comfortable there. Back in Kufa, I immediately sent for Saba. She and I had argued before she left and she was angry with me, but that was typical for us. I wrote her and told her to gather Jabir's notes and come to my home in Persia. She is the oldest of us and the most skilled in healing. I hoped that she would know how to cure him."

"But she didn't?"

He shook his head. "She had some ideas. From the beginning, Saba was most reluctant to drink from the elixired humans, though she never said why. Perhaps some ancient instinct warned her where our reason and intellect did not. We finally realized that Kato's body remained vital, but the human blood we forced on him did nothing for his mind. It was then that we tried our own blood. Since human blood did nothing, we hoped that immortal blood would help heal his mind. After all, Saba and I were both very powerful, very rich in amnis."

"Did it?" Carwyn asked. "If human blood no longer fed his amnis, did vampire blood?"

"It did help some." Arosh nodded. "He was less aggressive and seemed to have some recognition of us. You saw him with Giovanni earlier. It was like that. So, we tried blood of other elements. I tried giving him Samson's blood, but it showed no improvement. I found other vampires. Older ones. I killed them if they refused. Drained them of life in the hopes that it would do something for my friend. It didn't matter. Their blood did nothing. Finally, it was Saba who suggested that it was Kato's own blood in *us* that had helped him the first time."

Giovanni lifted his eyes from the fire. "His own blood?" His eyes darted toward Carwyn's and he could see the expression in his friend's eyes sharpen. "You mean that his own blood *did* revive his amnis? Restart him, in some way? Is his sire—"

"Kato's sire is no more. We suspected, as you do, that the untainted blood that had sired him could heal him. Remake him in some way. It only existed faintly in those he had exchanged with, like Saba and me, but we had one other hope. If his own blood in us could heal him, then the blood of his direct line could, as well."

Carwyn broke in again. "So, since Lucien's amnis is damaged—dying, as it seems it is—if we could find Saba, his mother, he could be healed?"

"I believe he could, yes. Has he tried to contact her?"

"He has, but…" Carwyn shrugged helplessly.

Arosh nodded. "She appears when she wants. I know this better than any other."

"But *Kato* had a son," Giovanni said. "My father. Did he have any other children?"

"None living. Your father was the only living child of his line, and at the time, he had sired no children. His blood would be undiluted and strong. He was our best hope to heal our friend. Kato had cut Andreas off years before, so I was the one who sent for him."

Giovanni let out a measured breath. "So, that is the favor you asked of Andros. His blood."

Arosh leaned forward. "I invited him to my home in Persia. I asked him for this favor. I never dreamed he would refuse. I considered killing him and taking his blood, but who knew if one ingestion would be effective? Saba and I had given Kato our blood many times over a period of months. But your father was unwilling." The ancient leaned back and shook his head. "I should have kept him captive. I thought Kato would regain his strength as time passed, and I didn't want the irritation of Andreas as my captive. He was annoying and rather surprisingly powerful."

"So you took Kato away and asked Ziri and Saba to tell the world you had killed each other."

"The last thing I wanted was Andreas to come back and try to assassinate his father. I wanted to give Kato time. I believed, in my arrogance, that no affliction could weaken my friend for long. After all, he had been as strong as I was! Surely, he would heal."

Carwyn said, "But he didn't."

Arosh cocked his head and stared at the fire. "No, he didn't. I brought him here. I made sure he was safe and left him in Samson's care along with a few trusted humans. When I went back to my home in Persia—this was after the word had spread that we had killed each other—" His eyes lifted to Giovanni's. "My home, particularly my library, had been ransacked."

Giovanni closed his eyes and clenched his hands in anger. "And that is how the book came to my father."

Arosh nodded. "Saba left Jabir's manuscript and notes in my library. I doubt your father had any idea what he took. Maybe he discovered it. Maybe he didn't. He was always a bright child, however detestable his character was."

Giovanni slumped back, exhausted by the revelations. Had his father known? Did it even matter? The damage had been done. The poison had already spread, and Arosh was staring at him.

"So now, Giovanni, son of Andreas, you will ask me for your favor again, and I will tell you what you must give me in exchange."

Giovanni leaned forward and stared through the fire to meet the ancient immortal's gaze. "Arosh, will you expose this truth, and my grandsire, to stop this evil from spreading? Will you take Kato to Rome and show the immortal world the true price of this 'cure?'"

Arosh's gaze was guarded. "You ask me to expose my closest friend, Giovanni Vecchio. You ask me to show the world what he has become. To show them his weakness?"

"To stop this? Yes. I ask you to expose the dangerous secret that you, Kato, Saba, and Ziri hid."

He could feel the heat from the other vampire roll from across the room. "Why do *you* not kill this vampire and take the city? Destroy the book. Destroy those who know of it. Why should I expose my friend to scrutiny? To spare you the inconvenience of battle? I fought many battles I didn't choose because I had to. What makes you above me?"

The flames threatened to burst from his collar, and it was Carwyn who answered while Giovanni fought to maintain his control. "This elixir, Arosh, this *secret*, has been released into the world! Who knows whom Livia has told? Who knows if there have been copies of the book or the formula made? We don't need to just stop the elixir, we need to tell the world the *truth*. Enough secrets! Expose the danger. That is the *only* way it will be stopped."

Giovanni managed to push back his own anger as he rose to his feet. "You have warned us of the dangerous fire of pride. This secret that you and your friends created has remained hidden for too long. Others have been hurt. Killed. Saba's own child has fallen ill from it. Do not let your pride blind you to what must be done to stop this."

Arosh gave him a long, measuring look before he rose. "You are asking this of me?"

His heart gave a quick beat. "I am."

"Then you know what I will want in return."

"Yes."

"Your blood, Giovanni, son of Andreas. Your blood to heal your grandsire. For as long as he needs it. Your blood and the blood of your children. The blood of any and all of Kato's line." His eyes flared, and he stepped through the fire toward Giovanni. "Promise me your blood, and I will grant you your request."

CHAPTER TWENTY-SEVEN

Residenza di Spada, Rome
November 2012

Beatrice had spent most of the day in the bath. The house was quiet. Lucien was sleeping. Gavin and Jean were due back any night with the truck that held the ELIXIR shipment, but it was anyone's guess when they would actually show. Dez remained in the hospital on bed rest per her doctor's orders, so Ben and Matt spent their days there and Beatrice wandered the halls of Giovanni's house with little to do.

She had kept away from Livia, letting Emil take the lead as more and more vampires flooded into Rome. News of the Roman noblewoman's startling announcement had quickly spread through Europe, and the Roman court was suddenly the most active in the Old World. Most European leaders had either sent delegations to Rome to investigate Livia's claims, or had issued statements praising her. Emil Conti could no longer pretend to be impartial. The lone voice of dissent, he had come out weeks before with a strong public statement, warning those who would listen about the unknown dangers of any formula that claimed to cure bloodlust.

Distinct lines were being drawn and, unfortunately for Beatrice, the personal grievance of a young American vampire received little notice to the major players of the European immortal community, no matter what her connections were.

She dabbed at her face with a towel as she walked back into the bedroom and saw Giovanni stretched out on the bed. He reached an arm out as she walked toward him.

"Come. Lay down and try to rest, Tesoro."

She blinked back tears and dropped the towel before she went to lay next to him. "That's it. I've finally lost it, haven't I? I'm hallucinating."

He tucked her into his side and wrapped a warm arm around her. "Hush. You're dreaming."

"Thanks for trying to make me feel better, but I don't really sleep anymore." She closed her eyes, resigned to the illusion if it let her imagine he was next to her again. "I haven't slept at all since you've been gone. It's okay. I'm okay with being crazy."

"You're not crazy."

"I am," she said. "I am, but that's okay because you're here."

Warm fingers trailed up and down her arm as she reveled in his touch.

"Dreaming, I tell you. Not hallucinating."

She opened her eyes and looked up at him. "You're not really here, are you?"

He gave a sad shake. "As much as I may wish it, no."

"I guess I'm okay with crazy then."

He tapped a finger against her forehead. "Not crazy."

"I am, a little. Why do you love me like you do? I've never been able to figure it out. I'm really not that special."

Giovanni smiled mischievously and tapped her forehead again. "Maybe I like crazy."

"Told you."

"No." He breathed out. "I recognized you. Here." He leaned down and kissed her forehead, then let his finger trail down her nose, over the slight bump and down around her lips. His fingertips danced across her bare skin until they rested lightly over her heart. "And here. I recognized you. Your mind. Your heart. We recognized each other."

"Like Aristotle said."

"One soul. Two bodies. My soul recognized its own. That is why I love you as I do. All the mysteries. All the secrets. That is the one truth we can hold to."

She sighed and buried her face in the crook of his warm neck, inhaling the ghost of scent that covered him. "You are my balance in this life. In every life."

He tangled his hand in her hair and held her closer. "In every life. Remember that, Tesoro mio."

She took a deep breath and dug her fingers into his arms, desperate to hold him there. "I can't do this without you. I'm so lost. Nothing is right without you."

"You are exactly who you need to be."

"Not without you. Never without you. Come back to me." She closed her eyes and tried to stop the tears that welled up. "What if you don't come back to me?"

"Then you will go on."

"I won't want to."

"But you will."

She felt his lips on her forehead, softly pressing kisses along her hairline, down across her cheek until his face was buried in her neck and he could breathe in her scent. She twisted his hair around her fingers as their hearts beat together and they breathed in unison. In. Out. She inhaled the scent of sweet smoke and held it as long as she could.

"You can't leave me."

"I didn't want to."

"Please, Jacopo."

"Why did you send me away?"

She choked on her cry. "Please... please come back."

"Whatever happens, you will go on, Beatrice."

"No."

"Yes."

She closed her eyes and held him close, but when she opened them a pillow was crushed to her chest, and the ghost of his scent barely clung to it.

Night had fallen when Ben tapped on her door. "B?"

She was still holding the pillow and wrapped in the sheets that held the last of his scent. "Yeah?"

"Jean's here. He's in the library."

"Gavin?"

"I guess he's guarding the truck wherever they left it."

She grabbed the dark handkerchief she kept by the bed and swiped at her eyes. "I'll be down in a minute, okay?"

"Okay." She heard him hesitate. "You all right?"

Beatrice sat up and swung her legs over the side of the bed. "I'm fine."

She heard Ben walk back down the stairs, and she rose to walk into the closet. On impulse, she grabbed one of Giovanni's black Oxford shirts and threw it over a black tank and a pair of jeans. She slipped her old boots on and pulled her hair back into a quick knot. Then she took a deep breath and walked out of the bedroom and down the stairs.

She heard Jean's deep voice as she approached the library. He was chatting with Angela and complimenting her on the wine. When Beatrice entered, he rose and offered a guarded smile. "Beatrice."

"Hey, Jean. So, what's the news?"

Angela slipped out of the room, probably to join Ben, who she could hear in the kitchen on the ground floor.

"Well, as they say, do you want the good news? Or the bad news?"

She sank into the couch and Jean took the seat across from her. Leaning forward, she tugged at her hair. "Can't we get one, single break, Jean? Hit me with both. Whatever."

"We have the truck. We have the boxes of ELIXIR. But we only have four of them."

"And there were five in the shipment."

"*Oui*. Whoever was holding the truck for us in Zagreb must have taken one off. Or Livia managed to get one of her people in."

"So, there's one box of this stuff floating around?"

He shrugged. "Chances are, she also had people watching, though she does not have as many *interesting* associates as Gavin and I do. Prior to this, the majority of her business has been legitimate."

Beatrice bit her lip. "What's your best guess? I'm bowing to the experts on this one. Do you and Gavin think she has it, or is this the kind of thing that was randomly stolen?"

Jean squinted and took another sip of his wine. "Honestly? If it was ordinary thieves stealing from a truck carrying what appeared to be high-end cosmetics... I suspect they would have taken all five boxes. Things like that are easily sold. Thieves would know this. I suspect that this was a single individual, one probably sent to fetch a box for Livia when she realized we had located and stopped the truck. A human who could only carry one before being detected. There was no scent of another immortal lingering in the area."

"So, chances are good that she has a box of ELIXIR now."

He nodded. "I would work from that assumption."

A voice spoke from the hallway. "I'm going to Castello Furio." Beatrice and Jean turned to see Lucien enter the library. He was paler than normal and appeared exhausted, but his voice was strong.

"Lucien, you can't."

"Yes, Beatrice, I can. I am no longer waiting for my mother. I don't know when, or even if, she will show up. And I am through hiding the truth of my illness."

Jean stood and held an arm out. Though Lucien was still strong, he often seemed to have strange sensitivities to light or sound. His balance was no longer reliable because the strange fugues that took him could hit at any time. Jean helped him to a chair and gave him his own glass of wine.

"My friend, may I send for some blood?"

The earth vampire only shrugged. "I am not hungry."

He was never hungry.

Beatrice reached out a hand. "Lucien, please—"

"It's been a year. I took the elixir a year ago and this is what it has done to me. I have lived thousands of years, and it is defeating me." He shook his head. "I will probably die anyway; what use is my pride? My reputation? If any of my enemies wanted to take advantage of this to harm me, they will anyway."

"Lucien, you know that we will take care of you, no matter what." As much as she tried, Beatrice couldn't help but feel like part of this was her father's fault. If Stephen hadn't shown interest in the manuscript, would it have drifted into obscurity? Would Lorenzo have damaged or destroyed it, ridding the world of its evil? It was useless speculation that still haunted her.

Lucien shook his head. "No. Enough. I spoke to Emil to let him know I am in town, and he told me the clamor of praise grows around her every day. The enthusiasm is boundless. I need to tell people the truth of what has happened to me."

"Did Emil put you up to this?"

Lucien scoffed. "I'm not that far out of my own mind, Beatrice. I can make decisions for myself."

Jean said, "Hold, my friend. We are only concerned that you may be endangering your—"

"I'm dying, Jean!" He clenched his jaw. "I am *dying*, and she would offer up this poison as a cure. Our kind must know the truth. Beatrice, take me to her. Take me to court. I will speak before I die. While I still have a voice, I will tell the truth."

Beatrice couldn't ignore him. "Okay, Lucien. If that's what you want, I'll take you." She could see Jean begin to protest, so she held up her hand. "It's his choice. Can you and Gavin guard the boxes of elixir until we get back and decide what to do with them?"

Jean nodded. "Of course. Should one of us stay here at the house with your humans?"

She nodded. "If you could. I don't trust anyone in this city right now. Matt and Dez are at the hospital, and I'm pretty sure of the security there, but the house is too big to be left without at least one of us here."

"I'll let Gavin know. We won't leave the residence unguarded."

"Thanks, Jean. Now." She rose and walked toward the door. "I better call a car if we're going to make it there with enough time for some ass-kicking. Lucien, you need anything before we go?"

He took a deep breath, and she noticed that he looked peaceful for the first time in weeks. "Nope. Just point me in the direction of the asses. I may pass out, but I'll try to get a few kicks in before I do."

Beatrice wanted to laugh, but it stuck in her throat.

This wasn't going to end well.

It took over an hour to reach the castle. When they pulled through the lavish gates, she noticed the number of uniformed drivers and luxury cars that crowded the lawn. Beatrice got out of the car and debated wearing her *shuang gou*. Unfortunately, there was no way she could carry the weapons inconspicuously. She tucked a few daggers into her boot and put the rest of her weapons away.

"Look at them all," Lucien murmured as he looked around. "This is insane."

"Well, Gio did say she loved it when people came to her."

"He's right."

"He usually is. It's very annoying."

Lucien chuckled. "Let's make sure we have an introduction. Do you think the party's inside?"

"In this weather?" She looked around at the damp mist that was falling. "Yeah, they're inside."

"Does she still have that grand hall where she likes to sit like a queen?"

"Yup."

"Lovely."

They stopped inside the gates of the castle grounds and flagged down a servant. They asked for someone to give their names to Emil Conti while they waited under the watchful and plentiful eyes of Livia's guards.

"When did she get so much security?" Lucien asked.

Beatrice looked around. Her back itched where her swords would usually hang, and she twisted her leg to the side, taking comfort in the solid press of metal against her ankle. "She really started piling them on after Lorenzo showed up and she arrested Gio."

He frowned. "Where is she getting them? These do not look like young vampires." He trailed off, muttering as she watched for a sign of Emil. Within a few minutes, she spotted a blur crossing the grounds and Emil stood before them. He nodded toward Lucien and bent to greet Beatrice with a kiss. He did not look pleased.

"My dear, this is unexpected. And probably quite foolish. Livia has taken advantage of this reception to announce what she is calling a 'partnership' with a few other vampires. I'm really not sure this is the proper place to—"

"Hey, don't look at me." She raised her hands, palms-out. "Lucien insisted."

"Lucien, your call this afternoon was very unexpected. What do you have to do with all this mess?"

Lucien took a deep breath. "It's the elixir, Emil. They found the truck, and there was a box of elixir missing. She has it. I know it—it..." He drifted off and Emil looked between Lucien and Beatrice in confusion.

"Lucien? What are you talking about?"

"He's taken it, Emil." Beatrice took Lucien's hand and held it as he drifted.

Emil's eyes grew wide. "The elixir? Lucien has taken the elixir?"

"He drank from a human who had taken it. Now, he is... ill. We're not sure how or why, but that is where Gio and Carwyn have been. They've been trying to find more information from the vampires who helped develop it. And hopefully, they'll find some kind of cure for Lucien, too."

She was still reluctant to detail Giovanni and Carwyn's attempts to find Arosh and Kato. For one thing, she had no idea whether they were having any success. They hadn't heard any news from them in weeks. For another, the vampires they were looking for were supposed to be dead.

Emil was staring at Lucien in confusion. "So, Lucien drank from a human who had taken this drug and now he is... what?"

Lucien blinked and came back. "I'm still here. For now. But my mind is not right. I must tell the court what this elixir does. I must warn them."

Emil shook his head. "My friend, I know how trustworthy you are, but I can only vouch for you as my friend. Many of the younger Romans do not know you. They don't know your sire or your reputation. There is no guarantee they will listen to you when Livia and her three associates have been telling them they hold the keys to a miracle."

Beatrice's eyes darted away from Lucien's disappointed face. "Associates?" she asked. "What associates?"

"She has just announced that she partnered with Matilda from Germany—"

"She's wind."

"Bomeni from Ethiopia."

"Earth," Lucien said.

"And Livia holds water." Beatrice's eyes darted back to Emil's. "Who else?"

"Oleg, the Russian."

Lucien said, "Fire."

Beatrice nodded. "And she's got her four now. We knew she'd have to find willing donors."

Emil asked, "Do you think they know the effects?"

Beatrice nodded, even though they were far from sure. "She knows. Lucien has tried to contact them with no success. They're obviously avoiding him." Though Lucien raised an eyebrow, he did not correct her.

He said, "Whether she knows or suspects, I must have an audience to speak to the vampires of the court. I must at least try, Emil."

The Roman nodded. "I understand. And I will introduce you tonight so you may speak. Beatrice..." He looked toward her with an apologetic expression. "I think it would be better if—"

"Not on your life," she said. "Lucien's not going anywhere near that bitch without me. I don't make the same mistake twice."

Emil sighed. "I will introduce you. Please understand though, the matter of your friend—"

"Is a minor human problem according to these guys," she said. "I get it."

"I am truly sorry. It would not happen if I—"

"Not your fault, Emil. Let's let Lucien have his say so I can get him home. The last thing we need is to be stuck here for the day."

The three started toward the castle, and Beatrice couldn't help but notice how many more guards were dotted around the grounds. "Are Ziri and Tenzin inside?"

"I believe so. Tenzin is with the remnants of the Chinese delegation, though I believe most of them are leaving or have left already. Ziri is... around."

"Somewhere?"

"Yes, but I've only seen him once tonight."

They sped over the grounds and, in no time, they were climbing the stairs toward another of Livia's glittering parties. And once again, Beatrice was distinctly underdressed. She caught the stares of the vampires inspecting her jeans and tank top covered by her husband's shirt, which draped her body almost to the knees. The stares didn't bother her. However, the idea that a good number of these vampires could be going out of their mind if Livia had her way did bother her.

She glanced sideways and caught Emil's frown. "What?" she whispered.

He spoke in a whisper. "Why does she want this?"

"Money? Power over her enemies? Who knows?" Beatrice kept walking through the whispering crowd. "Currently, she's the one that has the knowledge, and knowledge is power. People have fought for this. Died for it, even." She tilted her head toward Lucien. "What would you sacrifice to hold a power that could turn your keenest enemy into a shadow of himself?"

Lucien whispered, "I'd be offended if I didn't agree with you so much. Emil, imagine a bottle of this in the hands of your enemy. They wouldn't even need to attack you. They could influence any human you drank from and send that poison back to you with a healthy flush on their face. You would have no idea."

She didn't miss the hairs that lifted on Emil's neck as they made their way through the crowd. Still, his face was impassive and his stride was purposeful. Many of the vampires they passed seemed to want his attention, but didn't feel confident enough to approach him. He acknowledged the crowd with a polite nod, though he did not stop his steady pace. Beatrice smiled. She had chosen a good leader for Rome.

As long as putting him in power didn't get them all killed.

They arrived in the main hall, which was teeming with vampires. Glittering lights dripped from the ceiling and the rich colors of fall decorated the room. Red and orange dresses were everywhere along with purple, green, and gold decorations. The human servers carried flutes of champagne and tiny hors d'oeuvres as they moved through the crowd. Other humans held up wrists that Beatrice saw more than one vampire take advantage of as they mingled. A thought suddenly struck her.

"You know, all she'd have to do is dose up her donors, and she'd have everyone here under her thumb. Think about it, Emil. None of the younger immortals drink from anyone live unless it's here."

She could tell he'd never considered the possibility. "My god, you're right."

Beatrice heard Lucien say, "This is ridiculous. All this ridiculous protocol. Have we become humans after all?"

Lucien pushed them both back and strode toward the front of the room. "Lucien!"

He didn't stop. The crowd parted and she could see Livia seated in another richly draped chaise at the front of the room. Lorenzo was beside her, along with Matilda, Bomeni, and a scowling vampire Beatrice did not recognize.

Livia rose as Lucien approached.

"Lucien," she said, clearly shocked, but trying to cover it. "What a wonderful surprise to—"

"Shut up, Livia."

Livia didn't just shut up; the whole room did. If there had been a record playing somewhere, Beatrice imagined it would have made a screeching noise. Lucien raised a hand and pointed toward Lorenzo as he sat at her side.

"Did your errand boy tell you he's given out samples of your great discovery?"

Livia's face was blank, and Beatrice suspected she hadn't known, after all. No matter, Lucien was still speaking, but he had turned to address the crowd.

"Oh yes, my friends, I have tried this elixir she calls a miracle! Lorenzo gave it to cure a human under my aegis. Then he told me of its other benefits." His eyes swept the room and Beatrice could tell the ancient vampire had the attention of all in the room. "I drank from her. I drank from her over a year ago. Do you know what it has done to me? Shall I tell you, or perhaps I should just wait here with Livia until I fall into a coma and do not wake?"

The muttering began to circulate around the room. Livia stood, doing her best to keep the peace.

"Lucien, my old friend. Whatever are you talking about?" Her laugh was brittle. "If you have received something purported to be my elixir, I apologize, and I will make sure the finest healers see to you, but this cure has been tested, my friends!" Her gaze swung away from Lucien to the crowd that surrounded her, trying to reassure them. "This is not some magic potion; this is science. A breakthrough of historic significance..."

Beatrice's eyes drifted as Livia started her sales pitch again. She searched through the crowd to examine those who surrounded the water vampire. There was security, definitely. A lot of that. And her three partners stood next to her. None of them looked shocked in the least. All their faces were very carefully blank.

She continued to scan the room. In addition to the tiered fountains that dotted it, a discreet channel of water had been built since the last time she had visited. To most, it would have looked like a very beautiful water feature, but Beatrice knew what it really was: a weapon. Luckily, it was a weapon for more than just Livia. She stepped closer to Lucien and the wary vampires of Livia's court kept their distance.

"Livia!" Lucien was shouting over her. "Stop your speeches and listen! I'm willing to believe that you may not have realized how harmful this all was, but for the good of your people, you must stop this madness now. Admit that this elixir is harmful. Stop the production until more research can be done. What kind of leader are you if you cannot look past your own self-interest to the good of Rome? To the common good of our kind?"

Beatrice noticed a flicker on the edge of the crowd. *Tenzin.* Her ancient friend nodded toward her and Beatrice slowly relaxed. She glanced at Emil and noticed that he was subtly making eye contact with a number of other vampires in the room who she guessed were his allies. There were more than she had expected.

Livia's eyes narrowed. "Lucien, perhaps you are ill. Or at least ill-informed. Apparently, your association with…" Livia looked toward Beatrice with a blatant sneer. "Less than trustworthy immortals has influenced your usually clear head."

"It's not Beatrice or Giovanni who have clouded my mind, Livia. That was done by this poison you are trying to convince—"

"Stop your lies!" she exploded. "Your reputation for questionable connections has long haunted you. You are no longer welcome in my home."

"I am not leaving until I am heard!"

"Guards, escort the vampire, Lucien Thrax, out of my home, along with his detestable companion. Emil, I cannot believe you even offered them an introduction here."

Silent vampires stepped forward and laid their hands on Lucien's shoulders, pushing him toward the doors. Beatrice saw him blink and stumble once.

"Lucien!" She rushed forward, only to be grabbed by several guards before she could reach him. She quickly grabbed the daggers from her boots and slashed out, cutting two of them at the throat. She could feel the blades meet their spines, but the bone did not snap. Blood sprayed out as guards rushed them and Livia shrieked.

"Murderer! She brings weapons to my home to assassinate me. Seize her! Arrest Beatrice De Novo. Take her away!"

Beatrice heard Emil shout out over the gathering furor. "Hold, immortals of Rome! Listen to me and hold!"

Rough hands grabbed for her. She whirled, slashing at any that came close. Two went down at her feet, their blood spilling over the marble mosaics on the floor as she severed their spines. Another. Two more. Beatrice cut and kicked at anyone who approached her as she fought her way toward Lucien. He was crumpled on the floor, and she feared he could be trampled as the crowd began to panic and churn.

She felt water dash her face and glanced over her shoulder to see Livia raise her arms to command it. Beatrice raised an arm, swiping the wave that Livia aimed at her back toward its source. As she did, she felt multiple hands grab her legs. She growled and kicked them away. She needed to get to Lucien, but kept tripping over vampires in her path. She looked around in confusion. The hall had turned into a near riot as humans fled toward the doors, but where was Tenzin?

Beatrice reached Lucien, only to kneel down and have four of Livia's guards dive on top of her, kicking her face and hitting the sick vampire in the process. She screamed and lashed out, but more still came.

"Seize her!" Livia continued to scream. "Seize her and bring her to me!"

It seemed as if dozens of hands grabbed her and tore her from Lucien's side. She was dragged in front of Livia, but the crowd still churned in confusion and she couldn't see Tenzin anywhere. Suddenly, Lucien disappeared from in front of her. Beatrice looked around in panic, only to see Tenzin hovering in a corner of the room, cradling the tall man in her arms. She relaxed for a second before they dragged her in front of the screaming Roman matriarch.

Emil was shouting over the crowd. "Livia, you must not do this! She is protected. Do not lay a hand—"

The crowd drowned him out and the guards pushed him back. Beatrice stood in front of Livia, secured by Livia's guards. The Roman was spitting mad, but Beatrice ignored her as she noticed the new addition to the room. Lorenzo. He was standing behind Livia, surrounded by guards, and his canny eyes watched the chaos breaking out across the room.

Beatrice finally caught his eye and grinned. She mouthed, *'You're next,'* and kicked at one of the bodies near her feet. Her boots were sticky, and she could feel the spray of blood cooling on her face. Giovanni's shirt hung in tatters and trailed thick drops on the intricate mosaics at her feet.

Beatrice no longer cared.

The hall finally seemed to quiet down, and she could hear Emil's shouts again. "Do not allow Livia's rash actions, immortals of Rome. Beatrice De Novo is the favored scribe of Penglai Island. She is the granddaughter of Don Ernesto Alvarez. A favorite of those in power across Europe and the East. Do not let Livia's vindictive actions go unchallenged!"

Just then, Beatrice heard it. The water in the fountain near her quivered and shook in excitement. A hush fell over the room as a gusting wind approached. She heard a commotion in the outer chamber and the smell of smoke reached her nose. Her eyes followed Livia's, glued to the giant doors at the back of the hall. They suddenly burst open with a rush of wind and fire. Humans around the room screamed as three immortals passed over their heads and the room filled with heat.

Carwyn dropped to her side with a crash. The marble floor burst open beneath his feet.

Tenzin circled overhead, hissing and spitting at any guard that drew near.

And coming through the crowd, blue fire swirling over his body, Giovanni walked. He looked for her, and Beatrice reached out a hand to her mate. Their fingers twined with a hiss as water and fire met, then both of them turned to Livia.

CHAPTER TWENTY-EIGHT

Castello Furio, Rome
November 2012

As his fingers tangled with hers, Giovanni thought that there was no other time in five hundred years of life when he'd had so much to say and so little ability to say it. He linked his fingers with hers as their friends flanked him. Their amnis tangled together, twisting in relief that mirrored the sense of relief he'd felt as soon as he entered the hall and sensed her.

The room was frozen in shock for a few precious moments until Livia screamed out, "Arrest him!"

Giovanni glanced up at Tenzin. She nodded. He let go of Beatrice's hand and shoved her behind him. Then he snapped both fingers, immediately bringing the fire to his hands. He threw out two streams of flame that Tenzin whipped into a circle, surrounding them, holding off Livia's guards and causing the vampires in the hall to skitter back in fear. He could hear the few humans left in the hall weeping as Livia bared her fangs and hissed.

She raised her arms, calling the water in the room. It rose up, a glistening shower over their heads, the tiny droplets poised to spear down on them, but then Giovanni felt Beatrice's amnis rise behind him and the water halted, suspended like a quivering chandelier, frozen as it scattered the light of his flames.

Matilda took to the air to face Tenzin. Bomeni crouched down in front of Livia. Giovanni recognized the Russian standing behind her, surprised to see Oleg in Livia's company. He met his fellow fire vampire's gaze and saw the other man's eyes narrow to a calculating stare. Giovanni's collar began to smoke as he caught the smell of the other immortal's fire.

He looked back at Livia as the hall reached a standstill. The once beautiful woman had never appeared more animalistic. Her fangs had pierced her lips and blood dripped from her mouth and down her chin, staining her intricate gown. He stepped forward, the fire moving with him as Tenzin tracked his pace.

Livia pulled back her rage and spoke to him in a low voice. "Why are you here?"

To kill you. Giovanni whispered to Beatrice. "Conti?"

"He's ready," she whispered. She held the water almost effortlessly above them.

Giovanni looked at Emil Conti, who stood at the edge of the crowd, eyeing Giovanni with suspicion. No doubt, the vampire was wondering if the fire vampire was there to take his place.

"Signore Conti," he asked in a respectful voice. "I would like to address the immortals of Rome."

Emil straightened his shoulders and nodded with a smile. "Please, Dottore Vecchio, the Roman court will listen."

Giovanni looked back at Livia, who was curling her lips in anger. "Step aside, Livia."

She bared her fangs. Giovanni could see black-clad guards pouring into the room from the two doors behind her. "Never," she said. "This city is mine."

"Admit that this 'elixir of life' is a poison."

"You are as ridiculous and delusional as the Thracian. I seek only the good of my people; you seek to deceive. No one will believe your lies, murderer." She raised her voice. "*Murderer!*"

Giovanni turned back to Emil. "Signore Conti, if you would send the humans out of the room?"

Emil nodded. "Immortals of Rome, this is a conflict among our own kind. Send your humans away. They are not welcome here."

Giovanni could see eyes darting around the room. Many of the older vampires looked to Livia for confirmation, but she ignored them. Then the few humans left in the room were herded toward the doors near the back.

"Oleg!" Giovanni addressed the Russian. "I have had no quarrel with you."

The Russian responded with caution. "Nor I with you, di Spada."

"This water vampire has deceived you."

Giovanni saw Oleg eyeing Livia with suspicion. The Russian had been sired from earth. He usually minded his own business and had never been the trusting kind. He had also been an associate of Lucien Thrax, who Tenzin had flown out of the hall earlier. The vampire was obviously reconsidering his alliance with the Roman aristocrat after seeing his ailing friend. Oleg looked up at Tenzin, then at Carwyn, and then over Giovanni's shoulder where Beatrice stood holding back Livia's water. Oleg looked to

Emil Conti and nodded. "I seek no quarrel with Rome or those who dwell here."

Oleg stepped away from Livia, and Emil called out, "Depart in peace, and consider yourself a friend of Rome."

"Traitor!" Livia screamed. "I will have your head for this, Russian."

Oleg only looked amused as he and his retinue headed toward the doors. "We shall see, Livia." The doors opened one last time as the fire vampire headed out the doors, then they slammed shut and a low murmur began to fill the room. Livia's guards surrounded them. Bomeni and Matilda guarded their leader. Swirling amnis charged the air, and Giovanni lowered the flames that surrounded him as he looked over the nearby vampires.

There were immortals from all over the Old World. Romans, but also those from the Middle East, North Africa, and Europe and Asia. Familiar, friendly faces and unfamiliar, suspicious expressions combined. Some of them had obviously cast their lot with Livia, and he could almost feel their anger floating in the air around him.

"Immortal brothers and sisters," he said. "I am not your enemy! I come here as one of you. Not to lead. Not to conquer. I come seeking the truth. I am the only son of the great scholar, Niccolo Andros, and I am here to warn you of a great danger." He reached over and grasped Beatrice's hand and her amnis met his again. "One that could affect all of us and all those under our aegis."

Emil Conti spoke. "Dottore Vecchio, your skills as a scholar are as renowned as your skills as a fighter. Please, tell us what you know of the elixir of life."

Giovanni nodded. "I learned of this elixir years ago. I know that Livia has told you it is a cure for the bloodlust that stalks us. That it is an answer to humanity's ills, as well. It is not."

His eyes swung back to Livia. "Step down now, Livia."

"Don't be ridiculous," she scoffed.

Beatrice squeezed his hand as he continued to address the crowd. "The vampire who leads Rome tells you that with this elixir, you will no longer be a slave to your hunger. She tells you that any humans you may care for will live forever, without pain or illness. We have all suffered from bloodlust. We have all lost human companions or friends that were useful or even loved. But I tell you now, this is no cure."

Livia began to laugh as more guards entered the room. They lined the walls, and he could see the vampires around him start to tense. Some with anticipation. Some with fear. The guards blocked the door. All of them were armed with swords, though none of the crowd appeared to carry any weapons.

"Last chance, Livia." Giovanni still wouldn't let her live, but he might kill her in a more private location if she complied. The problem was, she knew it, too.

Livia said, "You are a murderer, a liar, and a thief. No one believes you, Giovanni di Spada."

"You are right," he said. "I *am* a murderer." He heard the gasp that swept the room, but he continued. "I will hold back no truth! I admit that I killed my sire, Niccolo Andros, with the help of my son, Lorenzo, who stands behind you."

"You forced him to help you with amnis, Giovanni! He was only a human."

Giovanni laughed. "I did no such thing. Lorenzo knew of my father's cruelty. As did you. Andros's own sire had cut him off. It was only the rest of the world my father fooled."

"Andros was not cruel." She addressed the crowd. "He was a great immortal and my beloved mate. Let me kill this rebellious child who has admitted to taking him from us."

"Niccolo Andros had no more use for you than he did for his money purse, Livia. You were a tool. Nothing more. We both know it."

She screamed. "Liar!"

He narrowed his eyes and a smile curled the corner of his lip. "Perhaps you were deceived by him. Perhaps he fooled you, as well. Did Andros keep his secrets from you, as he did from us all?"

"Foolish child, Andros was my mate. We had no secrets from each other."

She had stepped into the trap with such ease that Giovanni had to force himself not to grin. His face was a picture of sympathetic understanding. "There is no shame in being the victim of deception, Livia."

"I knew him better than you ever did."

Perhaps not even Livia knew the truth. She had created her own history, and Giovanni would not fight it. In the end, it did not matter; she would burn with the rest of his enemies. "Then, my dear, you will not be surprised by our guests! Emil?" He turned back to the old Roman, who was watching the exchange with a guarded expression. "I would like to invite to the court three of our most ancient brethren." Giovanni angled his shoulders toward the door a second before they flew open. A few of the younger vampires rushed toward the open doors, only to be thrown back by a strong wind as Ziri flew into the hall.

The ancient wind vampire carried Giovanni's grand-sire, who looked around the room with a slow blink. Giovanni had fed Kato his blood before they left Arosh's mountain fortress, and the effects were immediately evident. The old water vampire was less aggressive and seemed to already have more awareness of his surroundings. Though he still did not speak, he seemed to exhibit a growing recognition of Giovanni and Arosh. He had even allowed Carwyn to remain in his presence.

The fire vampire strode into the room with a lazy gait and looked around in amusement. He ignored the whispers that began as he entered, and the crowd parted for him. He calmly walked through the circle of fire and came to stand beside Giovanni as Ziri landed behind him and set Kato on his feet.

Arosh looked around the room; then he nodded at Emil Conti and narrowed his eyes at Livia. His deep voice filled the silent hall when he finally spoke. "So, this is Andreas's woman who calls herself the leader of Rome?" He curled his lip. "We shall see."

CHAPTER TWENTY-NINE

Castello Furio, Rome
November 2012

At the mention of Andros's name, the massive vampire next to Beatrice bared her fangs and hissed. She looked up with wide eyes. This had to be Kato. He looked like the statue of Neptune that ruled over the Trevi fountain in the center of Rome. His hair flowed over his shoulders. His beard was long and curling, and he wore only a loose pair of pants. She clutched Giovanni's hand, but he calmly pressed her fingers between his own.

Despite everything, the blood in her veins sang. *He is back.* He was near! Her mate was next to her again, and her heart sped in delight and anticipation even as she looked at the frighteningly powerful immortal that towered over her.

The water in the air clung to Kato's skin. She could even feel it wick away from her as she stood next to him. The delicate skin of her lips cracked, causing blood to spring up. She shivered, and a small breath escaped her, but as soon as Kato heard her small gasp, he turned his eyes to Beatrice, and they softened. His fangs disappeared, and he lifted a large hand to touch her cheek. Her skin immediately plumped with moisture again.

"Gio?" she whispered.

"It's fine, Tesoro. He won't hurt you. He smells his blood in you. Remember, you are of his line."

"Isn't Livia, too?"

At the mention of Livia's name, Kato's eyes swung back toward the front of the room and he bared his fangs again. Ziri placed a hand on the giant's shoulder, and Kato calmed. Beatrice clutched Giovanni's hand in hers, determined not to be separated from him. She heard the long-haired vampire with the crackling energy address the crowd.

"I am Arosh. The vampires of Rome know who I am. I need no permission to speak to this hall."

Livia, as if sensing the situation slipping out of her control cried out, "This is *my* hall! And I do not—"

She was cut off as a sharp spear of fire shot out of Arosh's fingers. Livia pulled a guard in front of her, who immediately turned to ash.

"Shut up, woman. I am speaking."

Beatrice might have imagined the slight shake in Emil's voice, but she didn't think so. Still, Emil stepped forward with an outstretched arm that didn't tremble once. Beatrice was impressed.

He said, "Though you need no permission, my lord, I would welcome you to my city. We had heard of your demise, but I am very pleased to hear that the rumors were false."

Arosh waved a careless hand. "My thanks, Roman. I have come to your city in return for a favor granted by Giovanni Vecchio, the son of Andreas, sired of Kato."

The low chatter began as Kato's name moved around the room. This was the ancient king of the Mediterranean, she realized. As soon as he had stepped into the room, many of the vampires had probably recognized him. All of them had thought their legendary king was dead. And though he definitely wasn't dead, there *was* something wrong with him. As powerful as he was, his amnis, when he had touched her, had felt very wrong.

Arosh continued, "I come here with my friend, Kato, your ancient king, and our friend Ziri, who is often among you, to tell you what I know of this elixir that the alchemist made for us."

Beatrice held on to Giovanni's hand and felt his warm energy run up her arm. He stepped back and put his arm around her shoulders as she breathed in the rich scent of his skin. Then, she caught the bobbing blond head of Lorenzo from behind Livia's guards. He was watching them with narrowed eyes. She tensed for a moment, but then heard the soft, steady thump of Giovanni's normally silent heart. He was poised, but calm, so she tried to relax.

Arosh continued his speech. "I will not stay long. This is not my fight, but I do know this elixir and it is no cure. It is quite harmful and has made my friend, this ancient immortal before you, sick. Though it nurtures the body, it destroys the very energy that animates us. Do not believe this deceiver who claims to lead you."

The low chatter in the room grew louder, and Giovanni stepped forward to speak.

"Vampires of Rome, I was trained by my sire to be the most rational of our kind. He desired that I exhibit knowledge and reason alone. I did not subscribe to superstition or magic. I believed only in what could be tested and tried." Giovanni looked around the room, then down to meet her eyes.

"But some things, I have learned, have no rational explanation. Some things are far greater than what can be seen."

He looked around the hall. "We are not only creatures of the elements. Though these elements preserve our bodies, they are *not* the eternal energy of our souls. We are *more*. All of us. We are more than creatures of the physical world." Giovanni turned to his grand-sire, placing a hand upon the giant's shoulder. "We are creatures of the heart and the spirit. Of energy and things unseen. If we seek to preserve our bodies without accepting our need for humanity and what they offer us, *we will be lost*."

He turned to Arosh, who gave him a respectful nod. Giovanni said, "We are *not* all-powerful, my friends. Even the greatest among us have been forced to acknowledge this."

Arosh spoke again. "Be rid of this poison and be rid of your foolish pride. Though the great Kato grows strong again..." He glared at the vampires who surrounded them. "And will soon be as strong as ever—not even he could heal himself. Giovanni Vecchio has helped to heal him."

A brave voice called from the back of the room. "But Giovanni Vecchio killed his own sire!"

Arosh frowned. "If he hadn't, I would have. Andreas refused to grant me a favor."

The room fell silent again. Beatrice wanted to ask why refusing a favor was such a big deal, but decided that it wasn't the best time. She finally heard Livia speak. The favor thing must have been serious, because for the first time, the scheming water immortal's voice held a note of calculation.

"My lord Arosh, forgive my ignorance. And forgive my earlier outburst. I was enraged by the thought of my mate's murderer standing before me. But if you say Giovanni Vecchio has your good will—"

"I did not say he had my good will," Arosh scowled. "That is not easily bestowed. I said he had granted me a favor, one that his sire would not."

Livia nodded respectfully, her face a picture of accommodation.

Unbelievable, Beatrice thought, she was actually trying to get out of it. Livia continued in an ingratiating voice, "But if you would only forgive my earlier surprise. I had no idea that my husband had displeased you, or that his sire was in need of—"

"But Livia"—Giovanni stepped forward, still holding Beatrice's hand —"you just finished telling this court that Andros had no secrets from you. Arosh, did you not tell me that Andros knew of the elixir and its effects?"

The ancient king shrugged. "Of course. I told him when I asked him to help his sire. He knew exactly what the elixir did. And, I'm assuming he would have told his wife when he stole the book containing this formula from my library and brought it back to Rome."

Giovanni looked around the room. "Then surely Livia knew as well! For she and Andros had no secrets. Surely her 'dear friend' Lorenzo knew when he gave Lucien Thrax the fatal dose. They have deceived you, Rome. They hope to profit from this formula. To become rich as their enemies grow weak. They would use this elixir, not to cure bloodlust, but to kill us. To kill the humans we value. It is not the elixir of life. It's the elixir of death."

The water in the air that Beatrice had been holding began to shake again, as Livia quaked with rage. Beatrice pulled away from Giovanni and held her hands out, forcing the water away from the ring of flame that protected them from the multitude of black-clad guards. She eyed the one nearest her, measuring how quickly she could take his weapon from him.

Giovanni's skin began to heat, and she saw the smoke rise above his collar. Arosh was looking around the room in amusement. "I see great fear on many of your faces. I believe some of you have taken this elixir already. Foolish vampires! Is your sire alive to heal you? I hope so, for your sakes. Come, my friends, you have wise immortals among you." Arosh gestured toward Emil. "You are the people of the great sea! Kato's heirs. Rid yourselves of this poison she has spread and appoint a leader worthy of you."

Beatrice's eyes flew to Livia. She was livid. The appeasing expression on her face had vanished and her arms were raised over the crowd.

Beatrice felt Giovanni's hand tighten around hers and knew he had seen the insane glint in Livia's eyes, too.

Not good.

The water in the air crept along her skin. The flames around her surged. And Beatrice's heart sped for a moment, then fell completely still as Livia whispered, "Kill them all."

CHAPTER THIRTY

Castello Furio
November 2012

As if they had choreographed it, Ziri grabbed Kato and Arosh, then took to the air in front of Giovanni as soon as the words left Livia's mouth. He looked up and caught the other fire vampire's eye, and Arosh grinned as the room erupted in violence.

"Do not get yourself killed, Giovanni Vecchio! Remember, we have a deal."

So they would fight Livia and her guards without the help of the ancients. Giovanni wasn't surprised. Arosh and Ziri had their own agenda, and risking their lives in a fight that was not their own was not part of it. Giovanni could see Emil calling to those vampires loyal to him as they rushed Livia's allies.

His eyes swung toward Beatrice, but she had already leapt through the circle of flame, bashing in the head of one guard with a swift kick before she grabbed his weapon and the weapon of another guard she quickly beheaded. He felt a spray from overhead and looked up to see Tenzin with her scimitar out, locked in struggle with a ferocious Matilda. A moment later a long, pale leg dropped to the ground between Giovanni and Carwyn, and the earth vampire bared his fangs and grinned.

"Can't let the girls have all the fun, can we?"

"Never!" He dropped the circle of flames that protected them a moment before the water Beatrice had been holding showered around him, soaking him to the skin and dousing his flames. Carwyn rushed Bomeni, and the two crashed together like twin boulders before they rolled across the floor and the ground buckled beneath them.

Giovanni scanned the room. Where was Livia? The front of the room was a mass of swirling black as Livia's guards protected their queen. He cut through the crowd, slashing with the dagger he had brought, the same one she had plunged into his body in rage. He felt a sword slash at the small of his back before a spray of blood hit him. He turned to see his wife grinning with bared fangs as she took down another guard.

He took two strides to her and grabbed his mate in a fierce kiss.

Beatrice bit his lip and said, "Hey, handsome. Nice to see you."

He elbowed a guard that tried to attack them, grabbing the vampire's sword as the guard fell to the ground and Beatrice cut off his legs. Giovanni licked the blood from his lip and smiled. "I missed you, Tesoro."

"Same here. Now let's kill this bitch so we can go home."

She pulled him down for one more swift kiss before she spun away, slashing with the twin sabers she had stolen.

Giovanni headed toward the front of the room. He had a sword but no fire. His hair was wet and moisture clung to his body. Giovanni looked up for Tenzin and yelled, "Bird girl? A little wind, please?"

Tenzin curled her lip, but grabbed Matilda by her long blond hair and swung her across the room where the vampire was bashed against the wall and slid to the ground. Tenzin directed a strong gust that dried him as he walked toward Livia's position. The flames sparked on his skin, and Tenzin's wind fanned them higher as he looked for his prey.

A streak of red darted by and he saw Donatella Conti rush toward the back doors where she battled the guards who were cutting down those running to safety. Many of the younger, weaker vampires were desperately trying to escape the battle, so he abandoned his search to help Donatella. She saw him approaching and shouted, "The doors! They're oak!"

He nodded and summoned two streams of flame. With one, he blasted back Livia's guards. The other, he aimed at the giant arched doors that sealed them in. The smoke began to fill the room as the lacquered oak caught fire. Within a few moments, the doors were crumbling, and the drapes in the room had been set aflame. Donatella flung water from the fountains to douse the flames and quell the growing panic.

"Go!" she yelled, and the younger vampires ran from the room. Donatella plunged back into battle, her brilliant red cocktail dress slashed and ragged. She grinned at him as she ran past, grabbing a sword from the ashes near the door.

"I like your wife, Giovanni. *Fantastic* boots."

He gave a hoarse laugh. "I'm fond of them, myself." Donatella disappeared into the melee of vampires still battling, cutting toward her husband who was in the center of the battle. They were greatly outnumbered once the younger vampires had fled, but were still holding their own.

Tenzin was battling in the air. He didn't see Matilda, but some of her entourage were keeping his old partner occupied. Sprays of blood rained around him as Tenzin cut them down, one by one. Carwyn and Bomeni were evenly matched, and the floor buckled as each tried to best the other. Though Carwyn was as occupied keeping up the support pillars in the room as he was trying to best the other vampire.

Beatrice was cutting down the guards that swarmed near the front, slowly but surely making her way forward. Most of the guards were water vampires, but were no match for his mate's power. She slapped at them with the water from the fountains and spun gracefully. Giovanni saw her take out two guards with one slash of her sword.

But he still didn't see Livia.

As he walked through the room, he sent out his fire, trying to avoid allies while killing enemies. Battling in enclosed spaces had always posed a problem for him, unless he wanted to kill everyone in the room. He cut back a few guards with his sword as he searched. He caught a flash of blond hair and saw Lorenzo dueling with Emil Conti.

Just then, he felt water splash against his feet. Giovanni looked down to see a few inches of water had covered the floor.

A lot of water.

He felt the ground shake and looked for Carwyn.

Bomeni, playing to the strengths of his allies, had opened a crack in the floor, splitting the foundation and the earth below it. Giovanni finally spotted Livia. She was standing in the corner of the room, pulling groundwater from the river that flowed under the castle.

Too much water.

It splashed up around his feet. At the speed and power with which she was drawing it, the room would be filled in no time. The fire along his torso sizzled out. There was no way Tenzin would be able to dry him when she was battling six of Matilda's guards in the air. Carwyn was holding off Bomeni with one arm and keeping the ceiling from crashing down with the other. Emil was dueling Lorenzo, as his allies battled Livia's.

As Giovanni dispatched four of Livia's guards, he saw a red-clad arm float by. He spun just in time to see Donatella Conti take a deep breath. Her eyes were wide and hollow when the sword slashed her neck and her head sailed across the room, landing with a splash as Emil roared out at the death of his mate.

Giovanni's eyes sought Beatrice. She was holding her own, trying to make her way toward Livia, but he saw her arms were bloody and torn. The room continued to flood with water. They had lost one of their fiercest fighters. And the black clad guards poured into the room like a never-ending stream of death.

He needed to end this.

"Beatrice!"

CHAPTER THIRTY-ONE

Castello Furio, Rome
November 2012

She heard Giovanni call her name from the back of the room. Beatrice cut off the heads of the two guards in front of her before she sped back to where he stood. Livia's guards did not follow. They were completely focused on protecting their mistress, who seemed to be pulling water from the ground itself as the battle raged around her. Giovanni grabbed her and slashed at the vampires that fell on them.

"Beatrice, I need to end this. Now!"

"How?" she cried. "There's too much water!"

Beatrice glanced toward Carwyn. The earth vampire seemed to have finally stabilized the pillars that held up the room, so he turned his attention fully on Bomeni. The fierce immortal bared his gleaming white fangs and sprang on the her friend, but Carwyn caught him and locked his long arms around the man's chest, crushing his ribs with an audible crack before Bomeni howled in pain and fell to the ground. Carwyn stood over him, took the vampire's head between his hands, and twisted it off in a spray of blood and gore. Then he roared and started into the mass of twisted bodies where Emil still fought.

The room was filling with water. Massive blocks of marble had fallen in front of the doors, so they were blocked, and Livia's guards still outnumbered them.

Giovanni yelled, "Carwyn!"

The earth vampire turned and looked to them. Then he sped back, tossing away the vampires that followed.

"We need to do something!" he panted. "This water, Gio—"

"It's filling up the room." He shook his head. "I can't build any flame, and even if I could, our allies are scattered. It's not safe. I would kill our own people."

"Carwyn," Beatrice said. "Get to Emil. I'll try to push the water back, but I'll need his help."

Carwyn nodded, but before he could leave them, a drenched and tattered Tenzin appeared with Emil gripped in her arms. He was wounded and bleeding from a deep cut to the neck.

"Your son almost killed him, my boy. I managed to grab him, but I think Lorenzo has fled."

Giovanni said, "Forget him right now. We need to kill Livia. Can you get to her?"

She shook her head. "They're watching for me. She has guards that are covering her from the air while she pulls this damn water up."

"Go. Get as many of our allies as you can and bring them here to the back of the room. Then I need you to bring the wind."

Tenzin cocked her head. "Truly?"

Giovanni's voice was hoarse. "I need a hurricane, bird girl."

Tenzin narrowed her eyes, but nodded before she took to the air.

A kind of barricade built up as they killed and tossed the bodies of Livia's guards around them in the back corner of the room. Carwyn continued to protect them as Emil gathered his strength in the corner. Beatrice saw the ancient Roman grow stronger with each breath as the water grew higher. He grabbed a passing guard and bit his neck as the vampire screamed in agony. Then he broke his victim's spine and tossed him on the growing pile.

She felt Giovanni tug on her arm. "Tesoro, we need to end this. We have to kill her."

Beatrice wiped a spray of blood from her face. "How—"

"As soon as Tenzin gathers as many of our allies as she can, she'll bring a whirlwind to this side of the room. That will block her guards; they won't be able to get through."

"But the water. She's pulling from the river; there's no end to it. I've tried! I can't hold it back."

He turned to face her and shook her shoulders. "*Don't* hold it back! You and Emil must pull the water away from her."

"I can't!" Tears came to her eyes. She was exhausted, and Livia had not lifted a sword.

"You have to. Tenzin's wind will help. As soon as the room is dry enough, I can finish this."

A sick feeling rooted in her stomach. "How?"

"You will take shelter in the water. The wind and the water will protect you from the fire. You will be in the eye off the whirlwind with the water around you. The flames will *not* get through."

She hacked the head off two guards and spun on her mate. "What are you going to do?" she screamed.

Taking advantage of a brief moment of calm, Giovanni cupped her bloody cheek in his hand. In the background, she heard the fall of their allies as Tenzin tossed them to safety. Then the air grew eerily still as the ancient wind vampire began to stir the wind around them.

Beatrice looked up to meet her husband's eyes. "Gio, please…"

He leaned down and pressed his lips to hers as the wind grew stronger. Soon, Beatrice, Giovanni, and all their friends were surrounded by a screaming vortex that Tenzin whipped into a frenzy. Giovanni wrapped her in his arms, and Beatrice held him tightly, refusing to let go. He finally pulled away, and she could see his look of resolve.

"Pull the water into the whirlwind, Beatrice."

She choked back the tears. "You can't."

"I must." He stroked her cheek tenderly. "Pull the water in, Tesoro. Emil cannot do it alone."

She looked over her shoulder as the tears fell down her cheeks. Emil was pulling the water in, and the air around them grew damp and humid as he forced the water away from Livia and into Tenzin's storm. Carwyn's arms held up the ceiling as the floor trembled. In the distance, Beatrice heard Livia scream when she realized what Emil was doing.

"Pull the water in, Beatrice. You have the strength. *I love you*," he whispered. "So much. And you are exactly who you need to be. All of this has happened for a reason. Now let me do my part."

She sobbed as she reached up and clutched his neck, pulling his mouth to hers in one final kiss before she let go with a hoarse cry and lifted her arms. Beatrice felt the rage and the power well up from the very center of her being. She grabbed Emil's hand and held onto it as the amnis rushed between them and they pulled the water into the storm. The room around them grew dark as the lights went out, but they stood protected in the eye of the small hurricane. The wind around them grew thick with mud and ash, until all she could see was the swirling black of wind and water, and the grim resolve on Giovanni's face.

He caught her eye one last time before Tenzin plucked him from the center of the storm and lifted him up and over the wall of wind and water. Beatrice let go of Emil's hand and screamed in rage as she pulled at the river. She could feel the water around her, flexing and answering her call. It danced and sang, waiting for her command.

Immortals around her gaped in silent awe as strings of water reached down to touch each finger, and Beatrice lifted her face to see Tenzin floating in the air above. Her friend hovered for a moment with tears in her eyes, before she came and landed in front of Beatrice, who continued to hold the water in the wind.

"Pull it in, my girl. All the way. The room is dry, but he needs you to protect us so he can finish this."

"No!" Beatrice cried out in anguish when she saw Tenzin's tears.

"Yes," she whispered.

Tenzin placed one hand on her shoulder, and she felt Carwyn's hand press against her back, holding her as she reined in her element. Beatrice finally nodded, and the water rushed over her skin, comforting her and washing away her tears. Then she called the river over them. As soon as the vampires were enveloped in their watery sanctuary, the room around them erupted in fire, and Beatrice fell to her knees.

CHAPTER THIRTY-TWO

Castello Furio, Rome
November 2012

The air was dry and crackled with energy as Giovanni stalked toward her. Livia was trying to call the water toward her, but the river that poured from the gash in the marble floor was pulled with ever greater ferocity toward the storm on the far end of the hall.

Livia was no match for his mate.

He flexed his arms, and the fire burst forth.

Livia turned furious eyes toward him. "Stop!"

Giovanni kept walking, and the guards that rushed toward him turned to ash as he threw out streams of fire that enveloped them as they ran.

More.

The dry air fed the flames. He stepped over the bodies that littered the intricate marble mosaics on the floor.

More.

The flames grew higher. He could still hear the sound of voices calling from the eye of the storm. Once they were silent, he knew they were safe. That *she* was safe.

More.

Livia's guards scurried and ran around him, trying to find an opening to attack, but his fire only burned hotter in an ever-widening perimeter of flames.

The water rushed into the wind, pulled by his mate's extraordinary power. The flames along his body grew brighter. The blue fire singed his hair and the smell of it caused a rush of memories. Her cries when Lorenzo had taken her. The punch of a bullet as he fought toward her in the belly of a ship. Her tears on a lonely riverbank.

"You are my balance in this life. In every life."

Giovanni felt the last scraps of his clothes burn away as he walked toward Livia. With each step, the fire grew. He could feel it, the slow, angry shiver underneath his skin, quivering in anticipation, begging to burst forth. And at the core of his being, Giovanni realized he was exhausted. He could imagine no greater release than to finally release the fire he had suppressed for over five hundred years. He closed his eyes and thought of Beatrice.

The feel of her mouth on his skin.

Her soft sigh as she curled into his body.

The curve of her lips just before she smiled.

"I love you, Jacopo."

He met Livia's angry glare, and he could see the moment she truly began to panic.

"Stop!" she cried, giving up the water and snatching a blade from one of her guards. "Go no farther or my men will kill you!"

Giovanni came to a halt, but her guards no longer tried to approach him. The flames churned out, swirling and pulsing along the ground, reaching up the steps and curling around the legs of each vampire who screamed and fell away.

Livia's eyes narrowed. "If you do this, you will kill everyone in this room. Including your precious wife and friends."

Just then, the sound of the wind grew still. The room was utterly silent, and Giovanni knew that Beatrice had pulled the water over them. They were protected.

His mouth turned up at the corner, and Livia's eyes widened in terror as she loosed a feral scream. Giovanni whispered, "Enough."

Then he lifted his burning arms and released the fire.

CHAPTER THIRTY-THREE

Castello Furio, Rome
November 2012

Beatrice had no idea how long she screamed, or how long the fire raged around them. The barrier of water she had erected held against the flames, just like he knew it would. The angry, red glow lit up the room and pressed against them as they huddled in their watery cocoon.

Was it minutes? Hours? Suddenly, the room blacked out.

She rose from her knees, lifted her arms, and brought a fall of water. It fell over and around them, rushing along the floors, pulling black ash from the room as the river returned to its course. Beatrice walked forward and surveyed the room that had been burnt beyond recognition. Slowly the river receded and floating just along the edge of the room was the pale form of her mate.

"Gio!"

She screamed and pulled the water back before he could be swept away. The river answered her and brought his body to her hands. She clutched his naked form; it was cold and limp in her arms. There was a rush of energy, then Tenzin and Carwyn stood at her side.

"God in Heaven," Carwyn breathed out.

"He's alive," Tenzin said. "How could he be alive?"

"No," Beatrice shook her head and pressed her hands to his temples. Every hair on Giovanni's body had burned away. His skin was smooth and unmarred, but he was cold. Colder than she had ever felt. "I can't feel him. I can't feel his mind. What's wrong? I can't feel him!" Her voice rose in hysteria.

"Shhh," Tenzin soothed her. "He must be alive. He is here. He is unmarked. He must be—"

"I can't feel him!" she screamed again, clutching him to her chest. She bit her wrist and held it to his lifeless lips. "Please. Please, Gio, please."

A drop of red blood fell into his mouth, but he did not move to swallow it. She pressed on his throat, willing him to taste her blood. His blood. The blood that ran between them. But there was nothing.

Beatrice rocked him in her arms as the surviving vampires crowded around them. She felt Carwyn's hand on her shoulder and flinched.

"Darling girl—"

"Get away! All of you!" She pulled Giovanni's body toward the scorched stone steps and held him close, still rocking him back and forth and whispering in his ear.

"Come back to me, Jacopo," she said. "Remember, you said you would always find me. I'm here, love. Come back to me. I need you to find me now."

She could feel the eyes of the room on her. She could see the worried stares of her friends, but she ignored them and placed a hand over his heart. "They don't understand. They don't know. I can feel your blood in me. It *hasn't* cried out, so I know you're still there. You just need to come back to me. They don't know. But you do. *Ubi amo; ibi patria.* Hundreds of years. Thousands of miles." She choked back her tears. "Pain. Loss. It's so clear to me now. You are my home. You just need to come back to me, Jacopo."

He didn't open his eyes. He didn't make a single movement. He lay still and cold and lifeless in her arms. But a faint hum of energy sparked under Beatrice's hands, and Giovanni's heart gave a single thump.

"Anything yet?"

"She's stayed with him all day, but no."

Beatrice could hear the whispers outside her room, but she ignored them.

"No movement at all?"

"She says she can feel his mind, and his amnis is a little stronger, but he hasn't moved or opened his eyes."

The sun rose in the sky, she could feel the pull of the moon, but Beatrice lay still and silent next to her husband, willing him to return to her. Willing him to heal from whatever black void had taken over his mind.

"Blood?"

"She's tried, but it just lays on his lips. She keeps trying to force it down his throat, but nothing."

Beatrice and Giovanni lay in their bedroom of the house in Rome as the city continued its maddening march.

A day.

A week.

Emil Conti was slowly pulling the immortals of Rome back from the madness of Livia's rule. The immediate and vocal support of Terrance

Ramsay in London, Jean Desmarais in Marseilles, Oleg in Russia, and many other prominent immortal courts helped to ease the transition. Even more unexpected was the public support of the fabled Elders of Penglai Island.

"Any change?"

"No, and she told us to stop asking."

Lorenzo had disappeared again. This time, no one claimed to support him. Whatever connections he might have held, whatever sneaking influence he'd clung to, had been severed by the knowledge that the devious vampire had willingly supported Livia's quest for an elixir that could render even an ancient immortal helpless.

"She needs to drink. She hasn't fed in over a week."

"I know."

Ziri, Arosh, and Kato had disappeared as if their presence had been a dream. Though rumors of the ancients' appearance ran wild through Rome, the whole saga of Livia's defeat, and all that had led up to it, was quickly becoming more vague speculation than actual knowledge. Wild tales rose up, but the Roman noblewoman was no more. Dwelling in the past was useless. Emil Conti was the power in Rome, and despite the loss of his wife, he had quickly gathered a strong group of allies around him. There was no question who had control of the city.

"Anything?"

"I think we need to stop asking."

It was two weeks after Livia's defeat that Beatrice found herself standing in the kitchen, looking around blankly. She couldn't remember why she had come downstairs until the smell of a human reached her nose. She turned around with bared fangs.

"Whoa, B." Ben held up his hands, quickly walked to the refrigerator, and pulled out a bag of blood. He tossed it to her, and she caught it, biting into the thick plastic and sucking the cold bag dry. Ben watched her, then reached in and pulled out another.

"Looks like someone's hungry." He tossed her the second bag.

She bit into it, ignoring the stale taste of the preserved blood. It was enough to take the edge off.

Beatrice asked in a hoarse voice, "Where is everyone?"

Ben took a deep breath. "Most of us are… around. Jean took off back to France for political stuff. Gavin and Carwyn cooked up something to do with the last of the elixir, so Gavin's gone, but Carwyn stayed. And Angela's here, of course. Tenzin's even been staying here. All the family except for Dez and Matt. They're back at the hospital." She looked up in panic, but Ben was quick to continue. "The baby's *fine*, but Dez had some bleeding again, so they think they're going to do a C-section in the next couple of days. She's a few weeks early, but the doctors think the baby's big enough."

"Lucien?" she asked.

Ben's face fell. "He's in his room. It's not good. He's mostly just sleeping. Though, I guess since we know that Kato survived… There's still hope, you know?"

She nodded. "Okay. Good. Uh… you okay?"

He gave her a crooked smile. "Yeah. I'm good. Just been worried about you guys. Is there any… never mind."

She just shook her head. "No. Nothing so far. Everything's the same with him."

Beatrice turned when she heard a thump in the hall. "Who…"

Ben started toward the door. "It's early, but the sun's up; I thought everyone was asleep except for you."

Her eyes narrowed and her senses went on alert, but she could detect no unfamiliar scent. In fact, she thought she smelled Lucien, but he wouldn't be awake.

Then, she smelled the smoke.

She rushed toward the courtyard and pulled open the door, but reared back at the low light of dawn. No sunlight touched her, but she could still feel the agonizing heat from its glow.

Ben was right behind her. "What are you doing, B?"

"I think Lucien's in the courtyard!"

Ben's eyes grew wide. "Oh shit! I don't know if I can—"

"You have to drag him in. You *have* to!"

Ben ran into the courtyard while Beatrice held the door open, aching with the proximity of the light. Her skin wasn't burned yet, but she could feel the heat building. She heard a scuffling sound along with quiet curses, then Ben pulled a charred Lucien into the house, and Beatrice slammed the door shut.

His skin was blistered and smoking, and he clutched a letter to his chest.

"Ben, grab some blood from the fridge!"

Beatrice cradled him in her lap and rocked him back and forth. "Please, Lucien. Not you, too. I can't handle this. It's too much."

She saw his lips move and put her ear down to his charred lips.

"Rada," he whispered. "She is dead, Beatrice. The letter…"

She pulled the letter from his hand and smoothed it out. It was written in Bulgarian, and she could only read the date. It had been written the week before. She didn't try to stop the tears that fell down her face.

"Too much," he whispered. "I'm tired, B. I'm so tired."

She pressed a kiss to his blistered forehead and closed her eyes. "Please, Lucien, don't make me lose you. I'm so tired of losing."

Ben held out the bag of blood and Beatrice held it to his lips, mouthing the word '*Please*' again. Lucien's eyes held hers for a moment; then he closed them and bit. She watched as he forced down the blood she knew he didn't want. Lucien's eyes closed after a few moments, and he fell into a deep sleep.

Beatrice was just stirring to lift and take him back to his room when she felt the pulse of energy coming from outside the house. The hairs on the back of her neck rose, and she crouched over Lucien, immediately on alert.

The sun may have been rising in the sky, but her instincts told her there was an immortal only steps away. It was the oldest amnis she had ever felt. She looked at Ben, and she could tell he felt the strange energy, too. It hummed as if the very dust in the air vibrated. The scent of dark earth came to her nose. The smell of green and living things. Of soil and leaves. Moss and flowers. Her ears pricked at the sound of a light step in the courtyard.

Ben placed his hand on the knife he wore at his waist and walked to the door, but before he reached it, the door opened and a tall figure wearing a heavy cloak stepped through. It closed behind her, as if moved by an invisible hand. The stranger lifted her hands and pushed back the hood of her cloak as Beatrice gasped.

She was Saba. Beatrice knew it without question. She was earth and life. Her dark brown eyes were round and thickly lashed. Her black skin pulsed with energy, and her wide lips spread in a gentle smile. She was the most beautiful woman Beatrice had ever seen.

Beatrice couldn't stop the rush of joyful tears that came to her eyes as she looked up and whispered, "Mother."

Ben stepped back, even his weak human senses telling him that this was a creature of immense power. Saba stepped farther into the room and knelt down, placing a hand on Lucien's forehead.

"My son," she said. "My lovely child, what have you done?"

Beatrice was frozen as Saba gently lifted Lucien from her arms. The vampire rose and spoke to Ben. "Boy, you will show me where he may rest."

Ben looked at Beatrice, then back to Saba in confusion. "Um... yeah, okay. His room is up the stairs and down the hall."

Saba turned her eyes to Beatrice. "Daughter, you will follow me."

Beatrice rose without question, following them to Lucien's room where she saw Saba lay Lucien down on the bed before she came back to the door.

"Daughter, you will wait."

She shut the door, and Beatrice sat down in the hall just outside. Ben slid down to the floor next to her and asked, "B, who is that?"

"Saba," she whispered.

"How can she be out during the day? She wasn't burned at all."

Beatrice only shook her head. "Because she's Saba."

Ben frowned at her, then turned back to stare at the wall. Beatrice relaxed. For the first time in months, she felt complete and utter peace.

An hour or two later, Ben was slumped against her shoulder, napping. She heard the crack of the door; then Saba entered the hall. Beatrice quickly stood. Ben roused when his pillow moved and looked around, blinking like an owl. Saba smiled at him in amusement.

"Boy, you are faithful. Few know such strength so young. Go to sleep. Your time is not now."

Ben blinked again and stood up, stretching his lanky frame. He sniffed and rubbed his eyes. "Okay. B, you need me?"

She shook her head and placed a hand on his cheek. "Not right now. Go to bed, Ben."

He rubbed his eyes again, then turned and walked down the hall. Beatrice looked back at Saba, who was watching her.

"Daughter, where is your mate?"

Beatrice felt tears come to her eyes again, but she was not ashamed. Saba held out her hand and Beatrice took it, climbing the stairs to the third floor where Giovanni rested, cold and motionless in their bed.

The ancient healer entered the room and walked to him as Beatrice sat at the foot of the bed.

"Do you know what's wrong with him?"

Saba stroked his face and placed a hand at his temple. "He is tired."

Beatrice choked back a sob. "Will he wake up?"

"Do not be uneasy. He has earned this healing, Daughter."

Beatrice blinked and wiped the tears from her eyes as Saba sat next to Giovanni. She bit her wrist and held it to his lips. Immediately, he latched on and began to drink. Beatrice had to stifle a joyful laugh.

"How—"

"I use my power to make him drink."

"You can do that?"

Amusement colored the ancient's eyes. "Oh yes."

Beatrice stretched out next to him and put an arm around his waist, watching in fascination as Giovanni's lips moved. "I didn't think I would ever see him move again."

Saba's other hand stroked along her forehead. "Of course you will. I can feel your blood in him. Do not worry; he will come back to you, Daughter."

Beatrice stared up into her beautiful face. "Am I your daughter?"

"Of course you are."

"I've never had a mother."

The ancient smiled. "Now you do."

Beatrice watched Giovanni as he continued to drink from Saba's wrist. "Are you really the oldest of us?"

"I think so."

"Where do we come from, Mother?"

"Does it matter?"

"Yes," Beatrice whispered as she watched her mate. "It matters. The past matters."

She heard Saba draw a deep breath. "I have spent thousands of years searching for wisdom. I know enough now to know that I will never know everything."

"Does that mean you'll stop looking?"

She chuckled. "Of course not. And neither will you."

For the first time in weeks, she felt Giovanni's heart give a quiet thump. Saba withdrew her wrist, then paused, looking at Beatrice. She held it out. "Daughter, do you need to be healed?"

Beatrice looked at her, then at Giovanni. His amnis was faint, but it was slowly creeping over his skin. She put her hand to his neck and felt the warmth return. His green eyes flickered open for a second, met hers, then shut as he gave a great sigh and fell into sleep again.

Beatrice smiled. "You've already healed me."

Saba nodded with a smile. "I will rest with Lucien today. Your mate will wake at nightfall."

"Thank you, Mother."

She heard the door shut quietly, but she kept staring at Giovanni as the life returned to him. The warmth continued to spread over his skin. His hair, which had been completely burned off, began to grow before her eyes. First his eyelashes. His eyebrows. A faint stubble covered his jaw.

She felt an odd sensation under her fingertips and looked down. She couldn't stop the smile when she realized that Giovanni had chest hair, probably for the first time in five hundred years. She bit her lip, then laughed and buried her face in his neck. His scent wasn't exactly right, but his skin was warm. His amnis hummed, and she could feel the lively energy when she put her hands to his temples.

Beatrice laughed more. Then she curled into his side to wait until he rose.

When his eyes flickered open hours later, they immediately sought her own. She sat next to him, grinning down at his confused face.

"Where am I?" His voice was hoarse.

"At the house in Rome."

He kept blinking, looking around. A curl of hair fell into his eyes, and he frowned in confusion.

"What happened, Tesoro?"

Beatrice leaned down and brushed the hair from his forehead, tangling her fingers in the curls. She traced the shell of his ear before she pressed her lips to his in a gentle kiss. His arms reached up and held her to his chest, and Beatrice could feel the slow, steady beat of his heart.

"You found your way back to me, Jacopo. That's what happened."

CHAPTER THIRTY-FOUR

Crotone
Spring 1509

"What is your name?"

He looked up from tightening the fastenings on his leather jerkin. His father was standing at the door observing him as he dressed in the fine traveling clothes he'd been given. Tonight, he would leave the cold stone fortress. He was no longer Andros's student. He was his son. He no longer wore the clothes of a servant or the scraps of cloth he'd scrounged during his training. His jacket was richly embroidered, and his boots were made of the finest leather. His immortal body was strong and healthy. He had conquered the fire that burned within.

Andros stepped into the room and smiled at him. He asked again, "What is your name?"

The young vampire smiled back, amused by the old game his sire played. "Whatever I want it to be."

"Why?"

"Because I am superior to mortals."

Andros smiled at the rote answer and asked another question.

"Where is your home?"

"*'Ubi bene, ibi patria.'* Where I prosper is my home."

"Do not forget." Andros stepped close to him and put a hand on his cheek, smiling up at the child who towered over him. "Nothing endures, save us and the elements."

The young vampire smiled, feeling a surge of warmth for his sire. "I remember, Father."

Andros patted his cheek fondly before he stepped back and walked to the desk, paging through the books piled near his trunk. He carefully placed a few inside.

"You do need a name, though. You'll be introduced as my son, but the name you choose is up to you. You need something other than your mortal name. It was a peasant name, and you are a prince."

He ignored the old ache and pushed it aside. "I may choose it?"

"Of course." His father shrugged. "Haven't I taught you this? Your name is whatever you want it to be. Keep in mind that you will be introduced into the Roman court, so make sure it is something appropriate."

Andros began listing names. Aristocratic names. Fine names that would be acceptable for a rich merchant's son. A faint, human memory rose to his mind. The sweet burst of an apricot and the sound of trickling water in a stone fountain. He heard the buzz of bees in a summer garden and a woman's tinkling laugh.

"Giovanni! My Giovanni, sing me a song."

He could hear the echo in his mind. His uncle's lover teasing in a laughing voice before she was joined by another, who sang a childish tune. A song about a cricket that made a small boy giggle.

"Giovanni!" She laughed out his name. *"My love…"*

The young vampire blinked and looked up. His father was staring at him with calculating eyes.

"My name will be Giovanni," he said.

Crotone
December 2012

No one visited the cold stone building that jutted into the sea. Old women who passed by made the sign of the cross, and small children peeked at it from behind their parents' legs. Daring boys climbed the rocks that surrounded it to impress their friends, but no one ventured inside except a lone caretaker who visited the old fortress every few months. He slipped in silently then left after a few hours. The heavy locks that hung in the door were always in good repair.

Giovanni walked down the rocky path leading to his birthplace. The sound of the sea filled his ears, and the salt spray tickled his nose. It was a clear night, and the black outline of Andros's fortress rose ominously from the waves that rose and fell under the full moon. He walked to the front door, noting the broken lock, and pushed it open. Then he tucked his hands into the pockets of his overcoat and walked in.

He could feel the faint energy trace as soon as he entered. Giovanni took a deep breath and closed his eyes, then he followed the energy down the stone stairs. Down. Down. Until the damp walls around him pressed in and the haunting memories filled his mind. Childish voices seemed to echo off the walls.

"Paulo, give me back that book!"

He followed the hallway toward the ancient classroom, and he heard the mischievous laugh echo off the walls along with his steady footsteps.

"Cook says that I look like an angel."
"Then I congratulate you on your deception."
"She gave me a cake, too."
"Perhaps I need to speak more sweetly to Cook."

Giovanni turned the corner and passed by the room where his son had slumbered. He pushed it open, but he was not there.

"Will I ever be as tall as you?"
"I do not know. How tall was your father?"
"I never knew my father. I only remember Andros."

He entered the cold classroom to see his son's blond head bent over. Lorenzo was sitting in the center of the room, reading a book as the waves crashed against the stone walls.

Giovanni leaned against a stone pillar and watched him.

"What are you reading?"

Lorenzo looked up. "Virgil. *The Aeneid.* Book Four." He straightened his shoulders and lifted the book. "'But the queen, wounded by serious love, cherished the wound in her veins, and she was consumed by the hidden fire.'"

Giovanni stared at him. Lorenzo's face was gaunt. The shining blond hair he had always been so proud of was limp and hung around his face. His clothes were torn and stained with blood.

"She was so bitter with hate," his son said. "Maybe even more than me. It was easy to convince her that you had plotted to murder Andros."

"So you told her that I used amnis on you? That I used you to kill him."

"You *did* use me."

"You wanted him dead, too."

"I did." Lorenzo nodded. "I did. And she always hated you. I saw it even when you didn't. The way she looked at you when your back was turned. I knew it would not be difficult to fool her." A loud wave smacked the rocks outside.

Giovanni asked, "Did she know about the book? Did she ever really know the truth about the elixir?"

"I don't really know. She said that she did. When I went to her—after I knew what it was—she said that Andros had told her about it, but she thought it had been destroyed. She could have been lying. She was a good liar."

"But you knew?"

"Not at first. I only knew that Andros valued that book. It was one of the reasons I took the library. I heard him questioning Ziri once when we were in Rome. I was young, but I remembered the old vampire. After he was gone, I looked for the book that Andros was asking about. I didn't understand it. Not then, anyway."

"But you took it. You took it all."

"None of it would have been mine. All those years with him, and he would have given it all to you, his precious son."

Giovanni ignored the ache in his heart. "But you convinced Livia that she was included in his plan."

Lorenzo shrugged. "It wasn't hard. I played to her vanity. Told her Andros wanted them to rule the world together. With a weapon like the elixir, they could have subdued their enemies. In a few years, after the effects had taken hold, every immortal leader would have been under their thumb. Even the ancients."

Giovanni pulled a chair over and sat across from Lorenzo as the waves crashed up the walls. "It sounds like a plan Andros would have concocted. Nicely done."

Lorenzo cocked an eyebrow. "She's dead, of course. If you are here, then she is dead. She really was consumed by fire, wasn't she?"

"Yes."

"Good. I suppose that is good." Lorenzo sighed. "So all the secrets have come to light."

"Not all."

Lorenzo looked at him in surprise. "Not all?" Then he nodded. "Ah, the books. Of course, Andros's library."

"Where is it?"

His son shook his head and a bitter smile touched the corners of his lips. "Does your woman live, Father?"

"Yes."

"How happy you must be. You have everything now. You always did."

Giovanni's heart twisted in pain. "I did not kill her, Paulo. I did not kill your woman."

"It doesn't matter," he hissed.

"Yes, it does."

"No, it—"

"I drank from her, yes. But it was Andros who snapped her neck. He heard she carried your child."

He saw Lorenzo blink once before he spoke. His mouth opened, then closed again and he looked off into the distance, staring into the past.

275

"I had an irritating moment of clarity when we were in China," Lorenzo said. "Do you know what it was?"

"No."

"That infuriating Elder Lan asked me how many children I had sired."

"I remember."

Lorenzo looked up with a glare. "Do you know what my first thought was? *One*."

Giovanni's hands clenched in old anger. "Serafina's child."

"I sired one child. Her child."

"Andros never would have allowed her to—"

"She asked me—the night before she died—she asked me to run away with her. To leave this place. I told her I had to think about it. I had to weigh my options."

Giovanni took a deep breath of the salty air. He could hear the waves growing louder. "Would you have?"

Lorenzo shrugged again. "I like to think that I might have. In my sentimental moments, I think I would have run away. Started a new life. A normal one with her as a wife, raising our child."

"That's—"

"But I doubt it." A sneer lifted his lip. "I have no illusions about who I am, Giovanni. Mortal or immortal. I am who I am. But you and Andros took the one thing that was *mine*. And I wanted revenge."

"So you killed him, and I sired you. How long would you have waited to kill me?"

"I don't know."

"After I was dead, would that have been enough?"

The bitter smile spread. "No."

"If Livia's plan had worked? If you had ruled the world with her?"

"Not enough."

"If you had forced Beatrice to take the elixir so she was your puppet. If you could have taken my lover as yours was taken from you... Enough?"

Lorenzo yelled, "It was never enough! *Nothing* could be enough!"

Giovanni shook his head. "Then you have been consumed by the fire just as Livia was."

Lorenzo said, "I won't tell you where the books are, Giovanni Vecchio. You figured out where I would be, you'll be able to find them, too. Why— why did you keep this horrid place?"

"Why did you come back?"

"Because I want to die."

Giovanni looked into Lorenzo's vacant blue eyes, and his son spoke again. "Aren't you going to kill me now?"

"No," he whispered. "I am too much at fault for what you became."

Lorenzo rolled his eyes. "So dramatic. I am a creature of my own making, *Papà*. Don't overestimate your influence. Tell the truth, why aren't you going to kill me?"

He took a deep breath and lifted his eyes over Lorenzo's shoulder. "Because she is."

Giovanni had felt Beatrice enter the castle. She'd waited longer than he'd asked her to. Her elemental energy had filled the fortress, drawing the angry waves as he and his son had spoken. He knew Lorenzo had felt it, too. The amnis of an immortal as strong as his wife was unmistakable.

Lorenzo smirked, then tossed the book he'd held and darted down to grab his sword, which was tucked under the chair. He spun toward Beatrice and their blades clashed together.

His son was good with a blade, Giovanni thought as he watched them from the corner, trying not to intervene. But his wife was better.

Beatrice spun and twisted; the *shuang gou* she carried moved as if they were part of her own body. Sparks lit the dark room as they battled. Lorenzo ducked and darted around her, but Beatrice moved at a languid tempo as she parried with him. The room was utterly silent except for the sound of colliding metal. The two exchanged no useless chatter as they dueled.

She slid one blade down and swung it toward his legs, leaving a deep gash in his thigh. Lorenzo hissed and parried. He swung his blade up toward her face, but she only ducked away.

She was playing with him.

Her tempo slowly built, and he could see Lorenzo struggle to keep up. Even without the benefit of her element, she controlled the fight, forcing him around the room, pushing him into the corner.

"Because I want to die."

Even if it was true, when faced with a mortal adversary, Lorenzo was battling as if he wanted to live. Giovanni wondered whether he had changed his mind.

It didn't matter. Beatrice would have her revenge.

She looped one of the hooks of the *shuang gou* around his long hair and pulled, jerking him toward her and opening a gash on his neck as a chunk of his hair fell to the floor. The blood sprayed across the room, and Giovanni could detect the moment Lorenzo knew he was going to die.

A strange calm fell over his son's angry face, even as his sword reached up to block Beatrice. Sparks scattered across the floor as she lifted her blade again. She brought it down against his, and the sword flew from Lorenzo's hand.

He fell to his knees, weaponless, as Beatrice circled him. The tears streamed down her face as her blades ran around his neck, slowly deepening the bloody cut. She came to a halt in front of Lorenzo, and he lifted his brilliant blue eyes to hers. She crossed her swords at his neck, the hooks of the blade curling around the softest, most vulnerable part of his neck.

Giovanni could hear his son whisper as he looked into the face of his killer.

"Let it be enough," Lorenzo said.

Beatrice pulled back her arms, and the curved blades caught his neck, slicing off Lorenzo's head in one smooth stroke. Giovanni felt the sharp ache pierce his heart as the son of his blood fell to the ground, crumbled into a lifeless heap. He was frozen for a moment until he heard her sobs.

His mate dropped her swords and stared at the body of her enemy. At her father's murderer. The vampire who had thrown her world into chaos. Then, Beatrice pulled her foot back and began to kick.

She sobbed as she struck him, screaming into the silent room and stomping on Lorenzo's body over and over again, mashing it to a bloody pulp. Giovanni ran from the corner of the room and pulled her away, so she turned on him, striking his chest as she continued to scream.

"Let it be enough!" he whispered, pulling her close so that her fists could not strike. She sobbed into his neck until—finally—she wrapped her arms around her mate and let out a deep breath, exhausted by her rage.

He closed his eyes and whispered again, "Let it be enough, Beatrice."

Her rasping breath echoed off the walls of the cold chamber. The waves still bashed against the rocks outside. But her racing heart slowed as her anger turned to grief, and she let him hold and comfort her as she wept.

Giovanni kept whispering as he stared at the broken body of the child he had sired five hundred years before. Lorenzo's eyes stared from the corner, and a bitter smile was frozen on his face.

"Let it be enough, Tesoro. It has to be enough."

CHAPTER THIRTY-FIVE

Outside Florence
December 2012

Beatrice arched her back as she moved over him, and her eyes caught the skylight they'd uncovered at dusk. A thousand brilliant stars shone over her head as his warm hands stroked over her shoulders, cupped her breasts, then trailed down her body until he grasped her hips in his hands. He groaned in pleasure and rose up, kissing along her collar as her hands tangled in his hair. The amnis sparked between them wherever their skin touched, and their pleasure built as they slowly made love.

His hands trailed down her spine, teasing the small of her back as his mouth met hers and his tongue traced her lips. Then he flipped her over so she was under his body. Beatrice smiled as she wrapped her hands around his wrists, and they moved in ancient rhythm.

Rise and fall. Push and pull. When she felt the wave lift her, she looked into her husband's eyes. Her mouth opened, and a soft breath escaped her lips. Giovanni leaned down and captured the small exhalation of pleasure before he pulled back, rocking into her faster as his eyes darkened in desire.

The wave crested and she pulled him closer. He reached down to lift her up and press their bodies together in one, final thrust before his back arched and he cried out in release. Then he leaned down and pressed his lips to hers in a long, luxurious kiss.

She rolled them on their side, and his fingers reached up, tracing the line of her nose. Her chin. The curve of her eyebrow. She smiled and looked at him from the corner of her eye.

"You're staring at me," she whispered.

"Yes."

"Why?"

"Because you are beautiful, and I like to look at you."

She grinned and turned to face him. "Then I guess I can stare at you, too."

Giovanni smiled. "You are allowed."

"Bet your ass, I am."

They laughed quietly, enjoying the peace of the house. Giovanni's home in Florence reminded her of his home in Cochamó with a few major exceptions. One, it was huge. An estate more than a home. It was in the country and one wing of the house had no electricity, which made it easier for Beatrice to rest. She had even been sleeping a little more, which was nice.

It was surrounded by an olive grove, so it was private; she could see them spending many, many months there in the years ahead, enjoying the isolation and the quiet hills. She sighed in contentment, and Giovanni stroked her skin, tracing the small scars where he had marked her years before when she was still human. Her fangs dropped when she heard his low growl, and her hunger began to rise again.

Just then, a sharp cry pierced the silence of the room.

"What did you do?"

There was a clatter in the living room below them.

"Nothing!"

"Well, you must have done something. She wasn't crying before."

"Tenzin, I was just sitting here, and the baby started crying. I didn't do anything."

"Well, I didn't do anything, either. I was just looking at her. She's not a drooler. That's good."

"Well, how do we get her to stop crying? It's gonna wake Dez up."

More footsteps came from below them. "Oh there, precious girl. Let me have you." Carwyn's deep voice rose as the baby's cry grew desperate. "Why didn't one of you try picking her up instead of squawking about whose fault it is?"

"I don't know what to do with babies! I'd probably break her."

Tenzin's voice replied, "That is not my child."

"Shhh." The vampire soothed the baby, whose cries began to die off. "There you are, Carina. No more crying, love. Uncle Carwyn is here, and he isn't a bleeding idiot."

"Hey!"

Matt's voice came from a distance, whispering down the hall. "Hey, Carwyn, is the baby hungry?"

"I don't think so. Let Dez sleep. I think she just woke up and realized she wasn't by her *mam*."

Matt's voice drew nearer. "I appreciate you guys helping out, but should I—"

"No, no." Carwyn interrupted. "She's *fine*. See? She's falling right back to sleep. Let Dez rest a bit. I'll call you if she starts to fuss again."

The baby's cries had turned into pleasant gurgles, and Beatrice smiled when she heard the low hum of activity level out. Carwyn sang a lullaby to the baby. Matt returned to sleep. Tenzin and Ben wandered off to a different part of the house, probably to start another fight. She turned when she heard Giovanni's low laugh.

"What?"

He shook his head. "Our friend is singing a drinking song to that child."

Beatrice couldn't contain her smile. "Well, it's a very *soothing* drinking song. Besides, probably better that she gets used to him now."

He only closed his eyes as his shoulders shook with silent laughter.

"I mean," Beatrice continued, "that baby's going to have the most messed up sleep schedule in history with all these vampires doting on her."

"Carwyn does indulge the child."

"You're just as bad! I saw you reading her a book at two in the morning the other night. Isn't she supposed to be sleeping at that hour?"

"*The Runaway Bunny* is a classic of children's literature, and an allegory of unexpected depth."

"Sucker."

He couldn't hide the smile. "It's not a... conventional family."

"But it *is* ours." She grinned and tucked her head under his chin as he wrapped his arms around her. "And conventional is boring."

"It is. Though... perhaps we could use some boring."

"Maybe just a little."

By the time they'd returned from Crotone, Saba had disappeared, taking Lucien with her. If anyone could cure the vampire, it would be Saba. Giovanni appeared to hold no lingering effects from the strange coma that had held him for weeks, except a deeper sense of peace and contentment than Beatrice had ever seen from him. He no longer struggled to control the fire within him. It was always there, bubbling under the surface, but the tension, the ever-present stress of it no longer seemed to affect him.

He was finally at peace.

As was Beatrice... as much as she could be. The wound from the loss of her father, from the loss of their friends and allies could only heal in time. But they had time. And though the cost of the battle had taken its toll on all of them, when Matt and Dez brought home their tiny daughter, the whole household seemed to heave a collective sigh as they looked to the future instead of dwelling in the past.

Only one mystery remained.

Beatrice lifted a hand to stroke along Giovanni's cheek. "We should get ready."

"What time is our appointment?"

"Ten o'clock."

"Yes, we should leave soon. It's a bit of a drive."

Citta di Castello
Perugia, Italy

When they pulled through the gates of the isolated country house, Beatrice noticed the glowing lights that welcomed them. It was a large home, and when she had called the number listed, the curator did not seem surprised by her request for evening hours. The polite woman had simply asked for their names, put her on hold for a moment, then asked when they would like to make their appointment. She would be at their disposal.

The front door opened, and an attractive woman wearing long slacks and a blouse waited for them to exit the car. She had curling brown hair and a friendly expression. Her name, records indicated, was Serafina Rossi. She was thirty-six, and a graduate of the University of Ferrara. She had worked for Lorenzo for ten years.

"How long had he owned this?" Giovanni asked quietly.

"The house was built about two hundred years ago, but the renovations were done just before he hired the curator. So about ten years or so."

"A few hours from one of my own homes," he mused before he stepped out of the car. "A few hours…"

The curator stepped forward and greeted them in Italian. "Dottore Vecchio, Signora De Novo, it is a pleasure to meet you both. I am Signorina Fina Rossi, welcome to the collection."

"Thank you so much for meeting with us," Beatrice answered. "I know it's late."

"Oh," she waved a hand. "We are accustomed to unusual hours here."

"Signore Bianchi would visit frequently?" Giovanni asked.

"Not frequently. He often traveled out of the country." She smiled. "Occasionally. But I always enjoyed his visits."

"I see."

"Signore Bianchi gave me your name, Dottore." Her eyes flickered. "He said that if anything were to ever happen to him, that I should contact you. Were you a relative of some kind? Has something happened?"

Beatrice looked into the woman's eyes. She didn't appear to be under the influence of any kind of amnis, but at the same time, her cautious expression told Beatrice she knew her employer was something other than what he seemed. Nevertheless, she appeared honest and forthright as she spoke with Giovanni about the collection. Her husband broke the news to Signorina Rossi that her employer was no longer living.

The single home belonging to Paulo Bianchi had been buried in Lorenzo's files. It wasn't particularly noteworthy. A large country home in the province of Perugia. A weekly caretaker and a single employee who lived in the cottage on the grounds and received a generous, but not extraordinary, salary. In their search for Lorenzo's more illicit investments, the mundane had simply escaped their notice.

A shout drew their attention to the small cottage at the side of the house.

"*Mama?*" A small boy of nine or ten appeared in pajamas. A cloud of light brown curls covered his head and he blinked as he looked up at them from the open doorway. "*Chi e qui?* Has Signore Paulo come to visit?"

Signorina Rossi gave him a sad smile. "No, Enzo, we have other visitors. Go back to sleep; I'll be with the books if you need me."

The boy waved once more, then turned and went back in the house, closing the door behind him. Signorina Rossi gave them a sad shrug. "I will have to tell him tomorrow. Signore Paulo was a favorite of his. He would usually visit with Enzo when he came to see the books."

Beatrice frowned, curious if there were more humans on the property. "His father?"

The woman gaped. "Oh! No, no. Paulo was just a friend. Enzo's father... well, when Signore Bianchi gave me this position after university, it was very unexpected. A godsend, really. Not many employers would be so understanding about a single mother bringing a baby to work."

Beatrice glanced over at Giovanni, whose face was carefully covered by a polite mask. "Signorina Rossi, we don't want to keep you any later than necessary. If you would only show us—"

"Of course. I'm sure your time is limited. Though you may stay in the collection as long as you like, of course. I'll show you how to lock up. If Signore Bianchi trusted you, you are most welcome."

She ushered them in the door and Beatrice breathed in the cool, dry air that was so familiar and welcome. The smell of old paper and ink assaulted her. Vellum and the faint must it always held. The curious vanilla smell of old books and dusty covers. She looked around in awe.

Though there was an entryway of sorts, and she could see a small office to one side, the house had been renovated into a vast library. The vaulted ceilings sheltered row after row of dark, wooden bookcases and the arched windows were covered in smoked glass to protect the room from the harsh light that would shine through during the day. Signorina Rossi guided them through the room.

"In my ten years, I've had the privilege of curating the collection here. We rarely have visitors, though I do coordinate the loan of some materials to private institutions and universities. Most of the collection is private. I will confess, I almost feel guilty that many of these items are not in a museum, but that is not my decision, of course."

She guided them among glass cases, which displayed pieces of the collection. Beatrice grabbed Giovanni's hand and felt him clutch her fingers tightly as they walked among the treasures.

A finely preserved Asian scroll with red lacquer finish. Papyrus leaves pressed between clear protective sheets. A vividly decorated manuscript of intricate Arabic script that glowed with gold-flecked illuminations. A collection of small clay tablets marked by tiny cuneiform writing.

"Most of my time is spent organizing the collection. It was not in any order when I was first hired, and I am still organizing parts of it. It keeps me very busy!" Dottore Rossi laughed before she turned. As if she could sense the waves of emotion around her, the librarian halted and fell silent. Her eyes widened and she took a deep breath. "I'm sure you would prefer to examine it at your leisure. I'll leave you here. If you have any questions, please feel free to knock on my office door, but I will allow you your privacy."

Giovanni was silent, but Beatrice stepped forward and took the woman's hand, shaking it and sending a subtle message for the woman to go to her home and leave the key on the desk near the door. The friendly curator smiled and nodded before she left, and Beatrice waited until the door swung shut to turn to her husband.

He was overcome, and Beatrice was rocked by conflicting emotions when he pulled her into his chest. Sorrow. Joy. Relief. Anguish. Even pride. Giovanni looked around at the books that had caused so many trials and so much pain. A mystery that had brought them both the greatest joy and the deepest suffering.

"Beatrice..." He could not seem to form the words, so he held her hand and wandered among the rows of bookcases, stopping occasionally to open a manuscript box or scan the stacks.

Beatrice said, "This collection... Gio, it's priceless."

"She's right," he mused. "Most of this needs to be put into larger libraries or museums."

"But not all at once."

"No, not all at once."

He looked around at the collected treasures of his sire. Of his grand-sire. Centuries of wisdom hidden away from sight. They strolled among the lost books, and she could see him breathing in their scents. They would donate the most valuable pieces so the world could share them. Slowly, over many years, Andros' collection would belong to the world again. They had time.

Just then, a familiar volume caught her eye. Sitting unobtrusively on a shelf across the room, it was tucked among the others, but the scent of her father's blood marked the worn leather cover. She dropped Giovanni's hand and walked toward it. Then she reached over, picked up Geber's manuscript, and clutched it to her chest. Giovanni approached her from behind and placed his arms around her waist as the tears fell.

"Do you want to destroy it, Tesoro?"

She shook her head and patted her eyes with the handkerchief he held out for her. "It's just a book, Gio. It's just a book. It's not a secret anymore. It can't hurt us."

He reached around and plucked the small book from her hands, placing it on the table before he turned her and enfolded her in an embrace.

"That one goes home with us."

"Yeah," she sighed and buried her face in his neck. "Good idea."

After a few minutes, they parted to continue exploring. The library was arranged around a central reading area containing sturdy wooden tables and chairs, which was lined with glass display cases. Leading away from the reading tables, there was a long corridor down the center of the room, and two rows of bookcases lined either side. Small benches were placed at intervals, but the corridor was cloaked in darkness.

Beatrice looked for a light switch and spotted one on the far wall. She flicked it on with a pencil that lay on one of the library tables, and her eyes darted toward the single glowing light that lit the back wall.

"What is it?" she asked, blinking into the brilliant glow.

Giovanni's voice was soft when he answered. "San Lorenzo protecting the Holy Chalice."

An enormous stained glass window covered the back wall. Large and intricate, the yellow light shone from behind as if the window was lit by the afternoon sun. The scattered rainbow of colors dripped down the center aisle and Beatrice walked toward the light as Giovanni followed behind her. On the far wall, under the vivid stained glass, was a brass plaque with a Latin inscription.

Beatrice stepped closer to read it. "There's a quote here."

Desine iam tandem precibusque inflectere nostris,
Ne te tantus edit tacitam dolor et mihi curae
Saepe tuo dulci tristes ex ore recursent.
Uentum ad supremum est.

"What is it?" Giovanni asked.

"It's from Virgil. The last book of *The Aeneid*."

His voice was soft. "What passage?"

"It's when Juno and Jupiter are making peace in the end. 'Now cease, at last, and give way to my entreaties, lest such sadness consume you in silence, and your bitter woes stream back to me often from your sweet lips.'" She paused, blinking back the tears as she read the final line. "'It has reached its end.'"

Beatrice heard him gasp, and she spun around. Giovanni's jaw was clenched tightly, and he was staring up at the window. She could feel his energy reach out toward hers as he held out his hand. She walked over and his arms encircled her. She closed her eyes and held him tight.

"Has this reached its end, Gio? Even after all the evil, he did some good, too. So much lost, but so much gained. We found each other. The past is gone, and no one can take our future. You asked me once to let it be enough." She nodded and pressed her cheek against his chest. "It is. For me, it is enough."

Giovanni pulled back and cupped her face in his hands. His eyes searched hers before he nodded. Then he leaned down and pressed a kiss to her mouth. "Yes, Beatrice, it is enough," he whispered before he kissed her again. "It is enough."

The light behind the stained glass glowed brightly, a reminder of all they had searched for and all they had found. Beatrice pressed her cheek against Giovanni's as they embraced, and she could feel their hearts beat together in a slow, steady rhythm. The two lovers held each other as the light poured over them, and everything was illuminated.

THE END

A LOOK AHEAD

Dear Readers,

Thank you for reading Giovanni and Beatrice's story.

Thank you for your emails, notes, and other words of encouragement.

Writing these books and publishing them has been one of the most rewarding experiences of my life. I've met or corresponded with so many people who have been touched by my words and connected with the story and its characters. And many readers have asked me, is this truly the end of the Elemental Mysteries?

Well, yes and no. Giovanni and Beatrice have told their story. So for them, the books are over. But I think this world has more stories to tell. I hope you'll come back and find out what they are.

And if you really want a look ahead… well, just turn the page.

My sincere thanks,

Elizabeth

Five years later...

It was late Saturday night when Ben strode through the kitchen door. He put his motorcycle helmet on the kitchen table and tossed his backpack on the floor. Then he opened the refrigerator to grab a beer before he listened for who was around.

The only sound of life was the television in the study. It sounded like someone was watching an old kung fu movie with the volume turned low. The corner of his mouth turned up, and he walked down the hallway toward the noise. Tenzin sat on the couch frowning as she watched the screen. She didn't even glance at him.

"These movies are horrible," she said.

"Then why do you keep watching them?"

"I don't know."

She fell silent for a few more minutes.

"Are you done with your tests at school?" she asked, still staring at the screen.

"Yep."

"So you are done with the human schools?"

"For now."

"Good."

Ben propped his feet on the coffee table and looked around at the familiar room. He took a drink and stared at the screen. Then he looked at the small woman sitting next to him on the couch.

"Tenzin?"

"Yes?"

"I'm bored."

She turned from the television, and he smiled at the gleam in her eyes.

"Me, too."

ACKNOWLEDGEMENTS

There were so many this time I had to put them at the end!

First, I'd like to say thank you to all the professionals who have worked on the publication of these books.

Amy and Cassie at The Eyes for Editing, thank you for your professional work, your encouragement, and your ability to edit, proofread, and format all while nursing bodily injury. Your keen eyes and insight have been invaluable to this process.

Corey at Flash in the Can Productions, thank you for your excellent and unique cover work. Your vision sets you apart from all others.

To the many book bloggers and reviewers who publicized the books, featured me on their blog, or spread the word on social networks, thank you so much. You work incredibly hard for the love of the written word, and that makes you rock stars in my eyes.

To my pre-reading girls, many of whom have stayed up late and sacrificed sleep and the good will of their spouses to help me with my writing.

Kristy, my first reader. From the beginning, you have been the encouragement and voice of calm that I needed to keep going on this journey. The fact that you were so dedicated that you read and left notes on an entire book from your *phone* will never be forgotten. So much love to you and your amazing family.

Lindsay, who is well-acquainted with my neurotic, pre-publication jitters. This Hendricks and tonic is for you. I'll be Windy City-bound before you know it.

Sarah, who has coined more inventive swearing when I leave her on a literary cliff than anyone else I know. "Holy &%!#@-waffles!" remains a favorite to this day.

Molly, you are the voice of reason. The critical eye who challenges me and makes me better. The librarian action hero who really likes the bloody scenes best (don't try to deny it). I can't wait to return the favor someday.

Sandra, who reins in my repetitive prose and tells me when a gasp should really be a sigh. Your obsessive eye for detail has straightened out so many mistakes I feel like you should be a stage manager for my characters. Sexy chefs and Brussels sprouts, baby.

Caroline, who asks me why. Thank you for the chats and the brainstorming sessions that were so crucial when I was plotting this series. I hope I can return the favor for you. Also, Romero love, zombie-girl.

Paulette and Dale, who read, loved, and kept me supplied with avocados. I love your family like my own. Thank you, thank you, thank you.

To my own family, who are the reason I am the way I am (for good and bad), and especially those who read and gave me suggestions on my writing.

Kelli, best friend and sister of my heart. I may be a writer, but there are not enough words.

Gen, my sister. My friend. Your strength amazes me. Your enthusiasm and optimism inspire me. And to Shawn, who knows his transmissions and reassured me the books weren't too girly. Thanks!

Morgan, who knows how to pronounce Mandarin and gave me guidance and encouragement on all things Chinese. I'm serious about the Silk Road trip.

Dad, who is always proud of me, when I was changing diapers and when I was publishing books. It means so much more than you know.

And to Mom, my very first editor and teacher, who doesn't read vampire books, but did because they were mine. I'm incredibly happy (and relieved) that you like them.

And especially to Colin, who tells me the stories now. I love you so much, kiddo.

Eternal thanks to God, who gave me the mind to think, the family to nurture me, and the grace to live—truly live—my life.

Turn the page for a sneak peek of Carwyn's book:

BUILDING FROM ASHES

WINTER 2012

For a thousand years, powerful earth vampire Carwyn ap Bryn has served others. God. His family. His friends. But tragedy and loss disrupt his peaceful existence, causing him to question everything he has committed his eternity to.

Brigid Connor has known about vampires since they rescued her from a painful childhood. But not even their vast elemental power can save her from the demons that torment her.

As loyalties are tested and new paths are forged, a lurking danger slowly grows in the Elemental World. Carwyn and Brigid learn that even secrets revealed can come back to haunt you when you least expect it.

Wicklow Mountains, Ireland
June 2010

He emerged from the earth, the acrid smell of smoke hitting his nose as he brushed the loose soil from his face. He could see the flames licking at the houses, and hear the shouts of the humans as they ran, some rushing to safety, and others attempting to drown out fire that had already turned the main house to rubble.

His daughter sat at the edge of the garden, staring into the flames, leaning toward the heat as if drawn by some ineffable force.

Carwyn stalked toward her. "Deirdre."

She looked up, her eyes feverish in the moonlight. "I kept everyone away. As soon as I realized... I kept them all away. No one's been hurt."

He pulled her up by the collar of her singed shirt. "What have you done?"

"As soon as realized... She's still alive. She must be, I think. The flames keep coming, and I feel... But I knew as soon as she woke—"

"What have you done?" he roared as the roof of the barn adjacent to the farmhouse started to burn. He glared at her, the blood tears staining her cheeks, and her auburn hair wild around her face. His grip on her throat softened.

"I couldn't..." Deirdre's whisper could barely be heard. "I couldn't lose her, too. Not her." More shouts came from the houses, and somewhere near the dairy barn, a child began to cry.

Carwyn's face fell, and his rage fled. "My daughter," he groaned, "what have you done?" He let go of her collar, and Deirdre's long legs seemed to crumple under her as she sank back into the cool soil of the summer garden.

He waded through the mass of people running away from the smoking farmhouse. The old building was in ruins, the top having collapsed onto the ground floors. Through the rubble, he could see the black doorway where his son had dug into the hill so many years before. The cozy passageway now gaped like a tomb, and rough stones had fallen in front of it, partially obscuring the entrance.

Carwyn walked toward it, listening for any sounds that escaped the scorched earth. He lifted his hands to move the rocks and toed off the shoes he had been wearing, sinking his feet into the earth to feel for her. The air hung thick with smoke, but a faint waft of amnis, carrying the smell of charred hawthorne, drew him closer.

As he entered the dark passageway, he could hear her; her shallow breaths echoed off the worn walls. He followed the trail of her scent and energy, trying to keep his heart under control, knowing that any hint of danger could result in a rush of suffocating fire. He opened his mouth to speak, keeping his voice quiet, so as not to startle her.

"Brigid?"

A small hitch in her breath.

"It's me."

The panting picked up speed, and he scoured the past for a snippet of something that might calm her. The soft refrain of a Welsh lullaby came to him, and he blinked at the memory of a solemn young girl sitting next to his lost son in the library. The girl's dark brown eyes rose to Ioan's, frowning to hear the immortal singing a childish tune. Carwyn paused at the memory.

Brigid had always been too old for lullabies.

Nevertheless, he began to hum the tune, and he could feel her energy change. At first, it smoothed out, drifting in waves, but then the waves began to grow, the peaks and valleys broadening as he came closer. Her breathing stopped, and he could hear her heart pick up speed.

"Brigid?" he called again.

Carwyn turned a corner, still humming the soft tune, and brushed away the remnants of a burned oak door, blinking away bloody tears as he entered the smoky chamber.

The furniture had been pushed to the edges of the room by the initial blast. There were still flames teasing the edges of a bookcase and a dressing table, but the rest of the sturdy oak had been torched. He saw a huddled figure glowing through the smoke.

The small woman was sitting in the center of the room, curled into herself, utterly still. Her knees were drawn up to her forehead as she bent forward, and her arms wrapped around her legs. No trace of clothing remained on her delicate frame, and no hair covered her head. She was naked as the day she had been born into the world, the red-gold flames swirling along her skin having burned away any trace of the human she had been.

She did not breathe, but her heart was beginning to race. He stopped humming and glanced around the room as he felt the slow draw of air gathering around her body. Suddenly, Brigid looked up and opened her eyes, and Carwyn gasped. The golden amber gaze had burned to ash-grey around the edge of her irises, and streaks of blood and soot covered her heart-shaped face.

The flames along her arms began to lick up her neck. Carwyn held up both hands.

"Brigid..."

Her face fell in pain and confusion, and she opened her mouth to let out a feral scream as the fire burst forth.

In the space of a heartbeat, Carwyn lifted his shoulders and pulled the mountain down.

ABOUT THE AUTHOR

Elizabeth Hunter is a contemporary fantasy, paranormal romance, and contemporary romance author. She is a graduate of the University of Houston Honors College in the Department of English (Linguistics) and a former English teacher.

She currently lives in Central California with a six-year-old ninja who claims to be her child. She enjoys reading, writing, travel, and bowling (despite the fact that she's not very good at it.) Someday, she plans to learn how to scuba-dive. And maybe hang-glide. But that looks like a lot of running.

Her contemporary fantasy series, *The Elemental Mysteries*, is a paranormal romance available in e-edition and paperback at all major online retailers.

Learn more about her writing at ElizabethHunterWrites.com or visit the Elemental Mysteries fan site at ElementalMysteries.com. She may be contacted by e-mail at elizabethhunterwrites@gmail.com. Follow her on twitter at @E__Hunter or on Facebook at her page "Elemental Mysteries by Elizabeth Hunter."